ON THE DRAGON
...*A TALE OF MERLIN*

THE GLASTON GIANT
...*A TALE OF MERLIN*

Jenny Hall was born at the end of WW2, spent her childhood in Essex and most of her adult life in London. Her grandfather, having lost a leg in WW1, came to live with the family in his old age and delighted Jenny and her two sisters with his prodigious storytelling, mainly about his life as a blacksmith in Walthamstow and Wickford and the "larks" he and his mates got up to in Victorian England. The storytelling rubbed off and Jenny, in her more mature years, now does the same. Jenny has two sons and one granddaughter and now lives and writes on the south coast of England.

Other tales of Merlin
by the same author

On the Dragon's Breath
The Glaston Giant

The Place of Shades

...a tale of Merlin

But those who seek my life, to destroy it,
Shall go into the lower parts of the earth.
They shall fall by the sword:
They shall be a prey for jackals.

Psalm 63 vs 9-10

JENNY HALL

THEOPHILUS BOOKS
EAST SUSSEX

First published in 2008 by
THEOPHILUS BOOKS
13 Eastwood Road,
East Sussex TN39 3PR, England

www.jennyhall-talesofmerlin.co.uk

A catalogue record for this book
is available from the British Library

ISBN 978-0-9545423-2-0

The famous short pieces that appear in this novel are
extracted, once again, from the works of that celebrated bard,
William Shakespeare, to whom I am very grateful.

Produced and designed by members of
THE GUILD OF MASTER CRAFTSMEN
EVERGREEN GRAPHICS
11 The Drive, Aldwick, West Sussex PO21 4DU
Cover Illustration by Tony Masero
Design and Typesetting by Cecil Smith
Typeset in Minion

Printed and bound in Great Britain by
CPI ANTONY ROWE
48-50 Birch Close, Eastbourne, East Sussex BN23 6PE

For my mother,
Clare,
with love

ACKNOWLEDGMENTS

First of all I want to thank my granddaughter, Lauren, who asked if I would write a book about pirates. As it was such a great idea (and I have loved writing about them) I hope she and you will enjoy the read. I am much indebted, once again, to Claudia Holness and Jill Barnes for all their hard work and patience in reading and re-reading my work and correcting those typos and errors that always seem to creep in unawares and to Jacqui Barnes for her help with the intricacies of the computer (I'm not too clever with all these modern gismos). Many, many thanks to Jonathan Staplehurst for putting my web page together for me (yet another thing that baffles me)! Finally, I've drawn on many fond memories of my old dog, Sandy – her character and sense of fun appearing once again in my hero's hound Cabal.

JENNY HALL
East Sussex
2008

ONE

'La la la la la la laa, la de dah de dee. I'm back, I'm back, I'M BACK! Ha ha! HAH! Powerful again!' she chuntered on whilst skipping round the room, oblivious to the pots and plates crashing to the floor as her weight disturbed the floorboards and anything resting upon them. Did she for once imagine that she looked like a happy and pretty princess? Yeah, right! In reality, the younger woman, who was keeping as quiet as possible, thought she appeared more like a ridiculously ugly, grimy and even pregnant hippopotamus that was trying to dance on its back legs. 'I've finally got it all back!' Then her mood changed. '*Now* they're all going to pay! Yesss, not long and they'll all be sorry!' Her face darkened with anger as she hissed these words. Dressed in a bedraggled and formless gown of, possibly, blue cloth, the witch swirled around the smouldering cauldron almost felling the poor woman who stood stirring the bubbling brew with the awful stench that emanated from every part of her being. The younger woman was trying hard not to gag on those rank fumes when the witch suddenly collapsed into her chair. With her legs flicking automatically into the air as she fell, her mood changed once again as she let loose her renowned maniacal cackle whilst considering her plans – her breath adding to the revolting odours that already permeated the room.

Retching, and trying hard not to be sick, she had wondered on more than one occasion why this awful woman did not wash; how could she live with that terrible stench all the time? Had she no sense of smell at all? She had no idea at that time that the witch had always believed that by bathing she also washed her power away; unless it was by accident, no water or soap came within ten feet of her. So, unfortunately for poor Honey, it was only going to get worse!

But right now, though, through streaming eyes, she wondered at the screeching, crazy woman – an experience she had not had since she'd been brought into this castle. Now when had that been? She'd tried many times to figure out how she'd come to be here but each time she'd struggled to recall it, a blinding headache had made her give up. She always remembered back to the time she'd been selling her jars of honey by the roadside but then it had all gone blank and the next thing that jumped into her mind was this weird woman giving her some water in this very room – almost a kitchen but carved out of rock, with ceilings of cathedral-like proportions that disappeared into the darkness high above – very mysterious – terribly frightening. The awful thing was that she also couldn't remember anything of her life before she was selling the honey – except for her name and, also, the fact that the woman had told her that as she'd bound herself as an novice to the witch for life, if she disobeyed in any way she'd first of all contract the vomiting malady – something that the witch had already implanted into her, she'd said, and which would automatically spring into place if she defied her – and she'd sick herself up out of her own throat and away – eventually disappearing completely as she ended up as a pile of vomit in front of what had once been herself, but then she couldn't be in front of herself as she wouldn't be there, would she? When she told her this the witch once again found it very amusing and had fallen about laughing, growing redder and redder in the face till Honey thought she must either explode or pass out with the effort but, no, she eventually got herself under control, though she did have an unmanageable twitch near her eye that seemed to take ages to disappear. Up to now, she'd done everything the woman had told her to, though, so far, that hadn't been too bad. But, in the back of her mind, she was afraid she might have to do something one day that she wouldn't like at all. As for the vomiting malady, just getting a whiff of the mad woman almost made her throw up and it was with difficulty she managed not to – it might not stop and she'd end up that pile of vomit in front of what had once been herself. The poor woman was very confused and scared almost witless – a state that the witch was very gratified to see.

So when she had finally got herself under control the mad woman, in what she considered a playful way, cuffed Honey behind the ear, commanding her to delight in her joy. 'It's not everyone that experiences a witch returned to her power, Honey; come on – smile, laugh!' Honey tried to smile and hoped the witch wouldn't see the crooked, false, twitchy smile she tried to force onto her face, feeling her lips pulling down every time she tried to force them up, and all the time rubbing her ear and head to alleviate the pain caused by the witch's smack. Although her head hurt, Honey felt no fear this time; what on earth would it feel like if she really meant it! 'Come, Honey – rejoice – everything is now as it should be! And you will have the benefit of being one of a very privileged few people to see me reinstated as the most powerful person in the whole world. Queen Mab! My, that sounds grand.' The woman was obviously completely mad and Honey tried hard not to let her thoughts show; however, it was extremely hard to force a laugh and, even to her, it sounded hollow and empty and she could feel her mouth pulling downwards again – what an awfully false grin must be showing on her face! Fortunately the woman didn't seem to notice as, skipping and jigging she shook the floor whilst tra-la-la-ing around the room. '*This*,' thought Honey, '*is something she definitely shouldn't do*,' as yet more pots smashed to the floor from shelves and tables that vibrated to her violent prancing.

Finally coming to a halt as a thought entered her brain, she turned to the younger woman, 'Come – let's see what my crystal can tell me! It's been many a month since it revealed anything; I feel powerful today so, come, come,' she beckoned playfully, finally making a grab at the frightened young woman's shoulder before dragging her across the floor. Drawing back the moth-eaten velvet drapes that sheltered a corner of the room, she lighted two candles with a taper she'd lit from the leaping flames that licked around the sides of the cauldron. With one candle placed on either side of the crystal ball, she pulled Honey inside, sat her down on a seat opposite her and closed the curtains. It was stifling in there and Honey wondered how long it was going to be before she passed out from that terrible, all-encompassing body odour.

'Now, watch,' she commanded the frightened woman. 'My special cauldron must be discovered at some time or other. If you see it before me, let me know immediately. I know they have it, but where have they hidden it?' She muttered on for a few more seconds before, scowling, she lapsed into silence.

Both women concentrated on the crystal; it looked for quite some time just like any other crystal ball – clear, solid glass, completely round and resting on a black onyx base – obviously magnifying and misshaping everything within it – and Honey's eyes grew wide as she stared into the one bulbous eye that rolled around and glared back at her from the woman on the other side – until, suddenly a mist began to swirl within it, thankfully obliterating Mab's scary eye. Both women concentrated as they stared at the ball – one woman expectantly, one fearfully.

'Aha!' the witch exclaimed, making Honey jump out of her skin, and then carried on quietly gazing intently at the crystal until, 'There,' the witch grabbed hold of Honey's shoulder, dragging her round to sit next to her. 'There – can you see it?'

Honey nodded, trying to squirm out of that painful, rancid grasp, almost passing out as a sweaty armpit brushed against the back of her neck. She was too scared to speak even if she'd been able – her mouth had dried up so much that she couldn't make any noise at all; she wondered what would happen next.

The vapour within the crystal began to clear and a picture was taking shape. At first it was motionless but then, as the mist swirled away completely, things started to move. The noise began low down but gradually crept upwards before a satisfied bellow erupted from the witch's mouth.

'Oh, how wonderful! The spell must have worked, even though I never felt anything, which is strange,' she added, a confused look momentarily passing across her face. 'But look, girl! Look!'

So she looked into the crystal's depths and stared wide-eyed at what was taking place before her eyes. Within its confines a sea heaved as the little galleon rode the waves. When the vessel came more into view, it could be seen that unusual colours flapped from the mast – still too distant to be made out – while a motley band of men ran hither and thither about the decks. From a lower level, many oars, looking like matchsticks from this distance, protruded from large holes set in its sides, oars that moved in unison to aid the galleon's progress; faintly, on the breeze, could be heard the beating of a drum and, yes, the oars moved to its beat. The galleon appeared to sail nearer to the two women and the sailors could now be made out individually, and a frightening bunch they looked too; dressed in all manner of clothing, they ranged from some wearing just leggings and bandanas – like urchins, to others in leather breeches, frilly shirts and feathered hats almost like gentlemen, but hardly anyone wore shoes. Some looked drunk, others stared frighteningly, two or three were gambling with stones on an upturned barrel, while others appeared to be sleeping. As the crystal's power increased, their view progressed until they felt they were almost on board and walking along the deck and it soon became apparent that this was no ordinary ship; the two women's eyes travelled up a short flight of steps to a higher deck at the ship's aft where they met a pair of large, floppy brown boots; as their gaze moved higher, a pair of knitted blue tights covering muscled calves came into view, topped by garters just below the knee made of black leather and studded with silver which were holding up the tights and holding down a pair of green baggy breeches – *hardly colour co-ordinated*, Honey had thought! As their eyes climbed higher still, he could be seen to be wearing a frilly white shirt, open to the waist around which he wore a wide, brown leather belt and a slightly curved short sword sporting a red silk tassel was thrust through it. He wore a jaunty black hat with a wide brim and a large red feather, which curved up and over the crown of the hat, down its back, finally dusting his shoulder as he moved his head and almost brushing the thick black hair that curled beneath it. At that moment he had both hands – very large hands with hairy backs and hairy fingers – on the wheel as he concentrated on steering the ship; he had been looking over the port bow but now, slowly, he turned his head back to starboard and looked straight into their eyes.

Honey jumped as their eyes met before she became focused on the man's face. He was grimacing. Could he see them? It seemed as though he was returning their stares. Mab whispered threateningly at Honey to stop shaking. 'We don't want to lose this and every time you shiver the picture shakes and threatens to disappear! He can't see us, you dolt' she scolded. Honey tried hard to keep still, though her knees trembled wildly beneath her skirts. A sudden and sharp cuff round the ear didn't help either.

The man turned away from them and was once more staring straight ahead.

'See the flag up there on the mast, Honey? This is marvellous,' she chuckled. 'It's a pirate ship! Now, let's look around. What on earth have I done without realising it? I must be so powerful now that my magic is happening without me even having to do anything. And this looks very exciting.'

Honey looked up at the flag at the top of the mast. She didn't really know what to expect but was very surprised to see crossed white swords on a black background; above the swords was the skull of a hog. Well, she though it must be a hog as it had tusks. She felt her eyes dragged away from the mast as Mab somehow moved the picture along the deck.

They were now travelling back down that short flight of steps and were heading along a lower deck toward the hold. But no – they passed the entrance to the hold and were drifting down through another entrance. The drumbeat, which had been muffled by the decks, could be heard more distinctly now and then a scene most horrible met their eyes. Well, it was awful for Honey who, when she saw it, glanced quickly at the witch, expecting to see some compassion in her face. What she saw on that face was, perhaps not so surprisingly, almost glee. The scene before them was terrible, but the witch's obvious pleasure in it was incomprehensible! How could she enjoy such misery?

Looking down into the dim interior, they could see row upon row of men manacled to the oars; some were groaning, while others gritted their teeth and strained as they pulled. There were many rows of men and even some women, with three men to each oar and one narrow gangway down the centre between the oarsmen.

Facing them and at the far end of the centre gangway was a burly man who was beating a drum with a large mallet in each hand. The men had to keep rowing to the beat; if they failed they were flogged by a another muscular man who was, at that moment at the other end of the gangway, facing the drummer and holding his whip across his folded arms. The men looked miserable and without hope; some were old – or were they? They might just look it because of all that was happening to them. Some looked no more than boys. Maybe they were older but just looked like boys because they were so skinny and small. But it was just all too awful to look upon.

'I bet it stinks something awful down there, don't you?' the witch gave a playful punch to Honey's shoulder as they stared at the crystal. 'Being chained like that night and day, you wonder just what they do with all their body waste, eh?' She chuckled as her mind dwelt on that awful thought.

Honey, on the other hand, wondered if the witch would be able to smell anything past her own disgusting stench, wishing she'd buried the thought before letting it loose in her mind; the witch stared at her with one raised eyebrow for a good twenty seconds before switching her gaze back to the glass.

Honey had often thought she could to read her mind and had, on more than one occasion, told herself to guard her thoughts.

But now, thank goodness, they were moving back out of that place of misery and onto the deck above but not before the witch had observed something that excited her exceedingly.

'Oh Honey,' she cooed, 'you don't know how *completely* satisfied I am! If only you knew how long I've had to wait to get my revenge you would be happy for me as well. But you will learn, I have no doubt. You'll have too much to lose if you don't, won't you my dear?' she leaned across and whispered into the frightened woman's ear. 'And I always get my revenge however long I have to wait! Just look!' she turned and pointed at one of the rowers.

Honey, just about stopping herself from holding her nose, looked away wondering just what she might lose as, to her mind, she didn't have anything at all – well not anything she could remember however hard she concentrated. She turned back as she heard the witch's great sigh of pleasure.

'Did you see the boy?' she asked the younger woman.

'I saw a few boys, or at least I think they were boys,' she replied.

'Ah, but did you see the boy with the scar near his eye?

'You mean the one at the back near the man with the whip?'

'Yes, my dear – that's the one,' she grinned, rubbing her hands with joy.

'What about him? Do you know him?'

'Ah yes, I know him,' she cooed, staring off into space. 'But if I remember correctly,' she then growled, her mood rapidly changing, 'it's always when he's around that things go wrong. But not now, eh? He's well and truly out of the way now – trussed up like a chicken. In fact, if I'm not mistaken, the sea that that ship was sailing on will keep it going back and forth *ad infinitum* – it is not on this earth, you see!'

'Not on earth, mistress! Then where is it?'

She stared at the younger woman for some time – building up the suspense before replying. 'Under it, Honey, my dear – under it!' she chuckled, hiccoughed and then went off into peals of uncontrollable laughter, slapping her thigh and eventually having to wipe away tears from her face with the hem of her dress, leaving those inevitable cleaner track marks upon her otherwise filthy cheeks as she did so whilst rubbing her chest as the hiccoughs gained momentum. Panicking as the picture started to shiver and fade, she held her breath for as long as she could until the hiccoughs stopped.

'Under it?' Honey, after swallowing a few times, was eventually able to speak. 'How?'

'It's a place from which no-one returns; the place of the lost – the place of the dead!' Her lips twitched with mirth once more but she managed to keep hold of herself, if just to stop the pain in her chest.

'Then they don't ever come back?'

'No! Well, I've never seen anyone return, and I've been around a long time, you know! The ones who are sent there are usually scheming villains, wrongdoers in some way or other, murderers, thieves or people who are stupid enough get in the way of someone else's plans – they are all, therefore, accursed, and the only people I know who can put them under a curse are magicians, sorcerers, witches and the like; powerful people – like me! But if it was me – and I can't for the life of me remember doing it – then when? That's the annoying thing as I would love to have been the one to send him to the Place of Shades and am sure I should remember doing that! But I can't.'

She screwed up her face in concentration, jiggling one loose brown tooth with her tongue as she did so, but nothing came back to her mind. Shrugging her shoulders, she merely added, 'so, all of the people you saw on that ship are doomed from the galley slave right the way up to the pirate captain. I wonder if any of them know it! Well, I reckon the galley slaves know but I wonder if that captain thinks he's really in command! It's a laugh, eh?'

'But, you said you knew who it was in that ship! The boy – who is he?' Honey knew she was taking a chance in asking anything of the witch but, after being with her now for some few months, she was beginning to understand her a little, that is, if anyone could ever really understand this nutty woman. However, she knew that she adored being flattered and loved to tell tales about how she had triumphed, especially with regard to a complicated spell or potion, and even more so if it was over someone like Merlin or some other adversary.

'Ah yes,' she giggled, turned back to the crystal and whispered, 'so, how are you feeling now, young Percy? I got you, eh? And there's no way back!' Even knowing he couldn't hear her, she pretended that he could. As the picture faded she slid off her chair, fell to the floor kicking her legs in the air whilst using the hem of her dress to wipe away the tears of her uncontrollable mirth.

Honey turned away from the crystal, the woman and the stench as she tried to search in her memory for the name the witch had uttered. 'Percy,' she rolled the name around in her brain. '*I know that name – it rings bells in my head. But where have I heard it before?*' She gave up as the inevitable headache threatened. '*Perhaps it will come back when I'm not trying so hard,*' she thought and left it at that.

As the witch wiped the tears of laughter from her eyes she determined to return on the morrow to continue her search for the cauldron. They couldn't hide it from her forever!

TWO

Two years had passed by so quickly since my dad had rescued me from an almost watery grave at Tintagel. Or had I almost drowned? When I was younger, it was very hard sometimes to know if things in my past had actually happened or whether I had had very realistic dreams. But by now I knew that my adventures with Arthur and Cabal *were* real and not a figment of my imagination, though sometimes reality and fantasy twisted themselves together in a crazy dance and I had to really think which was which. No, now I knew that these were real happenings – not dreams or nightmares – and that there were other people and beings from another time – some who had become real friends and some that definitely had not (I shivered as I thought of Mad Mab). One of the best, of course, was Merlin and I knew that if and when he needed me again, well, he would call and I would go. There were no two ways about that! Some days I would be sitting in my class at school, possibly bored out of my brain and wishing he would save me from the tedium, when I would hear a soft voice echoing down through the corridors of time and into my mind telling me to "get stuck in and learn – I don't want an imbecile as my right hand man". And so I would try and do my best; what was the point of trying to get out of the learning when it was so much easier to get on and do it? Well, I mean, it really was so much harder to think up plans and excuses to not do the work than it was to actually knuckle down and do it. Also, if I believed he was talking to me still, then there was hope that he would call me back again soon; and then only if I was ready. So, I was obedient.

Quite often I would try to think of what they might be doing back in the Dark Ages, while I was here in the 20th Century. Might they be suspended in time until I got back? Or, like me, was Arthur still at his studies as well? Or was he full grown and now asleep in that secret place at Avalon until Britain needed him again – then Merlin would awaken him and he would once again be High King and save us all. Who knows!

One thing I did know, and that was that Mab had been relieved of her powers but I had no idea how long it would be before she got them back – if she ever did. Well, let's hope she didn't. Some hope! She always did! (So wasn't I soon in for a shock?) The giant was nothing more, now, than a huge pile of rocks on the beach at Bedruthan Steps, along with the white dragon who'd suffered a similar fate. The only thought that still troubled me – at that time at any rate – was wondering what had happened to Sir Niel. I'd really liked him – he was fun – but it looked very much like he'd perished in the sea.

After being scolded more than once by my teacher for daydreaming, I shook my head and, obeying Merlin's distant command, got stuck into my lessons.

By now I had reached the ripe old age of 13½ – and had to laugh at myself as I remembered Cabal scoffing at me for placing so much importance on that half year – while Arthur would be almost sixteen and Rhianne – I looked around at my classmates to see if any of them had noticed if I had gone red or not (I actually had of course; I could feel my face burning from the collar of my shirt upwards) – I thought, would be almost seventeen. Another, almost blasphemous thought entered my head – was my best friend, Cabal, still alive? I pushed that thought away. He was a strong, almost indestructible animal – wolfhound of the first degree! No – I'd know if that had occurred – I was certain I'd feel something if anything happened to him, so I was absolutely sure he was still with us. Remembering how shocked I was when he had first spoken to me, I had to chuckle to myself at thinking how normal it now seemed to have conversations with a dog. Well, no ordinary dog I must admit and, of course, no ordinary conversations. I don't think many people would have believed me if I had told them that I could converse with an animal through our minds and that those conversations sounded as though we were actually speaking, although no-one, or almost no-one, could hear except us. They'd probably think I'd suffered some brain damage when those two bullies had attacked me when I was only nine. Then again, they'd probably think the same if I told them of my time travel back to the Dark Ages. No, this was something I'd had to keep to myself and just enjoy those adventures as and when they came along. *Oh, come on Merlin, when can I come back?* Now, would I ever regret making that wish?

Jack, with his hands on his lower spine curved himself backwards before straightening up – the effort of chopping so many logs while at the same time recounting another story to his two grandsons was beginning to take its toll. As he stopped, they, too, took a break from piling the logs onto the trailer.

'Granddad,' Daniel, a sturdy youth of fourteen summers, asked him, 'you said that the witch had recovered all her powers but then you said that she couldn't remember how you got into the galleon.

How's that? And was it her that sent you there?'

'And also,' Ben, Daniel's slightly older brother interrupted, 'is Honey Mead and Hive's sister? How did the witch get her? Do Mead and Hive know? And where's Merlin? Surely he wouldn't let you get sent to a place of no return? And if that's the case, how will you get back.

Jack burst out laughing. 'Surely you don't think I'm going to give anything away,' he spluttered. 'You should know by now that the stories of my adventures get told in my way and in the correct order. I'm not going to give away the end at the beginning, am I? Also, I think you should both get going now; it's almost time for your mother to come home from work. Wouldn't it be lovely if you had a nice pot of tea ready for her?'

'Oh, OK,' they chorused. 'But we'll be back tomorrow.'

'Then it's half term so we'll be here every day after that.'

And so, jumping onto their bikes, they raced away home.

Jack, with a happy smile on his face, watched them disappear round the bend till the hedgerows hid them from view.

'*So, I might be dead, eh?*' Cabal stared up at Jack.

'You know I didn't mean it,' he stared down at the hound before ruffling his neck. 'It would've broken my heart if you had been.' He gazed down at Cabal and remembered, once again, when the hound first "mind-spoke" to him, advising him that obviously he couldn't talk like humans, as he didn't have the "equipment". He also recalled one of Merlin's weird concoctions that had enabled him to travel with Jack to the 20th Century and remain – something that others – including Merlin, Rhianne and, thank God, Mad Mab, had been unable to do. All well and good but the most marvellous thing about it all is that Cabal just didn't seem to age. He'd obviously gone a lighter shade of grey but apart from that he's as agile in body and mind as he ever was. He'd live forever, barring accidents or the witch. But he determined to put those thoughts out of his head – she sometimes crept into reality on just a quick thought!

Cabal started sneezing as, following Jack's reminiscences, he remembered the witch.

'*Ah, yes,*' Jack mind spoke, '*but autumn is approaching and, if you recall, that's when she gets active. You will remember she managed to recoup most of her powers after the giant was mineralised and the boys are going to be most surprised at the tale I'm about to tell them but, even so, don't ever underestimate evil – especially hers. We will always need to be on guard.*'

11

THREE

My back felt like it was on fire. The ship had by now pulled into port and I could hear the sailors' bare feet slapping on the deck above my head as they ran to and fro with heavy barrels and crates, shouting and whistling as they heaved them over the side onto the jetty. We were all slumped over our oars, completely exhausted and trying hard to catch some sleep – it would be another gruelling day tomorrow and, talking about gruel, that was almost all we got to eat – that, together with a mug of water, if we were lucky. However, we got very excited once a week as a large chunk of black, hard bread was added to the otherwise unvarying fare. Thinking back – how could one get excited about that? Everything is relative, so they say. The man chained next to me was twitching and mumbling as he lay across the oar, while the man next to him sobbed quietly, occasionally calling a name – his wife, I presumed. But ours wasn't the only miserable row – everyone else down there was suffering in his own way.

Being on the gangway side of our oar, I was one of the unfortunate people near enough to taste the lash from the whip on more than a few occasions; I didn't even have to do anything wrong, it just happened. Today was one of those days as the whip master was punishing the man next to me and so I got some of it as well and my back now stung; it wasn't a deep lash, in fact in merely raised a welt without cutting my flesh, but it burned and I'd had to waste a little of my precious water cooling it down.

How on earth was I going to get out of here? *'Merlin, where are you? Cabby can you hear me? Salazar? Anyone?'*

I strained my mind to reach out to them and listened for an answer – nothing! Had he forgotten me? I tried the same with Rhianne but, once again, there was no response at all. It was as though I was in a vacuum – my thoughts and cries for help just mocking as they echoed back at me and bounced around inside my head. Perhaps I had to rescue myself from this hell – but how? The manacle around my ankle was thick, heavy iron, kept in place by an enormous rivet driven into the floor. I couldn't even remember how I'd got here in the first place. Could that be it? Would remembering save me? I strained my mind to remember what had happened previous to my being chained here but it was hopeless! There were many thoughts and visions zipping through my brain but because they were all disjointed, they didn't make sense: James was smiling down at me and beckoning me to climb up to where he was sitting in a tree; mother was kneading dough and telling me off for pinching a biscuit but smiling at me nonetheless; dad was running away from me and I was trying so hard to catch up with him but my legs were like iron weights made of rubber, I just couldn't move them and, with tears running down my cheeks, I watched helplessly as he disappeared from sight. I tried so hard to call out to him but it was as if my throat had burned all my words away. As I drifted off to blessed sleep, one final thought comprising many words intruded in my search for answers – "water, cool, spots, shade". None of it made any sense, so giving up on all these confused ramblings, I allowed the oblivion of sleep to pull me into its caressing embrace.

And then the whip master, shouting for us all "to oars", caressed us with a different embrace – that of the whip – and I woke up. I would find that over the next few weeks, every time I tried to remember something – anything – I would fall into confused sleep. This, therefore, I reasoned, must be an enchanted place or perhaps the enchantment was only on me. Perhaps I needed to do something to enable me to stay awake – but what? Perhaps, if the strain of rowing wasn't too much, I might be able to think during the day. At least if I fell asleep then, the inevitable whipping would wake me up and I could continue with my thinking. Yes, even at the risk of being flogged, that was what I must do.

The days and weeks rolled into a never-ending, joyless monotony. I had hoped to be rescued long before now and could feel myself nearing my wit's end. My hands had miraculously now stopped bleeding, the calluses on my palms and fingers having hardened and thickened to a degree even I had thought impossible. I had lost weight due to our unvarying, insufficient diet and believed I could see my backbone through my concave stomach, even though, in different circumstances, I might have been proud of my rippling biceps; anyone pulling on those oars for up to twelve hours a day couldn't help but grow them. Adversely, though, I felt myself becoming quite brain dead in that hot, airless, dark and rancid prison. Was this it? Would I end my life here? Would I catch some awful sickness, like the man two rows in front who'd died in the middle of the night? I tried to shut out the picture of him being unshackled and dragged away, his heels trailing along the ground as he was pulled past me, and, more awful, the splash as he was thrown over the side. Would that be my end? I made sure I ate all that was given me, licking out the bowl to make sure there was absolutely nothing left and drinking all the water I could, even though some days it was extremely brackish and looked as though it had suspicious things swimming about in it. I tried to save just a little – enough to wash my hands to try and stave off any germs that might be trying to make their home in my cracked and calloused hands or other more unmentionable places. I had by now got used to the awful smell around me and wondered if even my pathetic attempt at a little piece of hygiene in all this filth would help; staring down at the awful mess I was sitting in made me think not. One thought kept creeping into my brain – perhaps I might wake up soon! So far I hadn't! And I still had no idea how I'd got here as I continued to fall asleep if I thought too much.

And then, amazingly, one day my luck changed!

'Ooo 'ere can read? Phwoar!'

A head had stuck itself through the hatchway and was calling out to us. The head retreated at the shock of the stench that attacked its nose. Nevertheless, it took me a split second to tune my almost numbed brain in to what was being said when, before anyone else could respond, I cried out that I could. My voice sounded awful, even to me. It was harsh and cracked and, because it hadn't been used for such a long time, almost non-existent, so, coughing loudly, I then almost shouted that I could read.

'Release him,' he commanded the whip master. 'Hose him down and find him some clothes. Oh, gross,' he retched as, stumbling backwards up the few stairs, more of the smell from the lower deck wafted up with me. 'You stink!'

I squinted as I came out of the darkness and into the light of day – a peculiar light, I considered much later, that was bright but had no sun, even though the light caused shadows. Where on earth – if I was on earth – was I?

As I approached him, the man turned away holding a hand over his mouth and nose before ordering me to present myself to the captain as quickly as I could. 'And don't you dare go into his cabin until you smell like a daisy,' he commanded. 'Shave off his hair, Pick – it's jumping. Can't let the cap'n catch lice now, can we?' He guffawed at his comment as he strolled away.

Pick, jumping to carry out his orders, made me strip off – peel off more likely – my leggings – which was all I had on – and, turning a barrel on its end, pointed at me and then at it, to show me that he wanted me to sit on it. He made a few grunting noises and then, as if to explain himself, opened his mouth and pointed inside it. I felt myself blanch as I realised he was telling me he couldn't speak and the reason, which was all too obvious to me now, was that he had no tongue! Had he been born without one or had he had it removed. I stopped thinking about that as it might be quite possible that whatever had been done to him, could be done to me. Quick, think about something else or don't even think at all! So I just sat blankly and obeyed orders.

Before I sat down upon the upturned barrel, I was surprised to find that calluses had formed upon my backside as well – must have been something to do with all that rowing backwards and forwards – and I could feel them as I walked – they seemed to rub against the tops of my thighs – hmm, at least I hoped they were calluses! Weird! My mind, however, was quickly brought back to the present by the sound of Pick sharpening his short sword upon a stone. My hair, greasy and stuck to my head and neck, stood on end! Surely my tongue was not about to be removed! But no! I felt relief sweep over me as he started to scrape off my hair.

I can remember when I had first been shackled to my oar – well to tell the truth I can't really remember first being shackled to it but remember when I first recalled being shackled to it – how quickly it was before the lice from my neighbours' heads soon began to make their home in mine; perhaps they'd eaten all that their heads had to offer and mine had become a source of new and tasty fare. At first I thought I would go crazy with all the biting and itching: I scratched until my head felt sore and would then try to ignore the movements that carried on unceasingly from one side of my head to the other; I soon stopped scratching as the lice went mad for the blood that I raised up; it felt quite often that country dancing or the hundred yard race was going on up there. I eventually gave up the fight and allowed my head to be bitten and chewed to whatever it was' hearts' delight.

Even though I reckoned I would look completely stupid with a bald head, the relief at having all those parasites removed as well was bliss. No sooner had my hair been removed than I was told to stand while Pick and a couple of his mates took great delight in hosing me down – two of them pumping the water from the barrel while Pick aimed the jet. I was beyond being embarrassed at my nakedness; though I was overwhelmingly grateful to be clean and out of the dark – and smell. My skin tingled from the sting of the hose as it scoured off the last of the scabs of filth that had adhered to my body and then I was clean – oh bliss. '*Mother, I'll never again answer back when you tell me to go and get washed in future!*' I promised. I recalled a film I'd watched with my brother some few months before – at least I believed it was a few months before as things were awfully confusing at the moment – called "Sea Hawk" or was it "Captain Blood"? – I was getting confused again. It starred Errol Flynn whom I thought was fantastic; his sword fighting and acrobatics were amazing and I just wanted to be him. He, too, had been shackled to an oar and – from the length of his beard and that of some of the others down there – had been there for a long time. I recalled that when they escaped, apart from looking a little sweaty, they didn't appear to be too dirty. Well, even though I thought it a brilliant film, I now realised that those filmmakers had got it very wrong! I was covered in filth – I hadn't been allowed a toilet break from those oars for the whole time I'd been manacled down there – I not only stank but you could see why as it was plastered all over my backside, up my back and down my legs making me look and smell awful. But they didn't! Well, I couldn't smell them because it was just a film but you would have a good idea of the smell if you saw the mess, wouldn't you? And there wasn't any! Another little thought rushed in and out of my mind – how could that awful witch not wash? Then – was she at the bottom of all this? But even those thoughts rushed away as things moved on.

I ran my hands over my bristly head, shaking off the water that glistened on my skin and then dressed myself in an oversized pair of blue knee-length pants which I secured with a piece of rope and a red and white striped vest that Pick held out to me. The clothes stuck to my wet skin but soon fell away as I dried quite rapidly in the day's warmth.

Pick, after rolling the barrel back to its place, grabbed me, but not in an unfriendly manner, and pulled me along the deck towards the captain's cabin. He knocked on the door and, without waiting for an answer, opened it and shoved me through. I was so weak that I tripped and fell to my knees, just keeping my balance by grabbing the edge of his desk before raising my eyes to look over its edge at the man who was in charge of this evil ship. I had never seen him up to the present moment as I had only ever been in that miserable pit; in fact I can't even remember being put there – it seemed as if I had always been shackled to that oar; any thought about the ship before that time was completely outside my memory.

'So you can read, boy, eh?' he boomed. He was a big man, even though I could only see that part of him from the chest upwards, seated as he was behind an equally huge desk.

Looking up, I stared into deep-set black eyes covered by thick black eyebrows that met in the middle, making him look as though he had a permanent frown. He, too, like me, had no hair. I wondered if maybe the ship was overrun with head lice. Then I almost laughed as, hanging from a hook just behind his chair, I noticed a huge black hat, which sported not just a sweeping red feather on the outside but also a curly black wig on the inside. I told myself to keep myself under control; I was also amazed that I had managed to salvage some humour from a brain that had almost died from boredom. Oh well, the ability of youth to recover and overcome! (This, all in a matter of a few seconds.)

'Yes sir,' I responded.

'Then come here, sir!' he boomed again, standing up and, towering over me, almost filling the cabin. He pointed to a spot next to his chair and I made my way round to the other side of the desk. I kept my eyes on him all the while until he took me by the shoulders and turned me towards the papers spread out upon his desk. 'So, what do they say? What does all this mean?' He sat down again and awaited my response.

I looked down at a very neat hand and was surprised to find that I could understand what was written there, even though I knew it was in a language I had never learned. However, it still took me a while to get my head round it before all became clear.

'Well, boy,' the captain prompted me. 'What does it say? You'll be sorry if you've lied to me.'

'No, sir,' I responded. 'It's just that it's written in a strange way and it'll take me a moment or two to decipher and translate it and then I'll be able to let you know exactly what it says.'

We both remained silent for at least a full three minutes and then I turned and told the captain that I was ready to read it. He urged me to carry on without any further delay. I read:

"He who is the storyteller will guide you safely past and
beyond the Wailing to where the great treasure is hidden.
Beware the coursing sea, which swirls to drag you down.
Beware the Guardians: though blind they still watch over the
channel are still angry and are each built like a colossus.

Though they cannot see, they will know when you are
near and will sweep the sea with a mighty arm to dash you
to pieces against the rocks. Only trust the one who knows.
Whoever owns the treasure owns all things."

'That's it.'

I stopped reading but daren't look up – I just stood there and waited
as I listened to the huge man breathing deeply through his nose. After
a while, he asked me if there was anything else or if there were any
other clues as to where this place was.

I shook my head, telling him that that was all there was.

'OK,' he said as, shouting for Pick, he dismissed me into his hands,
telling the man to take me back to my oars.

Then I panicked. Once freed from that hellhole, I didn't want to
even *think* about going back there, let alone actually physically return;
I was so clean now even though the stench of my imprisonment was
still in my nostrils; I just couldn't bear the thought of all that filth
again.

Taking my life in my hands, as I understood that anyone even
talking to the captain without being invited to do so could be thrown
overboard without so much as a by-your-leave if he was in a bad
mood, I decided I had to speak. To my way of thinking, being shackled
back to that oar was not the better option – I think I would have
preferred to be thrown over the side. Now that I had tasted relative
freedom, I really would, at that time, have preferred taking my
chances in the sea.

'Sir,' I spoke just above a whisper. 'You may need me again! When
you get to your destination, there might be another direction that
you'd want me to read. Or, perhaps I could read the signs in the sky
like the Great Bear; you could put me on deck to make out those
signs.' I was, by now, blithering and could see I wasn't really getting
anywhere whilst desperation began to clutch at my head like a vice. 'I
don't think anyone else can read and if I die down there, like Chovie
did last week, there won't be anyone left to read anything else if
needed.'

Pick was still standing in the doorway waiting for instructions. I
held my breath, not wanting to make any sound in case it caused him
any annoyance and thus seal my awful fate, until I thought my lungs
would burst. All stood still for what seemed an eternity before the

captain, who'd been chewing the inside of his lower lip, let out his breath in a long sigh and ordered the other man to set up a bed in the alcove outside his door so that I would always be on hand day or night and to position me at the prow of the ship during the day to look for my "signs".

Oh, how happiness is relative to where you are and what is happening at the time. I was still a slave upon that awful ship and there didn't appear to be any sign that that would change in the near future but I was freed from the awfulness of being shackled to an oar, almost starving, in semi-darkness, under the threat of a whip and from sitting in my own and my neighbours' ever-spreading filth and from everything else that was foul. Now I was happy. How long that would last I didn't know, but I was determined to enjoy it while I could and try never to return below decks. So it was that I set out right there and then to make myself indispensable.

Pick threw a few fairly clean sacks into the corner outside the captain's cabin before beckoning me to follow him up the stairs and onto the deck. As we moved forward I luxuriated in the wind as it caressed my face and flapped through my clothes. I looked up and saw the effect it had on the sails and was surprised at how fast the ship was travelling. As I looked over the side I saw the ends of the oars that were never seen from below decks and felt pity for those poor souls stuck down there, even though they were resting at the moment – they didn't need to row when the wind was favourable; but there was nothing for them – no future, no hope, nothing – just despair, death and a watery grave!

Determining not to think about them too much – my own misery was still too raw – I concentrated on getting myself fit.

The food was a million times better than that which I'd had to endure below decks and it wasn't long before I started to fill out again. Over time my hair started to grow and my sickly pallor gave way to a slight tan. Even though I didn't trust or even like the captain very much, I was working very hard to keep in his good books, doing those little jobs that no-one else had wanted to do or even thought of and doing things for him that he didn't even know he wanted done in the first place; sometimes answering questions that I knew the answer to, even when I knew he was only talking out loud and was really only asking himself. Before long he started to trust me and then, as the days went on, I found out how we came to be where we all now were – well almost!

FOUR

Lying on my back upon the hard wooden floorboards barely softened by the itchy brown sacks that Pick had thrown down as my bed outside the captain's cabin, I tried to put together all the little bits of information I'd somehow gleaned from him over the five or six weeks I'd been with him – well away from those oars, I mean; it irked me that I really still couldn't remember how long I'd been shackled to that oar.

I'd asked him for some paper, ink and a quill; I said I was going to try and map out where we'd been for future use so we'd be able to find our way back quickly; what I really wanted was to keep notes on the shoreline for myself and also everything that he or anyone else said in order to see how I might be able to find my way back home if it was at all possible and if an opportunity ever arose to escape.

He thought a map a good idea and told me that I could use his cabin to do this while he was on deck.

So, here we go. Well, I thought "here we go" but we didn't really seem to be going anywhere. I'd thought, when I first came up on deck, that there must be some sort of mist between us and the sun, as although there was plenty of light we never actually saw the sun. It was the same at night – there were no stars let alone a moon; I couldn't make it out. When I had been with Sir Ector and his men or Arthur, they had pointed out the different constellations in the sky and before long I was able, on a clear night, to know exactly where I was at any time of the year and could even plot a course. But here? Nothing!

I gathered up my courage at the end of that first day of searching for clues as to where we might be and asked the captain why there were never any stars and the name of the port we had recently sailed from.

'Well, boy,' he replied, leaning back from his desk and balancing himself on the two back legs his chair, 'it's like this. I took over this here ship a good many moons ago – er, that is, if there was a moon.' He screwed up his face, looking perplexed, before continuing. 'Come to think of it, there's day and there's night but no heavenly bodies. I'm sure there used to be, but not now. Now I wonder why that is; I've not really thought about that before.'

'Then how do you know where you're headed?' I asked.

'Ah, that's easy! Come see!'

Grabbing his hat and wig and hastily plonking it atop his head, he took me up on deck; I had almost to run to keep up with his deep strides. I nearly laughed, then, when I noticed that both the wig and his hat were slightly askew. Considering it, I don't suppose any of his men ever mentioned it or, if they did, I wondered if maybe some of them then ended up where I started off or even over the side. Catching up with him I leaned over the prow of the ship to see what he was pointing at. I couldn't believe it. I'd seen many a ship with a carved figurehead before but they were at best beautiful – a lady looking something like an angel or a goddess, or at worst powerful – a warrior or something – but this was ugly – a hog with huge tusks. Looking aloft I could see it was almost the same as the ship's colours except this was not a skull but was painted as if it had skin – blackish-grey with yellow tusks; and then I saw its eyes – huge, bulging, green eyes, shaded with long, straw-like lashes, that stared straight ahead just as if they were real. The light was now fading rapidly as evening drew on but I could still make out its ugly features.

'Ah, I can see you've noticed,' the captain almost chuckled. Come to think of it, no-one smiled, let alone laughed, in this place – well, not a pleasant laugh anyway – except at someone's misfortune or expense. Everyone was not exactly miserable but not happy either. But getting back to the captain, 'He takes us to where we should go. We check him at the forenoon watch every day, not that we need to, but it's part of the ship's discipline.'

'But how do you know you're going in the right direction?'

'If, by some chance, we stray, we hear two loud clangs as he shuts his eyes. He does that when we're going in the wrong direction; so we manoeuvre the ship till he opens them again and then we know we're headed in the right direction and move on.'

'So it's not you that makes the decisions as to where you're going then?' I asked – carelessly, with hindsight – but he didn't take it amiss, fortunately for me. I had thought I might have overstepped the mark as I saw his face darken. Thinking as quickly as I could, I spluttered, 'but perhaps he is so in tune with your mind, he knows instinctively where he *should* be going.'

His stiffened shoulders gradually relaxed until, clapping me on the back, he guffawed that he was obviously a clever chap to have picked out an intelligent lad like me, and not to worry about where we're headed because we always got there!

'*Phew!*' I thought. '*But get where?*'

I was still at a loss to know how to make my map when, for all I knew, we might be sailing round in circles – the hog's head only ever pointing in the direction it thought we should be going – so I'd had to make up a map somehow and keep some sort of a log as to where we'd been, what had happened there, where we thought we were going, what we were going to do; also what was it all about, where was I really and why was I here, but, more importantly, how was I going to escape? These latter points would definitely *not* be entered in the log or marked on the map even though I knew no-one else could read; but you never knew who might come on board who could.

The wind had fallen and, wincing at the muffled sound of the drumbeat and crack of the whip, I felt the ship leap as those poor men down below started to pull on their oars. I felt so sorry for them but, at the moment, what could I do? I must have been looking quite perplexed and almost jumped as the captain asked me if anything was amiss.

'Oh, no sir,' I replied. 'I just wondered how long it would take to get to where we are going next.'

'Well, to answer your previous question, the last place we sailed from was called Crowsport and the next one, I feel sure, will be Raven's Harbour – named after me (he puffed out his chest), where we shall use some of our treasure to buy some new men for the oars. Some of them are worn out now and are almost no use, especially if we come up against another marauding vessel; almost didn't get away once, when the Jackal caught me unawares. No, I'll have to buy some new ones.'

My face must have shown my horror at the thought of buying and selling people. It wasn't right! However, he must have thought I was worried about being captured by the Jackal as, patting me on the head, he assured me that that ship hadn't been seen in these waters for nigh on two or was it three years and that I needn't worry. 'Must have sunk, I reckon,' he grinned, shoving me along in front of him. Noticing the unhappy expression that remained on my face, he chuckled, 'So what's the problem?'

FIVE

'The problem is – I can't seem to find him however hard I search,' Merlin groaned as he stared at the swirling mists within the empty Glass. 'I reckon Mab's back on the prowl and has had a lot to do with this!'

'Surely she'd still be incapable of using her powers! She was in a pretty sorry state when we left her on the beach at Bedruthan Steps,' Salazar stated as he moved across the room to search the Glass over Merlin's shoulder, remembering the woman they'd left there, soaked to the skin, wailing and babbling incoherently.

'Don't be complacent where she's concerned, my friend,' he replied as they watched the Glass darken. 'She is mad enough to think she can do something, even if she can't, and sometimes that's even more dangerous than when she knows what she is doing – that is, if she ever knows what she's doing.'

Both men turned away from the Glass – a huge frosted mirror that hung on the wall in Merlin's cave. He had several caves dotted around Britain and one or two others also had a similar Glass in them. It had many purposes but one of them was to search. If, for instance, he wanted to look for me and thought I might be with Arthur at Sir Ector's home, all he need do would be to look into the Glass, think of a place at Sir Ector's, like the Great Hall, concentrate until it came into view and then look around to find me; however, it had a much more powerful use. I recalled the time he needed me to go back to the witch's castle and so he'd asked me to concentrate on something – I chose the cauldron in her kitchen – and as it came into view he sprinkled some dust over me and I was immediately transported there. But at this time they couldn't find me in all the usual places.

'So what do you propose we do?'

'Well, we've searched the Glass to no avail and you know that we need to be able to see the place clearly in order to be able to travel there through it; neither I nor Cabal – nor you, I believe – have been able to see him in there or reach out to him with our minds. And Rhianne is beside herself with worry. You and I know where Percy really originates from and I suppose it won't be long before Rhianne and Cabal will have to know. I've been searching through the readings for clues as to what might possibly happen in the future and I've seen that that witch will one day be able to successfully travel through time.

So far, I have been unable to do that but I am going to need to be able to; she is determined to destroy young Percy, whether in these days or in his own time. You and I will have our work cut out to find a way and the means to travel through time before she can.'

Cabal rushed into the main chamber of the cave where they were conversing. He saw two men, both tall and slim and about the same age, roughly mid-thirties, although Merlin had from time to time changed both his age and his appearance. Both were extremely elegant. Merlin, with his Celtic colouring, was dressed in a long midnight blue robe that came down to his feet. I still cannot say if he really had any hair as I never saw his head other than with it being covered by a tight fitting skullcap; this was also midnight blue and was decorated in silver swirls, whorls and hieroglyphs and sported a silver badge at the front embossed with the head of a merlin. He had a staff, etched with similar hieroglyphs to those on his cap, which was almost black and made of some very strong material, the front of which also sported the silver embossed merlin's, head. And the birds, on both his headgear and staff, which at that moment was resting against the wall beside the brightly blazing fire, had glittering rubies for eyes. I say I've never seen his hair – well, that's not quite true: when he changes himself into another character, he looks completely different – he was once a very old, bent man and had long flowing white hair that came almost to the floor, but I don't think his characters count really, as all of him then is so different. Also, he always told me that it was all just an illusion – he always looked the same but everyone else only saw what he wanted them to see. Which makes one wonder if he really even looks like I've just described him – I mean he could be a green, horned alien who's made himself look human. I really thought that once, as I'd been reading some American science fiction comics at the time and my over-active imagination had almost everyone I knew as monsters or aliens inside human bodies – even my mum and dad! I hid from them all day one Saturday, believing my dad to be a warthog-headed troll with a bludgeon that he was about to flatten me with and that my mum was just like the fairy on the Christmas tree but as soon as she touched me her mouth opened really wide with huge teeth that dripped blood and skin from the previous person she'd eaten and that she was about to do the same to me; I was convinced they'd eaten my real parents and were about to zap me off to a planet in another galaxy. I think I had mumps at the time!

Salazar, with skin of ebony, was dressed in clothes the like of which had never before been seen in Britain. He wore a long, loose white tunic that came to his feet. His head was adorned with a turban made of the same material; it was extremely elegant. Set into it and just above his brow glowed a huge blue-black shiny gem that flashed when the light caught it. The sash at his waist, also dark blue, held a long scimitar, and a cloak of similar colour, which he slung around his shoulders, complemented the whole ensemble. His footwear looked as though it must wear out in hours if worn outside but, ever since I've known him, the soft leather sandals remain as new.

'*I've been hunting in the forest*,' the hound announced as he trotted over to Merlin, tongue lolling out of the side of a grinning mouth, which belied what he brought. '*The news I bring is terrible. Terrible*,' he repeated.

'Tell me at once,' Merlin demanded.

'*Both Percy and Arthur have been taken*,' he replied.

'Arthur too? But where? How? Who?' Merlin cried, shocked. 'How is it you know and yet I don't? I'm sure I would have known. Come here, Cabal, and tell me all. Don't leave anything out!'

'*I was chasing this squirrel through the woods on the north side of Sir Ector's stronghold. There are quite a few of them making their homes in the large oaks at the edge of the forest. Before the chase, I suppose I counted at least four males, let alone how many nesting females there might be…*'

'Cabal – STOP.'

The hound jumped as he looked up at Merlin, tilting his head enquiringly to one side.

'When I say, "don't leave anything out", I mean tell me everything that pertains to Arthur and Percy's disappearance. I don't need to know the mating habits of squirrels or any other species of animal come to that, just what's happened to our friends. OK?'

Cabal nodded – an unusual feat for a dog but one that he had managed to learn.

'OK, then. Get on with it.'

'*I was hunting in the for…*,' He stopped and corrected himself. '*I came across Queen Gisele of the Faerie who, with a company of her soldiers, just happened to be on her way to see us. She didn't return with me as she was extremely worried about her subjects and once she'd given me the news she hurried back to them. King Ogwin is calling in his troops as it looks like there is going to be a lot of trouble – a war she called it. They don't know what but they feel it and so do the spiders. Anyway,'* he continued hurriedly when he saw the look on Merlin's face, *'both Arthur and Percy have been mesmerised by the witch who has captured them and sent them to the Place of Shades.'*

'Place of Shades?' Salazar enquired.

'No!' Merlin uttered, shocked. 'Not there!' His brow furrowed as, deep in thought, he considered the news brought by Cabal, and searched his mind for the where, how and what could be done about it. 'It's the place of the dead, or should I say "undead". They've been taken to a place – a place of no return, kept for the wicked until judgment day. Oh my poor, poor children,' he choked as he thought of them.

'But how can you say that they are there, when it is a place for the wicked? They are not wicked; in fact Arthur, who follows The Way of Christ, is the opposite! Surely there must be some way to liberate them from that place?'

Holding his head with both hands, Merlin cried out in distress, 'my thoughts are racing, searching all the rooms in my mind to find a way to them and bring them back, but nothing – NOTHING. I cannot find a shred of hope! We can't travel there through the Glass because we have never been there and so there's nothing for us to concentrate on. I can't think of any way that we can go there!'

'But I can!'

Merlin lifted his head and raised an enquiring eyebrow as he swung around to face his friend, hope suddenly taking wings.

'Do you remember when Jasmine and I travelled throughout Britain? The time we went searching for standing stones? Well, there were several – in fact many – stones that were just that – stones; they held no warmth, no signs of life and no hope for anything other than something to lean one's back against to rest. There were several dragons, like Moon Song, but whereas we know she lives, the life had left most of them completely, though we came across at least six that were still sleeping – all of which were down the west coast of the land from Scotland, through Wales and down as far as Cornwall. But, and this was the worst, there were also several that emanated awful vibrations. It felt as though there were invisible hands within those stones trying to clutch at us and draw us in.

'Merlin, I believe that some of those stones could be entrances – doorways into the bowels of the earth – that terrible Place of Shades that you speak of!'

'I believe you may be right! There's no time to waste!'

'But what if it isn't?'

'We have no other option Salazar – it is our only lead. Now,' he shouted, turning from the main chamber and rushing down a short corridor, 'let's look up all we can about this and then we'll go rescue them. Come, my friend; I need you to help me.' From despondency to exuberance in seconds! Merlin, once motivated, would never allow the grass to grow under his feet. 'And can you remember where any of those stones are situated?'

'Only too well, Merlin – there is one not two days' journey from here.'

'Then come, let us not tarry; there may not be much time.'

Cabal, lapped up a huge quantity of water and, as worried as he might be (especially about travelling through stones – a thought he tried to put out of his mind), curled up on the floor as close to the fire as he could get without setting himself alight to rest and store up what strength he might need in rescuing his friends. *'Don't worry, Percy. We'll soon come and get you.'* He listened, but there was no reply. *'I'll keep trying, my friend,'* he promised. *'Every day!'*

SIX

'Granddad! You said that Arthur's also been sent to where you were – the Place of Shades – I've never heard of that place before. But you haven't said anything about him. Is he there with you? Was he one of the rowers? Why can't Merlin see you in the Glass?' Daniel's questions tumbled from a voice that was currently breaking and it took all Jack's strength of character to keep a straight face as he listened to the deepening voice that was often interrupted by a high pitched squeak.

'Can't I tell a story without getting any interruptions just once?' Jack growled at his two grandsons.

They both laughed at his assumed angry disposition.

'Well, you must admit that sometimes you keep us on tenterhooks for just a little too long,' Ben argued.

'True, but it's such good fun! Anyway, all will eventually be revealed.'

'I'm sure that some of what you are saying rings a bell in my mind,' Danny mused. 'But anyway,' he continued, shaking his head, 'please go on, granddad.'

We sailed into Raven's Harbour in the early hours of a very dark, ominous and sticky night. The quayside was clear of people and clutter and the only sound that could be heard was the distant howling of a dog who'd obviously been disturbed – could it hear us? I doubt it – we were moving so silently.

Pick sidled up to me and, plucking at my sleeve, urged me to follow him down to the captain's cabin.

'Well, boy,' he gestured me over to him as Pick shoved me inside, and I thought, not for the first time, why has he never bothered to find out my name. He always just called me "boy" when he was in a good mood or, if I dared to upset him, "sir". 'Come and explain your map to me. I want to know just how far we are from Crowsport and where any other harbours might be.'

I gulped – and hoped he didn't notice. I would now need all my powers of inventiveness to try and convince this man that I knew what I was talking about. And he was no fool!

Walking with jellied knees to the other side of his desk, I spread out the sheet of paper, securing the corners with whatever heavy objects I could lay my hands on, one of which was a large bronze dagger in a weighty jewel-encrusted sheath; just getting hold of it almost gave me the shakes as the thought shot into my head that it could in the past have been used to kill or might even still be used on me. Pushing that thought aside, I grabbed another heavy object to help stop my hands from shaking. I took as long as I could in the hope that my brain might give me a convincing narrative.

As I spread out the sheet, he leaned over me, breathing heavily down my neck, and ran his hand down the coastline that I'd begun to draw from the top of the paper; it ran from north to south (even though there didn't appear to be a north or south in this mad place, or any other type of sphere or hemisphere for that matter) and at the present time finished almost halfway down the page. Near the top of the page I'd written the word "Crowsport" in my neatest hand, even though I knew the captain couldn't read, but you never knew if someone might come on board who could and thus give the game away. On the right hand side of the sheet I had ruled off a section where I could write up notes.

'That, I take it, is Crowsport?' he asked.

'Yes sir,' I responded.

'Can you draw a crow?'

'I think so, sir.'

'Then do so,' he commanded, clicking his fingers. 'There's hardly anyone on this ship, um, apart from you and me that is, who can read! Hold on, hold on – do it later. Now, tell me, where are we now?'

I pointed to a place on the map further "south" and almost to the end of my drawing – which finished just short of halfway down the sheet of paper. I'd marked out a cove and, quite artistically I thought, added a few dwellings, a quayside and an inn. I'd believed that if this place was called a harbour, it must be set within some sort of bay. And it was right at that moment I remembered some of the stuff I'd learned in geography and was so grateful to what Miss Owen had taught me. I had thought, as she taught it, that it was a complete waste of time – how wrong can you be? Isn't it weird how things that you've learned jump into your mind just when you need them?

'I believe we're now at Raven's Harbour, so I think perhaps I should write that just here?' I queried as I looked up at him.

'Excellent,' he responded, clapping me on the back. My breath shot out of my lungs as he did so and, once again, I wondered just how old I had to be before everyone stopped doing that.

'And don't forget to draw a raven above the name,' he ordered. 'I might not be able to read *very* well but I know what those birds look like! You can draw a raven, can't you? I know it looks a bit like a crow, but make it bigger so I can tell the difference.'

'*Vain or what!*' I thought.

He watched as I drew both of these birds in their appropriate places; I took my time, as I was not sure what was going to be asked next. I needn't have concerned myself.

The men, following the captains orders, spent the rest of the morning and much of the afternoon rushing to and fro, filling water barrels, purchasing stores and loading goods on board, lashing down anything that might roll or fall overboard. The noise was terrific and only slightly less so in the captain's cabin.

Pick knocked on the door and stepped inside all in one fluid movement. The captain didn't seem to be bothered that he didn't wait for the command to enter; however, I never took that chance.

As the captain looked up, Pick beckoned him to follow.

'Come, boy,' he said as he pushed me along in front of him – so did I have a choice? 'Let's see what's up.'

By the time we reached the deck, the day was well advanced. I was amazed that the square was just as I'd set it out on my map even though I couldn't recall ever having been to this place. Or had I, but just couldn't remember? Well, I wasn't going to start thinking about all of that again in case I fell asleep. But I made a mental note of the rest of the harbour and the town that stretched steeply ever upwards towards the hills, so that I could embellish my map when I returned to the captain's cabin.

The sailors had stopped their shouting as the captain came up on deck and were now busy eating, although they were keeping a wary eye on the delegation of men that was approaching the ship from the square's rambling edge. Though continuing to eat, the captain's men kept their weapons half-sheathed and were ready for anything.

'Now, they don't look overly-pleased to see us; I wonder what they want,' the captain murmured as he straightened the wig under his hat.

SEVEN

Merlin and Salazar, with Cabal and a select group of Sir Ector's men in tow, set off to find the standing stone at Avebury. Salazar had explained that the particular stone they were to use looked remarkably like a man – albeit a huge man – in deep meditation; it seemed as if it stood head bowed and with hands clasped behind its back. 'I'm convinced it's a doorway,' he added.

Cabal, of course, was really not that happy to be going with them; well, he was glad to be going as he, like the others, wanted to find Arthur and me – he just hated and feared standing stones. He once told me he wasn't sure what it was about them that gave him the heebie-jeebies, it was something to do with a weird heat that emanated from them, together with a deep vibrating hum that thumped up through some of them and gave him a headache. Obviously, since Bedruthan Steps, he now had added weight to his argument as the witch had almost succeeded in turning him to stone and it was only by the skin of his teeth he'd been saved.

I'd felt that warmth in one or two monoliths but had only ever experienced the vibrations from Moon Song's stones. Moon Song! Now wasn't she the most wonderful dragon in the entire world? Every time she comes into my mind I almost get lost in dreams of her and everything else just disappears from thought. Even now I can recall, as if yesterday, when Merlin caused the spell that made the circle of stones buzz, spark, hum and clatter as it came together to be joined once more into a living and breathing dragon, clothed in red scales and breathing fire. But she, Moon Song, was no ordinary dragon – she was as devoted to Merlin and obedient to him as to make one wonder why. I can remember asking Merlin once how he could make her do what he wanted her to do; he had looked at me with such a confused expression on his face that I felt ashamed at asking him my question, although I didn't know why. After staring at me for a very long time with that faraway look he eventually turned away, telling me that he might one day, perhaps, tell me, but only if he was absolutely sure that he really knew. I must admit that, like any youngster caught up in the current excitement, I soon forgot about it altogether.

But getting back to Cabal. The inevitable headache he ended up with when getting near the stones, together with an unfathomable foreboding, always kept him as far away from them as he could get.

However, the alternative was to be left behind and he'd thought that not knowing what was going on was much worse than chancing the stones, but the nearer he got to them the jumpier he became.

'You're getting worse, Cabal,' Merlin ribbed him. 'How many times must I tell you that as long as you are with me nothing can happen to you?'

'*What about the time I was turned to stone?*'

'Ah yes, but that was by that witch – nothing to do with standing stones or me as when it happened I wasn't there, now, was I?'

'*Hmm, suppose not. But if we hadn't gone through the stones in the first place I wouldn't have been in the position I was in to get turned to stone, would I? And they are dangerous though, aren't they?*'

'Yes, I have to admit they are but you will just have to trust me. I have made much preparation this time against all contingencies. And I wouldn't let anything happen to you, would I?'

'*Right! Or is that "famous last words"?*' This last thought with his barriers up.

Merlin went over a mental list, checking all they'd done over the last few days; preparing concoctions for or against this and that, practising spells and repeating them over and over in his head – Salazar doing the same – checking maps of the nether world, such as they were, and making sure there was at least one pouch full of dragons' droppings and a phial of naiad root, ready for all contingencies – that is, if they worked from there.

I have to laugh when I think of those two potions and always recall the look that must have been on my face as Merlin explained them to me. "Dragons' droppings have to be collected at just the right time – not too fresh and not too stale – otherwise it is completely ineffective. If it's too fresh, it is usually still damp and will rot if it is stored; on the other hand if it has been left too long it turns to dust and blows away – you will remember how I told you that those motes of dust you see drifting about in the sunbeams are really dragons' droppings." Considering what he was talking about I was surprised by the earnest look on his face; if I was explaining it I reckon I'd be laughing my head off. And naiad root is not a root at all! No – a naiad is a water sprite and although they are mischievous and play tricks on you they are usually quite harmless but the ones we'd come up against were not nice at all – in fact they were the complete opposite and would chew you to bits as soon as look at you. They were fast in water, which was their natural habitat, and not too slow on land either, if it was very wet but on dry land they had to pull themselves along by their front paws or whatever those claw-like arms were called, their back legs being almost useless out of water and dragged along behind them. If they didn't get back to water in time they would dry out and die and, when dead, shrivelled up and looked just like the exposed roots on some old trees – hence the name "naiad root". Dragons' droppings were ground into a powder and could transport people from one place to another when sprinkled on them but naiad root could maim or even kill – so it had to be collected and stored very carefully.

However, getting back to Merlin – he had polished and re-polished the head of his walking cane, along with the badge on his skullcap, until they shone like the sun, the rubies in the merlins' eyes flashing like lightening.

Merlin had wanted to leave as soon as he'd heard where Arthur and I had been taken but, like the practised sorcerer he was, he knew he would need to be ready for all emergencies and unforeseen events. The men he needed had been sent for and all arrived in the excitement and anticipation of another adventure, even though they knew how important it was to save Sir Ector's son. He left a note with the Lady Elise whose husband, Sir Ector and son, Sir Kay, were travelling back from Wales. He would have preferred their assistance in his venture but they were not here and so, as swiftly as they could manage it, a small force was soon made ready to travel into the unknown to rescue us.

'*And then we were ready,*' Cabal thought as he trotted alongside the men mounted, on this occasion, on very strong ponies. Heading west, they ate up the miles as they rode, mostly in silence toward '*who knew what.*'

'I wonder if the dragons' droppings will work the same there as here, Merlin,' Salazar queried as they rode along. 'We've been unable to see anything through the Glass; perhaps there is a barrier between that world and this and what works here doesn't work there.'

'Perhaps. But we need to be ready for anything. We'll try it out on a mouse or something when we get there and see what happens to it. Jasmine will be here to see if it arrives in my cave and will be able to let us know but not, sadly, until we get back.'

'*If we get back! Oops.*'

Merlin looked down with disapproval at the hound. '*Watch your thoughts, my lad. If you can't keep your negativity in hand, just think of who else might be listening in. And who knows – we might not even be able to get there, let alone get back!'*

'*Sorry!*'

'Hmm.' Without changing his expression throughout our exchange of words, he turned back to Salazar. 'As I was saying, it might change its properties and do something completely different. We'll just have to be careful.'

The other men took it in turns to ride alongside the two Druids, asking whatever questions came to mind and receiving instructions from them as to what they intended them to do and how they reckoned they'd accomplish it. The men all believed in Merlin and were positive that their goal would be achieved and, thus, they'd all get home safely, so it was not too despondent a party that travelled towards Avebury and a very particular stone.

The party spent merely one night under the stars before breasting the rise the following evening; they squinted down at that vital megalith. With the sun setting behind it, it looked ominous. Cabal started shaking and was chastised roundly by Merlin. However, it was going to take something more than a telling off to stop those shakes.

The men rode slowly down the hillside and, with Merlin raising his hand, stopped some hundred yards from the stone.

'OK men, we'll camp here for the night and make our move at first light. Wite, I'd like you to position sentinels – two hours at a time will do it and then everyone should get a decent night's sleep. But I'll take first watch and Salazar second. You can sort out the men after that. I know we shouldn't be disturbed but we are on no ordinary quest and who knows who or what might be ready to attack. Perhaps you, Brosc, could light a fire and start cooking supper?'

The men set about their tasks, the ponies were rubbed down, fed and watered and before long, after supper, they were all settling down to sleep.

Cabal went hunting, but obviously nowhere near the stones; it was gone midnight before he returned, after successfully consuming a fairly large portion of the rodent population of that area. He found Merlin and Salazar deep in conversation beside a fire that blazed merrily but which hardly lightened their sombre mood.

As Shake Spear took over guard duties from Tailor, Merlin and Salazar stood; telling Cabal to stay by the fire, they added that they were going to examine the standing stone. Cabal did not need telling twice. 'No, don't worry; we're only going to look, not touch! We'll be back in no time.'

The hound, with head lowered and tail curled under his belly, watched them walk to the edge of the ditch and down its steep sides as they disappeared into the darkness. *'This was not good. He'd known something like this would happen. He'd never see them again or, worse, he'd have to follow them through into the stone portal – on his own – so as to save them! Then, when he got through, he wouldn't be able to find them. He'd be lost – by himself; encased forever inside that cold, stone tomb. He'd never be found again. It would be just awful to try and breathe, crushed as he would be inside the rocks. Remembering his experience at Bedruthan Steps, he just knew he'd be forever looking out at them but they wouldn't be able to see him; they wouldn't even know he was there. Forever locked inside. Walking the endless corridors – searching, searching! Never finding anyone again! A lonely hound walking through endless loneliness – never thought of again! Lost! Or, he might end up being broken up – into many pieces, never to be joined back together again! Then they'd all be sorry!'*

'Cabby! Stop!'

Merlin's voice, making him jump, echoed around his head; he was sure he'd put up his guard but, probably because he was so scared, he hadn't or he'd let it slip. Shaking off his fears, he tried his hardest to think positively. That was very hard. Giving up, he settled himself down onto the ground, laid his head on his crossed forepaws and determined to go to sleep but believing he wouldn't. So it was with surprise – and delight – that he was awoken by the sound of the two wizards talking quietly once more as they approached the now dying fire, with morning peeping through the trees.

'Yes, it is definitely an entrance to that other world, but as to which part of that world it will take us to is quite another matter,' Merlin whispered to his companion as Cabal manoeuvred himself into a position of being scratched. Merlin idly obliged as the two men continued discussing their plans.

As they talked, it became more and more obvious to Cabal that that which he had feared was almost upon him. He was going to have to go through the standing stone with the rest of them. What on earth would happen to him? Starting to shake he was immediately scolded by his master.

For the sake of the men, Merlin addressed the hound through his mind. *'Cabby, you know you don't have to come! If you've made up your mind not to, then I suggest you head back to Lady Elise and*

Rhianne immediately! If you decide to stay, however, then I would urge you to strengthen your backbone right now and behave like the hound you are supposed to be! I mean, look at the size of you? I've seen more attitude in a Yorkshire Terrier!'

Feeling mightily ashamed of himself – and who wouldn't? – well, just look at the size of him compared to a Yorkshire Terrier – he replied that he was very sorry; Merlin should remember that in reality he was ready for anything and would face anything or anyone – except those miserable stones – and that he would try his hardest to overcome even that fear.

Merlin took pity on him, ruffled his head and replied that he knew he could count on him. How could Cabal do anything now other than try to live up to Merlin's expectation?

The sun, melting the enveloping clouds and mist with the warmth of her smile, was now clambering over the distant hills when the men, slapping the rumps of the ponies as they sent them home with Cooper, watched until they'd disappeared through the trees and then followed Merlin and Salazar down the slight incline. Wandering around the ditch that surrounded the stones they came eventually to a gentle gully and made their way up to the flat platform upon which stood those magnificent boulders. They approached the huge monolith that rose majestically out of the last remaining swirls of mist – a vapour that didn't seem to want to let go of that particular stone; clinging to its feet as though its life depended upon it – but die it eventually had to as the sun's warmth uncurled its clutching fingers and watched benignly as it sank down upon the dew and breathed its last.

Each of the men considered what had been told them when they were awoken at the crack of dawn, when Merlin had gone over his plan. With grim but determined faces, they listened as Salazar first, then Merlin, told them, such as was known of it, about the place they were about to visit – and what was known was very sketchy.

'And visit I hope it is,' Merlin had interjected, 'as I have never met anyone who has returned. Therefore, men, I won't think badly of any of you if you feel you cannot go on as I cannot promise you will ever get home again.'

This didn't help the worried look on all their faces.

'I have only met one man,' Salazar interjected, to Merlin's surprise, 'and he was slightly mad; he told me that the place was being run by almost every bad person he'd heard of and loads that he hadn't. When they were ashore they congregated at an inn called The Blue Pelican and a couple of other hostelries where they were always trying to get the better of each other, but even when they did, it wasn't long before someone else got the better of them. Also, there were people popping into their world all the time; he said that it wasn't at all like people being born – and come to think of it, there weren't any really young people or babies there at all – but they just arrived, sometimes dropping out of the sky – disturbing that – more than one person had been crushed by a gigantic person falling on top of him; or appearing in front of you without a by your leave or any warning whatsoever – apart from, maybe, a rushing noise from those that fell; even if you stopped to consider what the noise was, it was always too late to do anything about it before you were flattened; or you were possibly just staring into space and then zing – there you were, blinking at each other, sometimes thinking you were the interloper. That often caused a fight, he'd added. But mostly the newcomers were in a state of severe shock for many days before their old characteristics took hold again and they became what they were before they'd arrived there.

'Everyone but everyone was trying to get the upper hand and, if they were strong enough or cunning enough, that usually worked; however, it was usual that the physically strong ones were powerful enough to get their own way but, on the other hand, it was the physically weaker ones that were, of necessity, becoming the more wily and got the upper hand by their cunning – and so it goes on. They were always searching for the treasure but the man couldn't tell me just what the treasure was; however, they were forever after food because there was never enough of it to go round. The man had said he'd met someone who'd spent a month or more chained in a galleon and that the food there was virtually non-existent. The only way out of it was to die – then you were thrown overboard. The problem with that, the man confided to me, was that because you were in the place of the dead already, you just couldn't die and that after a short while – and in the case of this man – he said he'd woken up at the bottom of the sea – you finally came round. He said that he'd walked a long way along the seabed but because he didn't know in which direction he was walking he had had to swim to the surface and then just keep swimming until he came to shore. Neither experience in the sea was pleasant because of the serpents, but he said he couldn't tell me why as he couldn't remember. The man I spoke to said he'd found a huge cave in which, at its heart, stood a large grey menhir. After spending a long time considering the stone he eventually plucked up enough courage to examine it; it hummed slightly and, reaching forward, he could feel warmth emanating from it.' (Cabal started shaking again at this point.) 'Then it all became confusing. As soon as his hand touched the stone, everything seemed to happen at once. He was pulled through the smooth rock and into its heart.' (By now Cabal was almost hyperventilating!) 'The inside of the rock itself felt hollow but seemed to crush in on him from all sides at the same time and as soon as his foot touched the floor he was propelled up and up and up, swooshing heavenwards like the pebble let fly from a catapult. And then he told me that the very stone we are looking at now was from where he was eventually ejected. He said it wouldn't have been quite so bad but he was thrown up into the air some twenty feet before falling and landing, quite badly, on his head, since when he feels he has lost a little of his sanity and a lot of his marbles.'

Salazar finished his discourse and lapsed into contemplative silence. (Cabal had staggered off into the trees!)

'Yes, well, we'll have to remember to land correctly if we come back this way,' Merlin added.

'*If we come back*,' Cabal thought, staggering back.

Merlin cuffed him round his ear.

'*Blast!*'

'Salazar,' Merlin queried, disdaining the dog, 'did the man say where this cave was situated?'

'Well, he said that there is no north or south or any maps that could tell you where you might be; there is no sun, moon or stars, even though there appears to be night and day; but he did say that the cave was above Raven's Harbour – if you look one way you will see the swamplands and opposite it, just visible on the horizon, an island called "No Hope Island" which is where they send the double-damned, although the amusing thing is, they don't appear to realise that they are all damned anyway whether damned or double-damned. If you look over the roof of the Blue Pelican you will see the Endless Hills stretching away into the distance under which you will find the cave.'

'I wonder why he was sent there in the first place, then,' Brosc speculated. 'And even more, how on earth was he allowed to escape if it's supposed to be a place of no return?'

'Unless we meet this man again,' Wite answered him, 'we'll never know.'

'Why do they call them the Endless Hills?' Shake Spear speculated.

'They must have a starting place, which, if you are coming from the other direction, will be the beginning or if you are going the other way, the end! So how can they be endless? Or is it that once you go into them you just keep going round and round in circles? But that can't be so because someone would have had to come out of them to let everyone know that they are endless – or not, in this case! So, all in all, none of it makes any sense!'

They all looked at him for a few moments before, without commenting and as if he had not spoken, returning their gaze to Salazar.

'Is there anything else can you tell us about the place or anything we should be wary of?' Merlin had asked. 'Specifically, might there be any clues as to where Arthur and Percival could be held captive or who might have them?'

'None, I'm afraid. The balance of power in that place is so tenuous that it changes almost daily. He did tell me one very important thing, though, and that is that most people are afraid of one particular scoundrel who is known as the Jackal. People were afraid to talk much about this individual because they believed spies were all over the place taking back information and, thus, the names of anyone who might possibly be an enemy and also whatever they may have said. They couldn't take that chance, so there is not much I can tell you about him, save that we would need to keep a wary eye out for him – or could it be her? *Whatever happens, Merlin, I believe we should only ever communicate through our minds when mentioning the Jackal?*'

'I expect they called the Endless Hills that name because they had to call them something,' Wite suddenly changed the subject back to Shake Spear's previous query. 'I can remember my dear old mother answering me on many an occasion when I'd asked her why something was called something – I was always asking questions when I was very young, you see – that you couldn't call everything "earwigs". When I asked her why – again – she told me that sentences just wouldn't make sense if most of the words used were "earwigs". I would sit for hours trying to work this out, making up a sentence where most of the words were earwigs and thus having to agree that saying "earwigs on the earwigs were earwigs fighting earwigs" just didn't make any sense, but it wasn't till I got a lot older that I realised she'd been fobbing me off with one of her pet phrases just to shut me up.'

'I wish you'd shut up now,' Brosc commented rather unfairly, as

Wite rarely contributed anything – all his curiosity and excitement having been curtailed by his mother who was obviously not "my dear old mother" but someone not very nice and really quite unhelpful! Merlin duly took Brosc to task.

By that time they had walked toward and were now standing within four feet of the stone. Cabal couldn't help it; he was shaking like a leaf but Merlin, with a firm grip, held onto the ruff on his neck. They had been given their orders, that they should, if separated, make their way to the Blue Pelican Inn at Raven's Harbour, where, hopefully, they would all meet up again.

'Remember, men,' Merlin whispered, 'you have to decide now – we might never return or, if we do, we may never have right minds again. So – are you with me? If not, return home with my blessing.'

They all stepped through.

EIGHT

Plop, plop, plop. Merlin and Salazar, together with Tailor, fell into the sea just yards from the shore. 'How extremely annoying,' Merlin grumbled, shaking the water from his robe. 'Wouldn't it have been just a little bit possible for us to fall onto dry land?'

'And break some bones?' Salazar rejoined.

'Yes, well, perhaps you are right,' he responded rather ungraciously, continuing to shake out his robes that, to their surprise, dried almost immediately.

'It's extremely warm here!' Tailor exclaimed, straightening his jerkin.

'Well it would be wouldn't it? Considering where we are!' he responded.

Tailor stared at him for a long moment before asking, 'and just why would it?'

Drawing the edges of his patience back together again he sighed deeply before replying to the man in a much more even tone, 'Hell, the Place of Shades, the place of the dead! Let's just hope it's not as bad as it's been painted, or as hot, or make us unable to get back!'

They all looked around at the deserted beach that, apart from sand, pebbles and larger rocks, was merely the beginning of a barren and bleak landscape bereft of almost all vegetation. The sea hardly moved and, even as they gazed out over it, a warm mist began to rise, almost completely obscuring the horizon, so no ships or other land that might possibly be out there could be seen. Turning to face the land they observed that it sloped away in one direction but that hills could be seen in the other.

'I think we'll need to go that way,' Merlin pointed. 'They could be the Endless Hills near Raven's Harbour.'

They spent a short while searching and calling out for the other men and reaching out in their minds to Cabal but Merlin eventually said they'd have to give up, adding that they must have landed somewhere else. 'They know where we've agreed to meet up so let's go,' and without any more ado, they set off.

It was nightfall before the little party entered the outskirts of the sprawling harbour town where they moved carefully down towards the quayside through steep, narrow, cobbled streets. Many of the houses almost met overhead, some of which were in darkness and nearly all sported huge and heavy bars and bolts (against what?) that a king would be proud of. The sounds of rowdy singing and some shouting could be heard in the distance; it would appear that the only places displaying any signs of life were the inns and hostelries on the waterfront.

'Let's see if we can find the Blue Pelican,' Merlin whispered. This town, especially in the steep, evil-smelling alleyways, was giving off such bad vibes that he felt that speaking out loud might trigger off something very unpleasant indeed and heaven knew (if one could use that expression here) just who might be listening. The three men continued walking ever downwards through the lanes and alleys towards increasing but still dusky light and human noise, eventually stepping out into a square quite near its edge by the harbour. As they turned into it, Tailor, the first round the corner, jumped back, almost felling his companions as two men – punching the lights out of one another – careered into him. There were dozens of men and a few women cheering them on as, spilling out of the doorways, they occasionally pushed one or other of the men back toward the other when he fell against them. The fight continued for another two or three minutes before one of the men was knocked completely unconscious. With much cheering, moaning and laughter, several of the crowd clapped the victor on the back, exchanged coin and disappeared back into one of the three inns situated around the square to carry on their drinking – and fighting.

'Look, Merlin,' Salazar pointed to his left. They stared at the handful of men who were disappearing through the doors of the various inns before their eyes were drawn to the creaking sign swinging above the one facing the sea.

'The Blue Pelican!' Merlin's whispered exclamation hardly reached their ears.

The sign itself bore no writing but it was plain to figure out that the sea bird painted thereon was nothing other than a pelican, albeit blue. The inn itself looked dilapidated and unkempt. But, then, so did every other building around it. There was a lamp, also above the door but to its side, hardly illuminating it, but Merlin reckoned it was placed there, like the ones above the other two inns, just to shed some light on the occasional fight.

The other two inns, which faced each other at right-angles to the sea, were called "The Minstrel" and "The Nest"; singing, of a sort, could be heard coming through the cracked windows of the former, while the Nest looked dark and secretive, as though trying to keep itself to itself; it certainly didn't appear to be inviting custom and the men returning to their drinks seemed almost to creep back inside in a very furtive manner.

Merlin, pulling the other two men back into the shadows of the alleyway, turned towards them and explained that they couldn't possibly enter any of those hostelries dressed as they were. 'They'd attack us for sure,' he told them. 'We'll have to disguise ourselves – enough to fool them but not ourselves; we need to look more like they do but be able to recognise each other at the same time. Come,' he said, ushering them into a deep doorway. Holding his staff aloft until the ruby eyes glowed dully, he uttered strange words that, even as they left his mouth, were whipped away by a sudden stiff breeze until, with one almighty flash of red smoke, they stood blinking at one another until they could see clearly again.

What a sight met their eyes! Tailor, usually immaculate as befitted his trade, stood lopsidedly – one leg now shorter than the other which would obviously give him an awkward gait – as he stared at the other two men. His hair had grown exceptionally long in that short time and, though looking dirty and tatty, was tied behind his neck with a gaudy yellow-coloured velvet bow. The rest of him, like his hair, was very scruffy: an open-necked, green and yellow striped shirt, ripped in a dozen places, just about covered his grubby and matted chest hair, while black velvet knickerbockers – which had probably been extremely elegant when new – hung down (much too far) below the knees of his skinny legs. Cracked brown shoes – again too big – just about stayed on his feet and would obviously flop when he walked.

'Don't worry, Tailor, it's all an illusion – a figment of the imagination! You won't be uncomfortable I assure you. You are as you ever were; it's just that others will see you looking like one of them. Our dress, too, is the same. Again, it's merely how people will see us. Go on, try and walk – you won't feel the limp and your shoes will definitely not fall off.'

Salazar and Merlin then looked at each other as Tailor considered their appearance before taking a few tentative steps. Then he grinned at them with blackened teeth – where they existed!

Merlin appeared to look quite evil: from the top of his head to his feet he seemed like the pirate from hell. He wore a large blue hat that sported a silver badge which shaded a pale, shaven face – a face that had a scar running from the edge of his eyebrow down the side of it and which pulled up the edge of his lip, making him appear to be perpetually smirking. It was still unclear as to whether he had any hair underneath that hat! A waistcoat of deep blue covered both a massive chest and a frilly white shirt ruffled at his neck and strained over bulging biceps that any bodybuilder would be more than proud of. His trousers, also deep blue, were tucked into black leather boots. The whole ensemble looked donkey's years old. His sword – slightly pitted here and there – appeared extremely heavy, straight and at that moment was thrust through a scarlet cummerbund, the handle sporting a silver bird with two rubies for eyes.

Salazar looked almost the same as he always did except for very subtle differences. He still wore his turban, but without its stone and it was threadbare in more than one place. His long robe had been replaced by baggy, tattered trousers, which were still in the same material as before. Also, he kept his scimitar but it was rusting terribly and his feet were bare.

'I think we should see exactly how the land lies here before we make any decisions. Let's look into the other two inns before we see if our friends have arrived at the Blue Pelican. Come, it doesn't look at all inviting but we'll try the Nest first.

Stepping carefully alongside the buildings and over the still unconscious man who'd been propped up against the outside wall of the inn, they arrived at the doorway of the first hostelry to be met by two revellers falling out of it to the jibes of some of the men inside. Merlin, holding open the door, waited until, trying to keep one another upright, the two men moved drunkenly way. He ushered his two companions inside, urging them not to drink anything, and followed them into a smelly, dank and smoky dark room filled with, almost to a man or woman, drunken, cheroot or pipe-smoking pirates. Apart from one or two who were too drunk to notice, most of the men stopped what they were doing to stare inhospitably at the three strangers who'd just entered.

'Drinks are on me, men,' Merlin cried, as, cutting through the heavy atmosphere, he adopted a merry stance and flung gold coin onto the counter before the innkeeper – an enormous man with a yellow thatch of hair shaped, not surprisingly, like a bird's nest. Their hearts stopped in their chests as they waited to see the outcome. They needn't have worried. With cheers and much backslapping, the men held up their tankards and toasted his generosity. 'Let's find out anything we can,' he whispered to the others as he swaggered over to join a particularly ugly monster of a man seated at one of the furthest tables. 'See you outside in an hour,' he mouthed over his shoulder.

Tailor was beckoned over to join a group of men by the blazing fire, while Salazar, standing next to him, merely leaned against the mantel; looking to all the world like he was staring into the fire, he spent this time surreptitiously surveying the room and listening in to many conversations – and thoughts.

The hour soon passed and it was not long before the three men said their farewells and one by one drifted outside. They had, in a very short time, been accepted as great mates and left to the ringing sounds of, 'come back soon me hearties', 'thanks for the beer', 'so long shipmates', and the like. Merlin had put on a great show of being extremely inebriated as he fell against men and tables alike. However, they took it all in good part as they, mostly, were in a similar condition. 'Fare ye well, my friends,' he slurred as bowing low and crashing his shoulder against the doorframe, he backed out into the square. Their raucous laughter followed him outside where, gathering Salazar and Tailor to him, they swaggered towards the edge of the water to compare notes.

'The three inns are very similar to three warring countries,' Salazar told the other two men as they strolled along the quayside.

'Yes, Black Dog said as much.'

'Black Dog!' Salazar and Tailor chorused.

'That ugly so-and-so I was sitting with,' Merlin clarified. 'He said that he should have had his own ship when the Year of the Dog started.'

'Year of the Dog?' the other two chorused again.

'You'll have to stop doing that!' Merlin responded. 'It's very off-putting!'

'Well, if you would be so kind as to explain things a bit more clearly, we should appreciate it,' Salazar requested.

'Certainly, if you would both be so kind as to stop interrupting. Sorry – that was rude of me. But, well, what I have learned is this. There are several "Years" in this place and until a short while ago it was the Year of the Dog. At that time people who had dog-like names – well, like Black Dog, for instance – were the ones in charge – usually as sea captains. It is mostly a dog-eat-dog place down here you know!' Merlin's lips twitched – he couldn't help it – 'dog-eat-dog?' he repeated, raising his eyebrow as he looked at the other two, spluttering as the laughter exploded from his lips. 'Funny, eh?' he gasped, trying to get himself under control. Eventually succeeding and noticing that the other two didn't appreciate his witticism, he carried on with the information he'd come by. 'Yes, well, Black Dog and the rest of the captains – er, Wolf, Griffon and Spitz and a couple of others I can't remember, had come to meet here in the square to see if the previous Year had ended – and no-one really knows when that is because as well as no compass points or any type of direction there is no time down here. So, when they meet they have the Contest to see if it's time for another animal name to take over for the coming year. There are several animal types: the Dog, the Bird, the Rodent, the Reptile – which apparently includes dragons – the Horse, the Cat and the Insect and some others. Now, the Insect is the worst, apparently, but Black Dog couldn't or wouldn't tell me why.

'Well, when it was the Year of the Dog, it appears they were one ship short and it was Black Dog who missed out.

'Anyway, word gets around and almost a year ago they met here in the square and, apparently, there was a bit of a dog fight.' Merlin couldn't help it. 'Dog fight! Get it?' he choked as the laughter erupted from his throat.

The other two men stood patiently waiting for him to get himself under control although a small, reluctant smile could be seen on both their faces.

'Sorry,' he apologised, coughing as he pulled himself together. 'Well, after the Contest Black Dog went into a severe depression as his Year didn't win again. It appears that it is now the Year of the Bird – I reckon I'd be in that category if they knew who I really was. There are several captains – some of whom are still at sea – and one or two ashore, as can be seen by their vessels in the harbour,' he pointed. 'The Raven is the captain of that ship there and I understand he is ready to move off at first light. He's off to find the treasure, I believe.

'What treasure,' the other two men spoke again in unison.

'You really must stop doing that! Hmm, no-one knows. All they say is that there is a fantastic treasure on an island shaped like a rainbow.'

'But that's an old fairy tale,' Tailor said. 'Everyone's heard of the treasure at the end of the rainbow but no-one ever reaches it. If you go to try and get to it to dig it up, the rainbow's always gone before you get there, so you can't find it.'

'That's very true, Tailor,' Merlin responded. 'However, this is, apparently, not a real rainbow in the sky but an island possibly shaped like a rainbow or something on an island shaped like a rainbow – they're not quite sure. Many have tried to find this island, Black Dog explained to me, but nobody ever has as it's too well hidden.

'Anyway, to get back to the Contest to see what year it is and who would take over – Black Dog, as a defending contestant, and the other captains in his year got themselves ready and faced the other captains. There were about fifty men in all, all kitted out with bludgeons, swords, daggers, scimitars, balls and chains, cutlasses and the like, champing at the bit as they waited for the whistle for them to commence the fight. Each section tried to keep itself together as it's the year that had the most men standing that wins. He said that if you were cut off from your friends, you would more than likely be cut down. No, they had to stick together to win. However, this time it didn't work. It was obviously the Year of the Bird as by the end of an hour there were more birds standing than any other Year. Ships were always handed over together with all they contained including men, slaves, treasure, goods and food. The two men from the Year of the Bird were The Crow and The Raven: these men had the pick of the ships and, once chosen, had their names painted on the escutcheon. The only thing they couldn't change was the flag at the top of the mast, which is always the same as the figurehead. These had to be kept as they were, so that it would always be known what ship it had been in the first place. There are six ships in all and so the other four captains from the winning Year would then draw lots to see who got whichever ships were left, except one ship was still missing. Anyway, what did you learn?'

'Not much more than you,' Tailor responded. 'Except that there is someone called the Jackal who's gone missing on that other ship you just mentioned. The Jackal's ship sailed out of harbour over two years ago and has not been seen since. The Magpie was apparently very annoyed about this because when the Birds took over their vessels the Jackal's ship should have been his – so, having no ship, he's had to kick his heels in the Minstrel for the past year. Also, it looks as though he'll not now get a turn as the Year of the Bird is almost up – that is, unless they win the contest again the next time round. If that happens and he wins the toss, then one of the other Birds will have to stand down if the Jackal is still missing.

'That he is still missing, to us, would probably mean that the ship had foundered and everyone had drowned or been shipwrecked on an island somewhere. However, here, they can't accept that as, believe it or not, no-one ever dies and even if a ship is wrecked it still joins back up again some time later – though sometimes that takes many years!'

'Ah, yes,' Merlin nodded. 'This is the Place of Shades, or, to put it more aptly, the place of the living dead. They're dead already! But how is it that they don't know it?' He shook his head in wonder.

'Also, I was talking to a sharp little man called Hornet; apparently he captained one of the ships some three or more years back. He was extremely bitter that he hadn't won it back at the annual fight. He blames another of his compatriots, a man called the Mosquito, saying that he was becoming quite the coward. Well, a lot of his men were drinking with him and some of Black Dog's men were there as well. He told me that it was fairly quiet tonight but sometimes the place goes mental if someone says something about the men from the other sides.'

Salazar added a little more by stating that the men at the inn were getting excited by the fact that in a few weeks' time it would once again be combat time. 'They were a little agitated by the fact that the Raven was setting sail for places too far off to be able to return in time and had hoped to stop him from going, telling him he would be gone too long and would thus be breaking the rules of the game. But they were far too drunk to do anything or even, in that state, really care. Apparently there isn't much to do on land except get drunk. They say it's the only way to forget themselves.'

'Come, men, let's try The Minstrel and see what we can learn in there.'

NINE

I watched as three men left one of the hostelries and strode across the square towards the opposite inn feeling a stirring of recognition but before I had an opportunity to set the cogs of my brain in motion my eyes were drawn towards a larger group of sailors who had spilled out of the same inn and were now stumbling towards our ship.

The men were approaching us recklessly; I mean, our ship was, by now, fully loaded again and it and the men aboard were prepared for anything. My eyes searched in both directions and I, for one, would not dare to attack any of the evil looking men peering down at the approaching delegation. It was soon apparent that they were terribly drunk and thus no threat at all. Their leader stood with legs splayed and hands on hips as he rocked dangerously backwards and forwards before trying to remember what it was he wanted to say. With a face showing a great deal of confusion it was with gratitude and much shaking of hands and slapping of backs that he received enlightenment from one of his not quite so inebriated comrades.

'We're looking for work. Do you have a place for my mipmates and she?'

'Shipmates and me!' one of the others corrected him.

Staring at the other man for a few moments, he grinned, turned back to us and corrected himself. 'Do you have a place for my mipmates and him?' he pointed at the other man, who merely nodded. 'We're eshellent deckhands and don't eat too much, though we do like the occasional drink,' he slurred.

'Occasional!' the Raven scoffed under his breath. 'They look like they've been marinated in the stuff!' Then, loudly, 'Come up me maties and we'll see what you're made of. As if I'd accept dogs on my ship.' This last comment made under his breath.

Only three made it up the gangplank; two fell off it into the foaming water between the ship and the dock where they seemed to sink without a trace to the huge delight and jeers of the men on board but no-one else seemed to care. The rest, obviously not quite as stupidly drunk as the others, decided to return to the inn.

As soon as the spokesman and his two comrades came aboard they were quickly assessed by Pick who nodded at the captain when he examined the latter two men but pulled down his mouth at their spokesman. Then it was all dealt with fairly rapidly. It would be with some confusion that two men would wake from their drunken stupor later that day and find themselves in a stinking hole and shackled to an oar along with almost eighty other poor souls. Not so for their leader, though, as he was quickly despatched over the side where, like the others before him, he sank like a stone and was followed down by at least three diving serpents.

'Won't need to go to the slave sales now,' the Raven chuckled. 'We only needed two replacements and now we've got 'em. We'll set sail before dawn Pick. Sort it out! Boy – follow me.' He strode ahead and then down into his cabin chuckling quietly, 'nothing like volunteers.' Then, bursting with uncontrolled laughter he walked through the door, sat down at his desk and beckoned me over. Wiping the water from his eyes and nose with the sleeve of his coat, he gradually stopped, holding onto his side as he rubbed away the stitch that was forming there.

'Right, boy,' he croaked hoarsely, 'early tomorrow we'll head off to sea and see where we are taken. The figurehead knows we're off in search of the treasure. I understand from whispers brought back to me from shore that it is near here somewhere and worth a king's ransom and I'm certain that the Jackal is the key – so find him, find the treasure. When it comes to battle, no-one – and I mean absolutely no-one – can best me.'

I didn't know about the Contest for control of the ships at that stage; all I could think about was keeping myself alive and above decks and, therefore, doing what the captain ordered. He hadn't asked me to do anything wicked, so far, and I wasn't quite sure what I'd do if it came to that. However, those thoughts, when they tried to find entry into my brain, were quickly banished – how do you know what might happen if they are given admittance?

'Right, boy, as soon as we leave harbour, you go up on deck with the map and add to it whatever you see either to port or to starboard. I don't know how I didn't think of any of this before. I am a genius; I believe I'm the only captain with a mapmaker on board. So, when it comes to fleeing, I shall know every creek and gully I can hide in; then I'll be able to attack them unawares,' he added so as not to sound as though he might be running away and hiding like a coward. 'Make sure you position every headland and every bay – especially the ones well camouflaged. I don't intend to give up this ship. I am *not* going to take part in the next Contest – but I shall fight anyone who tries to take this ship from me – and I shall win! If the Jackal has done it, well so can I!

'For now – we'll search for the Jackal. Get some rest, boy – you'll need all your wits about you for later.'

I left his cabin and took up my place outside his door. A softer blanket had replaced the sacking and as I curled up in my little cubby-hole it wasn't long before the comfort of it and the gentle sway of the ship began to rock me off to sleep. Isn't it funny how some thought that has slightly troubled you during the day but has hibernated for a while, suddenly presses a button, shoots into your brain and sleep runs away like the darkness when a light is switched on? Wide-awake now and getting extremely excited I reached out in my mind to Merlin.

'*Hush now! I hear you. But this is a different sort of place to what we are used to. Be careful – there may be many who can hear. I will come for you as soon as I can. Keep a low profile. Our friends are with me and also the large animal, although he and some of the others must have landed elsewhere. However, our "future leader" – mention no names – is here and also needs to be rescued. Have you seen him?*'

I knew he meant Arthur and a cold shiver went down my spine as I thought he might be a slave (or worse) on one of the other ships.

'No!'

'*Well, we shall strive to do so. We will catch up soon. Speak in riddles if you have to speak at all – I'd prefer it if you didn't try to contact me but only answer me when I speak to you. If you are desperate or in any sort of trouble or you find the one we are looking for, just say my name and I'll do the talking. Do you understand?*'

'Yes.'

'*Or you can call me,*' Salazar whispered into my mind.

'*Or me,*' Cabby added from wherever he was.

'*No, not you,*' Merlin spoke so that both Cabal and I could hear. '*But I'm glad you are safe,*' he added.

'*Can I join in this game?*' a strange voice tagged itself on to the end of our conversation.

'*Barriers up!*' Merlin ordered and all communication ended – apart from this strange voice that kept trying to speak to us. The probing went on for hours before he finally gave up.

I wondered if he – and I believed it was a he – would try again later or tomorrow. Who was it? Was it someone near or someone far away?

It was an extremely baggy-eyed boy that crept up the stairway to the prow of the ship as it set off just before dawn. I must keep alert; I must draw the map that the captain wanted – and without missing anything. I must keep my mind closed off to the prying voice that was trying to make contact. How could I call Merlin without it tagging on or, worse, knowing it was me?

The wind, which had been blowing into my face for most of the day and keeping me awake, lightened and then stilled completely; the drumbeat started up and soon the water swished to the rowing of the oars.

Earlier, two unrecognised voices started yelling to be let out from below decks: they didn't belong there, they shouted; there had been a huge mistake; just wait till their captain heard about it; and it stinks down here. Then the swish and crack of the whip – and I winced at that terrible sound – before a few loud cries preceded an awful silence. My time below was still too raw for me to be unaffected. Even though I was desperately tired, the awful thought that I might be forced to return to that dark, smelly pit kept me wide-awake and drawing my map until night fell. It was with dragging steps I eventually fell exhausted onto my blanket to be tossed about by painful thoughts and plunged deep into agonising nightmares – and no-one had made contact, but in only one respect was I pleased about that. Making sure my mental barriers were in place I had wondered, as I first drifted off to sleep, whether Merlin would be able to contact me without that intruder knowing.

TEN

As Merlin and Salazar strode through the doors of The Minstrel that first evening, they all collided into one another when Tailor, stopping abruptly, brought them up short behind him just inside the inn. Their eyes, gradually adjusting to the dimness, rounded in surprise as they watched Shake Spear entertaining at least a dozen men and two or three serving maids. He sat upon the end of the rough-hewn bar, legs dangling and, with hands upon hips, almost sang his story to the crowd. There was much laughter during the fable and raucous applause at the end. Some of the more rowdy element jumped up and pulled him off the bar, all the while thumping him on the back as they congratulated him on his excellent tale. With loud shouts, much pounding on the tables and drunken exclamations, they ordered the landlord to fill their tankards and laughingly thrust a brimming mug into Shake Spear's hands, urging him to tell another.

'I must rest a while,' he spluttered through the froth of the beer. 'A bit later my friends, while I think up another.'

'Shake Spear,' Merlin's voice was low as he made his way through the crowd to his friend. 'Is there somewhere we can talk more privately?'

'Certainly, good sir,' he replied, taking the three men into a room at the back of the inn. 'Follow me.'

After sitting them down at a small table beside a roaring fire and offering them refreshment, he leaned against the mantelpiece, lit a short clay pipe and waited for them to speak.

Merlin, a little troubled by Shake Spear's demeanour, cleared his throat and, with a growing discomfiture, asked, 'Are the others with you?'

'Others?' he replied, eyebrows raised. 'What others?'

'The other men and Ca... er, the dog? Friends of mine,' he responded, deciding to give no names.

'I'm sorry, sir,' he answered, 'but I don't know what you're talking about or, for that matter, who you are! Have you got me mixed up with someone else perhaps? It happens a lot, you know! Or have you just arrived here? Maybe it would be best if we introduced ourselves, eh? I'm known round these parts as the Minstrel, and the inn is named after me,' he explained proudly. 'I own it but hire the landlord you see out there to manage it for me so that I can be free to entertain the customers,' he pointed to the main room in the inn. 'I also have the privilege of conducting the Contest. Will you be around to watch? It's going to be held when the giant tree – the one you would have seen in the square – blossoms. It blossoms for one day every 365 days or thereabouts and while it's in flower the captains and their men fight for the privilege of gaining the ships for a year.

'However, it's beginning to be a bit of a problem.' He screwed up his face in consternation as he considered what had been happening over the last few years. 'Things ain't been going right. The Jackal has disappeared with one of the ships and hasn't been seen for nearly three years. That means that one of the captains who should have a ship when it's their Year's turn has to stand down and that causes so much trouble. And, not only that but now the Raven has decided to set to sea just as the tree is budding and from what I understand he's going to be gone for much too long. Why he didn't wait until after the Contest, I really don't know. Or perhaps I do know: I reckon, like the Jackal, he wants to hold on to his ship forever. That's going to cause problems, you know, as there are only six ships and no more can be built. Well, they tried to build one but it never got finished: every night, when the builders – if you can call them that – they were just anyone, you know – went off to get drunk – and get drunk they did – something happened, so when they got back to carry on building the ship, well, one day it just wasn't there!

'So, in the end they gave up and left it with just the six ships they already had. The men draw lots to see who's going to be captain and once in every few Contests the captains can be challenged to see if they can be beaten and then a new captain takes over – and that's also due to happen this year. Well, that's it! It's the Raven's turn to be challenged and he doesn't want to fight, I reckon, because he wants to stay captain of his ship. Eagle has put in a challenge – and they are usually bloody affairs, you know – and he's going to be furious if he doesn't get his chance.

'Be that as it may, it will cause riots if they are two ships down. Not only that, but their Year will surely not win with so many sailors absent. So another Year will win and not have a ship – or two – to sail in. It makes my job so much harder! But, I am being rude; I've told you who I am and haven't given you the opportunity to introduce yourselves.' He stood, waiting expectantly for their reply.

During all the time of Shake Spear's discourse, Merlin had been thinking rapidly. If the man in front of them was not Shake Spear, then he, Merlin, was a monkey's uncle. What on earth was going on here? He had noticed, whilst sojourning at the other inn, that a man had just appeared – yes, had literally taken shape before his eyes. The man had looked extremely surprised at arriving in such a place and had stood blinking rapidly before falling back into a chair and trying to make sense of his new and sudden surroundings. '*Another of the living dead,*' Merlin had thought. '*Must just be sent here when they die on earth,*' he had assumed. '*Must happen really quickly, though – in the twinkling of an eye I reckon: one minute you're up there,*' he raised his eyes to the rafters, '*and the next you're not!*'

Another more important thing he and Salazar had noticed was the large bump behind Shake Spear's left ear. '*Had he sustained that when he entered this place through the stone?*' he had wondered.

'*I expect he did,*' Salazar assumed. '*This is an extremely weird place. He speaks as though he's been here for years and the bizarre thing is, everyone else here seems to think he has as well. I wonder if you make up your own story as you go along?*' he mused.

'*I think you must be right. However, I believe we should be very careful. We'll have to try and get Shake Spear away from this place to see what we can do for him but, in the meantime, we, like our clothes, need to be incognito.*'

Merlin just about stopped Tailor, who had opened his mouth and inhaled a large lungful of breath, from making the introductions, 'Mr Minstrel…'

'Er, just Minstrel will do,' he interrupted.

'Minstrel,' Merlin said, more loudly, effectively stopping Tailor from continuing, 'My name is Ambrosius and these are my friends,' he added, swinging around and introducing the other two, 'Prince and Stitcher.'

Tailor almost burst out laughing but Salazar, watching him like a hawk, trod very heavily on his foot before, moving him away from Shake Spear with apologies and 'let's see what the damage is,' telling him to keep quiet. He soon realised he needed to be more circumspect.

Minstrel bowed politely to each in turn. 'Is your man all right?' Then, 'where are you staying? We have some spare rooms that you are welcome to,' he added, his voice trailing off as he watched a very large, surprised warlord start to appear in the fireplace. The others, hearing the sudden noise, turned to see what he was looking at before they, too, with staring eyes, became mesmerised by this materialisation.

The warlord, like others before him, carried on doing what he had been doing just a few seconds before – which was obviously taking part in a very bloody battle by the way he carried on thrusting with his sword and defending himself with his peltae – and then looking completely stunned; with a yowl, he hurled himself out of flames that had risen to his waist as they feasted upon something more tasty than their usual mundane fare of logs, smacking himself on the backside to make sure the fire did not take hold.

Unlike the man in the Nest who took some time to materialise, this one became visible within seconds. *'Must be something to do with the speed at which they die,'* Merlin thought as he stared at the hole in the man's chest.

After patting out the flames and staunching the flow of blood from his chest, blood that was drying up and disappearing as quickly as he had appeared, the man stood before them and, with troubled eyes, asked the obvious, 'Where am I?'

Shake Spear – or should I say Minstrel? – didn't seem to be at all put out by this manifestation and, bowing once again, introduced himself and told the man he had arrived at the best hostelry in Raven's Harbour, following the information with:

> "To-morrow, and to-morrow, and to-morrow,
> Creeps in this petty pace from day to day,
> To the last syllable of recorded time;
> And all our yesterdays have lighted fools
> The way to dusty death.
> Out, out, brief candle!
> Life's but a walking shadow; a poor player,
> That struts and frets his hour upon the stage,
> And then is heard no more: it is a tale
> Told by an idiot, full of sound and fury,
> Signifying nothing."

Merlin's mouth dropped open as he listened to Shake Spear's verses and wondered just what had happened to the man.

Shake Spear – or was it really Minstrel – went on to tell the man to straighten his chain mail and go through to the bar for a large tankard of ale as he always gave new customers the first one free and he looked as though he could really do with one.

The man, still looking confused, wandered off clanking into the other room where, we later discovered, he soon became drunk and fell asleep, propped up in a corner of the room.

'So, Ambrosius, what do you say about those rooms?'

'It is very kind of you, Minstrel, but I have to look for three of my men. I have one other inn to search in this town and if they are not there then I will have to search further. However, I shall keep your kind offer in mind and shall let you know one way or the other if I find that I have to leave town. Perhaps you might like to join our search, for a change of air, perhaps?'

'Perhaps I may,' he laughed. 'I believe I like your company.'

The three men made their goodbyes and walked over to the last hostelry in the square hoping they would not find the others in similar condition to Shake Spear.

They pushed open the door and, coughing at the smoke, swaggered inside.

'Granddad,' Daniel interrupted as Jack drew breath to carry on with the story while Ben helped him make a pot of tea and slice the fruitcake. 'Was it really someone who looked like Shake Spear or was the Minstrel really him? Come on, you must tell us this time; it really won't spoil the story. Oh, come on granddad.'

Laughing to himself as he stoked the fire and added a few more logs, Jack nodded. 'Yes, they are one and the same. You probably got a clue from the fact that he had an enormous bump behind one ear. Though what that normally does is make people forget things, not make them think they are someone completely different! But we were all really glad that that happened, as you will see as the story unfolds.'

ELEVEN

Our ship had headed away from the harbour and for the next three days I made notes and drawings of the land as we travelled south and with the help of some of the more knowledgeable crew, named one or two islands that we had passed on the port side. They were very small and, therefore, couldn't be Rainbow Island, but I marked them on my map anyway. It wouldn't be long before I came off the end of the page; perhaps the captain would give me a bigger parchment so that I could re-do the chart and make a better job of it?

I'd gone up on deck on the third morning to find that the wind had begun to rise and, therefore, the rowers were not required. I could still remember the feeling of relief at being told to stop rowing and not having to do any more of that backbreaking work for a while; I can also remember the boredom of doing absolutely nothing. And the hunger! At least when I was rowing it took my mind off it. Shaking these thoughts away and as it was noon I leaned over the side to look at the hog. This was now one of my duties and I was relieved to see that it had its eyes open, so we were, thankfully, going in the right direction – wherever that might be!

I was about to sit down again when my eye was caught by an unusual sight. At first I was merely curious because there were so many new and weird things to see in this peculiar place but within a few seconds that awful companion of mine – Fear – began to climb up my spine to see how much of my still very short and bristly hair it could try to stand on end once it had finished tightening my stomach and loosening my bowels.

'Whirlpool,' I screamed, before realising that the sound had not actually left my throat. Pick – how was he aware of my panic? – rushed up beside me, climbed up the side ropes and peered in the direction of my shaking finger. Jumping down, he ran over to the ship's bell, ringing it frantically until the captain, hat and wig askew, emerged from his cabin and strode over to the prow.

'Is it a tornado?' I asked the captain.

'No, boy! It's much worse than that: it's the Unsettled Sea's vortex!'

'Vortex?' I asked.

'Yes! We'll soon see it – the whirlpool – very dangerous.' Turning around he began shouting at the men. As the wind whipped up, the waves began to lash at the ship and spill over onto the deck causing the vessel to roll frighteningly from side to side. It was becoming a very hazardous place to be. I twisted my arm through one of the side ropes and, like several of the others, held on as instructed by the captain.

'Hard a starboard,' he yelled through the gathering storm. Tighten those ropes! Tie up the sails. Turn the ship! Get those rowers rowing. Faster, man!'

I listened to the dreaded beat of the drum as I glanced quickly over the side to watch the oars start moving. How glad I was that I wasn't down there: the cold wind and sea water would be crashing through the holes; the strong current would make it extraordinarily hard to pull on the oars and it wouldn't be long before their backs felt like they were breaking – and that before any whip landed across them – and their hands would soon be bleeding. My heart went out to them. But worse – what if the ship sank? They were manacled and would not be able to escape! I went cold with fear at the thought of being pulled down with the ship and all that water waiting to drown me. How long would I be able to hold out before I had to breathe it in? Even now I found myself holding my breath. Eventually, with lungs almost bursting, I let it out thinking, oh, how glad I was not to be down there! Then, again, was it less painful to drown by being up here than it was manacled down there? 'Stop it!' I told myself as another old companion – Panic – clawed at my thoughts.

But we were losing the battle.

I looked over my shoulder toward the stern and every time the ship dipped, to my horror I could see us being drawn ever closer towards the rapidly expanding swirling water. It wouldn't be long before we were at its edge – if that were to happen we would be gripped and soon be sucked down through its centre.

Three of the Raven's sailors jumped over the side to try and swim away from it but ended up being sucked into it more swiftly than the ship. Watching them swirling around in ever decreasing circles, the last I saw of them was a mass of arms and legs moving like the clappers and horror-struck faces as they called out for help. We couldn't hear what they were saying for the noise from the force of the storm overrode everything else. All eyes were fixed on them as they disappeared down through the centre of swirling water and terror was on every face as the sailors contemplated their fast arriving fate.

I found myself, once again, praying to Arthur's God.

Those that hadn't jumped or been washed overboard were all by now soaked to the skin and merely hanging on to whatever they could for dear life. Was that life about to be extinguished? For goodness' sake – I'm only 13! *'Merlin – help me!'*

'Merlin, eh?' that strange voice interrupted my thoughts.

I looked down to see Pick grinning up at me and, because I had not closed my mind properly or because the truth of it was writ large upon my face, became aware that he now knew it was me that had been talking before.

'So who is this Merlin? No, no, don't try to hide it! I know it's you who's been doing all this talking inside your head and now you know that I can do it too. So, who is Merlin?'

'He's my friend.'

'Ah, a friend! Is he aboard this ship? No?' as I shook my head. *'You don't know how great it is to have a conversation with somebody. Since they cut out my tongue all I've been able to do is make awful sounds and some of the sailors treat me very badly because of it – they think because I have no tongue I have no brain. But now, you and I can have wonderful talks, eh?'*

I was really not sure if I'd like that or not but seeing as our present circumstances were likely to cut short any close friendship with him – or anyone else come to that – I merely nodded. My face had by then gone a curious shade of green and, puking, I was only vaguely aware of what the odd man said.

'It's all a nonsense, really,' he chuckled. *'We'll end up going down into the whirlpool – men, ship and slaves – but then we'll all be spewed up again somewhere – men, ship and slaves – and then have to find ourselves and each other again. I expect the Raven will be extremely annoyed because he's set his heart – if he's got one, that is – on finding the treasure. Now it looks like everything's against him and he'll have to fight in the Contest anyway. Hmm, I wonder if that also happened to the Jackal.'*

'But how do you survive?' I asked him. *'If you all drown, how can you possibly come back again?'*

'Drown? Oh yes,' he grinned. *'We might drown – not a pleasant experience, I can tell you and worse things do happen at sea – but we don't die! We're dead already! I thought you knew that! Well, maybe you don't know – some of them here just won't accept it, you know; they live in complete denial and others haven't even thought about it.'*

'But I didn't die!' I explained. *'I think a mad witch sent me here to punish me or get rid of me. Does that mean that if I end up in the maelstrom I really will die?'* I groaned.

'*Hmm, that's a hard one,*' he answered but I could see he thought I must be one of the dead who was living in denial. '*Perhaps you will.*' He stroked his chin while he considered this and then, brightening, '*But then you will join us anyway.*'

'*But I can't do that! Surely I would be out of time and that might cause really serious problems. Perhaps that's why this is happening now,*' I almost sobbed as I thought of the uselessness of any of these arguments, due to our present hopeless circumstances and imminent death – well *my* imminent death!

We were getting too close for comfort now.

'*I know what we can do,*' he answered, grinning and patting me on the arm continued, '*Come with me.*'

I followed him to the lower deck where all of the stores were kept. Most had fallen to the floor where it bobbed about, some being partly submerged by rising seawater. Two or three barrels were rolling about uncontrollably and it was to one of these that Pick made his way as he waded through the waist high water.

'*Help me empty it,*' he ordered me and after prising open the lid we tipped its contents – hundreds of what looked a little like apples – into the swelling water.

'*OK – we'll need to get this on deck. Help lift it onto my back and push the bottom of it as I go up the stairs. Don't forget to bring the lid.*' We struggled up the few steps and along the gangway until we could make our way out onto the deck.

The captain was still shouting his orders and didn't seem to care what we were doing. '*By the way, Pick, what are we doing?*' I asked.

'*Well, the only thing that can be done! So far as you are concerned, you have to be thrown overboard!*'

'What,' I screamed out loud and then, '*You can't do that! I'll really die!*'

'*Well, there doesn't seem to be any argument,*' he responded. '*We have two problems here. The first one is that if you disappear down the whirlpool with the rest of us, although we'll eventually be OK – you won't – you'll die! But then you'll be one of us as you'll be dead but then, again it's possibly not your time and you'll cause mayhem – probably! And it's mayhem now, isn't it? You know, it's been really interesting talking to you. It's been so long and I'm going to miss you but I expect that if we can save you, we'll meet up again and you can trust me to keep your secret because I can't talk and I certainly can't read let alone write! No, you have to go over the side because that's the* second problem – you're bad luck and I reckon this is all your fault. So, if you will be so kind as to climb inside this barrel, I'll secure the lid and make sure it's watertight, then – over you go! If you don't break up, you should land somewhere safely enough. Come on now; this is the only chance you have of really not dying and there's not much time!'

I was really not very happy about this. However, we were by now at the very edge of those swirling waters and I felt very much like someone stuck between the devil and the deep blue sea or, as I'd read recently in my Greek mythology book, Scilla and Charibdys – literally.

Climbing reluctantly into that tight-fitting barrel, I chickened out and jumped back up; Pick, beckoning two others over, helped them lift me and squash me down into it. I sat then – did I have an option? – arms hugging my knees with head bowed onto them as the lid was lowered over me and hammered into place. Darkness settled on me along with despair as I felt myself lifted by more than one pair of hands and settled onto the ship's side before, stomach churning, I was tossed over its side. I hit the water with a clunk and then felt myself bobbing mostly upside down or sideways on its surface.

Within seconds, like a switch being pulled, the storm abated and deathly silence smothered me. Was I a Jonah? Was I, like him, bad luck and, once thrown overboard, everything was put right again? – well for everyone else it was at any rate! Had my prayer to Arthur's God brought me to this? Would the barrel be smashed and I'd get eaten by the huge whale of the Bible, or the nine-headed monster of those Greek tales? All I knew was that all the others were in the ship and I was not. I heard, faintly and getting fainter all the time, the beat of the drum and swish of the oars as the ship moved away, while I, suddenly caught up in that dying but still swirling eddy, gradually started to spin around. All other noise was finally drowned out by the roar of those crashing waters as they took hold of me. The whirlpool was disappearing, getting smaller and smaller but I was still caught up in it and nearing its centre and then, spinning faster and faster, I was finally sucked down into it. This was absolutely awful. Would I die? No, I mustn't! I'd end up one of the living dead! 'Merlin – help me!'

TWELVE

Salazar pulled opened the door, pushed back the blue feather and bone curtain that hung just inside it, and stepped through, closely followed by Tailor and Merlin. Once again, just as before, all conversation in the hostelry stopped as, to a man, everyone turned and stared at them. There was not one friendly face among them.

Merlin, just like before, produced gold coin as if from thin air and tossed it carelessly onto the counter, inviting all the men to "have a drink on me".

They were not quite as receptive as those in The Minstrel and it was only after one or two of the more drunken element had swayed up to the bar and slurred their thanks that the atmosphere relaxed a little.

'*You would think it was them doing us a favour!*' Merlin winked at Salazar. '*Can't see any of our men in here, though,* he continued as his eyes swiftly surveyed the dark room. '*Find out what you can and we'll meet outside in an hour. Make sure Tailor is with you!*'

'Well, what a closed-mouthed bunch!' Merlin exclaimed as they left. 'I got absolutely nothing from that lot!'

'Me neither!' Salazar added.

'Apparently they're waiting for one of the other ships to come in. They reckon it went further than Crowsport, as it believed Rainbow Island was in that direction. It's been gone a long time now and apart from the fact that it has to be back in time for the Contest, they said the captain was certain he could get his hands on the treasure before anyone else had a clue it was there; apart from that, as so many other people had gone up there anyway, he felt sure he'd be able to pick them up and sell them back here in the slave market. They hold them every ten days – that and selling fresh livestock (if there is any) and there's one in two days' time,' Tailor added.

'Well, you seem to have had more success than us in finding out what's happening,' Merlin said, a bit miffed. 'Anything else?'

'Yes.'

Merlin waited, almost patiently for a few moments, before sighing and asking, 'Well, what?'

'Oh, yes, well the really drunken one said something about Arthur.'

The other two men's ears pricked up. 'Well why didn't you say before? Well come on then, what about him?' Merlin demanded.

'Well, it really didn't make much sense. Something about the Endless Hills.'

'Yes, go on! Endless Hills! Is he there? Is he lost? On his own? Captured? Come on! What?'

'He said that it was a pity that nice bloke Arthur'd got it into his head to go into the Endless Hills. He said he was just sitting there one day.'

'Who was just sitting where one day?' Salazar interjected.

'The man said Arthur was just sitting there in the inn one day when he nodded and said, "OK". When he asked him what was going on, he said that someone had whispered into his ear that he had to get up and go into the Endless Hills. He told him that was mad as no-one ever came out but he just smiled and said that everything was all right and not to worry.'

'Was it our Arthur?' Merlin asked.

'I reckon so,' Tailor answered. 'He said he wore brass or gold arm shields on his upper arms with red dragons emblazoned on them.'

Merlin's face went even paler than it normally was as he gritted his teeth.

'He said that was a month or so ago. Then he said that Bonzo had followed him not two days ago.'

'Bonzo?' Merlin and Salazar exclaimed together.

'Now I'm doing it!' Merlin added.

'Yes, that's just what I said. He said it was a huge dog. Sounded like Cabal, I thought.'

'*Cabby! Cabby, can you hear me?*' Merlin reached out to the hound. Nothing!

'*I wonder if the hills block our communication.*'

'*Could be! We'll just have to keep trying. It must have been him. I wish he'd let us know what he was going to do before he just went off and did it!*'

Tailor, becoming perplexed as he looked from one to the other of the frowning Druids, thought he'd done something wrong and, starting to apologise, asked if he should go back in to get some more information.

'No, no, Tailor. You've done well. I believe it was Cabal – obviously they didn't know his real name – and he's gone after Arthur. Although how they knew he was following Arthur is beyond me! Well, he'll have more chance of finding him if the trail hasn't gone cold and, hopefully, he'll leave a trail for us to follow. However, before that, I think we should try and see what we can do about Shake Spear and also find the other men. We'll more than likely need all the muscle we can get. Now where on earth could they have got to?'

THIRTEEN

Arthur had exhausted his supply of food and water some four days ago and was now becoming extremely disorientated. He had followed the funny little dancing man and had almost caught up with him twice but then he'd jump out of reach and skip on.

'Wait,' he'd called out many times but apart from turning round and with long bony finger beckoning him, the little man jigged on but had stayed well out of reach.

At first it had been a great game, he'd thought. He'd found himself laughing until the tears ran down his cheeks, leaning against any outcrop of rock or cliff and rubbing his side to ease the stitch that had doubled him up. What was going on was, to him, the funniest thing ever. No-one had made him laugh like this silly little man. Where had he come from? Arthur didn't know and didn't care. All he knew was that this was fantastic sport and the game had to be played. He *wanted* to play; he'd never had so much fun in his life and he didn't want it to end. He ran and ran after the little dancing man until his legs went like jelly and he wobbled to the floor, falling onto his back and laughing like a drain. For nearly a week this went on, day after day, exhaustion gradually slowing him down until with an almost permanent pain in his side he could go no further. The laughter stopped, the little man disappeared and sanity returned.

Arthur had come to the end of his strength. Wandering around for days without food or drink, he was now becoming weak and cold; on some of the higher slopes snow had started to lie. He had been fascinated at first as he watched the snow forming on the rocks because it didn't fall from the sky like normal snow; it seemed to just grow like moss, only quicker – a thousandfold quicker, forming deep drifts within minutes. He wasn't fascinated any more. The little man had not returned; he'd called for him but to no avail. Why had he followed him in the first place? By now he was finding time to ask the questions that before weren't important and, at the time, didn't seem to need asking let alone answering. When the little man had beckoned, it had seemed the most natural thing in the world to follow. It was great: a game; a wonderful time; the funniest thing that had happened to him ever. He wouldn't have been able to resist even if he'd wanted to. He just *had* to follow this Dark Ages pied piper! But now that he had the time to reflect, the dreadfulness of it all clutched at his mind like a vice: the little man wasn't funny at all – he was horrific. His fingers were long and spindly, as was his nose and ears and his teeth, also long, had been filed to sharp points; his body was green and covered in scales. Shivering every time he thought of him now, Arthur believed it must have been a demon. Why hadn't he seen all this before? 'Don't think of it,' he told himself every time his mind started to dwell on that apparition.

Now hungry, thirsty, cold and tired he tried melting the snow between his palms to drink it but it just wouldn't melt. All it did was make his hands cold. As soon as he opened his hands or dropped it, it shot back to its original place like a pin to a magnet.

'*This is a most peculiar place,*' he thought, trying to cool his hot, cracked lips with his cold hands.

The wind had got up; it howled around the boulders and over the snow setting Arthur's teeth a-chattering. Finding a narrow cleft, he wedged himself between the rocks out of the wind for warmth and before long found himself drifting off to sleep.

'No, no, go away,' he argued, pushing away the insistent hands that dragged at his arms. 'I just want to sleep! Come back in the morning; just leave me!'

They were not going to give up. Pulling at his arms, fingers, hair and ears they eventually got him to his feet. His lips and fingers were starting to turn blue. His resistance by now was very low and finally he mentally agreed with himself that it was going to be easier to do what they wanted than resist. He let them lift him to his feet and guide him away. With eyes half-open and panting heavily with the effort, he allowed himself to be taken to wherever they wanted. He was exhausted, hungry, becoming dehydrated and delirious. He didn't care any more. If he was going to die, well, so be it.

With eyes half closed and toes dragging along the ground, they took him away.

He didn't see that which his rescuers were determined to save him from.

Not two hundred yards away was something that could have only come from the pages of legend, as the like had never been seen in real life before – but, then, could this place be called real life? Many men – if, indeed, they were men – crept forward to carry out the dastardly deed to which they had been programmed. As they drew closer, Arthur's rescuers kept alert, frequently looking over their shoulders to make sure they kept well out of range.

Two groups of men – well, not really men but half-men – crept steadily forward, led by the green elongated little demon who was beckoning them on. To clarify – they were men merely from the waist up; from the waist down to their feet they were covered in long, coarse, grey hair; they had two legs which were shaped like the back end of a goat and finished off with cloven hooves – upon which they were able to stand, walk or run.

The first of these two groups, he would find out, were known as the Archers. They held a quiver of arrows on their backs but carried no bow. Did they throw them or stab you with them? No! As each one pulled his left arm stiffly forward, locked his elbow and spread wide his fingers, a bow formed itself out of his thumb and little finger; the rest curled round and held the shaft. They reached for the first of many arrows as they rushed forward to attack. But now, with cloven hooves clattering on the rocks, they were closing in.

Alongside the Archers, but set back slightly, were the Swordsmen. These were similar in build but had a different type of weaponry altogether: as they stiffened their right arms forward, swords shot out from the palms of their hands around which they closed their fingers and they, too, were then ready for action.

The little rescue party was finding it extremely difficult to get Arthur to understand the urgency of their plight. They pulled and pushed him along while their adversaries crept ever closer. Didn't he realise what a terrible predicament they were in? He dragged his feet, trying every few steps to lie down and seemed to be getting heavier by the minute.

They looked once again at their pursuers, who'd grouped themselves in a semi-circle around their prey; most were leaning back on one bent leg, giving the impression of coiled springs. Then, with one almighty roar, they rushed at them, swords flashing in the light and arrows soaring high before plunging earthwards.

Panic and fear giving them wings, they pulled and pushed Arthur with all their might. Would they reach safety in time?

A low cackle could be heard bouncing back and forth among the mountainous hills. It didn't sound human but, to Arthur at least, even in his semi-conscious state, it did sound familiar.

FOURTEEN

I was by now screaming myself hoarse and beating frantically on the sides of my barrel prison – though sanity might ask why! There was absolutely no-one out there to help me open it and, even if I got out I would most certainly drown or be pulled to pieces by the roaring waters – or worse! Although the storm had by now gone completely, I could feel myself being swept ever faster downwards into that spiralling whirlpool. What would happen when I reached its centre or the seabed? Would I be shattered, crushed to pieces, drowned, eaten alive by those serpents or what other horrible death awaited me? Well, I couldn't get out and I shook as I awaited my fate.

I'd stopped screaming and hammering on the sides of the barrel; for one thing I couldn't hear myself anyway and for another my arms didn't appear to belong to me anymore and were stuck to the lid of the barrel and, as I'd become frozen with fear with it twisting so fast, was on the verge of passing out. I felt very sick and wanted to throw up but the gravitational force kept me suctioned to the side of the barrel and thus, fortunately, the vomit stayed in.

I lost consciousness.

'Wow, that was something to be seen,' Cabal chuckled – well, for a dog it was as near a chuckle as it could be, albeit through his mind – as, grinning, he licked my salty and bruised face. *'There I was just sniffing along the beach trying to find Arthur, some form of life, be it another dog, something interesting to eat or maybe Merlin or one of the others, when suddenly, like a cork popping out of a bottle, there you were – flying out of the sea – well the barrel was at any rate. I just about managed to get out of the way before you flattened me!'*

'Well you could have helped soften my fall.' I grumbled, shaking my head to get some sense back into it as I sat upright rubbing one of the many bruises that would soon colour my otherwise pale body.

'Er, no way friend. I doubt whether I would have survived your weight! Talking of weight – you've got quite skinny! Well, your arms have muscle enough – have you been working out without eating? Not a good idea – you need a bit of balance with your food when you're training you know! Fresh food is best, whether it's fruit, bread or meat – now meat has to be very fresh – fish is best and then either a little red meat or chicken – and the nearer the kill the better...'

'Stop it Cabby,' I moaned as I picked off more broken barrel from my skin and discovered yet another tender bruise making its presence felt. 'I've been shackled to an oar for I know not how long and being fed on bread and water for months on end doesn't help!'

'Sorry! But it's great to see you. Why do you keep doing those disappearing acts? You've been gone for more than a twelvemonth, you know!' he mused. 'Where do you go when you leave for all that time? Surely you haven't been on that galleon for over a year? Mind you, you look very thin!' He had by now stopped licking my wounds and was circling round, making a note of all the changes to my body. 'You've grown taller though, or is that because of your hair? It looks a bit peculiar sticking up like that!' he commented at my bristly scalp. 'Stand up and let me take a good look at you.'

'And you've grown extremely bossy!' I replied, like him, through my mind as I stood to my feet. The stones on the beach were rough but my feet had become toughened by running about the ship and climbing its ropes with unshod feet and so they did not prove too much of a discomfort to me.

No-one interrupted our conversation – they were either too far away or, perhaps, thought it best not to chance being overheard by anyone who might have the gift – like Pick!

'And it's so good to see you again, Cab,' I laughed – partly through relief at still being alive but mostly because I had really missed him. Removing what I hoped was the last splinter from my palm I sat next to him with my arm round his neck and just hugged him for a few moments, unable to speak. But eventually we had to find out what had been going on from each other.

I spent the next half hour or so asking Cabby all sorts of questions about Merlin and the others, how had he found me and where we now were.

Imagine my surprise when he told me the answer to that one. 'Place of the dead!' I exclaimed. 'You mean I'm really dead – we're dead? How can that be? One of the men on board was telling me a little bit about it but I really thought I was still alive and he was just mad.'

Cabby kept trying to explain but, still reeling from my all-too-current adventures, my mind was in such turmoil and dread – I'd never see mum and dad again – well not until they died at any rate – but then this seemed an extremely wicked place and then I wondered if, horror of horrors, I'd gone to hell and what if they went to heaven?

Oh no – they were good (well I thought they were at any rate) and they'd obviously go to heaven and then I'd never see them again. I'd be stuck here with these awful people who only laughed when it was at other people's misfortunes, who were always fighting, treated some people (like those shackled to the oars) in a terrible way and were only interested in the treasure – that which they already had and the great one they all wanted to find which they thought was on Rainbow Island. I couldn't live like that! But then, if I really was here, then I was already dead! And I'd never see my mum and dad again!

It was when my thoughts had gone full circle and I was back at my mum and dad again that Cabal, who'd been trying very politely to interrupt me by mind speaking to me, took the only step he now could. Jumping at me and pushing me to the floor he pinned me to the ground with his huge forepaws on my shoulders and just barked, full blast, into my face. Well, it was very loud for a start and quite wet as splutters of spit shot out all over my face. He stopped only when he realised I was shouting at him to get off. Lifting himself off my shoulders he began speaking to me before I could succumb once more to my scary thoughts.

'*You're not dead! You are just in the place of the dead! If you were dead you wouldn't bleed and just look at you – bruising and bleeding all over the place. Merlin and Salazar and some of the men are here somewhere to rescue you and Arthur…*'

'*Oh dear! I'd forgotten about Arthur. How selfish can you get?*'

'*…yes – and Arthur,*' he continued. '*The witch has something to do with all of this but just what we haven't found out. Merlin did say, though, that we must make sure we don't get killed because if we do we won't be able to get back. Now, somehow we'll have to try to find the others. Well what happened was we journeyed to Avebury and then we all went through one of the standing stones there…*'

'What – you went through as well?' I interrupted him with a very shocked look on my face. I shouldn't have done it but it came out without me even thinking about it. Don't you just hate it when your mouth goes into drive before your mind has got into gear? I mentally kicked myself and resolved to try and stop doing that – a word, once spoken, cannot be retrieved. Like a tiny rudder, it is able to turn the whole ship and then a whole relationship can end up on the rocks. What devastation a tiny tongue can do, eh?

'*I understand,*' he spoke extremely haughtily into my mind, '*that bravery is not just going for it, but it's being extremely afraid of something and still going for it!'*

I felt ashamed and said so, adding, *'You're the bravest friend I know, Cab. Forgive me for being so rude and so wrong.'*

'Hrrmph, you're forgiven.'

Don't you just love dogs?

We walked on for some few moments before I could get him to continue with his story but with a bit of gentle persuasion he was only too happy to oblige.

'Merlin organised the men and got them to go through the portal first. He pushed me through with Tailor but we seem to have got separated from each other and Merlin and Salazar followed behind us. It was a weird sensation. We pushed ourselves up against the stone – well Merlin actually pushed me – and I could feel the resistance as I pressed against it, feeling my hair and skin flattening against my face and body as though we were trying to push the thing over or crush our noses in the effort. "We're never going to get in there," I'd thought. Then Tailor vanished into it, pulling me through after him as Merlin shoved me from behind.'

'It was weird in there, I can tell you. I saw the others, seemingly miles ahead or behind, and they looked like ghosts – they floated along and I saw Wite who had moved on some hundreds of yards in front of me just disappear. Tailor, floating well away from me now, suddenly shot up into the air – if it was air – and he, too, disappeared. Then it was my turn. The awful thing about being in there though, was seeing lots of weird people passing us, reaching out to us with horrific faces – they looked like they were being tortured; they tried to grab me with skeletal fingers as I passed them but they couldn't keep hold of me as I just drifted right through them; there were other weird things within it too – phantoms, grinning masks, disjointed bodies that kept falling apart and joining up together again. Lines and lines of people roped together and shuffling along with their heads bowed down. Heads floating around without eyes and then eyes – just eyes without heads – glaring at me – and awful noises – screams and the like. I just hope we don't have to go back the same way or,' he shivered, 'end up there! Anyway, eventually I came out the other side of the stone and – but you will probably laugh at me – my hair was standing out all over me.'

He looked across at me as I sat, still rubbing my bruises but I had learned a little lesson by now and dare not look up at him – let alone laugh. He seemed satisfied and continued his story. I did add, though, that different stones seemed to have different properties because with some of them I had been able to just float right through but with some of the others it had been extremely difficult – I had almost to force my way into them.

Cabby shivered again at the thought and then continued: '*I found my way into the town and, after hearing about Arthur started looking for him but I ended up here – been here for a couple of days now and haven't been able to get away. I kept thinking I'd gone in the right direction when I'd end up back where I'd been before. Perhaps it was because I was supposed to wait for you, eh? Anyway – I didn't like it inside the stone.*'

'OK Cab, let's try and find out where we are and where the others are. We have to meet up with them. We have to rescue Arthur. Let's see if we can contact Merlin or Salazar. By the way, which of the men did they bring with them?'

Even though we were in this barren and lifeless place, we were just so happy to be with each other again. I, for one, had missed Cabal so much. We carried on talking whilst intermittently reaching out in our minds to the others but so far there was no response. Cabal showed me the pathway between the cliff face that he had gone through to see if he could get off the beach and find the others. We tried it again but, like he'd said before, it did a circuitous route back to the beach. So, we had decided that the best we could now do would be to carry on along the beach and just hope we were going in the right direction. There was nothing to eat and it was only by chance that we found some fresh water as it trickled out of the seemingly endless cliff face. We drank as much as our stomachs could hold, knowing it might be some time before we found any more.

On the third morning we awoke to Merlin's voice calling out to us.

'*I know you're near. Come on wake up! I need to talk to you. Wake up! Wake up!*'

I eventually climbed the steep steps of interrupted sleep and, rubbing my eyes, pushed myself up and sat with my back against the cliff. '*Merlin, it's great to hear you.*'

'*Where are you?*'

'*I don't know but Cabal is with me and we've been walking for days along the beach with the cliffs to our left.*'

'*Ah, stay there! I'll find you. I'll be there shortly.*'

All was quiet for a minute; then amazingly he was with us.

'*Sorry about that,*' he chuckled as he materialised ten yards away. '*You know I hate just appearing as it causes too many questions, but you know me, so that's all right.'*

We were so happy to see him even though he looked weird in his peculiar disguise but, that aside, he was true to form as pulling a leather flask from one of his many pockets, he made sure we had as much water as we needed before offering us some cheese and fruit for me and a small strange-looking bone for Cabal that still held a great amount of meat. I didn't like to think of what it was he was chewing on but I think he was much too hungry to care. The main thing, though, was that Merlin was with us. How I'd missed him back in the 20th Century. He was obviously following my thoughts and I believe he, too, was just as pleased to see me.

However, he had lots to do and so cut my train of thinking short. *'Sit, sit, both of you,'* he grinned at us. *'You can eat while I get you up to date with what is happening. You'll feel so much better when you have a full stomach and when you know what's going on. Hmm, that's if I know what's really going on. Things are a bit too weird here even for me. But, I'll tell you what I know and then you can tell me your story.'*

I didn't know how wonderful such a plain meal of cheese and apple could be. My food had been quite good, albeit samey, on the ship once I'd been rescued from the gruel and water diet I'd had to resign myself to but after three days of absolutely nothing, this was nectar. I could see that Cabby was thinking the same as those gigantic teeth ripped the meat from the bone.

'...and so, once you've both finished, I'll throw some dragon's droppings over us and we should end up back with Salazar.'

'Should?' I asked.

'Well, there's no knowing what might happen down here,' he replied out loud, 'but this other powder worked OK in finding you, so hopefully the droppings will work in taking us back. Though where Wite, Brosc and Nell's son are, I'm still at a loss.'

My mind was whisked back to listening to Merlin explain about the powder he called "dragon's droppings". Well, it really was the droppings from a dragon – although droppings was a bit of a misnomer as when dragons really do "go" there is always an absolutely huge mound of the stuff and they only went occasionally which, thinking about it, was probably a good thing. Merlin had explained how he had had to sit and wait – sometimes for days – until the mountain of droppings was ready to collect: when it was ready it glowed like phosphorus and had to be collected, bottled and stored very quickly. It's main use was for transporting people or things from one place to another, although Merlin had said that when mixed with other ingredients it could be used for a completely different type of magic altogether.

'Anyway, ready?'

And then, without even waiting for our response he sprinkled it over us and we were whisked away.

FIFTEEN

The rescuers were pulling frantically at an almost dead-weight Arthur who was rapidly losing consciousness, their task being hindered by the fact that he kept slipping from their grasp and this because their semi-spectral forms didn't allow them to get a firm enough grip. To their utter consternation, they watched as their pursuers advanced literally in leaps and bounds, the Swordsmen only holding back until the Archers had exhausted their supply of arrows, the noise of their pursuit becoming louder as their hoofed feet thundered across the rocky ground, all urged on by the evil-looking demon as he pranced and screamed along the top of the cliff. Only one of the rescuers had been hit, and that not too seriously but he, too, now had to be supported by the others as they fled.

Turning a sharp corner and rushing behind a large boulder; one of their number whispered a swift word after which they all appeared to be sucked rapidly into the tunnel – it closed slowly and silently behind them. The last two rescuers turned round and, unseen themselves, watched their pursuers running around in confusion while they tried to find their prey, the green man's piercing gaze, though appearing to stare right at them, was searching unsuccessfully everywhere.

Keeping watch, just to make sure, they stayed to guard the entrance until the last of the hunters had gone but not before they observed the swords becoming sheathed once more inside the arms of the Swordsmen and the bows retracting into the hands of the Archers. They also observed the Archers, as they trotted away from them, sprinkling some concoction or other into their quivers, after which miniature trees sprouted that turned within seconds into wood and then into sharply-pointed shafts. Their wait was a long one as the green demon sat perched on an outcrop of rock opposite them as he searched for his quarry; eventually, in a flash of smoke, he, too, disappeared.

When all was quiet again, the two watch keepers finally left their post behind the see through rock, squeezed through the almost closed entrance and secured it before following the rest of the party through the tunnel. The passageway itself sloped downwards through a gentle descent between rocky walls until they arrived inside a cavernous cathedral-like room well inside the cliffs and situated deep beneath the Endless Hills. Even in his semi-conscious state Arthur recalled later how surprised he had been at the size and illumination of the place. Hundreds of huge braziers were scattered across the floor and many more torches were attached to the sides of walls that rose at least a hundred feet, finally disappearing into the darkness; but here below it had the appearance of day.

Some of the women began attending to Arthur: they had mopped his brow to cool his still rising temperature and were at that moment trying their hardest to get him to take some water – a very difficult task as, thinking they were trying to poison him, he kept pushing them away. But his strength had deserted him and eventually he gave in to their ministrations.

Finally coming out of his delirium some few days later he opened crusty eyes to stare upwards into a lovely face. She had been watching for him to wake up and now, as she saw him open his eyes, she smiled, albeit sadly, down at him. She was so lovely that he found it impossible not to return that smile. Trying to raise himself up he moaned as, falling back, he found that his strength had completely deserted him.

'Don't try,' she spoke very softly to him. 'You have been extremely ill and it will take some time to recover your strength.'

Her voice was very soft but strong, almost like a melody or the tinkling of bells as she spoke to him and then his eyes widened when he realised that she was to some extent diaphanous – he could almost see right through her. He shook himself in order to stop from staring.

Realising his thoughts, Tiala – she introduced herself to him – decided that while he was a captive audience she would tell him all about herself and the others. It would also give him extra time to rest – he was very weak. While she spoke she had him propped up on silken pillows so that he could look around at some of the people she would be telling him about, one of whom was Bohai, her brother – who was much the strongest person in that place – with whom she took it in turns to help him drink and eat a thin soup.

'Do you feel well enough to hear my story?' she asked him and he nodded. 'I have to tell you first that it was our intention to capture you. I hope you won't be too angry when you hear of our plight and the reason why we have had to resort to this but you will soon understand that we didn't have any choice.'

'But how did you manage that?'

'Oh, we didn't! It was someone else who brought you to this place, but we took advantage of it nonetheless and once we were able, we brought you here.'

Her pretty, almond-shaped eyes looked quite sad as she stared off into space, obviously remembering a distressing and frightening time.

'Not all of the people here come from my home country,' she whispered. 'They come from all over the world but you will see that there is a large contingent from my village in China.

'We discovered this place, under the Endless Hills, quite by accident, and have been here for many, many years. There were others here before us and many more keep arriving but we have organised our lives so that they are fairly bearable – that is if you can call it life! The evil one hasn't been able to get to us yet. First we thought she'd never come to this place – not while she lived at any rate and then we thought she'd given up because we hadn't seen or heard of her for so long but we were mistaken – she is here and getting closer.

'But let me start at the beginning,' she said as she smiled her heart-rending smile again.

'For many years we had been ruled over by an evil witch.'

'Not Mad Mab?' Arthur enquired with a croak, cleared his throat and then repeated his question.

'Mad Mab? I don't know that name! But then, we never knew her name.' She stared off into space again without speaking.

Arthur apologised for interrupting and asked her to continue with her story.

'Yes, of course,' she nodded but it was still some time before she could find the words to continue.

'My parents – over there,' she pointed behind her, 'were in charge of the nests of dragons' eggs. We had about...'

'Dragons' eggs!' Arthur exclaimed, interrupting again.

'Yes – white dragons to be precise,' she added.

'But I didn't think there were such things any more!'

'Oh yes. We hatched at least twenty every year, although many died. Of course, when they did, we suffered!' Her lovely face took on a look of such misery that Arthur thought she might cry. But she shook her head as if to clear it and then carried on.

'This particular year there was a serious drought and the stream that kept the mill going dried up. We tried to turn the mill by using our strongest men but even they eventually became exhausted. We still needed water and grain to feed them, so we had to send them miles away to buy barrels so that we could give the newly-born dragons enough to keep them alive until the rains came and to feed them from the grain from the mill which we had been forced to turn by ourselves – taking it in turns to walk the slats. But so, even with all our hard and exhausting work, that year the rains didn't come and only two dragons survived. It took our people almost all their strength and time to keep bringing barrels of water to keep even those two alive.

'Well the witch came, as we knew she would, but she was late in coming. I don't know how she travelled this time because usually she arrived on the back of Hellion but she didn't this time. She was extremely angry with us and flew into the most awful rage, striking down both my father and mother with fire from her fingers. I rushed over to them but they were both dead – scorched and smouldering – awful!

'"Now, you!' she screamed at me as I stood sobbing. 'You will raise these two sickly looking dragons and at least one of them will be ready for me when I return. If not – well you know the penalty," she crowed, looking down at my parents.'

'I've met this witch, I'm sure,' Arthur muttered. 'It must be Mab. I'm sure she had a dragon called Hellion. Though apart from him – and he died at Bedruthan Steps some years ago – there was only one other that I knew of – the beautiful Moon Song. But, obviously I must be mistaken. Sorry, please go on.'

'She stayed with us for a week. It was terrible! She wouldn't let me make any funeral arrangements for my parents; she made me leave them where they were "as a reminder" until she was ready to go.

'She spent that week concocting various potions and making spells. She threw things into the sky and stamped about chanting and muttering I know not what until she was satisfied that all would be well. On the sixth day it rained. She gathered the first of the rain into a huge cauldron in which she'd been stirring this and that until green smoke started to rise from it. She chanted and danced round the cauldron for most of the evening and night until she fell into an exhausted sleep during the early hours of the seventh day. She slept for a whole day but none of us dared go near her for fear of what she'd do if she woke up. When she did awake she charged me with feeding the last remaining dragons until they could make fire. Once that happened they would be able to fly and be strong enough to be used by her.

'She told me she would return in a month telling me that that should be time enough, warning me to take care of Gundestrup.

'Gundestrup?' Arthur enquired.

'It's the name of the cauldron she'd brought with her. The cauldron is very large and made of silver with faces and figures inside and out. She valued it highly – though why I know not – I thought it very ugly. I reckoned it must have magical properties but at that time I couldn't be certain.

'Well, immediately she'd left, my family and I rushed over to our poor dead parents and finally gave them a decent burial.'

'Um, sorry Tiala, but,' Arthur pointed at her parents who were just at that moment walking across the cavern,' didn't you just say that your parents were dead?'

She looked down at him with that sad smile again and nodded. 'Please let me tell the story in my way and you can ask me anything when I've finished.'

Arthur, looking extremely confused, nodded.

'We would normally have spent a month in mourning but things happened and we could not. First, we knew that we had to nurse the two remaining dragons and secondly, the rains again had dried up. We tried to feed them from the mixture contained within the cauldron and many of our people searched throughout the countryside for water but to no avail as the drought was very severe. At the end of the third week one of the dragons died, leaving us frantic with worry. By the end of the fourth week the last remaining dragon had become dehydrated and looked as though it would soon follow all the others. Then she returned.

'Can you imagine her fury? Her eyes almost bulged out of their sockets as she examined the dragons – one a corpse and the other barely clinging on to life. We stood around – deathly silent and quaking with fear. We didn't have to wait for long.

'In a matter of moments her wrath overtook whatever sanity she may have had left. Swirling around she felled every last one of us with fire from her fingers – she had, in less than twenty seconds, killed everyone in sight and we all ended up here.'

'Then are you telling me that you are all dead? That everyone here is dead?' Arthur could feel panic gripping and bile rising up as the story progressed.

'Yes, I'm afraid so.'

Arthur tried to recall what he'd been doing before he died but nothing came to mind. '*Surely, if I was about to die,*' he thought, '*all my previous life would flash before my eyes. But it hadn't. Or at least I don't think it had. And then, again, like Tiala, if she remembered what had happened to her just before she died, then why can't I?'*

Tiala had been watching Arthur and could almost read his thoughts, which were writ large upon his face. Putting him out of his misery, she added. 'We are dead, Arthur, but you are not!'

'I'm not?'

'No! I don't know why you are here but you are in the Place of Shades – the place where people go when they die – when they are bad! But when we found out you were here we knew we needed you to help us.'

'But you don't seem to be bad to me – in fact you are good! I can just feel you are good.'

'It's more complicated than that,' she answered; then trying to explain said, 'I believe you worship your God? Am I right?'

'Yes, I worship the Lord my God and Jesus my Saviour.'

'Then you are wise – you will go to be where your God is when you die. I, unfortunately, go where mine is. I chose unwisely. It's not so nice here, is it?'

'But you said that you had to capture me! Why?'

'As you can see, we are all, to varying degrees, wraithlike – without form. Some have more density than others: I expect that's to do with how good or bad they are or, maybe, how near natural death they might have been when they died. I'm not sure. But we cannot stay like this. Even if we have to stay here in this god-forsaken place it would be preferable to be solid.'

'And you say I can help you?' She nodded. 'But how?'

'When that witch killed us all – well, she left some of the others alive as they were out trying to find water but I expect she'll round them up to nurture that last remaining dragon or her next batch of eggs – she somehow managed to transport her precious cauldron along with us.' Turning, Tiala pointed to the centre of the cavern where the cauldron sat upon a dais surrounded by braziers whose flickering light caught the faces emblazoned thereon appear to come alive. 'She has been sending her spies and soldiers to try and find us – and it – ever since. She must be very frustrated – how could she leave real corpses and send us spirits to this place and at the same time send a real cauldron here? Does she just have a ghostly cauldron there I wonder? We need to be set free from our ethereal bodies; we need to be solid. We need you to go back to that witch and get her to take her spell off us or do something so that the spell is broken. If that happens, we will agree to let you return and take her precious cauldron back to her. If not, we will keep it here and see if we can figure out how it works. We also need our kinsmen on earth to be warned about her and to leave and move away to safety.'

'But you don't know what you are asking! Her sole aim in life is to kill me! Didn't you know that? She's almost succeeded on several occasions and might do so this time if I go back!'

'That is why you are warned beforehand. She won't try to kill you if she knows you can have her precious cauldron returned to her. You'll just have to make sure that when she has it in her possession you are well away. I believe we can help you there. We can't return! We're dead! But you can!'

Arthur found it very disconcerting knowing that he was talking to someone who was very beautiful, very dynamic but also, as she said, very dead.

'Do you have a plan?' he sighed resignedly.

'Sort of!'

SIXTEEN

Screaming, pulling her hair (she really shouldn't do that – there's very little left of it nowadays) and stamping her foot she whacked poor Honey round the head several times. The petrified woman had learned to keep out of the way most of the time during the months she'd been with the witch but, somehow, she hadn't ducked quickly enough on this occasion. Scurrying out of arm's reach, she cowered down in the corner and watched the fireworks from comparative safety.

'She's got it! I've seen it!' she wailed as she ran round the table, stopping now and then to glare into the crystal at its centre. Pointing a shaking finger at the ball she began to weep with frustration as her eyes travelled over the intricate designs shining back at her from a cauldron that appeared to mock her – she could see it but not touch it. She had to get it back! All her best spells were made within its depths. They always worked when she mixed them in there, even if she'd got it a bit wrong. She just had to get it back. And then she saw him! 'Arthur,' her whisper could just be heard. 'So he's there too is he?'

She rubbed her chin, absentmindedly plucking at one long hair that grew out of it, as she continued to stare into the crystal, taking in all that it revealed to her. She saw the wraithlike figures of those that peopled the cathedral-like cavern and curled her lip at what she'd done to them. 'Thought you'd try and get the better of me?' she asked but naturally got no reply, nor expecting one. 'Hobgoblin did well to locate you and your people – but, hah, now I have two bonuses!'

Flopping down onto her chair she sat for a considerably long time without moving – something very unusual so far as she was concerned. Honey watched from the shelter of her corner, not daring to even breathe above a whisper in case she reminded the witch of her existence and became, once more, the object of her wrath. At least half an hour passed before, 'Honey,' she screamed at her. 'Come here now!'

The scared woman pulled herself up from her hiding place and, expecting no mercy, moved over to stand beside the witch, her eyes following the pointing finger until she, too, stared at the picture displayed on the crystal's screen.

Quietly now, the witch, in undertones, spoke to her. 'We are going on a journey, you and I. It will take us some time to prepare,' her voice gradually rising in excitement and volume as she spoke before it reached a crescendo and then calmed. 'So, sleep now, my child,' she ruffled the cringing woman's hair, who'd thought another cuff round the ear was on the cards. 'Tomorrow we prepare our spells and potions.' Laughing, she swirled and danced, spreading her awful odour around the room like a blanket and almost felling poor Honey with its rankness.

The witch, misinterpreting as usual, told the other woman to rest as much as possible; she was obviously very tired as she could hardly stand on her feet! 'From tomorrow we may not rest for days – these preparations are very tricky and must not be allowed to cool until they are ready. If they go wrong we could be killed or maimed – well you might,' she amended, 'as it will be you doing the mixing. No, we will need all our wits about us so shoo, shoo, off to bed with you now.'

'*If she reckons I'll be able to sleep after telling me all that, well she's madder than she looks!*' Honey thought as, with dragging feet, she climbed the stairs to her room.

If the witch bothered, she might have noticed the puffy and bloodshot eyes that looked across the table at her the next morning. Even if she did, she said nothing.

'Right! Now, I want you to listen very carefully – for your own sake as well as mine!' she added. 'There is much to do and one of us has to be here all the time to keep the fire lit beneath this pot – oh I wish I had my cauldron back, or even had Mordred with me; why didn't I think of calling for him? No, stop worrying about it Mab – that's why we're doing this. Concentrate now,' she told herself as she smacked her cheeks several times with both hands, making a hollow popping noise as she did so.

'*Oh man,*' Honey blanched. '*She's really losing it. I'd best be very, very careful.*'

'Yes, that's right,' she pulled herself together.

Honey started trembling. '*Had she heard her?*'

'Stop shaking girl,' the witch admonished her. 'How do you think we're going to get through this if you splatter and spill everything? Do that, and you will be sorry! Right – go get me six buckets of water and when you've done that fetch me the large green pot with the slimy red toad in it.' The mad woman started to give her instructions and the room, for the next few hours, became a hive of activity – well it did for Honey at any rate (well a very fast rate actually) as the witch just sat back and gave her orders.

SEVENTEEN

We materialised beneath the sign of the Blue Pelican and, thankfully, just to the side of the inn's door, as two burly men crashed through it while trying their hardest to crush each other to bits in a bear hug. This set Cabby barking but he was soon silenced by a swift word from Merlin who went on to tell us that this was the norm here – there was always someone being punched through the doorways.

'This is a crazy and violent place to live,' Tailor remarked as he and Salazar followed the drunkards out, swiftly moving his leg out of the way as the fight travelled back towards him.

'Hmm, yes,' Merlin added. 'That would be correct, if they were alive in the first place, eh? But come – let's see if we can find the others. Perhaps they've arrived while we've been away. Anyway, we have to see what we can do for Shake Spear.'

'Why, what's happened to him?' I asked.

'Had a bump on the head and now thinks he's a somebody!' Tailor put in.

'That's a bit unfair, man,' Merlin chided him. 'He's obviously lost his memory or something has happened to it – probably when he arrived he hit his head – and we need to try and help him recover it.'

'What? His head?' Tailor asked, turning pale.

'His memory, you imbecile,' Merlin responded becoming exasperated with the man.

While Tailor had been talking I'd been taking stock of him and Salazar: where Salazar didn't look too different, Tailor looked wrecked. I must have been gazing at him with my mouth hanging open (again) because a swift jab in my ribs from Merlin's elbow made me realise my rudeness.

'It's only a disguise, Percy; like mine. So *please* close your mouth.' This said in a very weary manner. I suppose I should have learned by now – but surely even Merlin must admit he did look peculiar.

'So, Prince…'

'*Prince?*' I looked around to see who else might be with us.

'*Oh, Percy, catch up will you!*' Merlin exclaimed. 'Perhaps I'd better introduce you: this is Prince.' Salazar gave a short bow. 'This is Stitcher.' I almost burst out laughing at that one. 'And my name is Ambrosius. And you are called?'

'Percy,' I replied, 'and this is my dog Cabby.'

'Well, I suppose that's OK but I'll just disguise them; we'll just say "Percy" or "Cabal" but everyone else, except us that is, will hear a different name. What you have to remember, Percy, is that you will hear me called Merlin, but everyone else from this place will only hear our new names. But when they talk to us they will use our new names, so please,' he added as we made our way over to the inn, 'try to keep it in mind, will you? Now we've made our introductions, let's go and see what's happening in the Minstrel. Perhaps our friend has recovered his memory.'

I followed the others through the swing door into the hostelry now being run by Shake Spear. He was all joviality as we stepped through, shaking hands with Merlin and Salazar as though they were long lost friends – which in reality they actually were – and ruffling Cabal's head with one hand whilst thumping me on the back with the other. I won't even mention it! But surely I was old enough now to be a hand shaker rather than a receptacle for back thumping. One day! I gritted my teeth. Merlin looked at me with amusement, merely raising an eyebrow.

'So, my friends – are you taking me up on my offer of hospitality?' Shake Spear asked. 'There are enough rooms for you both, you know. And,' he turned and looked at me, 'for this one who's not yet old enough for a man nor young enough for a boy! And the dog,' he added, giving Cabal another pat.

'Yes, we'll stay one night. Tomorrow we need to depart to find our other friends. You haven't heard anything about them, have you?'

'No, I'm sorry – nothing. But they'll turn up,' he grinned. 'Everyone always does!'

I knew that! That young man who'd been thrown overboard as dead – yes, I'd seen him when the ship docked and he looked alive when I saw him again. Well, as much alive as a dead person could at any rate. I was still finding it hard to get my head around the fact that everyone – well almost everyone – in this place was dead.

And as if on cue, 'Ah, here comes another one,' Shake Spear pointed.

We all turned round in unison, hearing the wailing first, to see a weeping woman, hugging a bundle with one arm and fighting off an invisible assailant with the other, materialising in the doorway. She stopped crying when she started to notice her surroundings. 'Where am I?' she stuttered as, trembling with either fear or emotion, she stepped into the room. Then, 'Where's my baby?' she almost screamed whilst poking through the empty bundle as it collapsed in her grasp. 'Someone's stolen my baby,' she shouted as she searched the room with eyes that rapidly filled with tears. 'Where's my baby?'

'Ah, greetings, good lady,' Shake Spear cooed as he moved forward to welcome her. 'This is my humble hostelry, the Minstrel, which is also my title. Come in, come in.'

The woman, still dabbing at her eyes, moved into the room before adding, 'but how did I get here? And,' now pleading, 'if you've got my baby, please give him to me.'

'You're dead missus, like the rest of us.'

A scruffy, hard man that was leaning against the bar was immediately chided by his companion who told him to try and be a bit more compassionate to someone who'd just got here. 'Can't you remember what it felt like when you first arrived?'

'Best get it over and done with, I say,' he stated. 'Got to find out sooner or later! And there ain't no kids come here neither,' he added pointedly, rubbing salt into the wound.

'Gentler, man!' Shake Spear called across to him.

The woman had collapsed into a heap on the floor and wept bucket loads as she rocked to and fro hugging the empty blanket.

Shake Spear, shaking his head at the two men, stooped down and gently lifted her to her feet. Beckoning another woman over, he watched while she helped her up the stairs until they disappeared from sight; even after the door had closed, her sobs could still be heard for a long time afterwards.

'So you see,' he sighed. 'Sooner or later they turn up. Therefore I reckon it won't be long before your friends do too.'

'But they're not dea…'

I experienced a swift shooting pain as Merlin ground his heel into my foot, followed by, 'Sorry old chap! Thought you'd moved out of the way. *Keep quiet! You mustn't give away the fact that we are not dead! Now barriers up – just in case.*'

We spent the best part of an hour talking in a guarded way to Shake Spear to find out what he knew but he seemed to have lost his wit as well as his memory. Realising we were getting nowhere we gave up.

'Perhaps you would be so kind as to show us to our rooms, Minstrel,' Merlin asked him. 'We have an early start tomorrow and we'd like to get a good night's sleep.'

'Certainly. Follow me.'

We walked up the stairs, passing a door through which low shuddering sobs could still be heard, up a further flight and on into the roof space. There were three doors. 'You'll have to share with Stitcher and Cabby, Percy. But there's plenty of space. Try to get some sleep – all of you.'

It was quite comfortable. There were two mattresses on the floor and Cabby would, as usual, sleep across the doorway. I think I fell asleep as soon as I lay down.

Merlin and Salazar, however, had different fish to fry. As soon as night fell and the inn was quiet, they let themselves out of the side door and made their way back up through the steep lanes through the town until they reached its outskirts. There, Merlin set to with his powders and spells. Salazar, unpacking the cloak of invisibility and wrapping it around them just in case they might be observed – you never knew who might be watching – waited for his instructions.

Taking a deep breath before they set off, Merlin turned to his friend. 'Ready?'

EIGHTEEN

'We're ready at last,' the witch poured the last few drops into the phial before tapping the cork in with both a dirty finger and a filthy grin.

Now you would have thought that all that pouring, mixing, chanting, chopping and stirring would have produced bottles and bottles of whatever it was but there was merely a spoonful of the stuff in one small pot.

'This will transport us to the land of the dead,' she purred as, wickedly, she watched the effect her statement would have on her companion. With twitching lips, she eventually could hold it in no longer as she watched the blood drain from the poor woman's face before she collapsed onto the floor.

Howls of laughter erupted in the room; it was some time before either the witch or Honey came to their senses again.

'Now, now, my dear,' she eventually crooned to the poor woman. 'We'll be able to get back. Well, at least one of us will,' she added, looking closely at Honey. 'There is certainly enough to get us there; let's just hope there will be enough to bring both of us back.'

Poor Honey could only stare at her. What else could she do? She still hadn't worked out why she was here or what promises she'd made to her or even where she'd come from so it was useless – and painful – to even think about it. She'd just have to hope she'd get back. Then again, did she really want to come back with this awful woman? Perhaps the land of the dead would be preferable. Her mind was racing but, unfortunately for her, the witch was tuning in to as much as she could – which was not a lot, but enough. It really annoyed Mab that she couldn't mind speak very well but, as Merlin had often told me, the wicked couldn't.

'However, as you might already know,' she angrily interrupted Honey's train of thought, 'my cauldron has mystical powers and should I have need of them I am sure I'll be able to use them to return or, come to that, do almost anything I want. So, don't worry, my dear, we shall be together for a long time yet!'

The rest of the day was spent in packing this and that in sacks that Honey soon realised she would be carrying, and in storing whatever ready food they could lay their hands on in the tops of their bundles.

'And don't you dare eat any of that without my say so!' Mab growled over her shoulder as she collected the last things she needed.

'Come now,' she held her hand out to Honey. 'The moon is full in an hour's time – and it's witching night – just right for our journey. I want us to be on top of the battlements before then – or it might be too late.'

Now Honey thought it would have been a better idea if the witch helped her carry the three sacks up all those flights of stairs to the castle's battlements if she was in that much of a hurry – but, no, she had had to make all three trips herself, being urged to go faster and couldn't she carry more than one at a time and don't you dare drop them or crush them against the walls and come on girl pick your feet up. By the time she laid the last sack against its brothers she was boiling hot, exhausted and feeling as though she must smell as bad as the other woman as she dropped to the floor beside the bundles.

'Come, come, now. There's no time to dilly dally; you'll be able to rest soon enough when you're dead!' Yes, amused at her own joke, she collapsed once more with laughter, cackling away like the really not so old witch she was, falling to the floor and kicking her legs in the air as she screeched. But she was also well aware that time was creeping up on her and that the time to travel was imminent. Pulling herself together – with a little difficulty – she heaved herself up, grabbed Honey and made her stand directly in front of her.

'Now, my dear,' she hiccoughed, wiping her streaming eyes and nostrils with the back of her hand, 'grab hold of those sacks and stand still. I am going to place a blob of this potion on your tongue.' The thought of those filthy hands touching her tongue almost felled Honey once again. 'At the same time I shall place a blob on mine. We will then arrive, hopefully, at the same place at the same time. When we get there don't you dare do anything unless I tell you. You might be surprised, even shocked, but, as I said, don't you dare move or it really will be the worse for you. Come along now grab those sacks! It's time,' she uttered before carefully placing the phial she'd just extracted some mixture from into a pocket within the folds of her dress and buttoning it down! 'Open your mouth!'

It was frightening – weird – if she could feel her knees at all, she felt sure they would be knocking – but she could feel nothing except this swooshing sensation. She was flying through something – it wasn't air as it had more substance – and horrible things were flying past them. There were terrible faces that looked like they were being tortured; hundreds, even thousands of people who were marching along in chains, all with bowed heads and slumped shoulders, one or two of whom looked up at them as they passed by but their faces showed no emotion other than hopelessness. They flew on for several minutes through this murk – it seemed like hours – before they eventually broke out into a place that wasn't too unrecognisable.

The witch was searching and Honey, realising that they were both moving along with the witch's finger still on each of their tongues, hoped they would get where they were going fast as she felt sure she was about to throw up. Then they saw it. In the gathering dusk it could just be seen on the horizon – a ship. They flew swiftly across the waves until they reached it: flying from stem to stern they made their way, amazingly, through its wooden sides until they stood inside the captain's cabin.

Mab finally removed her finger from Honey's mouth and immediately clamped her hand over it – the stupid woman was about to choke or cough or something. Putting a finger to her lips, she frowned at her before removing her hand.

Honey, dropping the bundles she'd been carrying, wondered what on earth she'd ever done wrong to end up in this state. She was about to wonder that thought some more! *'And will I ever get rid of the taste of her hand! Goodness – and that's a misnomer – where on earth had it been?'*

The captain was slumped in his chair and his right-hand-man was slumped, well, beside his right hand as it happened. Both were intoxicated – the remains of their drink dripping onto the floor from an overturned bottle. He was well named, Mab had thought, having long legs that were, at that moment crossed upon his desk, his ears were also long and pointed and he almost had a muzzle for a mouth. The remains of the leg of some animal or other, not cooked very well either, sat on a plate in front of him.

'The Jackal,' she thought. Then grabbing Honey's hand she pulled her forward and pushed her towards the captain's servant. With much resistance from Honey – Mab had to clip her round the ear several times before she managed to achieve her goal – she watched with satisfaction as, with only slight resistance from the man, she forced Honey down upon him and within seconds she had blended into the man and became him. She opened her mouth to say something but was silenced by the witch's finger that she had brought once more to her lips.

With eyes like saucers, Honey watched as the witch went through the same procedure with the captain; sitting on his lap and forcing herself backwards she soon became one with him. Then removing her legs from the desk and standing upright, Mab walked over to the polished silver mirror above the washbasin and jug (which Honey bet she wouldn't ever use) and, straightened the cravat that hung round her neck.

'He's an ugly so-and-so, isn't he Honey?'

Honey knew the question was hypothetical but thought, rather recklessly, that the captain – the Jackal? – was a lot better looking than Mab and, thankfully, didn't smell half as bad! He was dressed almost entirely in Crimson, from a huge crimson hat with matching feather, through cravat, shiny waistcoat, belt, trousers and boots, these only being offset by a whitish frilly shirt. His face was sallow and was not helped by sandy-coloured moustaches, beard and eyebrows; though his eyes were small, they, like those of any jackal, glittered sharply.

Mab – the Jackal – oh this was going to get complicated – looked over her shoulder and glared at her, and Honey, once again, wondered if she could read her mind. It was disconcerting enough when Mab stared at her but now that it was Mab looking like somebody else staring at her – well, she felt sure she must be going mad?

'Sit down. We'll need to plan our strategy and I can see that you're completely bewildered. Come, come, pull up a chair. No, first of all, go and look in the mirror over there. Once you see what you look like, well I think all will become a lot easier.

Honey, after watching the witch metamorphose, had already wondered if that had also happened to herself; her worst fears were thus soon realised as she stared at herself for a long minute. She almost cried but managed to stop herself, before being ordered to return to her seat beside her mistress.

'There now, you don't look too bad do you?'

Honey had seen a skinny man with almost pale everything – eyebrows and eyelashes staring back at her. His face was pink – not a pretty pink but an unhealthy one – like a pig. His pupils were large and almost black but were encircled by thin pale pinkish-blue edged irises and his lips were thin and bloodless – he looked evil. His hair, surprisingly, was bright red. He was almost as tall as the captain but where the captain was well built, he was like a beanpole.

'OK Honey! Time to stop admiring your new looks! We've now taken over this ship. The men outside will not notice any difference: they will take my orders – or else! You will stay with me at all times unless you are running an errand. Until I can find out your name, however,' she mused, 'I will just have to call you "Man". So, your first job is to go and find out your name and the names of all those on board. Come nearer,' she beckoned her over with a crooked finger. Honey moved towards the witch who, without batting an eyelid or giving any sort of warning, punched her full and square on her temple. 'Now, you can go,' she said with a satisfied grin as she watched the huge bump begin to rise, 'and tell everyone that you can't remember who they are because you've hit your head and lost your memory. Come back to me when you've found out.'

Honey, with trembling knees, closed the door behind her, rubbing her swollen head as she went on her quest, but not before she noticed Mab start to eat some of the food they'd brought with them.

'*She didn't do any of the packing,*' she thought as she continued to rub her sore head, '*but she can certainly pack it away. I'll be lucky to get any of it.*'

'Get a move on,' was spluttered out of a full mouth and through the door. 'You can eat when you get back; that is, if you do your job properly!'

'*And if there's anything left! Oh, how I wish there was someone who could save me,*' she thought. '*I certainly am completely unable to save myself!*'

NINETEEN

'The witch has arrived in the Place of Shades,' Tiala informed Arthur. 'She was seen to arrive but since then has been able to hide herself. We must try to find out where she is but we must be very careful.'

Now how on earth – but then no-one here was on earth, were they? – she knew that the witch had arrived was beyond Arthur. So far as he could discern, no-one had left their hiding place and no-one had arrived! So how?

Thinking back to his arrival in this cavern – and he couldn't really remember much about that because he'd been in a semi-conscious state, but once he'd recovered somewhat he'd started to perk up and take stock of his surroundings – he'd been pretty much left to his own devices since then and had done much exploring.

He wandered around – hands clasped behind his back: it was just like living in a very brightly lit cathedral, though he couldn't see its height as it disappeared into the murky darkness way above him. He didn't know how they'd done it but the place looked astonishing. Steps, carved into the walls – some up the outside and some disappearing through it like tunnels, led up to homes that had been chiselled into the rock face itself – some were small, housing maybe one or two people; some were very large and were channelled deep into the rock, probably housing whole families. Tiala had said that the witch had destroyed almost everyone from her village so it wasn't beyond belief that whole families had arrived in this place.

Trying to stop himself from staring, it was, even after what he considered to be about ten days, very disconcerting to see someone who was fairly substantial talking or walking along with someone who was merely an outline or just a ripple – someone whom Arthur could see straight through – even their clothes were ethereal; but worse was if they stopped to talk to him – he then had to really concentrate on whatever part of them he actually could see! – or hear, as the less distinct the outline, the softer the voice – very, very weird!

But there were no children! Well, no young children at any rate; the youngest, he deduced, looked about eleven or twelve. Why was that?

The cauldron – the only really solid thing in the cavern – apart from himself – stood proud at its centre. Four fairly substantial guards kept watch over it at all times, only being replaced by others similar to themselves; they eyed Arthur suspiciously whenever he ventured too close, so he kept his distance.

'So how do you know that the witch has arrived here?'

'People are arriving here all the time – they just appear after they've died; that is, if this is their set destination. Not everyone who dies comes here as I have already found out but we've already spoken about that. However, things have been weird lately, as those people that arrived here who are not dead have caused tremors – not serious quakes but shudderings that cannot be mistaken for anything other than someone or other has entered here by a wrong doorway. Then it is only a question of time before someone from the network of spies and gossips lets us know who it is. And she is here! She's after Gundestrup.'

'OK then, what's so special about the cauldron,' he asked Tiala when she was strong enough to accompany him on one of his trips around the cavern and after he had regained enough strength to exercise his legs.

'The witch imagines it to be magical. I can't say if it is or is not as nothing exceptional has happened since we put it over there,' she pointed. 'I only know *she* does and so it's important to her. You, I think, believe in the powers of something called the Holy Grail?' she raised one delicate eyebrow in question.

'Oh yes. A travelling priest once told me and several of my friends about it when we were having instruction by Brother Geraint – how the Christ had drunk from it at the Last Supper – and my heart, I must admit, stirred within me. One day I should like to search for it. Perhaps I should make that my next pilgrimage! That is, if I ever leave this place.' His face screwed up and looked a combination of sadness, confusion and anger as he considered he might never do so. Then, shrugging off the melancholy that threatened, turned once again to Tiala and asked, 'but what has that to do with this?'

'All good things have their opposites. If there is one doing good there will be one who is evil trying to counteract the good. It is an authority thing I think – a power struggle – the bad trying to overcome the good and vice versa. Though, it's very hard to understand as there don't seem to be many very wicked people here in this cavern but then that would be just too awful, wouldn't it? Outside, I understand, it is very different.'

As Tiala had been speaking, her voice began to weaken; at the same time she started to fade. She sank down onto the ground and, with weakness overcoming her, leaned her back against the wall and closed her eyes.

'What's wrong Tiala?' Arthur, all concern, knelt down beside her.

'I really don't know whether it's talking about the Grail, the witch or the cauldron, but it seems that every time I do I lose strength. Let me rest a while to regain it. I'll find you when I feel better. Go now!' she smiled weakly as she waved him away. 'Let me rest.'

It was another two days, Arthur estimated – as time seemed to make no sense at all inside that cave – before Tiala was seen again. She drifted over to him, her small feet hardly touching the ground, and smiled her sad smile before remarking that he looked much better.

'But how are you now?'

'I've recovered, but I think I should tell you all that I know before the weakness comes over me again. So, I'll tell you now, then you can think about what I've said while I recover yet again – that is, if I do. It's quite frightening, really, as each time the weakness comes upon me, the longer it takes to recover and more scary than that is the fact that each time I recover less and less of myself – I am, literally, fading away. Well, it is going to take me about an hour to explain everything to you, so please try not to interrupt, as I shall completely exhaust myself. I know it's that witch who's done this to me. Please wait and ask me any questions at the end. Let's sit over there.' She pointed to a quiet corner of the cave where a long piece of rock had been carved into the shape of bench.

As they sat down, Tiala leaned back against the rock wall and closed her eyes, reassuring Arthur, when he asked, that she was well, just gathering her thoughts.

'The witch – and I don't know how old she must be – has been coming to our village now for at least three generations. She always arrives – apart from this last time, of course – on the back of a huge white dragon and if the wind is in the right direction we know she's coming because of the smell.'

'It *must* be her – it *must* be Mab! I know it! I can feel it in my bones. But her dragon has been slain – I was there and saw it happen. How did she get to you this last time then?'

'By sea. She stepped ashore – we actually lived close to the sea and had always been a village of fishermen and women – and she was ill for days. Once more, we smelled her long before she arrived. We understand she'd been travelling for almost a year to get to us and was in dire need of a new dragon. You can imagine her madness when she arrived to find that they were almost all dead. As I've already told you, there was, finally, only one sickly dragon remaining and I should imagine she must have used all her scheming and potions to make it well. But I don't suppose I'll ever know that. The dead cannot communicate with the living, you know, nor the living with the dead! Well, not in the usual sense,' she added. 'But this is not usual is it? Very confusing!' She hung her head before brightening. 'But you can go back to the living for us! You will be able to go back because you didn't die in the first place! But don't let that witch get hold of you because if she kills you here, I don't know what will become of you – or us.'

Arthur stared aghast at Tiala.

'Don't think about it. The laws down here are very different to where we came from – they are quite chaotic. But we can fight and we can win. Make no mistake about it, we will do all we can to keep you and your companions safe.'

'You keep saying "my companions". Who might these be? Are they some of your stronger men? Perhaps those guarding the cauldron?'

'OK. Let me tell you everything I know and then I'll set out my plan. This will take me some time and if I weaken again, please just let me rest and I'll come back to you when I recover.

'When we first arrived here – and we all got here within an hour of each other, you know – we were enveloped in a red mist – it's a very pale mist but you can always tell newcomers by it. They call it the death mist here. The mist stayed around for three days and then evaporated. It wasn't until then that we saw the state we were all in. The only other thing that arrived at the same time as us was the cauldron but it, unlike us, was solid. We knew that it was important but didn't know why. So, with great difficulty, we managed to drag it along with us and eventually hide it in these caves. We were in a very sorry state. We drew together for comfort and hope. We eventually received some comfort from one another but there is no hope down here, Arthur! None at all!

'Not until you came at any rate. We have nothing here, will go nowhere – even if there was anywhere to go, and will get no second chance. But you can go back and speak to our people – that is our hope. They must not help that witch any more! They must search for a better way! Perhaps you could tell them about your God of Hope, Arthur, and not ours. Also, you might be able to discover how we can make ourselves more substantial – and stay that way. However, I've no idea how you will be able to communicate that information to us –

but there might be a way and we will certainly know if it works, won't we?

'After several days, we moved through the Endless Hills.'

'Why are they called that?' Arthur interrupted.

'I don't know! They go on for a long way, so I suppose that might be why they're called that.' She shrugged her shoulders and continued. 'But that's not important. We hadn't gone far before we were attacked by those same beings that attacked you.'

'From what you've already told me, they must have scared the life – oh, sorry – must have scared you to… must have scared you!' he added lamely.

'Don't worry Arthur, we keep saying things like that, even though we *are* dead.'

'But why did you have to run? If you're already dead then surely nothing worse can happen!'

'It's not like that. Worse things do happen.'

'Like what?'

'Swords can slice you in two; arrows can pierce you; serpents can bite you. All sorts of things.'

'But what happens to you then?'

'Well, if you are sliced in two you eventually come back together again; swords can be pulled out of you and you can run from the serpents. There are other things that can happen as well but I don't want to get into that – it will take too long and I am weakening already. Suffice to say that all these things bring extreme pain – pain that takes a long time to go. It's the pain we try to avoid all the time. We might be dead but we still experience sorrow and pain.'

'Sorry, Tiala. Please go on.'

'It was then that we found this place. We were running from our hoofed pursuers when my brother tripped and fell. We couldn't believe our eyes! We thought he'd fallen through the rock! As quickly as our numbed brains would allow we followed. As you may recall, it was a very narrow fissure between the rocks and we managed to squeeze ourselves through. The cauldron was too wide so we hid it behind some boulders. Luckily it was still there when we eventually found our way out. Amazingly we could see through the rock and watched until those hunters had gone. Some of us who are less solid can actually float through it but the stronger and more visible ones cannot. We have since managed to break through enough of the rock and have therefore been able to bring the cauldron inside. The same entrance was used to bring you through.

'This is an amazing place, Arthur. When we arrived it was dark and shadowy. I don't know how they did it but some of our villagers managed to make it something like a home. We know it's a prison really but we are trying to make the best of it. They found light and they made houses in the rocks. We are not happy but for people with no hope we make the best of things.

'Then there's the dragon!'

'Dragon?'

'Hellion.'

'Noooo!' Arthur's long drawn out exclamation made Tiala turn and stare at him. She could almost see the way his brain was searching for an answer to her statement before finally asking, 'Did he come here, then, when he died?'

'I am not sure; if it is the same one that the witch used to fly to us in China then I'm afraid so. He looks different now though but if it is him he will probably be at the witch's command down here, just as he was on earth! But only if she is aware he's here,' she added.

'She doesn't know he's here?'

'No – not yet!'

TWENTY

'Come over here Prince,' Merlin called to Salazar.

They both looked into the piece of frosted glass that Merlin had brought with him. It was only a very small piece from one of the Glasses that hung in several of his caves; this piece fitted snugly into the palm of his hand but was sufficient for his purposes and slowly, very slowly, a ship's cabin came into view.

'*It's her!*' Salazar whispered into his mind.

'Speak out loud, Prince,' Merlin replied. 'Just in case; then if she listening in with her mind she won't be able to hear us. Are you sure it's her?'

'She's taken over the body of the captain but I know it's her – her eyes betray her. Don't know who the other one is, though, although his body has also been taken over as well. But it's another woman, of that I'm sure!'

'Do you know where they are or how far away they might be?'

'Not too far, I think, though distances on water are harder to determine.'

'Well, now we know she's around, I think we'd better see if we can find you-know-who and the other men.'

They stood for almost an hour concentrating on the piece of Glass, searching the land and the sea before, finally, the interior of a cavern came into view. They stared in awe at the sheer cliff-faces with houses chiselled out of them and watched as people climbed steep rock hewn staircases to reach their homes, marvelling at the myriad torches and braziers lighting the place until, suddenly, and to their relief that he was still alive, the Glass showed them Arthur who at that moment was fast asleep; they searched further and saw others – some easily discerned and others in various strengths of visibility.

'How far away are they?' Merlin asked.

'They're right here!' Salazar exclaimed, swivelling around as though he expected to see Arthur standing behind him. 'He's less than thirty feet away! But where?' His normally impassive features were marked by astonishment at the fact that what he thought he should clearly see just wasn't there.

'Find him, man,' Merlin's agitated response spurred him on. 'Which direction?'

But the picture faded and however hard they searched, and search they did for most of the night, all they found were rocks. Both Druids tried all the tricks and spells that came to mind but nothing happened and the Glass revealed no more secrets.

'They must be within these rocks somewhere,' Merlin stated. 'It must be this peculiar place – my spells don't seem to have the same effect as on earth. Well, we'll come back when it's light. Cabby can help us.'

Letting themselves back into The Minstrel about an hour later and just as it was starting to get light, they were surprised to see that it still held many people. Some were hunched over their tankards in solitary reverie, some of those were weeping, while others argued, tried to sing or merely slept.

'Perhaps they don't have homes!' Salazar exclaimed.

'Perhaps not,' Merlin responded, returning a merry wave that Shake Spear had sent him from behind the bar.

'Let's not get caught up in conversation, Prince; I think we should get some rest before we go back to those rocks.'

With dragging feet, both men disappeared up the stairs to their separate rooms where Merlin, at least, spent the next few hours dreaming weird things about Arthur, Mab and the Jackal and, surprisingly, because it had been a very long time, Nimue.

Merlin was awoken by the sounds of shouting and barking together with Cabal and me calling for him through our minds to come quickly and help us. Rubbing the sleep from his eyes he arose quickly and bounded down the stairs. Salazar arrived a few steps behind him together with Shake Spear who'd rushed out from the back room.

'What on earth is going on here?' Merlin's question vibrated throughout the room, silencing everyone and stopping all noise in its tracks. Again I noticed that he didn't have to shout – his voice was so commanding that it cut through everything; everyone turned toward him.

'Mind your own business,' a gravelly voice responded. All eyes now swivelled back to their original position to see what would happen next.

Taking in the scene, Merlin strode over and lifted the obviously very heavy man off his feet, making him lose his grip on Cabal.

'Oi, put me down you!' he yelled.

'Just what do you think you're doing then?'

'Taking the dog. It's my right!' he added striking a belligerent pose

– which he was finding it extremely difficult to hold; Merlin's grip forcing him to dance in the air.

'Tell me,' Merlin added sweetly, 'just what right is that?'

'We all agreed a long time ago that all animals, except breeding animals that is, were for food. I'd heard that this animal was in this 'ere inn, so I've come to take him to the slaughterhouse. It's my right!'

'And who gave you this right?'

'The law! The law gave me this right!'

'And just who would be able to eat him?' Merlin asked the still dangling man.

'Well, me,' he answered, adding, ''cos I found him – and my men of course. I ain't greedy!'

'You mean I wouldn't be able to have even a small slice of my own dog?'

I looked at Merlin and the man and then at Cabby who was alternating between growling and whimpering. I kicked him and told him mentally to stop doing both and just listen – Merlin was not going to allow any of this to happen.

'Well, er, I suppose you could have one slice – maybe two,' the man conceded with a nervous half-grin, thinking that Merlin would now let go of him and hand over the dog but, with a mighty whoosh, he was thrown across the room, hit the wall and, seeing stars, slid down onto the floor. I knew that Merlin had used some sort of magic to do this but he did it in such a way that everyone who didn't know him thought he'd physically thrown him and that, slim as he was, he must be extremely strong. The man's breath shot out of his lungs as he hit the wall and slid to the floor and it took him a good few moments before he could pick himself up, dust himself down and, with a breathless and wheezy voice, threaten retribution; he then rushed out of the inn and disappeared.

'You'll be sorry you did that to him,' Shake Spear ventured, shaking his head at the outcome. 'He's a very nasty piece of work that one – and his master, the Magpie, will no doubt be back to sort you out. He's been positively evil since he lost out on a ship at one of the Contests. It would have been him that sent him here in the first place. You see it's not very often that anyone gets fresh meat down here and when a nice piece is seen just walking around for the taking, well it's just too much temptation. If I were you I think I'd disappear for a while and take your dog with you. They soon forget, you know, as there's always something else to argue or fight about round here.'

'I wonder if you'd consider accompanying us?' Merlin asked Shake Spear. 'You tell a jolly tale and sing a merry song. It would be diverting and, if you know this place well, you'll be able to show us the sights. Also, you might end up with a new cheerful tale to tell.'

'Well,' he smiled, stroking his beard, 'you know I think I might just take you up on that offer. This place is, I must admit, getting very boring – apart from when those weird people keep appearing that is, as you don't know quite who is going to arrive next – and there was this interesting bloke the other day – called himself Sir Toby Belch and belch he did. Carried a tankard around with him all the time but unfortunately it was always empty. First thing he did was ask me to fill it up, which I did of course and we all had to admire the wonderful froth that rose above the rim, but, when he put it to his lips, it held no content. He was not amused, I can tell you. Reckon he liked his drink a bit too much but now it seems he's never going to get any. Dressed in the weirdest clothes he was too. But I digress. Yes, and they keep pressing me to tell tales; I've told most of them hundreds of times, you know – in fact, I think I'll start writing them down and then someone else can read them out – now why haven't I thought of that before? – or I'm continually breaking up fights. Yes, kind sir, I think I'll join you for a bit of a holiday. Give me two minutes to put some stuff together.'

Merlin spoke to me and Salazar in our minds to collect our stuff, including Tailor who must still be snoring his head off, and be ready as swiftly as possible. Cabby was to keep close to Merlin, as it was certain the Magpie would be back to claim his meat. Cabby shivered but didn't need to be told twice.

'Perhaps we will be able to bring Shake Spear back to his proper senses if we can get him away from this place!' he suggested.

Some few minutes later a little band of men and one large dog made their way up toward the Endless Hills. As we entered them I looked back over the rooftops to see a group of about twenty men, looking as small as ants, wielding swords and clubs and headed for the Minstrel. We'd only just escaped in time!

'Don't you trust me? We have not "just escaped" as you so eloquently put it or "only just in time"! It's all part of my plan.'

I often wondered whether he really did have a plan or whether he just took the credit for everything when it all went right. But even if I was thinking this at the time, I thought it with my barriers up!

'And we still have to find the other men! I wonder where they are!'

TWENTY-ONE

'I wonder where we are?' Brosc asked for the thousandth time.

'Oh for goodness' sake Brosc, it's no use wondering; no-one knows!' Wite moaned. 'If there were stars – that might help.'

'That would definitely help.' Nell's son responded. 'But there just aren't any and there's no sun or moon either. If one of those was to rise or set I could chart a course but there isn't: it just gets light or dark and that's it.' They lapsed once again into silent despondency, each remembering how they'd come to such a pass, taking it in turns to sigh heavily and sometimes all sighing at the same time – this was depressing!

They had all arrived at the same time but in different places on an island they would later discover to be called No Hope Island. They had also, independently of each other, tried to talk to the people there but with no success. Questions like "where are we?" would be met with responses like "does it matter?" or "how can we get off this island?" with "what's the point?" or "have you seen any of my friends?" with "who needs friends?" soon had them becoming nearly as despondent as everyone else.

It was some three days later that a very long-faced Wite turned a corner and literally bumped into an equally miserable-looking Brosc. Both men almost smiled but then thought better of it – it was so much easier to be depressed! In another two days they came across Nell's son but after searching for a further two days, mainly because there was nothing else to do rather than because they thought they needed to, decided that the others must have landed elsewhere. Even though they didn't see the point of it, they decided it might be best to stay together.

It took all their strength of mind and character to collect as much wood as they could, fix it together and make a mast and sail so as to try and escape that awful place. Brosc reckoned that the whole island population must have come out to watch what they were doing and offer discouragement.

'Waste of time doing that!'

'You'll never finish it!'

'The string's not that strong; it'll keep breaking – terrible if that happened at sea!'

'It'll break up as soon as you try to float it!'

'If it doesn't break up you'll just sail round and round in circles forever until it rots and then you'll sink!'

'Or you'll only end up back here!'

'Or at the bottom of the sea; the serpents there will sting you good and proper or chew you to bits.'

And so it went on. They actually did give up for a whole week; sitting around on the pebbles by the seashore. At one point Wite tried to skim stones across the water but gave up when Brosc told him he'd only strain his wrist and then his arm might fester and drop off. They fell into a morbid silence and, hardly speaking, it was by sheer mental effort that, on one particular night, they finished their raft and sailed off before anyone came down to depress and discourage them further.

Thus it was that at dawn the next day, they jumped aboard (well crawled, really, as they didn't have the mental or physical energy to jump) and paddled (very slowly as they'd almost made their minds up to stay) far away from the island, just discerning a few souls walking with hunched shoulders towards the water's edge where they stood shaking their heads disconsolately.

Then, amazingly, that awful despondent mood began to lift. The further they paddled away, the higher their spirits rose.

'It must be that place,' Brosc commented as the island finally disappeared from sight.

'Must be,' Wite agreed.

That was three days ago!

'I wonder where we are' Brosc remarked.

'Oh shut up!' Nell's son and Wite cried in unison.

And then they saw it! Just on the horizon – first just a ripple in the atmosphere and then something growing bigger and by the second they realised it was heading their way.

'What is it?' Wite asked.

Nell's son, who had the best eyesight of the three by far, screwed up his eyes and peered forward. 'I think it's a ship.'

'Oh dear,' Wite said, looking worried. 'Do you think it'll be a friendly ship or should we try and get away?'

'Get away? Where to? We've been stuck on this sea for so long that I think those island people were right! Whether they're good or bad, if we don't get rescued soon we're all going to die!'

'Well, good or bad, we'll soon know,' Nell's son remarked. 'They've obviously seen us as they're changing tack.'

All too soon the Raven grinned down at them and, throwing down a rope ladder, was welcoming them aboard.

Was it their imagination, or was that grin malicious? Oh well, they'd soon know!

TWENTY-TWO

'I'm sure this is where we felt Arthur to be close' Merlin, frowning, commented.

'It was,' Salazar replied. 'But there's no feeling or experience of him now!'

Cabby was rushing around with his nose to the ground as he searched out all the smells – some of which were quite tantalising – like squirrel – hmm, tasty!

'Cabby!' Merlin admonished him.

Pulling himself together he concentrated on that which they had asked him to do, eventually coming to a twitchy stop against a huge boulder.

I stood with the other four men and looked around, up and down but could see nothing except bare rock. There were, however, lots of hoof prints and other marks on the sandy earth round about.

'The entrance is here somewhere,' Merlin remarked, more to himself than any of us, as his hands felt over the rock. And then he stopped. 'It's a doorway,' he grinned.

I was stroking the rough hair on Cabby's neck as Merlin was speaking and felt his immediate response – raised hackles and shivering. Curling my fingers though his hair I grabbed hold of him and warned him to be brave. For goodness' sake, he'd been through enough "doorways" now to know that he came out the other side in one piece. The shaking subsided – almost.

Salazar, Cabby and I stood still and listened as Merlin told us what we were about to do. From now on it was imperative that they all assumed their new names. She – and we all knew who he meant – must not know we are here. He enveloped us all in a spell to make sure, adding that even if Arthur called us by our proper names, everyone else would only hear their new ones.

'What about me?' I asked. *'And Cabby?'*

'Well,' he pondered, stroking his chin. *'How about we call you Jack?'*

I was amused and shocked – he'd always said it was a name unknown in the Dark Ages and refused to allow me to use it; said I had to be called Percy.

'Don't get above yourself lad,' he responded. *'I was joking – we'll continue to call you Percy; anyone hearing it will hear another name*

– even Jack,' he chuckled. *'New names have to start somewhere, don't they? Cabby – well, when we call him they will merely hear "the dog"! In fact, why don't I do that for all of us, just in case any of us forget? We'll use our own names but anyone down here, including that mad woman, will merely hear our new names.'*

I felt Cabal bristle at being called "the dog" but he calmed down when Merlin explained – well to everyone else, not to Cabby; I mean, who would try to explain something to a dog? – that there were obviously other dogs around but that everyone should know him as Cabal or Cabby and not Bonzo! If certain others – and we all knew who – heard where he was, then he might end up on the griddle instead of beside it!

He was chastened!

'I wish someone would tell me just what is going on here!' Shake Spear exclaimed.

In our excitement at finding a possible way forward we had completely forgotten that he had still not regained his memory; not that even as Shake Spear, though, did he understand our gift of mind speaking. He'd always been there when we'd had our adventures and it seemed natural to just talk about anything with him included. Now it seemed we had a bit of a problem.

'Ah, yes,' Merlin turned round and smiled at the man. 'Well, we seem to have lost some of our number and the last we knew of one of them was that he was here roundabout. That was why we needed the dog – to see if he could smell where Arthur might be.'

'Arthur?'

'A young friend.'

'Ah!'

'Well Shake, er Minstrel,' Merlin amended, 'are you ready to join us in our exploits? It should be great fun and, you must admit, you will have a new tale to tell your boring friends when you return.'

'You're right! Just show me the way. He screwed up myopic eyes as he peered around.'

'It might be perilous,' Salazar warned him. 'We are not sure what dangers await us on our journey.'

'What! Do you think I'm afraid?' he exclaimed. 'If that be the case, good man, you don't know me! I have fought with the best! Just put a sword in my hand and you will then see what I can do!'

'No!' At least three of us chorused at Shake Spear's last remark. Merlin and Cabby – and I believe Tailor – could recall first hand the mayhem caused by the big man's short-sightedness, rushing here and there and fighting anyone within reach – even those on his own side – whenever he was armed and his blood was up. After chasing after and almost killing one of his best friends he had taken a solemn vow never to actually attack anyone again but to merely charge about, yelling at the top of his lungs and shaking his spear – hence the name that was eventually bestowed upon him. (In fact, I'd asked many a man what his real name was but none of them knew or remembered and so that was that – Shake Spear he would remain.) The rest of us had heard the stories; however, in his present state, he obviously did not remember his oath.

Merlin, not wanting the conversation to carry on in this vein – as he could see it was going nowhere and would just end in bad feeling – held up his hand to stem its flow. However, as he turned from the wall to look back at the others his eyes widened at the danger that was all too close. How come Salazar and he, or even Cabby come to that, had been unaware of its imminence.

'Quick! There's no time to argue! Follow me – NOW!'

He grabbed Tailor, Salazar grabbed Shake Spear and, yes you've guessed it – I grabbed Cabby as in pairs we pressed ourselves in through the boulder that was a "doorway" to another place, following Merlin as closely as we could. We could eventually see back through the rock as through a glass darkly but those creatures could not see us; they were running around but either did not see where we went or couldn't follow.

'What on earth are they?' I asked.

'They are the Swordsmen and the Archers!' a soft, tinkling voice replied from behind us.

We all swivelled round to stare at the amazing place we'd entered. How was it we hadn't noticed it when we arrived? I expect it was because we were so concerned as to what was chasing us that we didn't look where we were going, only worrying about where we were coming from.

We stared into the dark, sad, almond-shaped eyes of the young woman who stood before us. My mouth gaped open as I noticed that I could see almost straight through her. I got an elbow in the ribs for my rudeness. Closing my mouth, I looked past her, down a short corridor to some people staring at us from a huge, brightly lit room at the other end. At least a dozen men, less transparent than the woman, stood in a semi-circle around her with lances pointing at us. This was getting scary and I was beginning to tremble. 'What was this place? First I'm shackled to an oar, then I'm stuffed into a barrel, then I'm nearly drowned in a whirlpool, then they want to eat my dog, now I'm going to get speared. You couldn't make it up, could you?'

'Shut up Jack!'

'Who are you?' the woman asked.

'I know who they are, even if they are disguised,' a welcome and beloved voice broke in, as Arthur pushed past the guards and gave a mighty bear hug to Merlin, followed by a hearty shaking of hands with all four men, even though Shake Spear looked a little confused; I got thumped on the back! Hmmmm!

'Cabby, old friend: how are you?' he grinned as he hugged him round the neck and stayed with him, ruffling his coat as he started to talk to us.

Even Tiala and her people allowed a small smile at this meeting of old friends.

We all watched as the Archers and the Swordsmen sheathed their unusual weapons and gradually moved away; however, we didn't see the green goblin this time. Arthur explained who they were, even though no-one yet knew where they came from or who they worked for, if they worked for anyone, that is, or what their intentions were – well apart from capturing or killing that is.

'I don't think their intentions are for friendship,' Tiala remarked as she organised refreshments for our little group. One of the men passed around a tray containing cups of water and small, spiced biscuits. While everyone was accepting this repast, Arthur carried on talking.

'I have these wonderful people to thank for my rescue – for my life,' Arthur smiled up at Tiala as he thanked her for the food. 'Tiala has been a real friend,' he continued as introductions were made, Merlin interrupting to give them our assumed names. Arthur raised an enquiring eyebrow at Merlin but didn't argue with him.

For the next hour Arthur told us all that he knew concerning himself – not that he knew a lot about how he'd arrived in this place. Like me, I thought! How he'd been rescued and all that had happened since. Tiala then told them what had happened to her people and just who had been responsible for their deaths.

'Mab,' Merlin muttered. 'She has a lot to answer for.'

'But now,' Arthur's face darkened, 'Tiala needs me to go and parley with Mab so that those of her family that are still alive can be warned and those that are here can have this awful spell broken so they can receive their full physical bodies back.'

'No.'

'But I've promised! I didn't want to, but when Tiala told me what I had to bargain with, well I thought I'd stand a good chance of achieving it without being killed in the process.'

'Arthur, that mad woman will try to kill you if you are within spitting distance of her. It cannot be allowed. There's too much at stake!'

'Like what?' Arthur's face darkened as he stood to his feet and, with hands on hips, stared down at Merlin. The silence went on for some time until Arthur, turning, started to walk up and down – first with head down, rubbing his hands together in front of him and then with head up, shoulders stiffly back and hands clutched behind.

'Oh, for goodness' sake Arthur, sit down!' Merlin's exasperated tone broke through to the angry young man. 'You said you have something to bargain with? What is it?'

'Come and see,' he said as he pulled the older man to his feet. 'But don't get too close as it's guarded and Tiala might not be around to save you – the guards have their orders to kill anyone who gets too close; I think they were worried about the Archers and the Swordsmen breaking in and stealing it.'

'Stealing what?' I asked.

'This,' he replied as standing well away from the guards he pointed at the shining pot in the centre of the chamber. With flames from the leaping braziers situated around it bouncing off its many faces and facets, it glowed red, almost coming to life.

Staying well away from it and the guards, who were keeping a wary eye on us all, we circled it, remaining completely silent as we took in all its splendour. When we returned to the place where we'd started, we stood for minutes before anyone spoke. Then just one whispered word shattered that silence.

'Gundestrup!'

We turned and looked at Merlin as he stopped speaking.

'You know its name? How, Merlin?' Arthur asked.

'Oh I know about Gundestrup. But I don't think these people know exactly what they've got here.'

Arthur went on to tell us how Tiala had said about it being transported along with them to this place and knowing just how mad that witch must have been when she found it had gone.

Merlin's lips turned up as he smirked.

'So now I have to go and see her to get her to agree to leave Tiala's family alone and find some other way to raise the young dragons and to also set these people free from their ghostly state – and then we will give her the cauldron.'

'Oh no, Arthur! She must never lay her hands on that cauldron again. It could mean the end of everything good.'

'But I promised! It's part of Tiala's plan.'

We looked from Arthur to Merlin and back again, waiting to see who would give in first. Did we really expect any other outcome?

'But I have a much better way!'

TWENTY-THREE

'Where are you taking us?' Brosc shouted, trying to wriggle free from the grip of one of the frightening looking men that had taken hold of them.

'It's no concern of yours,' he replied, shoving him roughly along the deck and away from the captain.

Nell's son, from quite some distance before they were rescued – if rescue was indeed what was happening here – had already been aware of the kind of ship that had been bearing down upon them – apart from anything else he could smell it. Taking his courage in his hands he yelled that if he wasn't allowed to tell the captain certain interesting facts, then they would all be sorry.

'What are you going to tell him?' Wite whispered as they all crashed into one another when the first pirate halted.

'Search me,' he replied. 'But I'll try my best to think of something before we see him; that is, if they let us!'

The three crewmen conferred for a short while and then handing Nell's son over to the care of one of the others, the smallest of the three – and even he was huge, one of them went off in search of the captain.

'Thought of anything yet?' Wite asked.

'And I won't, if you keep interrupting,' he growled softly.

'Sorry.'

'Just please be quiet.'

'OK.'

Nell's son glared at him.

'Right. Come with me.' The other man had returned and, clamping his hand over Nell's son's forearm, dragged him behind him along the deck.

'What about us?' Brosc called after him.

'Yous just wait there. If yous be wanted, yous'll be called.'

Brosc and Wite just stared at the retreating backs of the two men and hoped Nell's son was as bright as they'd heard.

'Come in,' the captain called as Nell's son's captor hammered on the door. 'You can go,' he told the man who was rough-handling his captive through into the cabin. 'Pick, you can go too. Get me some vittles. And make sure you shut the door behind you!'

Waiting until the door had closed behind the man, the Raven, hoping to see fear in the man that stood before him, sat and stared at him through narrowed eyes. It soon became apparent that he was wasting his time; the man just stared straight back at him – he was either stupid or brave – he'd soon find out; so, clearing his throat, he asked, 'And just what is this important information you have to share with me?'

Now Nell's son had from a very early age spent more time in boats than he had on land. His father, a keen hunter and fisherman, had kept his wife Nell's kitchen at the inn well stocked with all manner of food from land and sea and had taken his only son out with him on every possible occasion to teach him to hunt, fish, sail and navigate by reading the stars and knowing the seasons. He'd proved to be a quick learner and in no time at all had mastered not only the rudiments of these arts but was able to note just where they were at any given time of the year by watching the heavens and it soon transpired that he had an almost photographic memory so far as the countryside and coastline were concerned. He'd become extremely clever at catching fish – and fish were cunning and slippery things – and he'd found that outwitting some men was very similar to outwitting fish.

Drawing now on all the things he'd learned and almost correctly discerning the type of man that stood before him he said, 'The other two men and I have been on the island where the treasure is buried.'

'You've been to Rainbow Island?' he responded irresponsibly, greed's ugliness spreading itself over his face as he gave away his secret.

'*So, I set the bait and you jump onto the hook?*' Nell's son thought satisfactorily. But without any change of expression continued, 'We have – and a dangerous place it is too. We just about got away by the skin of our teeth.'

'Well, where is it?'

'To find it you have to sail fairly close to shore. There is a certain promontory that sticks out from the rocks – like a pointing finger.' He had seen this weird structure as they'd drifted on the sea. 'When you get there you will need to turn in the direction of the pointing finger and sail in a straight line until you reach some red hills. Once there you will need to turn ninety degrees to starboard.' He did wonder whether he may have gone too far in that as there weren't any stars, might there not be a starboard, let alone red hills? But he had heard someone on No Hope Island talking about someone looking as bloody as the red hills, so he thought he'd use this while speaking to the captain. However, he needn't have worried, the captain made no adverse reaction, merely asking him to continue.

He went on to describe the Colossi – he'd seen them in a dream – that stood on either side of the entrance to the wide river on Rainbow Island that led inland through a tunnel and out to where the treasure was hidden.

When Nell's son had finished, the captain jumped out of his seat with excitement. 'So, which way do we sail from here? This way or that way?' he asked, pointing one hand after the other in both directions.

'We'll need to get close to land first. When we get there I'll be able to check out the coastline and know exactly where we are at that time and then I'll be able to direct you.'

'Good. I'll clear the cabin next to mine. You can stay in there.'

'Um, I'll need my men!'

'Why? What good are they? They'll be better off at the oars.'

'I cannot function without them sir,' he responded quickly. 'One of them looks after me, especially when the malady attacks and only he knows how to mix the remedy. Someone else tried to do it once and I almost died. And just in case I do die, well the other one is almost as good as me so far as navigation is concerned.'

'Perhaps I should just use him, then,' the captain mused.

'You could try,' Nell's son responded, 'but he gets homesick and then no-one can get through to him. He goes into a sort of trance for days on end. Lost in his own little world, I think.'

'Oh well, whatever you say. I must reach the treasure before anyone else – especially the Jackal. But hearken to this – if I find that you have deceived me, you will wish that I *had* shackled you to the oars! All who've tried to better me have failed and I have always made them pay. You will be no exception,' he grinned wickedly as he thrust his face right up to the other mans – however, it was he that looked away first.

'Go! Go get your men! Pick,' he called out to his man, 'clear out the room next to this one, behind where that boy slept; that will do for him and his men. Go with him first, get them and settle them in. Quick now. And hurry up with my food, I'm famished.

'I'll head towards land. We should be there late in the day tomorrow. In the meantime I'll get Pick to sort you out with some good and better clothing,' he almost sneered at the rags that just about kept the man in front of him decent. 'You can then rest but I shall want to see you all first thing tomorrow. That's all. Go.'

So he was dismissed and was barely able to contain the huge sigh of relief that he heaved as soon as the captain's door had closed.

Pick bowed himself out and closed the door behind him, leading Nell's son back to his men.

The two other very relieved men followed Nell's son into the very small room next to the captain's cabin and, watching him give a silent "shh" behind one finger, obeyed his warning to keep silent for the time being. Waiting until Pick had cleared the room, supplied some washing water and additional clothing and brought them in some victuals, they sat around in silence, eating and drinking, until they felt it safe to speak.

'What's happening?' Brosc finally whispered some time after Pick had left the room.

Nell's son, after silently opening the cabin door and making sure that the corridor outside was empty, soon got them up to speed with what had taken place in the captain's cabin, giving them enlightenment as to what he'd actually had in mind for all of them when they'd first come aboard. Within the next couple of hours they would hear for themselves the drum beat and whip lash of what they might have had to endure if Nell's son had not been so quick-witted.

'Thanks man,' Brosc said gruffly. 'Sounds awful down there.'

'We'll just have to make sure we remember our roles. If things look a bit sticky, I'll have to have one of my bad turns. When that happens, Wite, you will need to go to the cook and get whatever you think will make a healing brew. Think you can do that?'

'Course I can,' he responded.

'And you'd better make sure it's something drinkable. If you make up something that tastes awful, it will be the worse for you! In fact, I'm going to make you drink half of it first – just to be sure! Hmm, some rum would be good! Anyway, I'll stay here in this cabin when I'm supposed to be ill so you'll have to bring me some food as well. But let's not think about things going wrong until they do, eh? Sometimes I think that just thinking about them brings them on! What we'll really have to do is see if we can escape when we get near land.'

'How do you think we'll be able to do that?' Brosc asked.

'Well, we can all swim, so that shouldn't be too difficult, just so long as we're not too far from land and there's a beach or something to get out onto.'

'But what about the serpents?'

'Serpents? What serpents, Brosc?'

'When those men held us up against the bulwarks, one of them was leaning over the side and growled at the other one as he pointed down into the sea. We all looked over and saw about fifteen huge serpents swimming alongside the ship. I asked the sailor what they were, as he shivered when he saw them. First he was amazed that I didn't know anything about them, especially as we'd been drifting on the sea for so long. He told me that they weren't the biting serpents but the eating serpents. The sea, apparently, is infested with these things. There are some that are quite small and they move along the seabed; they nip your ankles if you are walking along there.'

'What do you mean, "they nip your ankles"? And what on earth do you mean by "walking along there"? Who walks along the seabed?'

Wite broke in here with, 'Apparently people here don't really die!'

'Don't die?'

'Listen. The men told us that it's almost impossible to die here, although they couldn't be completely sure as some people had disappeared and not been seen again, so they had to assume that maybe they did, but, then, maybe they didn't!'

'You're not making much sense. Are you making all this up?'

Brosc picked it up again. 'They said that the sea is one of the most dangerous places to be if you're not in a boat. If you fall into the sea and go down to the bottom of it, the little serpents nip your feet and that stings like crazy. The amazing thing is that if you sink to the bottom of the sea you can just walk about – you don't drown! But it's not pleasant, of course, because of the serpents. If you don't sink but try to swim, well the huge serpents who stay near the surface and who have six rows of sharp, razor-like teeth top and bottom, suck you into their mouths, chew you to pieces, which apparently hurts like blazes, and then digest you. When you eventually come out the other end – and that's not a pleasant thought is it? – your body joins up together again, almost as you were before but not quite the same!'

'Well, I should imagine you wouldn't be quite the same if that had happened to you!' Nell's son shuddered. 'Did he say if those people that it happened to were conscious the whole time?' Nell's son asked.

Wite continued, 'Apparently yes. One of the men said that a mate of his had had to wait nearly two weeks for the three toes on his left foot to be reunited with the rest of him as they had somehow got lodged within the serpent's innards and weren't passed through until then. He said that he'd been sitting in one of the inns with a tankard of ale when suddenly his three toes shot towards him through the door and attached themselves to his foot; he was still in shock at the time as he kept telling everyone that when he'd been inside the serpent he'd seen jumbled bits of himself floating past his eyes – well, one of his eyes at any rate, as the other one was wedged inside his ear at the time on the blind side – as his chewed up flesh and bones travelled through the sea creature's body.'

'Barbaric.'

'Enough! That's disgusting!'

Digesting this information, they were quiet for a while

'You're making this up, aren't you?' Nell's son finally asked them.

''Fraid not! Wish I was!'

'Then it's going to be extremely difficult to swim to shore, isn't it? Did they save our raft?' he asked after another long silence.

The other two shook their heads.

'They dragged it on board and Cook was chopping it up to use as firewood in the galley.'

'Then we'll just have to try and make another one. If we can put it together in here, then when the time comes we'll try and slip over the side. Perhaps at night.' Nell's son leaned back against the panelling and closed his eyes. 'When we're out and about we'll need to get hold of as much rope as we can; in the meantime, we'll loosen these panels so that when we're ready we'll be able to pull them down and lash them together. OK men?'

They spent the rest of the evening working out how, when and where they would be able to make their escape, before trying to get some sleep, sleep that was rudely disturbed by a call to arms early the next morning.

TWENTY-FOUR

Honey returned to the captain's cabin to find the witch had rummaged through every cupboard, drawer and chest, evidence of which could be seen by their contents strewn hither and thither across the floor. She'd stayed away for as long as she could, as though the sailors looked a scary lot they took her for who she was, which wasn't her at all, but someone called Mongrel and even though they were quite frightening, they weren't as bad as Mab! But, with dragging feet she felt it must be well past her time to return and so now reluctantly she was here.

'It's got to be here somewhere and where on earth have you been?' the witch, grumbling, shouted over her shoulder as she delved almost to the bottom of a large sea chest, oversized rump sticking upwards. Flushed with exertion she looked up at Honey again and called her over. 'I could have done with you here hours ago. Anyway, start from over there, what's-your-name?'

'Mongrel – they call me Mongrel.'

'Ha! And a mongrel you are!' she agreed, almost laughing. 'Start with that pile of stuff over there,' she pointed at a huge pile of literally everything from paper through ropes and clothes to sails.

'What am I looking for?'

'What are you – what are you looking for?' she spluttered. Always on the edge, with face reddening by the second, she lunged at the poor woman who, with virtually no time to spare, just evaded her grasp as she dived behind the captain's chair. Mab, falling against the panelled wall of the cabin, crashed her head against a glass lamp; seeing stars, she just about managed to keep control not only of her physical self but also of her mind. Rummaging about in the cabin and finding nothing – not even a clue – had rendered her almost manic. However, somewhere in the recesses of her spinning brain she told herself that, first, the girl clearly didn't know what she was looking for and, secondly, she really needed her help at the moment. Time was of the essence and unless she got to the treasure before anyone else – well that didn't bear thinking about. The time would soon come when she could amuse herself in getting rid of the woman; she really was irritating – almost as bad as that stupid brother of hers – Hide? Hive? *'Stop it Mab, stop it! Plenty of time to think of that another time!'*

Slapping the back of her left hand with her right and

straightening herself up, she looked down to see a quaking, skinny man hiding under the desk. 'Come, come, Honey – er Mongrel – I didn't realise who you were at first,' she lied. 'Now I need you to try and find either a map or directions to a place called Rainbow Island. Ah, but you can't read, can you?' She looked as though her temper would get the better of her for a moment or two as it bubbled just below the surface of her mind but, pulling her shoulders back and taking a few deep breaths, she continued. 'Right – I shall write the words "Rainbow" and "Island" and if you see either of those words written on anything, let me know. Understand?'

Still shuddering, she nodded.

The witch sighed, shaking her head, but still managed to keep herself under control – just. Finding some paper and eventually, after flinging all manner of rubbish off the desk, the inkpot, she wrote down the said words and pinned it to the panel behind the desk.

A knock at the door made both of them jump – an unusual occurrence for the witch. 'Enter,' she called, Honey noticing that her voice had changed.

A tall, scruffy-looking man entered, ducking in through the doorway and sliding the hat from his head in one fluid movement as he stepped into the cabin. 'Beg pardon sir, but there's a ship on port bow, headed this way.'

'Right, I'll be there immediately. Go, go – keep watch,' she ordered, waving him out of the room.

The man left as though rewinding the process, mechanically sliding his cap back onto his head as he ducked out.

'Mongrel, keep looking! Don't forget our new names – or else! I want to have that map in my hands before tonight. I must get the treasure,' this last muttered under her breath as she headed for the deck.

Standing beside the man at the wheel, she picked up the spyglass and scanned the sea, the sight alighting on a similar ship headed their way. She was still too far off to make out her name but it should shortly come into view. It didn't. It hove to, slackened its sails and waited.

Mab, turned the glass and could eventually read the name printed on the side of the other ship, 'It's the Raven, *Hello Percy!*' she chuckled, not knowing I'd escaped my shackles. '*Perhaps I shall soon get my hands on you, eh? And you won't even know it's me!*'

The two ships made no move to get closer, each one keeping a wary eye on the other for most part of the morning. As soon as half the day had gone, the Raven up-anchored and with all sheets to the wind, sailed away. Mab gave instructions to the men to follow but to keep out of sight; she watched the ship go but not until it could be seen no more did she return to her cabin.

'Well, Mongrel, have you found anything yet?'

The wretched woman crouched down awaiting the inevitable attack as she shook her head but was taken completely by surprise at the unusual evenness of the witch's temper.

'OK, we'll start again. You begin over there and I'll start over here – we'll meet in the middle!' she almost smiled. But Honey dreaded that meeting. What if they didn't find anything?

She needn't have worried. As the afternoon wore on the heat in the little cabin had increased to such a degree that Mab, mopping her brow, had been forced to take off the shiny waistcoat. Twisting to throw it onto the chair, Honey noticed some peculiar markings on its lining and so, standing up and with shaking hands – in case she was wrong – picked it up and stared at it.

'It's here, mistress,' she murmured, clearing her throat and repeating herself; she'd not spoken for so long, her voice had almost deserted her.

'Captain!' the witch shouted, just about stopping herself from cuffing the woman around the head. 'Call me Captain! Do you want to give the game away?' And then breathing deeply to control her temper she held out her hand, 'Give it to me!'

A quivering Honey handed the witch's waistcoat to her, moving as far away as she dare once it was taken from her.

'Yes! Yes yes yes!' she cried as she stared at the inside of the garment. 'To think I was walking about with it all the time! It's an omen! It was meant to be mine!' Swirling around in glee, she clutched the article to her chest while congratulating herself on her good fortune.

'Now, let's look at it in detail and see where we should go.'

Mab immersed herself into the map, checking this and trying to understand that, making a mental note of all the ports and harbours, hills and islands but there didn't appear to be a Rainbow Island marked there at all.

Honey watched her face turn from the redness of excitement to the whiteness of confusion and then from the whiteness of confusion to the crimson of fury. *'Oh dear, what was she going to do now?'*

The fury then subsided as she noticed another mark on the map: Dragon's Reach. This name had an "x" marked above it – very faint, but an "x" nonetheless. 'That's where we have to go!' she exulted. 'That's where we will find what we're looking for! Let's go on deck and find out if anyone knows where we might be at the moment and then how long it will take to get to Dragon's Reach.'

TWENTY-FIVE

It had taken the best part of two hours of negotiation, argument and frustration before Tiala, her brothers and some of the older men from her village agreed, albeit grudgingly, to Merlin's plan. However, the strongest and most able of the men stood alert, with swords at the ready, still extremely suspicious, while Merlin and his men approached the cauldron; they were certainly not going to allow it to be moved from its place of protection.

'Here's a list of everything that I need,' he handed the scrap of paper to me. *'Take Tailor with you and Cabby; make sure you're not caught. Oh, I suppose you'd better take Shake Spear as well; it'll be a bit heavy for just the two of you. Cabby – make sure you can find your way back here. Percy – be as quick as you can lad. We have the upper hand at the moment but just look at some of these poor people, some have almost faded away completely and, I hate to say it, Tiala is becoming more indistinct by the minute.'*

We turned then, with me giving orders to the other two men. I always felt a bit silly doing that. In my day – well, in the 20th Century I mean, I would be told off by my mother or father and sometimes even my older brother for getting above myself. "Know your place," my mother would scold. "Children should be seen and not heard," was another one of her favourites along with "Don't speak until you are spoken to," and I felt certain I could hear her telling me that I was getting a bit too big for my boots (which actually was quite true – they were starting to pinch) and tut tutting down through the corridors of time as she listened in, in my imagination, to me now. But here it was so different. I was accepted, through my friendship with Arthur no doubt, as one of the gentry and therefore it didn't matter how old I was; if I gave an order, well, the ordinary Joe Bloggs of the day carried it out. As I said, though, I still felt uncomfortable and half expected one of them to scold me at best or laugh at me at worst.

'Can't I go?' Arthur, stepping up to me, asked Merlin.

'No. It's too dangerous and I need you to tell me how you got here and what's been happening.'

'But I don't know how I got here. All I know is, I was following this ridiculous little man and laughing so much I thought... well I couldn't think! I must have been out of my mind. And the awful thing is I just can't remember how I came to be following him in the first place. These wonderful people,' he spread his arm wide as he turned and looked around the room, 'saved my life.' Choking back his emotion he faced Merlin once again, and I was shocked to notice that he was now just an inch or so shorter than the magician, and was about to continue his story when the Druid interrupted him to shoo us on our way.

We left, moving swiftly up the rough, sloping passageway until we could hear them no longer. Squeezing through the narrow cleft – rather than push ourselves through the boulder (which pleased Cabby no end, as I'm sure you must appreciate) – we stopped, listening for those strange man-goats or whatever they were, before moving on. All was quiet – perhaps too quiet? – or was that my imagination working overtime again?

Cabby nudged my arm with his nose as he edged past me. *'There's no-one around Percy. I'd hear their hooves clicking on the rocks if they were.'*

'OK – let's go. Shake, er, Minstrel,' I turned towards him. 'Lead on to where we might find that gypsum.'

'Hmm,' he held his hand up to his mouth as his brow furrowed in concentration. 'I think I know the best place,' he then grinned. 'Follow me.'

And we all did just that as we made our way back down toward the town. I hoped they'd forgotten about Cabby by the time we got there, but I needn't have worried; we arrived in the middle of the night and it was pitch dark when we finally made our way into one of the sheds by the side of the quay. Shake Spear jemmied open the lock and stepped inside. I was flabbergasted! I thought he'd take us somewhere where we could buy the stuff but no – he was actually breaking into this place to steal it.

Finally getting over the shock and recovering my voice, I asked him what he thought he was doing.

'Oh, don't worry about that,' he chuckled. 'Everybody does this all the time. It's the most peculiar place I've ever lived,' he added. 'Everyone expects to be robbed. They're always stealing my rum. I remember complaining once.' He stopped, a frown furrowed his brow, and then added, 'But everyone just laughed at me. I eventually found that it was a complete waste of time, so I stopped complaining and then did what everyone else did. So, young man, that's what I'm doing now. Now, how many bags did you want?'

We left the shed with six bags of the stuff over our shoulders –

Shake Spear carried two as did Cabal whose load was slung saddlebag style over his back, while Tailor and I carried one apiece – and, boy, were they heavy! Before long we were following Cabal back through the town's lanes and on into the hills. It was all too easy! We'd seen no-one in the town – not that we were wanting to and had kept close to the sides of buildings and alleyways – and no-one had spotted our departure. And was I congratulating myself on all of this? You can bet your life I was. Then I almost fell over Cabal who'd stopped so suddenly that I didn't have time to take note of the fact. His hackles were standing up straight on the back of his neck and his lips were drawn right back over his fangs. He looked frightening. Then I saw what he had seen. We were surrounded. How had we not seen them? How had Cabal not heard them? But then they looked as though they had just been waiting for us. Did they watch us go and just wait for us to come back? Probably! Well, we were in a right quandary. Tailor looked scared and turned to me for instruction. I was waiting for him to tell me! Well, he was a man and a lot more experienced than me wasn't he? But then again, I remembered that he followed orders, not gave them. Shake Spear had screwed up his face and was trying his hardest to see through those shortsighted eyes of his. Why wasn't he wearing those spectacles I'd asked Merlin to give him?

'What's happening?' he whispered.

'We're surrounded,' I replied.

'Surrounded by who?'

'I don't know what they are! Half-man – half-animal!'

'Any way out?' he asked.

I looked all around, my chest still heaving from the exertion of carrying that heavy bag and knowing that I had no strength left in me to fight. 'No. They've chosen their ambush very carefully. *Merlin – help us!*'

Nell's son rushed up the stairs behind the captain; Brosc and Wite were almost falling over one another as they followed close behind, Brosc's hair standing on end as he ducked at the otherworldly wailing sound that flew over their heads.

'What on earth is that?' he croaked.

'The dragon,' the Raven replied as he crouched beside him.

'Dragon?' Wite responded hoarsely as he and Brosc flattened themselves to the floor.

'H-h-horrific!' Brosc stammered.

'Wretched thing turned up a couple of years ago and has been making a nuisance of himself ever since. He tries to creep up on the ships when he can because he knows the serpents follow them. The serpents wait for bodies to fall into the water or be thrown into it, so they hang around and he knows that if he's quick enough he can catch one of the bodies before them or at least dive down and swallow up a mouthful of serpents before they know what's hit them. But I wouldn't be surprised if he tried to grab one of us if we were careless enough to stay out in the open too long.' Almost the whole complement of men had by now thrown themselves to the floor or hidden themselves in some way or other, staying there until eventually they saw the object of their fear flapping away towards the horizon.

Once the danger was passed, the Raven jumped up and dusted himself down before straightening his hat – and wig!

The rest of the men followed suit and, after watching the thing disappear, turned to see what the captain would do next.

'That looked surprisingly like Hellion,' Nell's son whispered to his two companions. 'But he's supposed to be dead; I reckon it must be another of the same kind!'

'S'pose so,' Brosc acknowledged.

'This is a weird place anyway,' Wite cut in. 'Anything seems to happen here; in fact I'm quite scared of even saying something bad in case it does!' He shivered, adding, 'I'm sure that I shouldn't even think bad things either. Perhaps I should start thinking good things and then everything will be all right. Perhaps then I'll wake up from this awful nightmare.'

'Oh shut up,' the other two mouthed at him.

The captain during this time was rounding up some of the men and shouting orders. He beckoned Nell's son over to him – the other two followed – and asked him to scour the sea all around to find out if he could discern just exactly where they were currently situated and did he think they were anywhere nearer Rainbow Island.

Of course, Nell's son had not the slightest idea where they were or where Rainbow Island actually was (or even if it really existed) but, shielding his eyes, he obediently searched all around for "clues". His two companions, as oblivious as the captain to what Nell's son knew or was actually doing, turned in unison with everyone else to see what he might be looking at.

Then that other ship came into view again! It was a very long way off and to the casual observer could not be seen but they had not bargained for Nell's son's keen eyesight. Even he had had to rub his eyes a few times to make sure that he was actually seeing what he thought he saw.

'Captain – it's definitely that ship we saw some days ago!'

The captain jumped up and, sending a man aloft, demanded he tell him everything. 'What do you see man?' he hollered, hands on hips and head bent right back as he stared aloft, almost losing hat and wig in the process. 'Hurry up man; hurry up.'

The poor man almost lost his footing in his haste to carry out his orders; all those on board gave a sharp intake of breath as he slipped just outside the crow's nest, but he recovered and was soon standing inside it. Everyone always jumped to the captain's commands for fear of what he might do to them should they appear to be procrastinating; the dread of being shackled to an oar was an ever present threat. The man leaned over the side of the crow's nest where, cupping his eyes, he strained aft, searching for what Nell's son had said he'd seen.

Yes, she was following in their wake, trying to keep out of sight but she was definitely following them. He told his captain so and was rewarded with a curt acknowledgment.

'Stay there, man, and let me know if she gets any closer or which way she goes if she sails off.'

The Raven strode up and down the deck for long minutes before, making his decision, he jumped up onto the bridge and started shouting orders. 'Beat the drum; get those oarsmen rowing – fast – double time; let's see if we can outrun them. See to your weapons men just in case – sharpen those knives, break out the balls and chains; bowmen – gather your quivers and fill them to the brim. No-one but no-one is going to cheat me of my prize!'

The three men felt a rush of excitement as sailors ran back and forth, sometimes falling over one another, in order to carry out the captain's orders; however, the exhilaration was tempered by the sorrow they felt for those poor men trapped below at their oars. And what on earth would happen to them should the ship sink – they were manacled to the floor for goodness' sake! All that water rushing in on them! It didn't bear thinking about!

It was almost nightfall before the man aloft confirmed that the other ship, though it had still tried to follow them, had not been seen for well over an hour. The captain ordered the man down, telling him to get some vittles and some sleep – he would be required to resume his post at first light. The man, rushing to obey, slid down the ropes to the deck, pleased to get a break from swaying aloft and also to feed and water his parched body.

Someone was sent down below; the drumming stopped, the swishing of the oars ceased and an almost deathly hush now hung over the ship.

Nell's son made his way across the deck toward the captain where, capturing his attention, they walked forward. The captain followed Nell's son's pointing finger, becoming quite excited as he saw, in the gloom, another pointing finger – the one of rock jutting out from the land.

'Great! Good! Excellent!' he exclaimed as, ordering the men to drop anchor, he made his decision to follow in that direction come morning. Rubbing his hands together with glee, he made his way down to his cabin. Shouting over his shoulder, they were all told to rest up for the start of their journey tomorrow. 'No gambling, no drinking,' he added. The Watch were given their duties and only two hours apiece so that they would all be fit for the morrow. 'And give the oarsmen double gruel – they have to be fit too you know!' he ordered magnanimously.

'What on earth is happening?' Brosc whispered to Nell's son as they settled down for the night.

'Search me,' he replied. 'I've given him some information but for the life of me I don't know what will happen when he finds out it's all nonsense.'

'Perhaps we'll get away before then,' Wite added.

'Perhaps.'

Then, as the ship turned so as to be facing in the right direction for their journey next morning, they heard two loud noises as each eye on the figurehead clanged shut.

TWENTY-SEVEN

'Cabby – run! We'll hide the gypsum here somewhere. Go tell Merlin what's happened. He'll know what to do.'

After we'd stuffed the bags into a fissure behind some large boulders, I watched as he went down almost onto his belly behind the rock and begin to crawl away. Almost pulling himself along by his forepaws I kept an uneasy eye on him while he crouched low and moved out of the circle in which we were trapped. Then, lurching to his feet, he sped off. I look after him satisfactorily until, with disbelief, I saw the arrow that arched high through the air fall and hit him. He dropped like a stone.

'Cabby,' I'd screamed as I'd watched the arrow fly and again as I saw him fall. *'Cabby – can you hear me?'* I cried out again, this time in my mind. Nothing! The tears started.

Our captors, directed once again by the evil-looking green demon, fell upon us and soon had us trussed and tied together in a line. Well, Tailor and I were in a line – if you can call two men a line; Shake Spear was being dragged along unconscious between two Swordsmen; he'd put up a great fight – he was just hitting out at everyone that came near – but didn't see the blow coming that ultimately felled him. Well obviously!

As they pulled me along I was past caring and took no notice of my surroundings or where we were headed. My wonderful Cabal had been shot by one of those Archers and now lay dead – all alone between those cold and lifeless rocks. No-one to tend to him. No-one to care. And now he wouldn't be able to leave this awful place – ever. *'Merlin!'*

The Archers and the Swordsmen dragged us over the sharp rocks and jagged countryside. If I didn't want to be completely cut to pieces I would have to shake off my grief about Cabal and start concentrating on where I was going and what I was walking on. I looked at Shake Spear, who was a little in front of us – he was still out cold so our captors were taking it in turns to carry the heavy man; Tailor was twitching as he was yanked along in front of me and looked scared to death. His eyes were as big as balloons. Then, again, I suppose mine were too. We were being held up by our shoulders by our captors and, with feet hardly touching the ground, had almost to sprint as they ran over the dusty and rocky terrain.

They spoke not one word. They seemed to click and to this day I don't know how they did it. They didn't appear to open their mouths or click their fingers. Perhaps it was something up their noses. Which reminded me of my granddad when he used to fall asleep in the armchair on a Sunday after a huge roast dinner – and, funnily enough, even in my fear, I was so hungry that I believed I could even smell my mum's roast beef and Yorkshire pudding. But, getting back to my granddad – when he fell asleep he was one of the only people I know whose mouth never dropped open. His cheeks would puff out and cave in as he breathed (he always removed his false teeth first, you see, and placed them beside his teacup and saucer – I was mesmerised by them!) but his mouth stayed resolutely shut; and then you'd hear this weird clicking noise. I can remember creeping up to him and listening hard to find out where the noise was coming from and I'm sure it came from one of his nostrils; I even tried peering up his nose to see if I could see what it was that was causing this weird click but could see nothing; and I never had the courage to ask him – even if I thought he might know in any event, being asleep when it happened, that is.

Anyway, returning to these creatures, even though they didn't speak, they all seemed to act as though being directed by someone or something – or the click! (The Hobgoblin had disappeared once we'd been captured – so it wasn't him.)

As night began to close in we breasted the rise and looked down at the waves breaking on the shore hundreds of feet below us and at two miniscule boats bobbing just offshore and one large galleon further out to sea. We were right at the top of the cliffs and I, for one, didn't think we'd be going to that beach – there was no pathway down – so I wondered why they'd brought us here. You can imagine my fear and the scream that rose up from the depths of my soul and out through my throat and the stomach churning that almost made me fill my pants as these beasts started to jump over the edge. 'Lemmings!' I thought – 'they're going to kill us all!' They seemed to have no fear and were as sure-footed as the goats that half their body represented. Hopping here and there and perching on the tiniest bits of rock, they quickly made their way down. No-one fell! No-one was injured! No-one died! No-one was going to believe this! Shake Spear was completely out of it anyway. Tailor was struck dumb with fear. Only I made any fuss and was convinced, afterwards, that my screams could be heard all over the world – well the world in which we were currently living at any rate – as they bounced back and forth from rock to rock on the cliff face and down to the beach.

As I have already said, Shake Spear was unconscious, so at least he wouldn't be composing a ditty to my shame at any time in the future. I only hoped Tailor was too traumatised to remember as well; it would be so shameful to have him recounting the story at some later date – that is, if we were actually going to have some later date to be able to tell anyone anything!

There were four men in each boat that drifted about twenty feet offshore and as they saw us cascading down the face of the cliff (or had been alerted by my screams!) they pulled on their oars and beached their boats. The creatures handed us over to the boatmen, received some heavy bags of something or other in exchange and returned the way they had come, hopping back up the cliff face as though it were no effort at all, even with all those heavy bags.

I'd been so caught up with my grief and fear that I hadn't considered what new peril I might now be in and it wasn't until the sailors started pulling on their oars that I began to wonder what was going to happen next.

Turning round, I searched the faces of the four men in my boat and then the four in the other boat. I didn't recognise any of them; they couldn't, therefore, be from the Raven's ship. Then whose ship did they belong to? I hoped it wasn't the Jackal. I'd heard he was a rebel and had disappeared for over two years and I believed he'd do anything to keep his ship, so perhaps it was. But why did he want me? Well, I thought resignedly, the way things had gone today so far, it most probably was him and would soon learn all the answers to my "whys". I shut my eyes and tried to block everything out, especially the thought that he might need extra oarsmen.

'Percy?'

I opened my eyes and found Shake Spear peering closely into my face. 'Yes Minstrel,' I asked.

'Minstrel? Are you all right, Percy? It's me, Shake Spear.'

I laughed. Yes, I actually laughed. 'You're back!'

He looked at me as though I'd gone barmy as he rubbed the new bruise that shone on the bump above his ear; I explained briefly what had happened to him. Well, he sat next to me and I whispered as quietly as I could, as I didn't want the rowers to hear anything about any of us. He continued rubbing the bump and nodded now and then as I told him my story.

'Sorry, Percy. I can remember getting into a bit of a fight with a man who bumped into me when he fell out of the door of the Blue Pelican. After that, I can't remember anything – except being the proprietor of an inn. And, yes, now you come to mention it, I can remember being the Minstrel. Oh yes – they liked me better than the old Minstrel who was, they said, a miserable old man; so they locked him up and I took his place. They really liked my stories and hoped I'd stay. They still called me Minstrel though. How weird I can remember all that!'

'Well, I'm glad you're back in your right mind now and maybe we can sort something out to try and escape whatever is happening to us – or is about to happen to us,' I grimaced as I saw the monster of a ship that we were approaching rising above us out of the night's gathering mist. 'Hope we can all stay together,' I added and looked over at Tailor. Realising Shake Spear couldn't see him, I explained that he, too, had been captured along with us and was in the other boat.

We were then hoisted on board and were greeted by a widely smiling Jackal who, for some reason or other, just couldn't take his eyes off me.

TWENTY-EIGHT

Merlin, deciding what might be the best way to extract the cruel, barbed arrowhead, barked orders, then quietly listing the herbs and potions, he waited as patiently as he could while Salazar mixed and boiled the medicine he knew was Cabby's only hope.

They had been alerted some few hours before by one of Tiala's guardsmen yelling from the mouth of the tunnel. He had seen something moving outside and called the guard to fall in before making out it was Cabal dragging himself toward them; they rushed out and carried him gently down into the cavern.

Merlin's face, always white anyway, turned paler as he saw the hound stretched out on the ground before him. Cabby was in a lot of pain and each indrawn breath rattled as he struggled to breathe, while his eyes, normally so bright, were beginning to glaze over. His breathing was becoming more shallow by the minute and his cheeks were hollowed; Merlin, lowering his head to the hound's chest, could feel his heart flutter rather than beat.

'Right – quick!' he shouted. 'Prince – help me!'

Within seconds Merlin had emptied most of the hidden pockets located within his robe and laid out the paraphernalia onto a flat rock. 'Bring him over here – gently!' he objected as the guardsmen went to pull him up.

Merlin took the cup from Salazar and sniffed its contents. 'A little more of that,' he pointed at the dried herbal bulb at the end of the bench. 'Just peel off one leaf.'

After adding this final piece to the preparation and stirring it once, he waited – not very patiently as could be discerned by his sighing and huffing – until it turned a deeper blue. Whilst waiting he kept whispering close to Cabby's ear, 'Hold on, old friend. Just hold on.'

Finally ready, the mixture was separated into two cups: the first, kept beside the wounded hound, was to be used to cover the hole that would be left in his side once the arrow was removed; the other would be trickled into his mouth, so that the remedy would work from within and without. Salazar was given his instructions to try and get Cabal to drink but if he couldn't he should smear the mixture slowly onto his tongue. Merlin would deal with the wound.

He bent over the jagged cut, separating the bloodied and matted hairs as carefully as he could, searching with gentle, probing fingers for the arrowhead; stopping only to turn and demand everyone move back. 'I can't see with all of you blocking out the light and you're making it deuced hot, you know!'

They moved back obediently but continued to watch from a distance, the more tender souls clutching their hands tightly or holding them over their mouths.

'Got it – no... yes, got it!' Merlin sighed as the offending piece of metal was finally removed – an awful looking arrowhead with a sharp point at the tip of the head and cruel barbs down the sides. Cabal didn't move at all. 'Prince – start giving him the brew; I'll sew him up and administer it here.'

They all watched as Merlin cleaned the area and then proceeded to tie strands of Cabal's own hair together across the wound until it was closed; hardly any more blood seeped out – but then, again, he had lost so much. 'Less likely to get an infection using his own hair,' he explained later. Then, taking over from Salazar spent the next half hour administering the potion as tenderly as he could. Cabal still did not move and it was with inward worry and concern over the next couple of hours that Merlin checked his breathing and heartbeat.

Arthur looked from one Druid to the other to see how serious the situation might be but their faces were inscrutable. Unable to contain himself any longer, 'How serious is it Merlin?' he asked.

'Well, we've done as much as we can. It's now just a question of time.' Merlin disposed of all his phials and packets back into the folds of his robe before moving over to the wall where he sat and leaned against it, staring across at the hound.

'Sleep, sir,' Tiala spoke quietly to him. 'I'll watch over your dog. If anything changes I'll wake you – I promise.'

'You're very kind. I will do that.' And without more ado he closed his eyes and slept the sleep of exhaustion but didn't rest – it was a very disturbed sleep and those watching the rapid movements behind his eyelids and the twitching of his body became quite concerned.

'I've hedged him around with a mist that you cannot penetrate- a barrier that only I can break through. So – all your bringing him here from times afar off was a complete waste, wasn't it? I knew you spoke to one another but you won't be able to do that now! Just you try! Go on – just try! Ha! See, it doesn't work, does it? I'm reading your mind, Merlin; I'm travelling down all those little corridors within it and picking out the best bits – your secrets, your spells, your potions, your

very being. In this Place of Shades the rules are different! So now I shall drain all your secrets out of you, you know – bit by bit. You will be left an empty shell. Empty, I say! Worthless! If you were ever worth anything in the first place! You will be mocked – a figure of fun – a nobody now! Relax – don't fight it – it's no use, you know! You are lost!'

'Wake up, wake up!' Merlin opened wild eyes and punched the air as he tried to fend off that which had taken hold of him and stared up into the concerned face of Salazar who only just managed to grab the fist that was flying towards him. 'What is going on? Are you well or ill?'

'Wait,' he replied hoarsely, pulling himself together. Holding up his hand to discourage any further interruption he strained to contact me. Reaching out with all his concentration, he called my name – and not only Percy, he even tried Jack – but to no avail. 'You try,' he ordered Salazar, knowing that he was listening in.

'It's no good,' he moaned after a few attempts. 'There is some sort of barrier there. What's happened? You were thrashing around like a crazy man and it took me and some of the stronger men some time to hold you down and wake you up.'

'I had the most awful dream – if dream it was,' he replied. Then, explaining the content of that dream to Salazar he waited to see what the African Druid might make of it.

'Hmm. Well, one part of it has obviously occurred – we certainly haven't been able to make contact with Percy. But I reckon the other part is a ruse – something to try and knock you off balance; something to try and make you ineffective. I suggest you take no notice of it. It's her, though, isn't it?'

'Yes, I reckon you're right; she's definitely at the bottom of all of what's been going on here. Well,' he brightened, 'at least she's shown her hand and made the mistake of letting us know she's here, eh? Now we can make our own plans to suit. I had thought we'd have to take Gundestrup back with us through the portal whereas now, well, perhaps we can do everything here. However, to be on the safe side, I think you'd better help me mix a potion to keep that witch out of my head.'

But then, that very second, before they had a chance to put something together, the headache hit him with a bang. Growling with the excruciating agony, Merlin held on to his head, twisting it this way and that to try and alleviate the pain, and then, mercifully, he passed out.

TWENTY-NINE

I took the last opportunity I had to speak to Shake Spear alone, before we were all dragged into the captain's cabin, to warn him to assume his old role of the Minstrel. As I did so, he gave me a quick wink and then there we were all staring at someone we'd only heard of in general conversation, but feared nonetheless – the Jackal.

It was true – he did look a little like the sly, wild hound that I'd seen in my geography books. But, weirdly, he still had his eyes on me and I began to feel very uncomfortable indeed.

I looked over at his servant – an unlikely companion – who kept his eyes down and his shoulders hunched. Was he, too, scared of this man? Probably. Was there some way we could escape? Probably not. What was this evil looking person going to do to us? Probably something awful, by the look of him. Don't think about it. I tried to put on a face that would give absolutely nothing away but was soon to be mentally knocked off balance and confused by the captain roaring with laughter as he still continued to stare at me.

'OK,' he said, finally, wiping his nose on the back of his sleeve, 'Let's see what you can all tell me.'

Well, I, for one, didn't know what he was talking about and, even if I did, I didn't think I'd want to tell him anything. I could feel Shake Spear and Tailor shifting from one leg to the other like me, probably thinking exactly the same. But then, there was something about the man! I knew I'd never seen him before in my life but there was something very familiar, something that jogged even my frightened memory. Now, what was it? What could it be? I could see him staring at me again as though he knew what I was thinking so I put up my barriers – just in case. But what was it about him? This was hard, as I knew absolutely that I'd never been anywhere near him before in my life!

'Right,' turning his head but keeping his eyes on me he ordered the other man – Mongrel he called him – 'take those two,' pointing at Shake Spear and Tailor, 'to the hold. I'll speak to them later.' Waiting while this was done, he merely stood and continued to look intently at me. I was, by now, feeling very uncomfortable indeed and extremely scared. I couldn't understand why he had picked on me or what he was now going to do. My stomach was churning – I needed the toilet!

Then we were alone.

I waited for an eternity before anything other than the stare took place. Then he spoke – well it was more of a purr.

'Percy!'

I jumped out of my skin. How did he know my name?

He laughed again. 'I'm going to tell you something that will make your teeth curl,' he said.

I was now shaking like a leaf.

'When I've had the satisfaction of telling you, I shall then erase some of it from your memory but, and this I love, you will still keep it in your mind but will not be able to do anything about it. You won't be able to share it with anyone. Now isn't that clever?'

I stood there stiffly, terrified to let myself relax as when I did my knees trembled and my bowels became loose. I waited.

'OK Percy, this is it. You thought you knew me didn't you? You've been searching your brain to try and remember where you've seen me before? Well, you have, haven't you?' he repeated when I didn't respond.

I almost nodded – more of a quick jerk.

'You do know me,' he stated. 'Are you ready?' he grinned.

It took me a long time but then again I nodded.

'I'm… ,' he waited a long time, lips twitching as he tried to hold himself in check, before completing the sentence. And then just like he might be saying "boo", said 'Mab!'

I definitely needed the toilet then! It was as much as I could do to hold it in as well as not to pass out! Then I remembered – it was when she'd wiped her nose on the back of her sleeve. That should have warned me but there was too much going on and it just skipped off down one of the corridors in my brain – in and out of my remembrance before I could grab hold of it. What a fool I was. But then, I would have got the same shock then as I had now. I think I went green!

I vaguely recalled Merlin telling me that whatever happens I must not appear to be afraid of her; easy enough to say but I was petrified. Shaking uncontrollably and trying my hardest to smile through my fear I was only too aware that my mouth wasn't actually obeying its instruction to smile but was grimacing and had dried up so much that my top lip was curled under and stuck to the gums above my teeth and I must therefore appear to anyone looking at me – in this case Mab – like a bug-eyed, deranged rabbit caught in headlights.

He, she, howled with laughter. This was going to get complicated again and I hope you will forgive me if I keep interchanging the "he's" with "she's" – but you'll know who I'm talking about anyway. Anyway, how could I get this information to Tailor and Shake Spear? But then, again, she said I wouldn't remember but would remember. What did that mean? I had let down my barriers again and she was able to catch some of my thoughts. Panicking, I quickly put up a screen against her.

'You will know when you remember but, obviously, you will not know when you don't remember. Oh, this is going to be so much fun,' she cried.

I didn't know what to do! Should I stand there and see what would happen next? Should I turn and run – but to where? I didn't know where they'd taken the others and I really didn't know what the situation was on board. Did the men obey her every command? Did they even like her/him? Did they know who she was? Then, again, where could I hide? We were on the high seas! She was watching me again and trying to work out what was going on in my mind. I'd let my barriers slip – a little – and now struggled to haul them back into place. My mind was becoming confused and tired. All these thoughts shot through my head in seconds but one thing was very clear – it was too late for me to do anything – even if anything could have been done!

'Now let me tell you what is going to happen,' she cooed. 'We are going after the treasure, my boy. It's hidden at a place called Rainbow Island and we are on our way there.' She screwed up her face as anger threatened to overwhelm her. I could feel myself getting ready to run. 'But there's another ship that appears to be headed the same way,' she croaked. 'I must get there first,' she stamped her foot. Then, more calmly, 'I will get there first! You wonder what that treasure is, don't you boy?'

I merely stood still, not answering. I knew this always got her back up. However, this time, she didn't seem to notice.

Continuing with her plan and lost in her own little world, she went on to tell me – well, I think it wasn't necessarily me that she was telling, it was just that she had an audience – about the silver spoon that was hidden there which was needed to mix the potions in the cauldron that she also didn't have. She was getting angrier and angrier by the minute as she realised that it wasn't going to be easy to do any of the things she wanted to do. She needed both to be able to achieve her goal but at the moment it was all pie in the sky, as she had neither.

'You know how you got here, I suppose?' she asked, red in the face.
'I'm afraid I don't!' I croaked and then repeated it again.

'Well, I made a spell – and an excellent one it was too – to send Arthur here. I'd been working on it for months. No-one knew I'd regained all my powers and so it was easy! Easy I tell you,' she yelled at me, two inches from my face – fortunately, as she was in this different body, she didn't smell too bad just yet, but I think she was working on it. 'Merlin must have lowered his guard over him thinking I was still out of action and it was just so easy to get it all to work. I'd tried it out on Honey… '

'Honey?'

'Yes,' she snapped, annoyed both at my obtuseness and at my interruption. 'That stupid Mongrel.'

I looked bemused.

'Oh, you dolt – my man – the one who was with me when you came in!' She was by now showering spittle all over her desk as she leaned across it to glare at me. 'That's Honey – disguised, like me! Concentrate, boy – don't interrupt me again.'

I tried to look blank.

Then she laughed. She was the weirdest person I've ever met in my life!

'The best part of all this, is that you won't remember any of it – yet you will!'

I still tried to look blank.

'Well,' she said, getting back to her story. 'I tried it out on Honey and she actually disappeared. I saw her standing by her honey stall waiting for customers and so decided that now was the time to try it out. I noted on my mystical map the place where she stood and placed a blob of the potion on it. I then placed a second blob – it was a different colour and contained different properties of course – on the floor in my room. The spell I used I shall not give you the satisfaction of hearing; suffice to say it worked. It has many different side-effects on people and I should be interested to hear what effect it has on you! She gets headaches when she tries to think. I wonder what Arthur gets! So what happens to you?'

She stared down at me and for the life of me I couldn't think of anything.

'Come, come, now,' she smiled. 'What happens when you try to think?'

Then I remembered – with my guard down!

'Ah, you fall asleep, eh?'

She was getting better at reading my mind – this thought with my barriers up. Or was it that she just could down here?

'Well, I suppose I shall just have to wonder what happens to Arthur but I might have time to ask him – before he dies, that is!' This last said as she shoved her face once more into mine.

I could feel myself starting to tremble as I remembered her sole aim in life – she had to kill him because the prophecy had been given to her that if she didn't, he would kill her. However, this wouldn't happen until he became king and then he'd run her down on his charger, trampling her underfoot, and thrusting her through with Excalibur. Therefore she just had to get rid of him before he was crowned.

With my barriers well in place I was thankful that she didn't appear to know that Merlin was here. She didn't seem to have connected Shake Spear or Tailor with him – or even why they were in this netherworld. I was certainly not going to bring her attention to that fact. It's funny – the more I looked at this person called Jackal, the more I could see the characteristics of Mab. Perhaps her disguise wasn't quite so effective after all.

'But I don't know how you got here. It doesn't really matter though. I expect you and Arthur were together when I applied the potion. I could see him in my crystal, but, somehow, I couldn't see you. Well, it's all of a nothing; more of a bonus eh?' she grinned as, turning, she opened her cabin door and yelled for Mongrel.

'Take him down with the others and then get my food,' she yelled at the unfortunate man – as though he was deaf, or should I say, she was deaf?

Mongrel took me outside and handed me over to two burly seamen (one would have done – how dangerous did they think a 13-year old boy was for goodness' sake?) who dragged me off to the hold where Shake Spear and Tailor were waiting to find out what I knew.

A quiet and still morning was just breaking and I'd noticed an almost glassy sea as I was dragged along the deck before being thrust down with the other two.

Before I could tell them anything my ears twinged and my heart flipped as I heard that awful sound – the drumbeat that broke out around us as its rhythm thrust itself up through the floorboards. Mab had ordered the men to row: the whip sang as it flew through the air before landing on some poor unfortunate's back. I quaked. Was she going to send us all down there? I just couldn't bear it again! I'd sooner jump over the side.

'Percy. Percy,' Shake Spear repeated. 'What on earth is the matter?'

I opened my mouth to tell him about Mab and what was going on but it didn't come out. Every time I tried, all that happened was I started talking about something else. And then I remembered! She said I would remember but would not remember. Perhaps that was what was happening to me – even though I wanted to tell them, my mouth wouldn't let me. I must find some other way to let them know what was going on.

'Pull yourself together man,' Shake Spear groaned, 'and tell us what's happening.'

THIRTY

What on earth is happening?' the Raven growled, as leaning over the side of the ship and staring at the figurehead, he wondered what this might mean. He scratched his head, slightly dislodging his wig, as he looked at the nearest eye – closed shut. Rushing round to the other side he furrowed his brow and chewed his lip as he contemplated another closed eye.

'We have to find the treasure but why has the hog closed his eyes? Surely he must know we need to go on!'

Nell's son felt slightly uncomfortable, believing his duplicity must be discovered at any minute. Shaking his head at his friends and showing by his expression that they should keep quiet, he stood waiting for the inevitable explosion.

Fortunately, the captain showed no signs of being duped. He stormed up and down for long minutes before, making up his mind, he ordered the ship to continue on course. This was something unheard of and there were more than a few gasps, grumbles and murmurings going on with the crew. But, he was captain, so his orders were obeyed.

The hog kept his eyes resolutely closed.

Sweeping out to sea, the Raven tried an experiment: 'Swing her around to face land,' he cried, then, because no-one obeyed him immediately he rushed across the deck and pulled on the wheel, in his impatience nearly knocking the wheelman off balance and more than a few pirates as the ship slewed sideways.

Everyone watched as the ship swung around, holding their collective breaths as they listened intently. "Clang, clang" – the two eyes opened. They smiled again, thinking their captain had regained his senses and was following proper procedures.

But no! His lust for power and the treasure was too much; even though he had no idea what that treasure was. 'Swing her about again,' he called, pushing the wheel the other way; this time succeeding in knocking the wheelman completely off balance. Didn't he know he was wasting time and time was of the essence? The poor man scrambled up from the floor and grabbed the wheel – which was turning slowly back the other way – almost spinning him round with it. Eventually order was restored and the vessel began to turn and head out to sea – "clang, clang" – obviously without the blessing of the figurehead.

'It can't be helped lads,' he called to the men. 'It's fortune and power or we will have to kowtow to someone else – and I have an awful feeling that that someone else would be the Jackal. Now, would you want to have to obey him?'

There were a few muttered "noes" but no-one sounded too enthusiastic although, to be fair, they knew the Jackal was worse than the Raven, so he'd felt fairly sure of himself in this regard.

The Raven beckoned Nell's son over and with bowed heads they spent a good part of the day pouring over maps that were secured by large rocks to a ledge at the bow. The Raven wanted to be the first to know they were going in the right direction, should the hog's eyes clang open. So far, though – silence!

The breeze had now died away completely and the Raven's face screwed up in anger and dismay as he looked at the hanging sails. The oarsmen were quickly whipped into action and the large vessel lumbered slowly forward, the beat of the accompanying drum soon having a mesmerising effect on every pirate on board; Brosc couldn't take his eyes off them – they all seemed to do everything to the beat – walk, talk, chew, breathe.

'*Moronic*,' he'd thought.

Being told of the whirlpool that had nearly sunk them a good week before, Nell's son took them on a circuitous route, hopefully well away from not just it but also the ship they'd seen following them the day before.

How was he to know that that ship contained the witch and the witch had thrown a spell – almost a homing device so to speak – at the aft of his ship as it had come into her view? How was he to know that all she had to do was almost literally sit back and enjoy the ride? How was he, or anyone else for that matter, to know that she was, even now (even though she'd made a detour to capture me and the others), just over the horizon and literally following in their wake?

As the light faded the anchors were thrown overboard and the ship slept. All, that is, except Nell's son and his two companions. As quietly as they could, and even they thought the whole ship must surely hear what they were doing, they loosened beams and panelling, shaped them and fitted them together, marking their positions so as to enable them to fit them back together when the need to escape arose, before replacing them; they then cut and joined rope and hid provisions – it was going to take them a long time to complete their task but they were determined that when the time was ripe – they would escape on their raft. Somehow or other they just had to get back to Merlin.

It took three more days – the wind whipping up by the third day, to the relief of those wretches down below – before they sighted land again. Land they'd never been to before. There were hills that came right down to the sea's edge, with, apparently, no cove or inlet in which to anchor.

'Looks like we'll have to anchor here and use the small boats to row to shore,' the Raven muttered under his breath. 'But, then, how will we get up those cliffs?'

'Perhaps we should sail further along,' Nell's son suggested. 'That way, we'll have a better idea of the coastline and will be able to see if there are any inlets.'

'Yes. I'm glad I didn't put you to oar,' he said, turning to the other man. 'You are of use to me.'

Nell's son looked away, back at the coastline, not wanting the captain to even think he might be lying. He, himself, always knew when people lied to him and, therefore, he didn't want to take the chance that the captain might be able to see how economical he was being with the truth. *'A man's eyes always give him away,'* he thought. *'I must be very careful!'*

As they neared it, he couldn't help but be surprised at the difference in the lie of the land to that which he had already seen. Whereas the other places, including No Hope Island, were bleak and grey, this place, as they sailed up to it, was still bleak but red – blood red, as though all the spilled blood in the world had seeped into it – and it smelled pretty bad too. They all just stared at the red hills with the red rivers cascading down through them.

He eventually looked around at the other men and could see the red reflected in their faces and eyes – yes, especially the eyes, as though they'd been crying and had rubbed them raw. *'What was this place?'* he thought.

Then they all saw it and gasped. From a huge eyrie set high on a crag behind those hills – which they hadn't notice until there was movement – it rose up, squealing mightily as it gathered pace and flew towards them, smoke – turning crimson from the reflection of the surrounding hills – billowing out of its nostrils as it swooped low, showing a fiery underbelly when it shot across their bows. To a man they all fell on their faces and quaked as the creature swooped down, each one thinking it would gather him up in its mighty claws and take him off to its lair and shred him to pieces for its dinner. They all waited with bated breath and then, collectively breathing out, lifted their heads and watched as it flapped away – out to sea.

The Raven was the first on his feet – well, he didn't want the men to think he was afraid, did he – shouting orders for Pick to send a man aloft to follow the creature's path and report back.

The same man as before, who was considered to have the best eyesight of the whole crew, scrambled aloft, bare toes as deft as fingers grabbed the ropes as he ascended, jumped into the crow's nest and peered out to sea. He watched unblinking, as the creature seemed to reach a point and then start circling. He stared and, opening his eyes as wide as they'd go, stared again.

'Ship a-following us, sir,' he shouted down at the captain. 'Same one as afore, I'm sure,' he called down. 'Creature not attacking it, cap'n; just a-circling.'

'Stay there and keep watch and let me know everything that happens.' He pulled one of the men over and instructed him to remain at the foot of the mast and bring him whatever news there was of the ship. Returning to the fo'c'sle he watched the shoreline as, moving slowly along, they looked for somewhere to shelter, now not only from the elements but also from whomever it was that was following them. He knew they were after the treasure – everyone had always been after it – but he was determined that he was going to be the one who would get it. '*Why should he get it the lazy way when I'm doing all the work?*' he thought.

Nell's son walked over to his two friends and, pretending to look over the side, whispered to them. 'You're right what you said about that dragon – it looks exceeding like Hellion!'

'I told you so,' Brosc agreed.

'You're right,' Wite added.

'But he's dead!' Nell's son exclaimed.

'Exactly.'

'This is a weird place. I don't think Merlin has told us everything about it. Now, men, I think at the first opportunity we must try to escape. But,' looking around at that awful place, 'I don't think we'll get far if we try to leave now, do you?'

They both shook their heads, staring at the blood red hills reflected in the sea.

'We'll have to bide our time. We'll know when it's right.'

The breeze finally dying again, the three men jumped as they heard the slow beat of the drum from below decks. Leaning once again over the side they watched the oars start their laborious and rhythmical dance to the sound of its beat and then looked concernedly at one another as a whip sang through the air followed by a sharp cry.

The concern in their eyes as they looked at each other's faces only made them more resolved to escape as soon as they could.

THIRTY-ONE

'Yes, oh yes, yes, yes!' she cackled as she watched the dragon circling the ship. 'Now things'll get moving; now we'll see who's top man – *well, woman I should say!*' She called up to the creature, expecting it to obey immediately. However, when it didn't, she felt a new and weird sensation – the tiniest nudge, could it be, of apprehension? 'Hellion,' she called, again feeling that slight twinge as it looked over its wing and down at her. It had changed! Where its once sluggish eyes had always held that resigned look of acquiescence, what she now saw was a look of belligerence – it wasn't too obvious, but it was there nonetheless. What had happened? *'Ah yes,'* she thought; *'we're in a very different place now, aren't we? I shall have to use all my wiles.'*

She waited until the dragon had made another turn above the ship before calling out to it again. But this time she got the shock of her life – it bellowed into the atmosphere, shooting fire straight up into the sky, before turning and staring straight at her. Then, *'You don't know how long I've waited to be able to do this, Mab,'* its words attacked her brain as well as her ears.

She screamed and the crew ran for cover thinking the dragon was about to attack, but her terror was much more frightening to her than that. If the dragon was merely attacking, she could have sent it packing by throwing a spell at it or a lightening bolt or even a curse sending it into another place or time zone; but no – her terror was caused by the awful rasping noise it made inside her brain when it spoke to her and the unbelievable fact that it had actually spoken to her in the first place; not to the others – they heard nothing except a loud roar – but to her it was a resounding, shrieking echo clanging around in her head.

'Now, Mab – there's no need to take on so,' it spoke again.

She screamed again. 'Stop, STOP! It's too loud – too loud!'

'Ah, yes,' it responded, more quietly. *'We are now not in the land of my kind or yours come to that but a place where nothing is as it seems.'* It screwed up its pug-like face and concentrated; now this in itself was bizarre as although it had always been extremely ugly but expressionless, now it was making faces – looking even more hideous. It mesmerised the witch, who, getting over her panic, couldn't take her eyes off him.

Eventually he spoke, although, once again, only the witch could hear what he said, the crew – still hiding, merely heard roaring noises. *'Is that better?'*

'Yes – much – but you could still tone it down a bit more.'

'I'll try,' he answered, *'though why I should bother, when it is so much more fun watching you squirm,'* he grimaced, but true to his word Mab found that she could almost quite happily converse with him – until he got a bit animated, that is. However, he soon learned to temper his excitement when Mab's screams once again broke through into his mind.

They spent the next half hour or so conversing until with a delighted look on her face Mab skipped very happily round the main mast in satisfaction as to its outcome – a sight the sailors had never seen their captain do before. Looking, eventually, at their shocked and bewildered faces, she cleared her throat and marched, as manfully as she could, through into her cabin, calling Mongrel to follow. 'There's lots to do,' she yelled for the benefit of the men. 'Get those men rowing again.' They'd stopped during the confusion caused by the dragon. 'And bring the youngster to me.'

The frightened pirates – obviously impressed at the fact she had not been scared of the dragon – rushed to obey her orders whilst keeping a watchful eye on it as it flew away. It eventually disappeared over the Red Hills and things started to return to normal, most of the men swaggering across the decks as though they hadn't been scared at all, although their eyes betrayed their bravado, so they kept them averted from one another as fear was still a stark and unwelcome lodger dwelling therein.

I was dragged back through the cabin door and thrust through, falling, unfortunately, after catching my foot in the edge of the threadbare carpet and landing in a heap before her desk. Mongrel rushed forward to help me to my feet but was stopped by the witch's unusually large masculine hand grabbing his shoulder.

'Let him get up on his own, you idiot,' she growled. 'If he's clever enough to fall down, well he's got to be clever enough to get up!'

Her logic was beyond me!

I scrambled to my feet and was told to stand before her desk while she finished arranging something on it. I stood watching her whilst listening to the drumbeat and felt my insides curdle. *'Hold on,'* I told myself.

Finally satisfied, she lifted her eyes and looked across at me.

'The dragon has told me where we need to go,' she whispered

conspiratorially. *Why tell me? I wasn't her best friend!* 'There is a narrow passage of water between the place of the whirlpool (I started shaking when she mentioned that) and the Valley of the Shadow.'

'The Valley of the Shadow?' I asked.

'Hellion lives near there – on the far side of the Red Hills. We will need to steer close to land, away from the whirlpool. About a two-day sail,' she started to say but screwed up her face angrily as she thought about the present calm, 'or four or five if we have to use the oarsmen!' Standing up and knocking her chair over in her haste, she began pacing the floor, muttering: 'I'll make them go faster – yes, they can use the whip a bit more if they have to; I'll put some of the sailors down there – no, better not, they might rebel. Can't have that.' She looked over at me. I blanched! Then she shook her head. 'No – need him in one piece!' Stopping her murmurings, she eventually sat back down in the chair that Mongrel had replaced upright, put her elbows on the table and, cupping her chin in her hands, stared into space – well stared straight at me really but I could tell she was concentrating on something else as her glazed eyes confirmed.

I had to stop myself from exchanging my weight from one leg to the other and tried to keep myself as calm as I possibly could. For one thing, if I made a nuisance of myself by interrupting her, she might send me to the oars; for another, the twitchier I got, the more my stomach curdled and then who knew what might happen? I just couldn't embarrass myself like that in front of her! She didn't move for at least twenty minutes. Even Mongrel got fidgety.

Finally, eyes brightening, she laughed. 'Hellion! He's the answer,' she grinned. 'He can tow us!'

Forgetting both Mongrel and me, she shot out through the door and could be heard giving orders to the men while, at the same time, calling the dragon to her, this last task achieved through the mind. I could hear part of what she called out to him but decided it not worth the effort and so switched off.

I look across at Mongrel and we stared at one another for some few moments before, eventually, he spoke.

'I know you are good,' she whispered. I felt uncomfortable at that because I didn't feel good at all – in fact, most of the time I felt I was pretty bad, I thought. If he only knew the plans to dispose of him that travelled through my brain at that moment, he'd soon revise his opinion of me.

'I'll say this quickly because I might not get another chance,' the words tumbled out of his mouth as though because they'd collected in there for such a long time they were all trying to spill out at once. 'You know I'm really called Honey?' I nodded. 'Well the witch forced me into the body of this man, just like she forced herself into the body of the captain. I only hope that I'll be able to get back to being me one day!' She almost started sobbing but with sheer effort of will and much swallowing kept herself in check. 'I've tried to figure out how I came to be here but my memory is virtually non-existent. But – and I haven't told the witch this – I have remembered one or two things. First, I can recall I have two brothers: one is called Hive and the other I think is called Mead.'

'I know them!' I blurted out. 'Don't tell me you're their sister? Honey! Yes, that makes sense – Hive told me he had a sister called Honey.'

'But when I try to recall them and anything about the life I had before the witch, I get terrible headaches. What I wanted to say was, if you try and escape, will you take me?'

'Of course I will,' I reassured her, feeling a little guilty that only moments before I would quite cheerfully have thrown her to the serpents. 'Perhaps we can help each other now, if we're careful. If you find out anything that you think might help me and the others – now how can we sort this out?' I asked myself, 'could you get a message to us somehow?'

She said she'd say she felt sick and have to go up on deck. Hopefully, she'd be able to speak to one of us there.

I said that I'd let the others know so that we'd always be ready to make contact with her and also take her with us if we did manage to get away. I hoped that I wouldn't be stopped from remembering that – hoping that it was only the things the witch told me that I wouldn't be able to tell or remember. Well, we'd soon find out.

We heard a rustling outside the door and Honey rushed back into her corner where she slumped down onto the floor and dropped her head onto her knees.

Then the witch swept into the room with a very self-satisfied look on her face.

'The dragon will tow us there,' she stated triumphantly. 'We'll get there without the help of that other ship. And we'll get there first!'

Merlin, recovering from his swoon, held onto the sides of his head and moaned as wave after wave of blinding pain shot through his temples. He stared sightlessly up at Salazar through eyes that were wracked with agony – the whites gradually turning red as myriad threads of blood cracked across them like some obscene crazy paving, his now black irises floating upon this new and aching sea.

Salazar didn't stop to find out what had happened. He knew! He hadn't been around that witch too little to know that it was she who was somehow responsible for what was now happening to his friend. Lifting him up and throwing him over his shoulder – and he was no lightweight – he managed to haul him across the cavern – almost dreading that the guards would stop him – until he lay in front of the cauldron. Taking two deep breaths he pulled him upright onto his feet, leaned him over the edge of Gundestrup and, lowering his head into the basin and whispering something under his breath, waited to see what would happen.

Arthur, meanwhile, knelt beside the cauldron with hands lifted towards the heavens as he prayed.

Except for the guards standing to attention and pointing their spears at Salazar, Merlin and Arthur, nothing happened for at least a minute. All who were able to see this drama being acted out in front of them stood still – waiting. Finally, with every person holding their breath, tendrils of bluish-green smoke began to rise slowly from within the cauldron's depths. They rose and fell slowly, then shot through the air at great speed, slowing down as they danced and swirled, curling up towards the ceiling and turning from smoke to ethereal shapes – some beautiful, some terrifying – before dispersing completely. All this time a battle was raging for Merlin's life as he tried to pull himself out of the cauldron – Salazar, on the other hand, was harnessing all of his strength to keep him in. Then all went eerily still and Salazar stood back. Another minute passed before Merlin moved: his body twitched and shuddered; raising his arms, he took hold of the rim of the cauldron and levered himself out of it, finally standing up. His back was toward everyone and they, still holding their breath, waited to see what would happen when he turned round. Eventually he did and all breath was released – he was back and he was as he should be.

Gripping Salazar's arms he was profuse in his thanks to his friend with praise for his wisdom and strength. Then turning swiftly towards a beaming Arthur he thanked him for his prayer. 'She almost had me that time, my friends,' he acknowledged.

'She will never get you,' was the reply.

'How did she know I was here?' he mused.

'I don't think she knows. I think she just sends out the odd roaming spell – just in case one gets you. And it nearly did that time my friend; it very nearly did. We shall have to be that much more vigilant. Perhaps we should use the old remedy that protects us from the barbs of the enemy?'

Merlin nodded as he stepped away from the cauldron – which was still issuing the odd wisp of blue smoke – and asked Salazar to start mixing it up. The guards, gradually slackening their over-protective stance, relaxed and watched the three men walk away from their precious treasure.

Then, remembering the hound, Merlin rushed over to see to him. 'It's worse than I've ever seen him before,' he whispered as he raised Cabal's eyelids. 'His eyes have slid upwards; he's well and truly unconscious. How long have I been asleep, or should I say unconscious?' he asked.

'Well over two hours,' Tiala, who had not left Cabal's side, replied. 'Your dog has not moved in all that time.'

Checking the wound, Merlin was happy with the result; it was still bleeding but sluggishly; it had almost dried up. 'I don't know how much blood he lost,' he admitted, 'but, even so, he should be coming round by now. Let's try some more of that mixture.'

'*But you know what too much might do to him,*' Salazar responded, not wanting anyone else to hear.

'*It's that, or he's going to die!*' he replied. '*Can't you feel his spirit trying to drag itself out of his body?*'

'*Can't we use the cauldron for him, now that we know what it can do?*'

'*It's too late! You took a chance with me, you know, but it worked that time. No, I think we should be cautious – we don't understand its powers yet and I think our old remedy will work.*'

No-one else present, except maybe Tiala who was looking at both men as they conversed in their minds, would have noticed the hesitation by Salazar, let alone sense the dilemma facing the two men; they were looking at the dog, not at the haunted expressions on the faces of the Druids.

'Gently; slowly; just a very small drip at a time.'

Salazar obeyed and everyone watched as he placed the smallest amount on the tongue that had been and was still hanging out of the unconscious dog's mouth. He waited for several minutes before adding another.

Everyone waited. It was very still. No-one moved.

A deep, convulsed and shuddering breath; an eye rolling and trying to focus; jaws juddering together in shock; a tongue trying to gather moisture; and finally legs locking trying to stand up.

'*Calm, calm, my friend.*' Merlin's soothing mind reached out to the hound. *Lay back down, rest!*'

Cabal stopped struggling and relaxed under the tranquil hand and the voice that continued to speak into his mind. He thought he knew that voice but couldn't quite put a name to it; it wasn't threatening but soothing and before long he relaxed.

'He's sleeping now,' Merlin advised the others. 'He's very weak but over the worst; he still has a long way to go. Tiala,' he looked up at the young woman, 'are you still able to keep watch over him or is it tiring you too much?'

'I am as well as I ever will be – it is no more exerting sitting here with him than if I was doing something else. In fact, I believe it is better for me. No, I will stay here and nurse your dog; my friends will help too.'

'I am obliged. Please just give him water should he wake.'

She nodded as she lifted the dog's large head onto her lap whereupon she started stroking his rough mane, speaking softly in a foreign tongue to him as she did so.

After sending someone to wait on Tiala and let him know if there was any change in the hound, Merlin and Salazar spent the best part of half a day with their heads together, whispering, making plans, nodding, mixing potions, testing spells until, finally, they agreed that everything was ready. Everything, that is, except the information that could only be got from Cabal.

So they waited until he came out of his long sleep. Merlin, usually a very patient man, couldn't help but pace up and down, most people watching anxiously as he did so. Arthur, on the other hand, sat down next to Tiala where they conversed quietly with one another.

Another shuddering intake of breath heralded Cabal's return to consciousness.

Merlin, rushing over to the dog's side, waited, all concern, to see whether he might now recognise him.

He did! And after Merlin's gentle prompting, gave him the information he required.

'Merlin, the gypsum is less than half a mile away. It is hidden – I would need to take you there! But I'm too weak!' The nearest to a canine sob and frustration racked the hound's brain.

'Not necessary my friend,' he replied. *'Calm yourself! Here is a portion of the Glass,'* he held it up. *'Look deep into it – show me where it is hidden.'*

Ignoring the confused looks of those that stood around, he waited for the still weak hound's eyes to focus on the Glass before, slowly, a swirl of fog cleared to allow a cluster of rocks to come into view. 'Ah, there it is! Tiala.' he called over his shoulder. 'Can some of your men go and rescue this for me? Do you see where it lies?'

The men, still wondering at what had just taken place, stared at the portion of Glass, discerned just exactly where the gypsum was hidden and left immediately.

'Now Cabal, old friend, tell me, what's happened to the others?'

THIRTY-THREE

Nell's son and the Raven missed cracking their heads together by a hair's breadth. Ducking to avoid what they thought must surely be the cause of their demise – although how the Raven might think he was anything other than dead anyway, was beyond imagining – they finally peeped up to see the dragon flapping off towards the other ship; it leered over its shoulder, curling its lips at the frightened men.

'Now what's going on?' the Raven grumbled, but uneasily, as he leapt to his feet.

Nell's son, jumping up at the same time ran to the side of the ship to watch the dragon's departure.

'Something bad's afoot!' Wite croaked into his ear, coughing to clear his throat, which had constricted with fear at the dragon's approach. 'What do you reckon's going to happen,' he asked.

Nell's son turned and suggested to the Raven that the man return to the crow's nest (he'd scrambled down on seeing the dragon head towards them) and let them know just what was happening on the other ship.

Scurrying back up the ropes he jumped back inside the crows nest and, shading his eyes, watched the dragon's flight as it headed towards the other ship. 'Dragon's a-circling cap'n,' he yelled down.

'And what's going on now?' the captain called back up some three or four minutes later.

'Still a-circling cap'n.'

'Let me know when there's a change,' he responded, turning back to his cabin and beckoning Nell's son to follow.

Ordering him to sit, the captain went through all the maps and plans he'd gathered, mainly by my hand, and asked Nell's son to pinpoint just where he considered Rainbow Island to be.

Nell's son became quite concerned, knowing that one small slip might be the end, not only of him but of the other two men as well. Gathering together bits and pieces from around the desk, he made straight lines with something as near a rule as he could find, marked off a right-angle, drew a few dotted lines and then put a cross in what looked like the middle of a huge bay.

'Are you sure?' the captain asked, not completely convinced.

'Absolutely!' There was not even a tremor in his voice as he lied.

'They say that's near the Colossi; they won't let us through!'

'What are they going to do to stop us?'

'It's not so much what are they are going to do as where they are! We've already made a detour to keep away from the Unsettled Sea. We were there some time ago and had to throw a lad overboard. He was very bad luck. We'd picked him up for a very reasonable price and put him to the oars but he could read and so proved quite useful. He even drew this map!' he added, turning round again so that Nell's son could look at it. 'I'm not very good at reading this foreign language, you see, so he drew it for me.'

As Nell's son looked at the drawings, with birds and the like on it, he thought it more than possible that the captain couldn't read at all. However, he thought it best he made no sign that he thought this.

The captain was continuing with his story: 'We had to put him in a barrel and when it hit the water – at that very instant – the wind slackened, the whirlpool evened out and as he was sucked into it we were able to pull away. That was a close one I can tell you.'

'So the boy died?'

'Huh, hmm I reckon so! Don't think much gets saved out of that situation! Percy – that was his name. Couldn't think of it for a while 'cause I don't think I ever used his name. But, yes, it was definitely Percy.'

The Raven didn't notice the pained look on Nell's son's face or see him jump when he said my name; he was too busy staring into space as he recounted his story.

'Well, we've done well keeping away from the Unsettled Sea but if we get too near the Wailing Rocks...'

'Wailing Rocks?' Nell's son interjected without thinking as his mind was still reeling at the thought of my death.

The Raven looked up sharply at the other man wondering, not for the first time, whether he really knew what he was talking about, as most sailors knew what happened at the Wailing Rocks. He determined, there and then, to keep a closer eye on him and his companions; he was now too long in the tooth to be duped by anyone. However, he pretended not to be concerned about Nell's son's question and answered readily. 'The Wailing Rocks cover the cliffs from the Red Hills to Dragon's Reach. They wail when a ship is near to warn the Colossi, though they are unable to do this at night. So we will see if we can sail up the entrance at night.'

'What do the Colossi do if they know we are there?'

'They will wreck our ship and send us all to a watery grave at best or the serpents at worst. Now – we have to get this ship under way. I'm sure that that other ship will be trying something. Reckon it'll be on its way soon to try to beat me to the prize but I'm determined to get there first. We'll have to get the oarsmen under way. You go down,' he ordered the other man, 'and get them moving. Now!' he spoke sharply as Nell's son still stood there.

He moved out of the cabin with leaden feet for more reasons than he could count. All he could think of was that I was dead! And if he was so upset about it, how would Merlin take it, or Rhianne and, of course, Cabal who, as my best friend, idolised me; not only that, but they were now in hot pursuit of something that he had heard existed and he'd told the captain how to get there – what would happen when he found out he'd been duped?

Then another thought penetrated his brain – that perhaps he must have known the way to the treasure somehow as the captain knew what the Colossi would do if they got close. Oh, his mind was in turmoil. And those poor men at the oars – they were to be whipped into pulling this huge ship along as fast as they could to somewhere he didn't really know existed except in his dream! Unless the captain had had the same dream, as he, too, was convinced of the Colossi. Oh how had he got into this mess?

The man in the crow's nest called down regularly as to what was or was not happening near the other ship: it could be seen on the distant horizon, just as they could most probably be seen by their counterpart crow's nest observer on the other ship.

The dragon circled that vessel for well over an hour before returning, scaring the life out of everyone on board their ship, and flying to its lair on the other side of the Red Hills. They couldn't see it after it landed but every so often a puff of red smoke would float high above them in the still air; its glow would become much more obvious during the night watches.

'Ship still not moved,' shouted the man from aloft as he saw its twinkling lights become visible when night drew on.

'Come down, man,' the captain yelled. 'It won't move now till morning! Come, eat and rest. You'll need to be up there again at first light.'

The man scrambled down and disappeared aft.

The captain, turning to the rest of the crew, ordered the watch to be set and retired to his cabin, Nell's son and his friends creeping past his door to theirs.

Lowering their voices as much as they were able, Nell's son told the other two of the conversation he'd had with the Raven. Brosc was near to tears when he heard of my demise and Wite had – well, turned white! They sat there despondently for long minutes before Brosc asked what they should now do.

'We've got to escape – and soon!' Nell's son responded.

'But how?'

'Well, it has to be near land – but not this land!' he replied. 'We're getting too far away from where we started! We'll just have to wait and see what opportunity arises. Just keep your eyes and ears open. Something will happen – I know it will.'

The drumbeat started up again at first light. The reverberation woke everyone. Who could sleep when that doleful sound vibrated throughout the ship?

As Nell's son stepped out onto the deck he noticed the man already aloft, peering out towards the other ship. The Raven, too, was abroad early and was checking the hog's eyes – they were still firmly shut. He looked a little worried but changed his expression when he saw his men looking at him.

Whoooosshhh!

They all ducked.

The dragon was back. They were almost sure they heard it give its version of a laugh as it watched their terror.

Jumping up as soon as they judged it safe, they ran to the side of the ship and watched it head back towards the other ship.

'Dragon's a-circling like afore, cap'n.'

'Let me know of any change. Get those oarsmen moving – double time,' he shouted and waited the split-second for running feet to confirm that his order was being obeyed. Giving a satisfied twitch to his nose, he waited again until the whistle of the whip, the quickening of the drumbeat and the groaning of some of the men let him know that they were picking up speed. *'We'll get there before him!'* he thought, whistling as he returned to his cabin where he hoped Pick had set out his breakfast.

However, all thought of food had fled the three friends; Wite, convinced that there was no escape from this awful place, was becoming more despondent by the minute. 'Why did Merlin bring us here?' he asked, more than once. 'Surely he could do what had to be done by himself!'

'Now, now, Wite,' Nell's son tried to encourage him. 'He needed us. No-one can do everything by himself! Everyone needs friends and helpers. He needed us!'

'I think we're going to be here forever! And I hate it! Percy's dead! And I think we soon will be as well! We must get found out! We can't keep it up forever!'

Shaking him, mainly because it would give the game away if he shouted, Nell's son tried to calm him down. 'Come, come my friend, we're all in this boat together.'

Brosc, who'd always had a weird sense of humour, sniggered and added, 'literally.' Nell's son just stared at him.

'Sorry.'

However, it had the desired effect and Wite stopped shaking and moaning.

'Let's be positive, Wite, and see what opportunities present themselves to us. I'm sure Merlin will do all that he can for us – I mean, he knows we're here somewhere. He'll save us!'

Wite didn't add, '*Like Percy?*' but he thought it as, probably, so did the others.

'Ship a-moving, cap'n,' came the cry from aloft and all hands rushed on deck.

All that could be seen for long minutes was the dragon heading towards them. Then, slowly – but gathering speed all the time – the ship seemed to grow in size and it wasn't long before it became all too obvious how that speed was being achieved: they'd tied ropes around the dragon's neck and it was pulling it along. The dragon was straining at first to get the ship to move, as could be seen by the grimace on its face and the sinews standing out in its neck when it first struggled to pull it along but, once the ship started, it soon began to gather pace. It wasn't long before it sped towards them and was near enough for even expressions to be seen on the faces of the crew.

'The Jackal!' whispered the Raven through clenched teeth.

The Jackal waved as his laugh bounced toward them across the rolling waves.

Then both the Raven and Nell's son saw me, but it was the Raven who whispered my name. 'Percy! – he's still alive. Well hasn't he got nine lives? But he's a jinx you know,' he smirked. 'The Jackal won't get far with that one on board. He might be laughing now but I reckon we've still got the best chance of getting there if not fast, at least safely. They might have managed to miss the whirlpool but, even so, if he gets to the Colossi during the day the Wailing Rocks will warn them and they'll all get smashed to pieces – has to happen with that one on board! Once he's been shipwrecked I'll just wait till night and then sail through.' He turned away with a smug grin on his face.

THIRTY-FOUR

I'd got a quick glimpse of Nell's son as we shot past the prow of his ship; we'd been heading straight for it but seemed to turn away right at the last minute. Thank goodness! Now, perhaps, we might somehow get rescued. I'd been holding my breath thinking we must certainly crash into one another; but, no, we missed by half a ship's length. However, I did see their hog's eyes blink open for a second and then immediately clang shut. Was it the draft from our ship that had caused that or did it actually know what was going on? Who knows! The other ship rocked madly as we shot past it and we could even hear the yowl that went up as many pirates were thrown all over the place like skittles.

Mab laughed like a drain as she stared down at the other ship's deck, slapping her thigh and rocking to and fro.

'*If she's not careful she'll fall overboard – with a bit of luck,*' I thought.

'*Not so, young man,*' she responded looking over her shoulder, one evil eye staring straight at me.

'*Barriers, barriers, barriers!*' I thought, now with them crashing into place. '*I must remember,*' I scolded myself. '*She's getting better; was it perhaps this place that made it so? And I bet she'll try to get her own back for my reckless thought!*'

We were by now a good distance ahead and I craned my neck to see who else might be aboard the other ship that I knew or who I could communicate with but I saw only Nell's son and he didn't have the gift, I thought despondently, barriers slipping again.

'*But I do!*' a voice edged its way into my brain and, as I looked, I saw Pick staring straight at me from the prow of the Raven's ship. '*You can always talk to me!*'

I looked up at Mab to see if she'd heard him reach out to me but she gave no obvious sign that she had.

'*That mad woman,*' he continued. '*Yes I can see she's a woman and not as those others who see her as the Jackal; that mad woman can't hear me! I've learned, how to fine-tune all my abilities – since the awful demise of my tongue, you know – and am able to lock it in, block it out and transmit it to whomever or whatever I want. I am able to talk to you without anyone else picking up on it, including this "Merlin" you keep reaching out to! Unless I want to, that is. Oh yes,*

I've been listening in! But even he doesn't know about me yet! I've also been talking to that dragon that's pulling you along. He hates that witch, you know! Hates her with a loathing that even he can't describe – he'd trusted her once but she didn't save him! Says he felt like he'd spent almost forever locked inside his own rocklike body on the beach at Bedruthan Steps until the life went out of him completely and he ended up here. He told me he thought, at first, that she'd come back and release him but she didn't. She sat on the sand quite close beside him but didn't give him one thought; all she could think about was that she was soaked to the skin and needed to get her power back. When she finally left the beach she didn't even give him a backward glance. His faith in her turned to disbelief, from disbelief to sadness and then to anger and hate! Since then he's been plotting his revenge. He somehow has to obey her but you wait and see, one day, when she's let down her guard, he'll have her. And that won't be a pretty sight, eh? No, I hear what you're thinking – I haven't let on to anyone any of this! For one, I don't want them to know that I have this ability – it's too handy. How do you think I've stayed alive for so long? Just as soon as danger concerning me comes to mind, I'm off and hidden until it passes – and there've been more than a couple of times that that's happened, I can tell you. And for another, I haven't found anyone else I can communicate with so far – just you!

'Well, you keep yourself safe, Percy. It's wonderful having someone to talk to again – thought you'd perished in that barrel, so I don't want anything to happen to you again, do I? By the way – she's planning something awful and not only for you – thought I'd tell you. She's after someone in particular – Arthur, is that right? – and she plans to make sure he doesn't leave this place alive!'

I shivered. *'How do you know?'*

'Ah, that's one of my little secrets! But I think I can trust you with it. I can, amazingly, project my thoughts and become like a little worm; it's very handy if I want to crawl through a brain I've decided to examine. Now, that has been quite a fun project at times as most people have certain hopes and dreams, some are cunning to a limited degree and some plot and plan to a wicked degree but some – most – don't have much at all. It's quite easy to crawl round inside the brain of the simpleton as the avenues are wide and mostly empty but with the odd cobweb here and there due to its not being much in use; the average person is much like me, I suppose – apart from my gift, of course – and the rooms inside their heads are filled much as mine are

– or were, once. Many are just worried about day to day things and man oh man are their brains chaotic – there's no rhyme nor reason to anything there and with those it's a relief to escape after having to climb over all the clutter and rubbish that's piled up in them and find the way out. Why can't people organise their lives? No wonder so many people go mad! But then people like Mab – that is, if there are others like her – let's hope not! – well, I can't stay in there too long; my head starts to ache like the devil. Oops, better not mention him! Not seen him around too much lately! Reckon he's too busy "up there"! He pointed heavenwards (or earthwards) – that is if there was a heaven or earth reachable from this place – but I got the picture. *'Gathering up as many as he can to send them down here!'*

'Can you tell me what it's like in there – in her head?'

'A little – before I had to evacuate! It is very dark in there – dark with precipitous edges here and there swirling with a red and green mist – waiting for you to step off; gnarled fingers that reach out of the different rooms in her brain to draw you in. I kept clear of them so I didn't get sucked into something or other that would hold me and devour me so that I wouldn't be able to escape. I had a sudden and vivid picture of me leaning against the bulwarks of my captain's ship with not only my tongue missing but also my brain – eyes staring out at I know not what because I wouldn't have had any sense to know what I was looking at. She would have been able to use my thoughts, my cunning, all the characteristics of my brain – suck it dry and empower hers! I would merely be a shell lying there – food for the serpents!'

'These serpents?' I pointed over the side.

'Yes – whatever you do, just don't get thrown overboard. The pain of being eaten by one of them is unthinkable let alone unbearable. My tongue is down there somewhere – the captain threw it overboard after he'd cut it out!

'Anyway, getting back to her brain: I started carefully to crawl along inside those cramped avenues in her mind and try to understand the wickedness of this woman when, upon looking into one room inside her head, I was startled and brought up short by what I saw.'

He was quiet for such a long time, I thought we were perhaps too far away to communicate but, suddenly, he was back and continuing his story; my hair, which had started to grow again, felt as though it was standing out from my head.

'A pile of nearly dead people – dead but not decomposed! – all staring out at me with agonised looks on their faces; unable to speak, unable to cry out, unable to finally, completely die. Their agony seemed to be eternal. There was a guard at the door of that room in her brain – a miniature Mab – standing, laughing, rocking.

'I couldn't bear it so I moved on. I suppose I'd looked into about three other rooms, all very different but all very similar in their wickedness until I came to a very narrow one. I expect I could easily have moved on past this entrance without even noticing it except I heard one word that stopped me.'

He was silent again for a very long time before continuing and I started to get a terrible foreboding.

'She said your name, Percy!'

I jumped then, turning round to see if anyone had noticed but no-one appeared to be looking my way; they were staring at the dragon and covering their faces whilst making choking noises.

They say that dead people – dead anything apparently – make a lot of gas as it builds up inside themselves when they start decomposing, and this dragon was no exception. As the ship was pulled along behind it and as it strained to pull it kept letting go great crumps of gas; those on board were suffering the full effect of each explosion – and it was not pleasant, I can tell you!

'Oh, phew,' choked one sailor, holding his nose and coughing. 'Does it have to do that?'

'Disgusting,' sniffed another, and then wished he hadn't.

Almost everyone covered their mouths and noses to keep out the stench.

So it was that they were more than fully occupied, although, as you will probably appreciate, it did not appear to affect Mab! So, as I said, no-one, thank goodness, saw me jump.

I turned my attention back to Pick.

'Why? What was she doing in that room?'

'She was making a spell. She is going to get her own back on you, my boy! What on earth have you done to her to make her so antagonistic towards you? Ah, really?' he responded, obviously reading my recalled memories in the split second they shot into and out of my thoughts. 'She needs two things to enable her to succeed, so I believe you must put everything in her way to stop that success.'

'How? And what two things does she need?'

'You need to stop her from getting to Rainbow Island! Well, before *we do, that is – we're going to get what she's after first. Though how you're going to do that with that dragon, I don't know. She has to find the silver spoon – and not many people know that that's what the treasure is. Even my captain doesn't know what he's after – he just knows that it's treasure. Now, nobody knows where it is and nobody knows exactly what it looks like but it, together with Gundestrup, will…'*

'Gundestrup!' I interrupted. 'I've seen it! What exactly can they do together?'

'Gundestrup is a cauldron that has very powerful and magical properties. It is brilliant on its own but when used in conjunction with the spoon it is almost invincible. It can kill or cure, it can add something to weak potions or spells and make them powerful, it is something every magician would give his right arm for and most probably would because he would know that he could make a potent spell to get it back again. Someone called Tiala has the cauldron and is guarding it; Rainbow Island has the spoon and there will be many barriers to cross before the island can be reached, let alone finding the treasure.'

'Do you know where it can be found?'

'Ah, that would be telling now, wouldn't it? I'm finding it a little difficult to reach out to you now, Percy. You're getting too far away and fading. We'll talk again.'

And then he was gone.

Switching off, I turned back to my present circumstances and stared at the witch's back as she watched our progress through the sea. The other ship had now been left far behind; I strained my eyes but there was no sight of it. The Red Hills, too, had disappeared; in fact, on looking around, there was now no land in sight at all. Then I saw the whirlpool! I started quaking in my boots. We got nearer and nearer; even the serpents had left off following us. The sea shot past us trailing the oars which were redundant while we were being pulled along by Hellion – I expect the oarsmen were more than relieved – but my eyes were glued to the swirling waters edging ever closer to our ship. I even found myself looking round to see if there was a barrel being made ready for my imminent departure. Oh dear, was history going to repeat itself again?

Then we were jolted swiftly to our right and I noticed I wasn't the only one relieved as we watched the swirling waters disappear past and then behind us.

Sailing on we travelled through the evening and into the night, the wind whipping up until morning broke on a stormy sea. Visibility was poor and men had been running about the deck lashing all loose objects down. The sea began to crash over the sides of the ship as it lurched backwards and forwards and from side to side and once – thank goodness only once – it took the concerted efforts of ten sailors to haul up and throw back over the side a twenty-foot serpent that had been washed onto the deck without being bitten, let alone eaten.

I was watching all this from a safe distance when, Grind! Whoosh! Crash! Creak! Crack! We all spun around as this new ear-splitting din attacked our ears. The noise drowned out everything else in our brains and many a man was rushing around screaming with his hands over his ears. We saw the effect the two mighty men created as a wall of water rushed towards us. Holding on to whatever we could we hoped and prayed that our ship, looking tiny compared to them, would stay afloat and that we would not be washed overboard. Even though I'd twisted a piece of dangling rope round my wrist and was hanging onto some side ropes for dear life, at one paralysing moment I was actually hanging over the side of the ship and very close to the water; I saw two of the pirates, who were fighting each other to get some purchase on another short piece of rope, shoot past me as they got washed overboard. The vessel was rocking from side to side with such force I thought we'd all get thrown into the sea and then, when it swung over to the other side, and me back to comparative safety, I saw the next episode in the drama. The serpents were now back in force and I nearly threw up when I saw one of those two men disappearing down into a huge, grinning maw. The other pirate, going like the clappers, was trying to swim back towards us but at least three other serpents were closing in. Whilst two serpents turned upon each other in an effort to fight for him, two more closed in for the kill – one managing to wrench the bottom half away from the other serpent who'd swallowed the top. Terrible screams were suddenly stilled and I hadn't even been able to let go of the ropes to cover my ears. I can still hear those screams inside my head today, if I allow that particular memory admittance.

Then – silence.

We had finally evened out. The wind had died down, the sea had regained her composure, had shaken out the ruffles and creases of her dress, smoothed down her outer garments and now sat serene, waiting for the theatricals to continue. We looked across at what had caused this mayhem. The Colossi had risen slowly out of the sea, water was still pouring down their bodies, and now, standing full height from those watery depths, stared down at us from sightless eye-sockets; swords raised they had severed the ropes that had attached us to the dragon and we watched helplessly as he flew, now unburdened, away over the cliffs, gathering speed as he left us to our fate.

Seawater, still cascading down the huge warlike statues as they stood guard in that day's eerie light, gave them the appearance of bronze. What they were guarding I had no idea unless this was the entrance to Rainbow Island and the treasure. They looked like they were made of stone but, apart from the fact that their feet were stuck fast to the seabed or whatever was under the surface, they could move as easily as a man; I wondered if they would be able to stand against the witch. They were obviously guarding something as could be deduced by the way they stood their ground – or, in their case, water! Legs astride and with swords raised they were dressed from their heads, which were at least eighty feet above the ground, to their feet in shining marbled battle gear.

The witch was furious and had almost completely lost it as she watched Hellion flapping off into the distance; stamping her feet and with arms waving like windmills, she roared at him and the two giants who were standing in her way. You know, she never ever felt that anyone or anything could or should oppose her; she always felt that she would win, get the upper hand and be obeyed by all and sundry. Bad as she was and sometimes defeated as she was, she always came back for more. Did she get stronger with each battle? Or was her mind affected in such a way as to damage it and thus make her think that she was more able and more powerful the next time. Who knows? Obviously, this time was no exception.

She yelled up at the two sentinels, 'Stand aside! Or it will be the worse for you!'

Bad move – very bad move!

THIRTY-FIVE

The oarsmen had been struggling now for the whole day when the shout went up for them to slow. Nell's son let out a deep sigh for those poor men's sakes as he imagined their relief – if they were able even to feel that – at not having to strain any more that day against a heavy sea with screaming, tearing muscles and bloodied hands.

'If I ever – *ever* – get my own ship,' he growled under his breath, 'I shall never – *ever* – treat my men like this.'

Brosc looked up at him and could see how badly he was affected by the misery of the men below decks. 'Perhaps we could get some of them on our side,' he whispered.

'Perhaps,' Nell's son replied. Then, shaking his head to try and clear it of the melancholy that was waiting to grip him, he continued, 'But, then, there is no way of going down there without being attached to an oar, I think. So, we shall just carry on with our plan, such as it is, for just us three.'

Almost everyone slept that night; some dreamed, some had nightmares, some cried, some died – again!

The morning brought splashes as two oarsmen, who'd not been able to cope with the previous day's rowing, were tossed over the side. The waters churned as many, always very hungry serpents fought for the prizes being offered them.

'*Prizes*,' Nell's son thought. '*More like sacrifices!*'

But the day brought some small relief to the rest of the crew (and Nell's son and the others, believing they might end up as replacements for the missing oarsmen) as an initially soft wind billowed the sails and, as it strengthened, sent the ship scurrying after the Jackal.

'This is a good sign! We'll catch him yet!' the captain grinned as he shouted his instructions at the men. Everyone obeyed: running hither and thither, up ropes, down decks, checking this, stowing that, slackening one thing, tightening another. After an hour the oarsmen were told to stop completely as the wind, picking up all the time, now had the ship almost flying across the water. The serpents, some fifty feet away, could be seen keeping up with its progress. Would they never give up?

They disappeared for half the day when the whirlpool was sighted a long way off to their left but, as luck would have it this time, it was too far away to have any effect on them. Everyone wondered, though, whether the Jackal's ship had been sucked down into it. It didn't really seem possible, though, as there was absolutely no wreckage to be seen anywhere. Then, for the rest of the day's journey, they were accompanied by a terrible wailing sound; it came from the cliffs over to starboard and some of the men believed that they could see the rocks moving; some said they could see people crying and begging them to come over and save them. No-one spoke much during this time but everyone kept a wary eye on those cliffs.

Surprisingly, as it was still some time before darkness would fall, the man in the crow's nest called down, 'Ship ahead, cap'n – and it's not moving cap'n.'

The Raven's face lit up as he stared at the man, crying, 'Same ship, man?'

'Aye, aye, cap'n. Same ship – no dragon! Statues, though, cap'n – huge statues!'

'Get up there at once,' he turned to Nell's son. 'Man's demented – got good eyesight but he's an idiot. Get up there and let me know what's going on. And while you're up there, let me know where we are and if we've any chance of getting to Rainbow Island before the Jackal. Hurry man!'

On reaching the nest Nell's son stepped up beside the other man and, with lowered voice, asked him what he thought they were.

'Statues! See – over there! Moving statues! They must be guarding summat, sir,' he replied. 'They've got massive swords and keep a-slashing at the ship when it gets too close.'

'What's happening on the ship?' Nell's son was shielding his eyes and straining to see as much as he could.

'Can't see, sir! Too far away!'

'Do you think that ship or ours will be able to get past them?'

'Dunno, sir! Reckon they need only to raise one of their feet, sir, 'n they could crush either one of us's ships underfoot.'

'I expect you're right! Captain,' he turned and called down, 'I think we might be able to engage with the enemy! It looks like two giant statues – well, they look like statues but they can move – are keeping the Jackal at bay. Are these the Colossi of which we have spoken?' He recalled the giants of his dream. 'Perhaps, if we overcome him, the statues might let us through!'

'Then come down, man. We'll get ready for battle. You, man,' he called up to the other man aloft, 'stay there till dark and let me know if anything changes.'

'Aye, aye, cap'n.'

Nothing changed as the light faded.

Then darkness closed in, wrapping her cloak around all that had once been visible. The wind had died completely but the ship's sheets quivered as the timbers groaned; had the darkness made them scared? Well, the ship's crew looked edgy enough and kept a wary eye as a mist rose up and crept along on silent feet across the top of the water, taking the shape of whatever each sailor feared most.

This was not a good night. Men were put on watch and, if anyone else walked on deck they could be seen with huge, bug-like eyes straining to see whatever might be ready to pounce on them from the shadows. Any barrel or pile of rope was an obvious place from which spectres and ghouls could pounce out and get them. Strange sounds, obviously from a great distance (or were they?), crept across the water – cries, howls, gnashings of teeth, clashings of swords, gratings of breath.

Then morning came. All was well! Nothing had appeared; no-one was missing; nothing had happened! Did it ever? (Well, obviously it did for those who died at their oars but the pirates never gave them a second thought.)

Our man had already shinned up the ropes and entered, once again, the world of the crow.

Anchors were weighed, sails were unfurled and, catching the strengthening wind, they were off.

The night before had seen the Raven, Nell's son, Brosc and Wite pouring over my map in the captain's cabin and making plans for the morrow. Nell's son had added quite a bit more to what I'd originally drawn and the mad thing was, neither of us had a clue what we were doing! It was almost a polar opposite to reality – instead of exploring the land and seas and making a map of it, it was like making the map first and the land and sea obeyed its design and just came into being! Still, as long as the captain believed it, all was well.

'We'll have the men ready and will strike without delay. As soon as we see the ship, we'll just head straight toward it and, without any warning whatsoever, attack. I know it's not the normal way of going about things but, well, the Jackal isn't normal and is, in any event, beyond the pale now! He's not obeying the rules of the Contest, so neither, in this case, shall I.' He cleared his throat as he remembered that for the last week or so, he, too, had disobeyed the rules, so he was pleased that none of the others appeared to notice as Brosc brought his question.

'The Contest?' Brosc enquired.

The Raven explained, very briefly, the rules of the Contest before continuing with his plans for the forthcoming battle.

And now they were headed straight toward our ship.

Almost hyperventilating at the effort of just about hanging on to whatever sanity she had left, Mab, the evening before, eventually turned a more normal (for her) colour before returning to her cabin. By that time she'd had to reconcile herself to the fact that it was she who was at the disadvantage in this situation and had mentally kicked herself a few times for not remembering how she'd enchanted the two marble men in the first place. Well, she'd now have to wait until morning when at least it would be possible to see what those two statues were doing. So after a restless night of either trying to relax, prepare potions to use against the Colossi or fuming in her cabin to try and discover a way past them Mab, still disguised as the Jackal and not looking her best, reappeared on deck.

We, or should I say Mab, had now been screaming at the two Colossi and throwing spells at them for the best part of two hours. She had tried, twice, to get the ship through, sending the crew over the side to muffle the oars so that the giants, blind as they were, would also not hear them rowing, but to no avail. That was a joke in itself as no-one wanted to go over the side for fear of the serpents but, after she'd had one man thrown over for disobeying her, they agreed hastily, shinning down the oars whilst watching him disappear down a wide, grinning throat. More than one of them was concerned at the current weird antics of their captain and so thought it safer to obey.

The Colossi, though blind, appeared nonetheless to be able to discern their positions whether it happened to be day or night.

There had been a mighty swish at the second attempt to sail between them when, without any warning, the crow's nest had landed with an almighty crash not two feet away from the mad witch. No-one was in it at the time but she'd had the poor wretch who normally stood watch in it brought to her, where she hit him around the head a few times and then had him thrown overboard – with the inevitable consequences, excusing herself by saying that if he'd been at his post he would have been able to warn them all – but he wasn't! – dereliction of duty and all that, she'd added. At this rate, there would soon be no sailors left (they were beginning to murmur but were, perhaps because they were a little worried about his newfound magical abilities, a little too scared of the captain to do anything about it).

Forgetting I was still on deck, she disappeared through the doorway. I stood for some time trying to figure out how I could let the other two know that it was Mab and not the Jackal. How was I going to do that? Every time I tried, I said something completely different. So I tried reaching out to Merlin again but to no effect.

I knew what Mab intended. She was only ever happy explaining her nefarious plans to those whom she believed would not live long enough to snitch on her beforehand and so be unable to do anything about it. She hadn't achieved them in the past; I wondered whether this time she would. Then, again, she'd always thought they'd work. I just had to get back to Merlin somehow. Returning to the other two and obviously without even now trying to let them know who the Jackal really was, I made them try to think of ways to escape. And so it was the witch found us later that morning – worn out with thinking of and discarding one hopeless plan after another before falling into an exhausted but restless sleep. And how I managed that with all that was going on around me can only be attributed to the spell she's placed on me before I was manacled to those oars.

THIRTY-SIX

The men guarding the cauldron, now trusting Merlin and Salazar a little more than they had originally, allowed the two men to mix various concoctions inside it, although they kept a diligent eye upon them and were always alert to anything happening that might seem suspicious. They spent the equivalent of a whole day, give or take an hour or so, in preparing whatever it was they needed before Merlin sat back on his heels looking satisfied.

'It will have to do,' he said. 'All we need do now is choose who will come with us.'

'I'll come,' Arthur was the first to speak out.

'No,' Merlin shook his head at the young man.

'No, Merlin – there's no "no" about it. I *will* come!'

Merlin looked up at him. The boy was now a man – almost! He was full-grown, tall and broad of shoulder, with muscles that rippled beneath his sleeves as he flexed his arms, and others that moved in his jaw as he gritted his teeth. His serious brown eyes bore into Merlin's black ones and the magician realised that he couldn't – and shouldn't – keep him wrapped up in cotton wool any longer. If he was indeed going to be king – and he would be king one day – he needed to start exercising his physical prowess as well as his mental authority.

'No,' Merlin answered. Arthur stiffened in anger but then released his pent-up breath as Merlin continued, 'you are right! I cannot forbid you any more. You are now almost full-grown – a man, no less! Yes, you will come.' He turned and looked at the rest of the people gathered about them. Tiala stepped forward but was stopped by the magician. 'No, young woman, you cannot come,' he said gently.

'No, I know that that would be impossible right now. I am still so weak and would only hold you up; but I was going to suggest that the guard could accompany you. They are the strongest men we have and, as you have seen, no-one has yet discovered our hiding place. I think we will be safe enough here without them.'

It took two or more hours to decide who else, apart from the guard, was strong enough and willing enough to accompany Merlin, Salazar and Arthur on their quest; it was not long before a small company stood waiting for their orders.

Having poured the mixture into several containers, corked them and laid them aside for the moment, Merlin turned to the nearest men. 'First, bring the gypsum; we must make a replica cauldron. When that is ready, we will head off after the others.'

'*What about me?*' Cabby interrupted.

Looking down at the still frail hound, but pleased to see that he was now recovering some of his strength, Merlin whispered to him that he should stay and guard Tiala and the others. 'I'm relying on you, old friend, to do this for me. You are getting stronger every day and, knowing you, a few more days, a week at the most, and you will have regained all your strength. But I need you to stay here to look after Tiala and the others and guard the cauldron. We will still be able to communicate, won't we?'

'*We will,*' he responded but could be seen to be not too happy at this outcome.

It still took another three days to complete their task; the gypsum was of an inferior quality and the first two attempts at constructing a cast were disastrous. Every time they tried to remove the mould from around the original it cracked and crumbled. Merlin was getting very frustrated and beginning to believe it a complete waste of time. They were running out of the fine powder before one of the guards suggested adding some powder they'd been using in the making of their pots. It worked! This time, as they removed the two sides of the outer casing, it stayed intact. The inside was going to be a different matter altogether as without cutting the cauldron in half it was going to be impossible to make a casting of it but, with some help from some of the more artistic among them, they might manage to work an almost faultless copy inside the replica. Merlin nodded his satisfaction; the outside would be perfect and he just had to hope that no-one would look too closely at its interior.

'Now, we need as much silver or silver metal as we can find,' Merlin called out. People went scurrying up into their homes, bringing out everything they could find that was metallic. The place was a hive of industry as fires were lit, pots were filled and molten silver and other metals were eventually poured into the moulds that had been made from the gypsum. Some few hours more and the replica cauldron was complete – almost perfect – inside and out.

Who could tell the difference? Standing it beside the original, they were the same, albeit the new one shone, whereas the original had been dulled by time. That, though, was soon remedied by a liberal application of dirt, soot and grime.

'Now, she'll never know the difference!' Salazar exclaimed.

Turning to Merlin, he asked, 'When do we head off?'

'At first light.' Calling all the volunteers to him, he laid out his plan, adding, finally, that first thing tomorrow they would all take a spoonful of the potion he and Salazar had prepared. 'It will protect you, strengthen you and keep us all of one mind as we fight the witch; I will be able to lead you without having to give directions – you will all know what to do as I will give you your orders telepathically: you and only you! It will wear off eventually but that won't be for a while yet, though I have another potion here that will counteract it, which we can use once our task is completed, if that happens before it does wear off. No-one outside the potion can possibly be included as we communicate with one another. If anyone is wounded, he will be transported back here immediately.' He showed them the phial containing the dragon's droppings. 'We cannot be held up by any injuries. If anyone believes he cannot take the potion, he should step down now. We must be of one mind.' No-one moved. 'Now,' he concluded, 'you all know what to do. Sleep well, as you don't know when you will get the next good night's rest.'

'We have to steal a ship,' Merlin spoke extremely quietly to Salazar when they were finally alone together. 'We'll make our way down through the town at first light – hopefully everyone will still be sleeping off their excesses of the night – and see if there is a ship available.'

'How will you do that?' Salazar enquired.

'We will have to silence the Watch before overcoming the rest of the crew. It will all come together, Salazar, you'll see. I know I can trust you to lock this information inside your head but I don't want anyone here dreaming about what we are going to do just in case that mad woman enters their thoughts. We need as much surprise as we can grab hold of without her knowing.'

They made their way down through the town very early in the morning, one of the more spectral of their company sliding ahead to investigate the harbour. Apart from a muffled scream and a window crashing shut, it appeared that he managed to scour the area without being spotted. However, if he had been seen by some of the more drunken elements from the inns, they would more than likely have thought him a figment of their inebriated imaginations.

They had all risen early, probably not having slept well at all, swallowed the potion, tucked a small twist of paper containing the dragon's droppings into their waistbands and, along with Arthur, awaited further orders. Well before dawn Salazar and Merlin had swallowed slightly different potions: 'Salazar, you and I are the leaders, they are the followers; we already have this gift of communication through our minds – so our potion merely needs to temporarily tune them in. I've prepared the antidote for them for when our work is done. However, this potion,' which he held in a barely-opened hand, 'will block out absolutely everyone else when I just need to speak to you or you to me.'

In the meantime, he had tried, once again, to communicate with me but to no avail. He was, he told me later, extremely worried that I may have been killed.

'So much for my faith in him!' I'd thought when he told me.

The guard, having earlier been instructed as to their roles now that Merlin felt it safe to do so, returned to say that there was a ship anchored offshore. Several little boats were tied up at the quayside and the two men guarding them were sound asleep, beside several empty liquor jugs. He believed that there were enough boats to carry all of them if they packed in tightly.

Speaking through his mind to the assembled company, within seconds they were all running on tip-toes, clenching their swords in one hand and holding their scabbards away from their sides with their other hand to stop them jangling. Arriving at the quayside they crept past the sleeping guards and lowered themselves down into the boats.

'Row slowly and silently,' Merlin ordered the men. The unconscious guards didn't even stir as the little boats edged away from them towards the silent ship.

It was as Merlin had thought – most of the men were ashore, drinking and carousing in one or other of the three inns. There were only four men left aboard to guard the vessel and they were all either drunk or sound asleep.

'Gag them and bind them up.'

Before they could utter one word, all four were trussed like Christmas turkeys and lowered into one of the little boats, which was then released into the harbour; they'd most probably be found by their furious captain later the next day. Merlin searched the ship, starting with the captain's cabin. 'The Crow,' he muttered. 'Well, he won't be crowing when he finds his ship's gone missing,' he chuckled.

He went out on deck and, nose twitching, followed it towards the unpleasant smell that was rapidly becoming a stench. 'What on earth is that awful smell?' he asked and one of the guards pointed downwards. Looking through the grill, Merlin's almost gagged at the smell but his heart went out to the multitude of huge eyes set in drawn faces that stared back at him.

Within minutes he had provided plenty of water and some food for the emaciated men (and a few women!) and, told them that if he could escape the town, he'd much improve their lot. Nodding between mouthfuls of real food and drink, they agreed to do what they could, though many of them, several minutes later, were groaning in pain as the unaccustomed food knotted their tender stomachs.

'Chew it slowly and only take a small amount,' he advised them. He then turned aside and, gulping in the relatively fresh air, started issuing orders: *'Up anchor. Let's get away from this place.'*

Even being in a situation of having no hope, there were looks of satisfaction on the faces of Merlin's men when they saw the outcome of their theft: someone had obviously spotted them as men were now pouring out of the hostelries (well more than half were swaying) and rushing towards the water's edge, though why they did that was puzzling – even if they ran as fast as they could, they were still not going to be able to retrieve the ship. The oarsmen had, at Merlin's request, started heaving on the oars and the ship was slowly but steadily easing out of the harbour; there were now no small boats with which to row toward it and even the fastest swimmer, serpents aside, would not be able to catch up with it, so why rush? The captain could be seen tearing off his hat and slamming it onto the ground – and then stamping on it – but what good would that do? Yes, it was satisfying – very satisfying indeed.

THIRTY-SEVEN

Brosc had been in with the captain now almost all day, showing him here and there on the map where they should be going, where he believed the Jackal was heading and discussing their plan of action as to how to get there first.

'Looks like he's determined to try to get to the treasure first! Hmm, with that dragon pulling him we didn't stand a chance.' He strode up and down inside the small cabin for a few moments before returning to the map. 'But now that the dragon's gone, he has no advantage – we've got the same chance as him!'

Brosc just stood; he didn't believe an answer was required.

'So how long do you think your master is going to take before he's well enough to join me here?' he suddenly asked.

'Well, sir, he was only slightly better this morning,' he replied, staring innocently ahead but crossing his fingers behind his back. 'It's the first day he's been able to keep anything down but his temperature is still raging. I reckon, unless he has a turn for the worse, he's probably still going to be out of it for at least another two or three days.'

'Blast!' he growled. 'Blast! Blast! Blast!' Each exclamation accompanied by the crash of his foot as he stamped on the floor.

Brosc got a little worried that perhaps he wasn't being quite as convincing as he should be. However, there was absolutely nothing he could do so he waited for the captain to calm down and just stood as still as he could just in case the fidgets gave him away.

'Well, there's nothing more that can be achieved here,' he decided finally. 'Let's get up on deck and prepare for battle. You go back to your master and try to get him well. Quickly!' he added, ushering Brosc out of the cabin.

Returning to their small closet next door, Brosc asked Nell's son, who opened only one eye to make sure he was alone and that the coast was clear, what he should do. 'The other ship is in sight and we are about to go into battle. I think you should have a miraculous recovery, man, and come up on deck. If we are going to escape, the only chance we'll get is during the fighting when no-one is watching us.'

'Perhaps you're right, Brosc,' he replied, pushing the blanket off and standing up. 'Percy's on that other ship. If we can get to him, maybe we can all get away.'

'How?' Wite asked.

'Oh, I don't know! Perhaps it will come to me once we get started! Things sometimes do, you know! Give me some of that grease,' he pointed at a jar in the corner of the cabin. 'Some of that on my face will make me look as though I still have a bit of a fever!'

And so it was that the three friends soon stood before a surprised captain to find out what orders he had for them.

'Best to seem willing,' Nell's son had advised the other two before leaving their small cabin. 'Puts people at their ease,' he explained.

'Statues are still swiping at the Jackal's ship, cap'n,' yelled the man from the crow's nest. 'Ship now backing away,' he added.

'Let me know if there's any change,' the Raven called back.

Most of the crew were watching, open-mouthed, at the scene being enacted some nine or ten ships-lengths away. Snatches of words, shouts and yells bounced towards them over the water, the Jackal's crazed roars drowning out most of the other noises.

It was obvious that he was not going to win. The crow's nest was gone and the main mast was askew. It was going to take them a good, long while before the ship was seaworthy and, even then, the Colossi were determined to stop them entering the channel they were guarding.

'I wonder if they will allow us through?' the captain mused. 'Perhaps they need their palms crossed? Perhaps that's why they won't let him through. Has he run out of money? Then, again, maybe they don't let anyone through.' He turned and called Nell's son over to him. 'Is there another route to Rainbow Island?' he asked.

Nell's son had to think quickly. If he said yes, they would be able to leave the area and, maybe, find a decent place in which to escape. If he said no it looked like they would have to fight not only the other ship but also those two giants guarding the channel. He compromised. 'I don't know! If there is, I haven't heard of it but that doesn't mean to say that there isn't another way.'

'Then we'll fight,' he stated, his face looking grim but excited at one and the same time. Shouting instructions, the men rushed to and fro as they got to their stations, opening up cupboards, taking out swords and sharpening them and other already lethal looking weapons, practising with balls and chains – more than one of their compatriots had to duck as a hedgehog shaped ball with wicked looking points attached swished over his head; others were shinning up ropes to cling halfway up, where they twisted their legs through the ropes to hang precariously and where some would shoot their arrows down onto the unsuspecting men on the other ship's decks.

All was hustle and bustle but everything looked well under control. The drummer from below decks was instructed to be ready to beat as they attacked the other ship but to merely row slowly and silently without the drumbeat until they got close.

The sea still churned with dozens of very excited serpents that were anticipating a great feast as they swam around both ships, while the Colossi, swishing the air with their swords, were trying to beat back the marauders. The wind had died out at sea and the Raven, his oarsmen still pulling slowly and silently, was now bringing his ship in very close.

The Jackal, on the other hand, had been so consumed with his fight against the two rock-like giants and with the red mist of madness that had fallen across his consciousness, together with the confusion aboard ship with no crow's nest and lots of obstacles strewn hither and thither, that he wasn't aware of the other danger until the sudden swift beating of the drum from the other ship made him finally realise it was not the beating of the blood pulsing through his temples but a new threat.

Too late he shouted for the oarsmen to row them out of danger; too late he gave his instructions to turn about and be ready for boarders; too late he made a grab at me to do I know not what – I'd ducked out of his reach and was heading towards the prow; too late the he that was really a she realised that her madness was once again her downfall. With arms flailing about like a drunken windmill she screamed hysterically, face crimson with frustration and bad temper.

Flapping wings! A trumpeting roar!

'Hellion! My pet! My angel!' (hardly!) she screamed as, grinning up at him, she allowed enormous talons to snatch her from the foredeck and whisk her away, but not before she managed to zoom down, grab me by my belt and thus with me dangling precariously from her hand transport us away.

Almost no-one realised what had happened. Most thought their captain and I had been taken to feed the dragon's young or the serpents if we were dropped. These things happened! As long as it's not me, was the general thought as most of them shrugged their shoulders and then forgot about us. They all knew the captain would be back, though. Just as soon as the dragon or serpents had chewed, digested and passed him through all the channels of its body, he would come out the other end (horror of horrors!), join together again and somehow rejoin his ship – if the new captain let him!

And, talking about a new captain, two men were, even now, fighting for that privilege – they didn't let the grass grow under their feet out here for sure! Obviously Mongrel wasn't one of them as he, or should I say, she, was right at that moment hiding under the captain's desk. Poor thing – what she'd gone through was something that no-one should ever have to go through and she thought it was never going to end.

The fight between the two men had, of necessity, to be quick as the other ship was now closing in very rapidly indeed. It lasted another minute and then, without a "by-your-leave" or an "oh, that really is not cricket, you know" or any other sort of warning or sense of fair play from anyone whatsoever, one of the fighter's friends merely crept up on the other one, knocked him out with a club and threw him over the side.

Splash!

Much splashing!

Burp!

'Well, at least he was unconscious!' the new captain's friend explained to a shocked Shake Spear, as if that was some form of defence.

The new captain – I never found out his name – sure of his strength, ordered the men to their positions, tried to turn the ship lengthways and waited for the other ship to come alongside.

Battle commenced.

Shake Spear and Tailor were huddled together in a corner. 'We've got to get onto that other ship. I think the Jackal might return to this one and we need to be away from it when he does.' Shake Spear rushed into the captain's cabin and, grabbing Mongrel by the hand, pulled him out and turned towards the stern. 'So what's been happening?'

'Mab's taken over the Jackal's body. Oh, I can say it! She'd stopped me, you see! She stopped Percy. She said every time we tried to say who she was, we'd forget. And we did. But now she's gone, the spell's broken.'

The other two looked sceptically at her as though she'd taken a knock on the head.

'It's true,' Mongrel added. 'She changed me into the Jackal's sidekick. I'm not really Mongrel, I'm Honey. You may have met my brothers, Hive and Mead?'

'Yes,' Shake Spear answered, still very suspicious. 'Though it's hard to believe it, looking at you. I mean, we've met your brothers but it's hard to, er, believe that you are actually, um, you!'

CRUNCH!

They were all hurled across the deck, Shake Spear holding on to Mongrel to save him being thrown overboard and Tailor, grabbing a rail on the bulwark, screamed as he was somersaulted over the side. Holding on to the rail for dear life he couldn't thank Shake Spear enough as he was hauled back onto the deck by the seat of his pants.

Yells and howls, screams and grunts were now the order of things. Arrows thudded into the wooden planks of the deck, while the mainly black-clothed pirates from the Raven's ship, after throwing over grappling hooks, thudded onto the decks after them and took up their fight with the mainly brown and grey-clothed crew of the Jackal's ship.

Tailor and the others crept behind a large barrel and covered themselves with ropes until this terrible battle was over but they could still see and hear all that went on.

'I've never seen anything like it in my life.' Shake Spear told me later. I'd been to the cinema and seen many a pirate film but, well, they were just films, weren't they? From what Shake Spear told me, it sounded just like a film I'd seen recently with Robert Newton playing Long John Silver. But Shake Spear told me he'd had to pinch himself more than once, thinking this must just be a dream. He realised, though, that there was a huge difference between dreams and reality. This was real and it wasn't fun at all.

He went on to say that there were swords flashing and crashing, arrows flying and other weapons of warfare humming and smashing everywhere – men were dying like flies – that is, if dead men can actually die! It was scary. He'd hoped and prayed they wouldn't be discovered.

He told me that poor Honey was shaking as she told him she thought she was going mad when, suddenly, as quickly as it had started, it was all over.

'Lay down your weapons,' they heard the Raven cry.

They peeped around the barrel and were surprised and delighted to see Nell's son standing beside the Raven but before any of them might say anything to give the game away, he screwed up his face with a "shhh" look upon it. Shake Spear, amazingly, saw this and nodded.

The Raven, after surveying the scene, turned and in his merciless way rounded up all the defeated crew.

'Fix the plank,' he ordered and everyone -the victors grinning and the defeated shivering with fear – watched as the requested item was fixed to the side of the ship.

'So – who's first?' he sniggered at the frightened men. 'Oh, come on now,' he cooed. 'Surely at least one of you is brave enough to take the plunge!' he chuckled at his own wit. 'OK, then, Pick – you choose.'

The men struggled as they tried to make their way to the back of the crowd before each was forced to walk the plank – the first one staring down bug-eyed at the grinning serpents jostling one another for the best catching position – but they were shown no mercy, being prodded along by the end of a sharp sword if they stopped moving forward. There were about thirty men in all and you could hear their screams echoing through your head, even after the serpents had silenced them.

Several of the conquering pirates moved away from staring over the sides of the ship – even they couldn't stomach too much, though one of the men relished it and gave a running commentary as he told as many as would listen about how even the serpents had to let at least seven men sink because they couldn't eat any more!

Tailor stood beside Nell's son for quite some time, trying to ignore the awful scenes happening in front of them, whispering to him about what had happened to them and the others, what they hoped Merlin was doing and how they might succeed in escaping when they almost missed the fact that Shake Spear was struggling and shouting as he was being pushed right to the end of the plank.

Nell's son and Brosc rushed forward at the same time, shouting at the Raven and pushing the sailor with the goad out of the way. Poor Shake Spear was balancing at the end of the ever-bending plank of wood, one foot in the air as his arched back leaned towards the ship. It took a little while for them to put the record straight and let him know that he and the others with him were all prisoners before, finally, the Raven gave the order for him to be released.

Wite made a grab and pulled him back onto the deck, just about saving him from more than a watery grave. Looking over the side he could see more large predators swimming towards the ship; they'd obviously been drawn by the turbulence caused by their thrashing friends. A quick thought jumped into Brosc's head, *'Would we, live people as opposed to the dead ones, taste much nicer?'* Looking at the hungry eyes and slavering jaws with their rows of sharp teeth in those awful creatures swimming below, he reckoned they would. He'd already turned his head and now, tearing his eyes away from them, he returned to Nell's son's side and forced himself to push that thought away.

Nell's son and the Raven were by now deep in conversation. As he now had two ships but only one crew there was a problem as to what he should do with the other ship. Should he halve the crew and sail both of them or should he scupper the Jackal's ship and sail on?

'But what would happen to his ship if you do sink it?'

'Oh, it will eventually come back. But who knows when, or where?'

'Didn't you say that there are only six ships sailing these seas and it is virtually impossible to build any more? That if you scupper this one, you can't be sure when it will come back and that the Contest is due to take place very soon?'

'True.'

'Then why don't you let me captain this ship for you until you get your treasure – which may be immense – too much for one ship to carry – and then you can find a place that only you know to hide it so that after the Contest, if you do not win again, you can retire to your place and enjoy it? It should only take me about half a day to repair the damage to the mast and the crow's nest!' Nell's son's face looked the picture of innocence as he made his suggestion.

Still, the Raven was not too sure. He had found in the past that he could trust absolutely no-one – not even himself at times – but the thought of all that treasure was just too much for him. He wasn't as avaricious as many (or so he thought) but, of course, he knew he had to have this treasure – whoever had it had power! So, fighting the conflicting emotions warring within his breast, he eventually, after staring at the other man for so long – a length of time that would have unnerved most men – decided that he could trust him – well, a little anyway.

Nell's son could almost see each chapter of his thoughts turning through the Raven's face and now stood waiting to see the outcome. Would the Raven fall for it?

'Right, you will captain the ship. You will sail alongside me – within hailing distance – and let me know where we are or where we're going. You will ring the bell every hour so that I know you are there in darkness or fog. You will not turn to the left or the right without my knowing or approval.' Then a crafty look came into his eyes. 'I will keep your men on my ship.'

'Ah, but I need them,' he responded. 'What if I'm ill?'

'But at the moment you are not ill. If you become ill that will be a different matter.'

'But who will know where we're going if I am unwell and Brosc is not with me to navigate?'

'If you are ill, then Brosc can navigate from my ship and I will come across to yours.'

Nell's son could see that he wasn't going to win this argument and that any further pressing on his part would only serve to confirm in the captain's already suspicious mind that he was up to something or other and might even give him a clue of their intentions to escape. He would have to await a further opportunity.

'That sounds good to me,' he agreed. 'But can I keep Wite so that he can minister to me when I fall ill?'

'No! You can have these two.' He pointed at Shake Spear and Tailor. 'In fact, I think that that's the best idea. As long as you are well, we will have a navigator on each ship!' these last few words being said with great emphasis and not a little sarcasm.

'So be it!'

The next few hours were spent in deep discussion between the two captains and their right-hand-men.

Using as many men as possible, the Raven shouted and threatened as the mast was heaved back into place, other repairs were attended to and the crow's nest – a little lower down than it had been before – was repaired. Several barrels of this or that were transferred between ships until the Raven, returning to his own, was satisfied that all was now ready.

Then, legs astride to keep his balance and with hands on hips, he looked starboard for a good few minutes before ordering the men to battle stations. 'Let's see if we can beat those statues,' he yelled. 'A tenth of my treasure to the man who breaks through!'

Then both ships' drums started beating and they were headed towards huge marble giants with staring eye sockets and raised swords held high at the end of great rippling, muscled arms, both standing motionless but ready to strike.

What on earth was going to happen now?

THIRTY-EIGHT

Merlin was as good as his word to the men rowing the ship. They were fed well – well, as good as anyone in that awful place – and their spirits revived as he unshackled them and allowed them to exercise or rest in the fresh air and also, mercifully, to wash. Once they'd recovered some of their strength and dignity they formed a line and spent a whole afternoon passing buckets of sea water to one another to try to flush out, for some, years of accumulated filth from the hold – an unpleasant and very smelly job which at first, as it dislodged the caked-on muck, made the stench ten times worse – and even though they couldn't rid the ship of all of its disgusting odour, they at least, eventually, made it more bearable. He didn't put them back in their shackles but trusted them to stay at their posts until they had achieved their goal. Merlin had told them he still had need of them but that when their quest was completed he would free them all.

When the oars were pulled, the drum would beat out its sonorous rhythm but it now didn't appear quite so desolate.

Turning, he ordered the men to set sail and, keeping the land on their right, make haste to move as swiftly as they could, knowing that every minute counted so far as the treasure was concerned. Mab would be making every effort to get to it first, though how she thought she'd achieve anything with just the spoon, if she got to it before him, was beyond him. It was also still beyond him how he was going to "allow" her to steal the fake cauldron. He knew once she had it in her hands it wouldn't be long before she discovered she'd been duped – especially as her spells would soon go wrong – but hoped that it would take her a long time to discover that fact. However, knowing her, she would have some nefarious scheme forming in that evil brain of hers to try to retrieve the real cauldron. No, Merlin knew every minute counted and so, even with a crew of dragon-raisers and men who'd obviously only pulled oars, he was able to get across to them the urgency of mastering the complexities of a ship as speedily as they could. Fortunately most of them were quick learners; others were put to work rowing, when required, and provided with food; some swabbed decks or carried messages and it wasn't long before good order prevailed on board.

Beckoning Salazar over to him as he stood peering over the prow, Merlin pointed out the figurehead and the closed eyes. 'What do you make of that?' he asked the other Druid.

'It looks like a sort of compass!' he answered. 'But not one that is drawn by any type of magnetic field; I think it's lured by some sort of personality rather than by a mineral force. Do you have any ideas as to its source?'

'Not yet, my friend! But I think it has a dual power in that it somehow tries to convince us that we have to go in the direction in which the eyes are facing; when we came on board they were open but since we've turned to face the other direction they have clanged shut. I think that everyone in this accursed place is being played like a game of chess but they don't know it; they're being used by a higher authority and even though some of them think they know what they're doing, they don't – they are merely doing what someone else is trying to programme them to do – like marionettes. Well, we are going to seriously mess up that programme, Prince,' he grinned. 'Let's get started!'

Leaving the foredeck, they made their way down to the cabin where Arthur was exploring. He turned as they came in and asked if everything was going to plan.

Merlin stared at him with a stern look and one eyebrow raised but was amused and pleased to see that where once Arthur would have backed down or even apologised, now he merely returned the gaze. Yes, he will make a great king!

'Hmm, well Arthur, we are certainly on our way but come, let us see if we can find any clues that the captain may have left for us.'

It appeared that the Crow was a much more intelligent man than many of the others in this place (though one might wonder, seeing as how he left his ship virtually open for the taking!) as the map on his desk had actual words on it. Merlin noticed that many he'd come into contact with appeared to have arrived from different periods of history; the Crow possibly from a time when many had been taught to read; the Raven, along with most, he reckoned, had not. The Crow was obviously looking for the treasure, though, like many, had no idea what it was – just that it would surely give absolute power. Merlin's eyebrow rose at that absurd idea. Even if they found it they wouldn't know its power, let alone know how to use it even if they did.

The map was headed up "Treasure Map" and Merlin burst out laughing. When asked by Arthur what had amused him, he, unable to speak, merely pointed at those two words. Finally getting himself under control, he explained, 'Well, what else would it be? I'm almost afraid to see if they have an "X marks the spot".'

Arthur, to Merlin's delight, joined in with the laughter; even though he was shaking his head and wondering at the Druid's weird sense of humour; it helped to lighten their mood – especially in grave situations like now.

'We certainly mustn't let these hard times get us down eh? While there's life, there's hope.

'Right! Let's get on,' Merlin swung around and got everyone searching the cabin, and they spent the next half-hour rummaging through scrolls, papers, drawers, shelves and chests.

'Well, apart from the map, there doesn't seem to be any other clues. So, let's examine it a bit more carefully.

'We've left Raven's Harbour and turned right – er, starboard – can we say that? I mean, down here there aren't any stars.'

'Merlin, I don't know,' Arthur answered, 'but we know what you mean so please just say either, we'll understand.'

'Right; um I mean good!' he shrugged, turning back to the map. 'The next thing marked on here is "Swamplands"; I think we saw them not long after we sailed and they lead up to the foot of the Endless Hills. Then, there,' he pointed, 'just south of No Hope Island – can we say that? "south of", seeing as I don't know if they have any south down here?'

Arthur sighed. 'Merlin – just say it! The top of the map can be north, the bottom south and so on – just like a normal map.'

'Right! Good! *Must stop saying right!* Well, just south of No Hope Island there is an area called the Unsettled Sea which holds a spot marked "whirlpool" – we'd better make sure we keep well away from that – and then a large inlet between "The Red Hills" at a place called "Dragon's Reach" and, can you see, he's put a small cross a little way inland, just along the river past Dragon's Reach?' He had a hard job keeping his laughter in.

'Yes,' Salazar and Arthur chorused.

'He's not written anything by that cross, so do you reckon that that's where the treasure is?' asked Salazar.

'I think that's a very good supposition.'

They ran their eyes over the map once more to see if there was anything they may have missed but all eyes were drawn back to the small cross.

'That's where we are headed then,' Merlin stated and then, sitting down in the captain's chair, brought out the small piece of Glass from a pocket in his robe. Arthur and Salazar made their way behind him to see what Merlin was going to bring into view.

Over his shoulder, they watched the swirling mist move slowly through the Glass before finally clearing. They saw two ships exchanging goods and crew and looked closely at the faces of the men, smiling as they recognised their friends.

'So, they're all safe, though I can't see Percy!' he sighed. '*Try to reach out to him, Salazar. I've been unable to make contact.*'

'Where do you think they are?' Arthur enquired.

'Whoa! What's that?' Merlin exclaimed. He had moved the Glass slightly to one side and almost jumped out of his skin as he found first one leg and then another, before moving upwards towards the body, the arm swinging a sword and finally the sightless eyes of one of the Colossi; then swiftly surveyed further to find his twin.

The other two onlookers drew in their breath as they, too, wondered at these marvels.

'They must be guarding the treasure,' Arthur choked. 'Might there be another way past them? They look terrifying.'

'I expect the only way to the treasure is up that channel,' Merlin stated, nodding toward the tunnel behind the two giants, 'and they stand either side of the entrance to it.'

'Still, now that we know they are there, perhaps we can make ourselves invisible so that we can sail past them,' Salazar suggested.

'But look! They're blind,' Arthur pointed. 'So they wouldn't see us anyway!'

'Hmm maybe – but perhaps they have some other type of sensory perception. We'll just have to devise something so they don't know we're there at all. Good thinking.'

Merlin listened to the other two men's comments before stroking his chin and frowning. 'Hmm, I wonder!' was all the comment he made.

They watched as the ships, now pulling apart, turned to face the two marbled men. It was obvious what they intended and Merlin's skin began to crawl as he saw one of the captains order them to attempt what must be a hopeless exploit. In his head he was shouting, 'No,' but he knew that his voice was not getting through as, mockingly and if to confirm his suspicion, it echoed back at him.

'*And I couldn't reach him either,*' Salazar broke into Merlin's thoughts confirming what he had already discovered. '*In fact, I didn't see him on either ship!*'

There was no further opportunity to search for me as the mists swirled in and the picture faded.

THIRTY-NINE

Nell's son and Shake Spear were going to take it in turns to command the second ship, Shake Spear having to rely on Tailor to be his eyes. The men on both ships had by now re-armed themselves to the teeth as they made ready to sail between the two Colossi, though what they thought they'd achieve was beyond Nell's son's imagination. How could tiny ants fight an elephant as that was obviously what the Raven intended?

Tailor looked up at the towering statues while his heartbeat crashed through his eardrums making him extremely giddy and not a little sick. '*We will never succeed in getting past them.*'

Brosc looked across at the other ship and could see Nell's son shouting orders at the men. Snatches of his voice bounced over the churning waves; how he wished he were there with him instead of here with the Raven. This captain was idiotic and must surely have a death wish!

As they got nearer the two marble giants became quite agitated; sounding like metal grating on stone they swung their massive swords lower and lower and nearer and nearer until the ship closest to the danger had to stop and try to pull back. Just out of range of those mighty men, it became obvious that they were not going to succeed. The Raven, almost out of control with frustration and rage, tore his hat from his head (and thus, his wig as well) and slammed it to the floor, remembering a split second later the state of his head. Diving to retrieve his head covering it was, in almost the blink of an eye, replaced, slightly askew, over a face flushed reddish purple with conflicting amounts of both fury and embarrassment.

Pick crept off into the shadows; he'd obviously seen his master look like this before. Brosc and Wite followed him – the clue had been too obvious to miss. Not so lucky were some of the others – the newer ones who, not having seen this side of their captain before, were unlucky enough to be passing too near him at the time; the serpents received another meal or two as he hauled them aloft and flung them over the side.

The rest of the crew made a dash for safety and kept well hidden until they were sure that his face had resumed its normal colour – absolutely no-one took any notice of him roaring for them to "come here or you'll be sorry" until all the redness had gone, everyone realising that they'd really be sorry if they did "come here".

Meanwhile, Nell's son had, after also watching and waiting for the madness of the Raven to subside, pulled his ship alongside and stood ready for orders.

The man himself, still spluttering but now in control of his emotions, called across that Nell's son should join him in his cabin. 'We are not going to get past them, so we have to find another route. Come, come, man – hurry! We need to find a way to get there before anyone else. There must be another way – there must!' He balled his fists and held his arms close to his side as, taking deep breaths, he tried to keep his control.

Finally, once Nell's son had come aboard, he gave orders to the other ship to pull back to a safer distance then disappeared into his cabin with Nell's son in tow.

They poured over the map and Nell's son, with artistic flourish, added a little more of the shoreline down to where they were now anchored.

'I think we should add those two statues to the map, captain,' Nell's son suggested. 'Even if we do find some other way to get to the treasure, we might need to come back this way!'

'Yes, do it! Though how we'd ever forget them let alone get past them I just don't know.'

He watched as Nell's son took his time to draw the Colossi as artistically as possible onto the map. He then drew the mouth of the river that they had glimpsed behind them, although this was sketchy as they were really not sure where the river led, especially as it seemed to run out of a huge cavern and goodness only knew where that might go or even if it came out the other side. But, come to that, he'd thought wryly, he wasn't really sure where anything was at all in this weird place.

'I think we should sail further along the coast,' Nell's son suggested. 'There might be another entrance – one that is, hopefully, not defended by such powerful guards.'

'Yes – we'll do that – now!' Wrenching open the door he shouted for his men to get ready to set sail at once. 'Go back to your ship, man; we'll leave right away. We have no time to waste! I know the Jackal has been dragged off by that dragon so who knows what will happen to him. It's possible, if he escapes, that he'll get to the treasure before me but he's on his own – well, he does have Percy with him I know, but he's only a boy – and a jinx. How could he possibly carry it all by himself? No, we have to get there first or, if not, intercept him and take it off him.' Still thinking out loud he strode on as he beckoned the others to follow him out onto the decks before sending Nell's son over to the other ship. 'Follow me,' he ordered the man as the ships drifted apart and, as they sailed away, watched the two mighty marble men sink back below the churning waves of the sea to their watery home. Soon all was calm and amazingly, within minutes, no-one would have known they had been there.

The thought did cross Nell's son's mind as to whether they'd rise again if they turned back. I suppose if the Raven's quest hadn't been quite so urgent he might have returned, but he probably thought that they'd only rise back up again, thus wasting valuable time in maybe finding another route, so he moved on.

And on, and on.

The Raven was becoming more and more frustrated as he sailed along the coast. There didn't appear to be any inlets or bays that he could visit, let alone traverse; the cliffs fell shiny and sheer into the sea – there was no foothold anywhere. On the third morning he realised that they had now gone much too far and were, in fact, moving further away from the treasure all the time. When the two vessels stopped sailing as night drew nigh, he called over to Nell's son and said that at first light they were going back. 'There is only that one way through – we have to fight those guardians – if that is what they are. Somehow we will succeed.'

Thus it was that as morning lightened the sky, they turned back.

Clang, clang, clang, clang!

The Raven was delighted; both figureheads opened their eyes as the ships moved off. 'This is a good omen,' he smiled for the first time in days. Whistling, he returned to his cabin, shouting for Pick to bring him his breakfast and shaving gear. He knew it was going to be a few days before he had to do anything else and so was determined to enjoy those days by refreshing himself in every way possible.

FORTY

We were whisked high above the colossi who tried to swipe at us with their swords but, fortunately, we were far too high. It would have been me that got hit in any event (something I feel the witch would have thoroughly enjoyed), as it was me that dangled the lowest. I could feel the sweat of fear breaking out all over me as we soared upwards, with me trying to hold myself as high up as I could, then we swooped, dipping down over the waves; drawing up my knees again as my feet did a tap dance, not only on the waves but also on the heads of some of those gaping-mouthed serpents we flew away from the sea and up over the Red Hills. Those hills were awful! They not only had the appearance of blood but had the smell of it too. Old blood! Like the smell you get from rotting meat. And streams of it, if it was blood, trickled sluggishly down the rocks that wailed and into the sea below, where quite a few serpents were drinking their fill. I felt sick! I hoped that Mab didn't suffer the same effects as I clung onto her legs while she held onto my belt; one sweaty hand losing its grip would be the death of me. But I needn't have worried – some few minutes later we landed further up the same river that had led to the sea – it had disappeared into a gaping cavern behind the Colossi but had re-emerged in a large valley a mile or so further inland. Hellion, who must have known the area well, had judged the landing for Mab but I suffered a few scuffs and bruises as I was dragged along the ground.

Dusting herself down, Mab had looked across at me and told me to stop whinging and follow her; she was leading the way into a dark cave almost hidden by a dense thicket. The whole area was made up mainly of caves and several ravines cut through the ground, having been carved out by a noisy waterfall that lay almost directly opposite the cavern into which ran the fast-flowing river. We were hemmed in! What could I do? There was nowhere to hide or run to! I had no idea where I was and, after seeing one or two serpents' heads (and they really looked so much like the naiad, I realised with a shiver) poking out of the river, I knew I couldn't try to swim for it either. So I followed her inside and decided that I would make an attempt to try and reach out to Merlin as often as I could. Obviously when she was occupied with something else and hopefully wouldn't hear! That is, if I now could!

'Now, I have to rid myself of this awful, confining body,' she was muttering as, delving into her pockets, she brought out a small phial. Looking over at me she turned up her lip and gave the most awful grin. 'Better look away Percy,' she cooed. 'You might not appreciate this!'

I turned away but, well you know what it's like, I couldn't resist looking back. Caught up in what she was doing, she didn't notice as I watched through my fingers. I wouldn't have believed it if I hadn't seen it for myself and I won't hold it against anyone for not believing me now, but what I saw is absolutely how it happened and made my stomach flip and my bowels churn.

She twisted the cork out of the phial and, sniffing it, lifted it to her lips, screwing up her face as the fumes went up her nostrils – and again I wondered how she could smell anything whilst managing to ignore her own usual fetid stench – but, ignoring its pungency, she downed the potion in one go.

Nothing happened for long seconds and then the show began: I was appalled as I watched what looked like two people having a punch-up inside one body; fists seemed to be pummelling out of his face, neck and stomach – in fact all over the body – and skin was being stretched like giant elastic bands, while the Jackal's countenance was twisted into many horrifying contortions as this fight was in progress. This went on for some time, during which I lost all pretence of trying not to watch and just stared bug-eyed and drop-jawed at what was happening in front of me, listening to the screams and grunts of a one-person wrestling match. Then all went quiet and still. The Jackal stood there, legs stiffened, arms akimbo and head thrown back – almost like a starfish standing up. He stood for some time like this as I, with unblinking eyes, watched to see what would happen next. Then I wished I hadn't.

She stepped out of his body, shaking her crushed skirts as she did so and almost felling me with that same awful, never-to-be-forgotten unwashed body odour that attacked my undefended nostrils as she swirled around! The smell, having been confined within the Jackal for so long, was concentrated and overpowering and hit me like a heavyweight boxer's left hook. It knocked me over onto my backside. Mab, just as I remembered her, had merely taken a step forward, out of the man, and was back to herself! Just like that! She looked over at me and laughed till I thought she'd pass out. But it was me who was almost doing that! Tears once more flowed down familiar dirty cheeks, leaving their inevitable washed-clean furrows. Mucous hung out of one nostril and even in the act of being sniffed back up again was quickly banished by the cuff of her sleeve – well, almost banished as it dried, puckering her cheek as it did so. She finally stopped, wheezing and snorting like an old steam engine until, supporting herself with hands on knees and gasping for breath, she told me that I was going to help her.

'You won't have an option,' she rasped. 'I can do awful things to you if you disobey and,' she looked around, pointing in every direction, 'there's no-one here to help you and, more importantly, there's no-one else here to help me!'

I looked down at the Jackal whose body had slumped unconscious to the floor after Mab had exited it.

'No – he can't help! You don't think I've been inside his body all this time to not know how his mind works, do you? He's an idiot at best and a madman at worst. No, Percy, it's you who has to help me.'

He was now coming round and had started to push himself up onto one elbow. Completely confused – but by now, obviously, completely sober – he looked around to see if he could understand anything. He couldn't and so, before he was able, Mab, with superhuman strength, grabbed one arm, almost flew towards the river and before he could do anything about it, was about to toss him into it, with the inevitable consequences, when I yelled for her to stop. I thought she was going to completely ignore me but she teetered at the edge of the fast flowing river and looked enquiringly over her shoulder.

'You might need to disguise yourself again with his body,' I croaked through my dried-up throat the first thing I could think of. I really didn't want to see anyone else die in that awful way – I had seen enough people being torn to shreds to last me a lifetime. Holding my breath, I waited.

She stood there for what seemed to be an eternity before, knocking the already weak man out with a jab to the side of his neck, she dragged him back and made me tie him up before he came round again. With lungs almost bursting, I let out my breath at last.

Mab threw one arm across my shoulders and stared at the man as I tightened the knots. 'I'll make a villain of you yet!'

I didn't know what was worse – almost passing out as I touched the unconscious pirate or gagging at Mab's rancid armpit stench as it once again assaulted my nostrils. Would I ever get away from this awful woman?

FORTY-ONE

Tiala smiled as Cabal, with feet hardly touching the ground, almost flew around the inside walls of the cave. He had regained all of his strength and was getting extremely frustrated at not being able to do anything to come and help us.

'*Is there nothing we can do?*' he asked her. '*I'm sure we'd be more help doing something rather than just sitting here. Did Merlin tell you to stay here or just stay with me until I recovered?*' Cabal stared at her.

Tiala, after ministering to the hound for the last few days, had found that she could almost understand what was going on in his mind. At first she thought it was something to do with her illness – that she was hallucinating because she was fading away. But, after one awful night, early on in Cabal's sickness, she felt sure he had thanked her or had been thankful, or something like that. It was when she had stroked his brow and wished him well that she was sure he had reached out to her with his mind. She didn't really think any more about it until the others had left on their quest and she was cutting up some food for him that she was now sure she heard him speak to her in her mind.

'*Please don't cut it up quite so small – I really need to chew on it to strengthen my jaws!*'

Now he had only been wishing it, not realising that she had the gift of hearing, and was pleasantly surprised when he looked into her face to see that she had understood.

'*You can hear me, can't you?*'

'Y-y-yes!' she exclaimed.

'*No, please don't speak out loud – the others will think you've gone mad! Just speak to me in your mind – I'll hear you!*'

'*What like this?*' she answered.

'*Yes; just like that!*'

Tiala smiled at him once she had got over the initial shock and the two of them spent almost a whole day telling each other about themselves and their adventures, fears and dreams. And speaking through her mind used up absolutely none of her energy so that pleased her no end.

'*What was that you were telling me about the ship they were trying to build?*' Cabal asked Tiala as they sat down to eat their evening meal.

'Well,' she said, settling herself against the wall, 'One of the captains – Black Dog – who had not had a ship for a very long time – not only did he keep losing during each Contest but we heard that he missed out when the Jackal didn't return with his ship; so getting really fed up with waiting he and a gang of men tried to build one. They had no idea that we were watching them as they built it and were making notes as to how it all fitted together and how it worked until it was nearly built, but each night we went aboard and coated the day's work with an amazing substance we'd discovered that would, when we were ready, make it invisible: we added this every evening to what they'd just built on the ship and then waited until the vessel itself was almost ready – then we stole it. We crept aboard – almost all of us did this – and gave it a final coating of the stronger compound we'd discovered, which made it completely invisible and so we sailed it away.

'No-one knew what had become of the ship; it was supposed that people had broken it up for their fires or had made carts or whatever. That's why the tale has gone around that no more ships can be built; but we know that they can! So, what they didn't know was that it had been taken by us.'

'You? You and the people here?' Cabal asked, looking around the cavern.

'Yes. We've been hounded by those Archers and Swordsmen for so long that we thought that if we could get away we might find somewhere safe; somewhere they couldn't attack us. We'd heard about Rainbow Island and understand that treasure can be found on it and that it's also an island of comparative peace. So, we've been waiting for this ship to be built so as to get away.'

'But where?' Cabal was getting very excited and quite agitated as he listened to Tiala. 'I haven't seen another ship anywhere, or heard of one either!'

'No you won't have!' she responded. 'As I've already said, it's invisible.'

'Where have you hidden it?'

Tiala laid her hand gently upon Cabal's brow and told him to stay calm; his agitation was beginning to have an effect on some of the others who had started to watch him closely; everyone knows that dogs have a sixth sense, especially when danger is around; it would not be good if they, too, became alarmed.

Trying to get himself under control, he promised not to interrupt if she would tell him everything about the ship.

Smiling her sad smile once again, Tiala said she would and spent the next half an hour doing just that.

'We waited until it was dark and people had either locked themselves in their homes or were getting drunk at the inns before we made our way to the harbour. We'd found that the Archers and Swordsmen never appeared at night and so, after a few nights of vigilance, decided to use more men (now that they didn't need to be on watch all the time) and move much more quickly to overcome what guards may have been left on the ship and then sail it out of the harbour and moor it elsewhere.'

'But where have you moored it?'

'Not far away. But let me finish my story.'

'Sorry.'

'After that first night, all we did was send someone during the day to hide and watch to see what they would do. We could have removed it quite early on but that would have defeated the object as we would have had to complete the building of it ourselves and we are just not shipbuilders. So we used the cauldron's magic a little!'

'How? I didn't think it could work without spells and things!'

'Oh yes. I don't know how we found out but I think it was much by accident. Someone threw something into it to start cooking food and it disappeared – well almost disappeared,' she corrected herself. 'Some of us could still see it as a pale outline, some couldn't see it at all and some couldn't see any change from what it looked like in the first place. So we worked on a formula made up primarily of water and were able, once it had been in the cauldron, to paint this over the ship that Black Dog was building. What happened was that until it was nearly built, they could see it as clear as day, as could some of us, but some couldn't; they thought that it had been stolen and that the others were mad, going out every day to work on it. However, it was finally ready and thus, when they added the sails, we got on board, painted it with a final coat of the solution we'd discovered and moved it away.

'Black Dog still hasn't recovered! He was as mad as you like for weeks and then went into a severe depression; however, he's managed to pull himself out of his despair and has determined to get one of the ships when the Contest takes place – and I understand that will be very soon as the tree's buds are almost bursting.'

Cabal was lying down, head on paws, next to Tiala as she told her tale, occasionally lifting his head and looking into her face. He could see in his mind's eye all that she told him, even to the bit where the ship sailed away, and it was then he asked again, *'but where is the ship? And what do you mean about the tree budding?'*

'The tree buds every so often and when it does all the captains are supposed to return to the Blue Pelican or one of the other inns and get ready for the Contest – to see who will be captaining the ships until the next Contest. It's only fair as there are too many sailors for too few ships. Also, we've brought our ship back to its berth in the harbour. No-one can now see it, except a few of us, of course, and we will soon be ready to remove ourselves from this place and try and find a new life on Rainbow Island.'

'But isn't that where Merlin is going?'

'I believe it is.'

'Why,' Cabal's thought sounded a little sad, *'didn't you let Merlin have your ship then?'*

'Well, I'm sorry about that Cabal, but it really wasn't up to me. Our people here have been working so hard on getting away from this place that it was decided we couldn't take the chance on our ship being wrecked in a battle. We believed that those who have left here with Merlin will be able to make off with one of the ships that might be in the harbour and will be able to get to the treasure but we couldn't take the chance of losing our ship.'

'But what if we follow them? What if we can help them? The more of us there are, the better chance you will have of finding the treasure.'

'I would have to ask the others; it is not just my decision here, you know!'

It took hours of discussion, during which time Tiala became very weak. It was only her argument for Cabal's cause and the fact that if they didn't agree with her soon she might cease to exist that they finally agreed. She came back, assisted on either side by two of the women, and sat down next to Cabal, merely nodding to him.

'So we could go and help the others now!'

'I think we can but we will have to be very careful.'

'Why? If no-one can see us we should be able to catch up with Merlin and maybe save the others.'

'Yes, but we still don't know whether we might be seen by someone who has the vision; then again, especially out on the open sea, even if they don't see us or the ship, if they are vigilant they will be able to see the ship's wake.'

'*Ah, yes.*' Cabal was silent for a moment before looking directly into Tiala's eyes and saying, '*But we must try!*

'*Yes,*' she responded, smiling sadly, '*We must try.*'

She turned, giving orders to some of the guards, who then ran to do her bidding. After a few hours of sometimes quite animated discussion – as some were for and some still against – it was agreed that they should help; in fact it was almost the plan they had agreed on before Arthur and his companions had arrived: as many as could be housed on the ship would go and as long as nothing bad happened to it, they would return to collect the others. '*Rainbow Island has been our destination – we shall now just be going there a little sooner and it looks like we'll be having an adventure on the way.*'

However, they would only sail at night so that no wake could be detected. But first she would see if she could summon some extra help and even though Cabal kept trying to break into her thoughts, she was adamant that, until she knew if they would come, she would not say more.

'*So let me get it all sorted out before I expire completely, Cabal!*'

So he lay down, placed his head on his paws and rested, with one ear cocked – just in case.

FORTY-TWO

The ship was now making excellent progress. Merlin went below decks and stared at the Glass to find out just who was where and what they might be doing.

Once satisfied, though he was still unable to contact me even if I was still alive, he and Salazar used the morning to mix and stir, chop and contain the different potions they were going to need and to consider which spells might be beneficial to their cause. It was going to take a day or so to reach their destination but one couldn't be dilatory – who knew when something powerful might be needed?

The afternoon was spent on deck, checking ropes, sails, barrels and men, just to make sure everything was shipshape. Turning his head towards the prow of the ship he smiled as he considered Arthur who was leaning forward keeping watch.

'Merlin, come here!' he called at last. 'Look – the Red Hills!'

'Then we are nearly there!'

CLANG.

Everybody jumped. Arthur, who was at the prow, leaned over and saw that the eye had opened. Rushing round to the other side he exclaimed when he noticed that the other eye remained shut. 'Why is that, Merlin? Why just one eye?'

'I have absolutely no idea. This place is too weird to have any understanding of it. All I know is that nothing down here makes any sense whatsoever; everyone is miserable and even things and people that die come back to life to go through all this hopelessness and misery again. In fact, I don't even know why we're here! If it weren't for the fact that you and Percy had been abducted, well, this is the last place I'd want to be.

'Anyway, let's check the map; I think the Unsettled Sea is somewhere to our left and we need to keep well away from there; then the next thing we have to negotiate is the channel between those two giant statues.'

Giving orders to the guards to exercise and feed the oarsmen, Merlin took Salazar and Arthur to the cabin, where they poured over the map and tried to discover just how long it would be before they arrived at the entrance to Rainbow Island.

'Unless we have a miracle, I think we may be too late to get to the treasure before Mab but we mustn't be too late to save Percy *if he's still alive.*'

A slight jerking preceded a more violent one as, wondering what was happening, they rushed crazily out of the cabin and were bounced from side to side as they hurried up the steps; they were soon met with the first howls of a violent wind – a wind which rapidly turned into a force eleven gale.

The crew, made up mainly of landlubbers, were struggling to keep the ship upright. Three or four of the oarsmen had sailed as crewmen before their incarceration in the bowels of the ship and before long were screaming orders over the howling wind to everyone else and it was a lesson of necessity soon learned to keep the vessel afloat. Some men were up in the rigging securing the sheets; some were trying to tie down or throw overboard anything that was crashing around on or below decks; some were just trying to stay on board.

It had turned very dark – an unhealthy, weird, red-darkness, even though it was still day, and what with the creaking of the boards, the howling of the wind whipping through sails that had still not been furled and the roaring of the sea, it was amazing that anyone was actually able to make out the whirlpool towards which they were heading.

Rapidly, Salazar lashed himself to the main mast and, holding one hand aloft that emitted a green phosphorous smoke, started mouthing words, which, even if anyone could understand them, were whipped away with all the other sounds assaulting their ears. Merlin had grabbed Arthur before he had taken one step on deck and dragged him back down to the cabin for safety. Arthur had wanted to go back up to help the others but stayed when he saw the uncompromising look on Merlin's face.

'Then I'll stay here and pray for your miracle, Merlin.'

He knelt on the floor and, recalling one of the passages from the Bible that Brother Geraint had made him learn by heart, started to recite it within his prayer:

> 'Where can I go from Thy Spirit?
>> Or where can I flee from Thy presence?
> If I ascend into heaven, Thou art there;
>> If I make my bed in hell, behold, Thou art there;
> If I take the wings of the morning,
>> And dwell in the uttermost parts of the sea,
> Even there Thy hand shall lead me,
>> And Thy right hand shall hold me.'

'Land ho-o!'

Arthur jumped up and chased after Merlin as he rushed out onto the deck.

The wind had died almost as suddenly as it had arisen and all was now completely calm; the darkness gave way grudgingly to the light, by which could be seen that there was little damage to the ship (which damage was rapidly being attended to by several oarsmen) but apart from that everyone else, as they disentangled themselves from whatever they had tied themselves down with, was staring ahead. Over to their left the remains of the whirlpool disappeared over the horizon. The sea looked like glass and, except for the odd swish and plop from their ophidian and constant companions, was now almost deafening in its silence.

Land could indeed be seen, reflected mirror-like in the unruffled waters. Slight hills from both the north and the south rolled down towards the shore meeting a huge cave entrance from which spilled a river.

'Isn't that where we saw the ships and those statues – you know, Merlin – in your Glass?'

'It looks like it, Arthur, but the place is deserted now – there are no ships, no statues, nothing! Fine! All well and good! So now we shall try to get up that river and find the treasure. It's all men to the oars now, I'm afraid, as there's no wind, so let's get rowing.'

The oarsmen went back to their stations below decks while several small boats were lowered into the sea and attached to the ship by long ropes; Merlin hoped that this could assist in pulling the ship along and also steer it through the channel and upriver.

With Arthur in tow, he strode around the decks checking to see if there was any serious damage. Satisfied that all was once again shipshape, as they say – a wry smile playing around his mouth at this thought – he moved on up to the prow and was only slightly concerned that the figurehead still had one eye shut, then, tut-tutting, he leaned across and removed what had been keeping the other eye open; he soon dropped it into the sea, where it was greedily swallowed by a cruising serpent.

'What was that?' Arthur asked as, leaning over the side, he watched this little play being acted out.

'You don't want to know!' he responded, hoping that Arthur had not seen the lower part of a leg, still with foot attached, as it slipped down the serpent's throat. He shivered as he considered what had been keeping the eye wedged open and what he'd just been handling, but not before the inevitable CLANG reverberated around in his brain.

Shaking his head to clear it of sound and memory, he was just about to give the orders to row when, with a mighty and thunderous roar, the two gargantuan statues rose up through the waters, almost causing a tidal wave as they broke and churned the sea about them; the ship was once more tossed around uncontrollably, while the little boats, being rowed hastily back to the ship by their terrified occupants, almost capsized. The huge waves gradually became less violent before they finally evened out and calm was restored.

Men ran for cover, some screaming for fear as they searched for somewhere to hide. Salazar just managed to save one man from being swept overboard to an inevitable and painful end. Arthur and Merlin grabbed a side rope and each other and stared at those two mighty men until, unbelievably, Merlin started to chuckle and then roar with laughter until the tears ran down his cheeks. Poor Arthur thought he'd flipped and quickly checked to see if he'd been hit on the head or something.

'No, no, Arthur – stop fussing, I'm fine.'

'Then what's so funny? I can't see anything amusing! In fact, I think everything is anything but!'

'No, of course,' he patted Arthur on the shoulder as he tried to get himself under control. 'I'll explain as I go along. Just watch and see what happens and then you'll understand. However, my tears were more of relief than of anything funny and it looks very much like luck is on our side; or it could be, Arthur, that your prayers have been answered after all and your miracle has happened!

'Hello,' he shouted, cupping his hands and calling up to the two giants.

'What are you doing?' Arthur shook him in fear. 'Have you gone mad?'

Shrugging him off he merely whispered, 'Trust me – I know what I am about.'

Everyone held their breath as the two statues stopped their cutting and slashing and merely held their swords to their sides.

'Which one of you is Castor and which one Pollux?'

The two statues appeared curious as one raised his hand to his mouth.

'Can you speak?'

He shook his head.

'Hold on!'

Merlin felt around in his pockets until he found what he was looking for. Grumbling slightly he opened the small phial and shook its contents into his hand. Nodding, he called up to the two giants. 'I am going to throw something into the air; I want you to breathe it in – you can breathe can't you?'

They nodded slowly.

'Good! I will shout as I throw it; breathe in immediately – I will throw it on the count of three. OK?'

They nodded slowly again.

'One – two – three.'

They all held their breath.

Merlin tossed the powder into the air, pointing his finger as he did so and watched as the shiny granules shot like an arrow ever upwards towards the faces of the Colossi; everyone was caught unawares at the violent inhalation of breath by the two giants and holding onto whatever was nailed down, it was as much as they could do not to be drawn up into those widely spread nostrils and mouths. Then it was still again.

With a gravelly voice, one of the statues spoke.

'Who are you?'

'It is I, Merlin.'

'Merlin. It has been a long time. How is it that you have been sent to this place? I believed you to be someone who would live forever.'

'Ah, I am not dead! And am I speaking to Castor?'

The statue nodded.

'I have come to rescue some people that that mad witch has enchanted and has somehow managed to send to this place.'

Castor and his brother became very agitated at the mention of the witch.

'You know our story, Merlin?' Pollux now spoke. 'When Castor, my brother, was slain, he was sent to hell, but I begged Jupiter and he allowed us to take it turn and turn about to be either in hell or enjoying life above.'

Merlin nodded.

Now Castor once again took up the story. 'One day, when we were exchanging places, she – and I refuse to give her a name as I don't even want to acknowledge her existence – ensnared us, telling each of us that the other would be stuck in hell for eternity at that very instant if we didn't immediately return there. As you can imagine, we love one another so much that the thought of the other one suffering was too much to bear, so we both returned. We met and were inconsolable when we realised the awful trick that had been played on us. It was good to be back together again but not to spend all of eternity in hell. Then, at our lowest mental and physical strength we met her! As you can see, she has done terrible damage to us: she has made us semi-stone by encasing us in this skin of marble; she has removed our eyes until we agree to her plan and she has secured our feet to the rock. Even though we would spend eternity here, we still tried to kill her when she attempted to sail between us; it would be better that that happens to us, than the world has to suffer if she ever lays hands on the treasure. But it seems that she is not meant to be slain by us.'

'That is true – the prophesy says otherwise. But she left the stars on your foreheads. Why is that? And what is her plan?'

'They are one and the same, Merlin. Until we agree to her plan we will not be able to move from here. If we agree to her plan then we will be freed but only to walk through that cavern,' he pointed behind him, 'and then, when we come out the other side, will be forced to shine our stars on the waterfall there. When that happens, well, you know what will happen.'

'Yes,' Merlin answered, a grim look to his mouth, 'a rainbow will appear!'

'And the treasure will be pinpointed,' Pollux finished the sentence.

'Then we have to get to the waterfall before Mab,' Merlin stated.

'Too late,' Castor and Pollux spoke in unison. 'She's already there.'

'But how? I thought no-one could get through here.'

'The dragon took her over the hills,' Pollux answered.

'And the boy, I believe,' Castor added.

'Percy?'

They shrugged.

'She might be there but she doesn't know where the treasure is, though, does she?' Merlin spoke under his breath.

'And she won't be able to find it without the stars. But we will let you through,' Castor said, interrupting his reverie.

'Then I've thought of a plan to help us all,' Merlin grinned. 'So just be patient you two,' he called up at them and for the next half hour outlined what he was going to do and what they needed to do in order that he might achieve his goal.

FORTY-THREE

Having argued her case with the other members of her family and friends, Tiala had by now become so tired that at one point during the day Cabal could hardly see her at all. She'd somehow found the strength to get everyone together and had spent the entire morning explaining what it was they were all to do, going over some points several times to make sure that everyone knew exactly what his or her part was that had to be played and it was all this effort that had drained her of most of her strength.

'I know that the wizards have taken some of our strongest men and women and I believe that they can accomplish what they have set out to do but we can help and shouldn't just sit around waiting to see what happens. Besides, they have Arthur and he is central to our plan – he must survive to go and warn those of our people in China that are still alive; so, if for no other reason than to save him should the need arise, we must go.'

So it was that on a very dark night – but then all nights were dark in that awful place – they made their way from their sanctuary, down through the hills and the town to the harbour, creeping warily through the deserted alleyways, skirting the areas behind the inns and then out onto their ship – the real cauldron being hauled along on one litter and Tiala, her strength almost gone, on another; Cabal, checking out the lie of the land and sniffing the air for any sign of trouble as they progressed.

The Archers and Swordsmen, thankfully, were not seen – but everyone still remained vigilant – and thus it was that with the few hours of night that remained they sailed silently out of Raven's Harbour.

Two women clucked and fussed to make sure that Tiala was settled into the hammock in what initially should have been Black Dog's cabin and one of the men – her brother, Bohai – left instructions that they attend her, commanding them to give her every care and let him know at hourly intervals how she was doing or sooner if there was a change.

Returning to the deck Shen, one of the guards, checked out the ship from stem to stern; it was quite disconcerting as some places appeared to be (if that could be the right term to use) quite invisible and he and some of the others found themselves checking the ground with their feet before placing them down firmly as they progressed, being able to see the dark, swirling waters far below them and, sometimes, the grinning maw of a huge serpent as it swam below them. It might have been amusing, if things were not quite so serious, to watch the serpents crash and flatten their faces against the underside of the ship. But it wouldn't do to think there was floor in front of you only to find that there wasn't and thus end up as dinner to one of those slimy sea snakes.

'I think they must be as confused as we are,' a soft voice spoke into his ear as, turning, Shen recognised one of the other guards who was also staring through the ship.

'It will take a while to get used to this, I agree,' he responded to the man, 'but I am going to check everything so that I know where everything is should I need to find something quickly. Will you join me?'

'I'd be happy to. I was one of the men who helped to coat this vessel with invisible paint so I know where everything is – especially the hiding places – one where the weapons are kept – you never know when you might need them!'

'Then let's go.'

The man introduced himself to Tiala's brother, Bohai, whom he had seen once or twice in the cavern but had never spoken to – suggesting they start at the prow and work back to the stern.

Bowing, Bohai returned the compliment and introduced himself.

Starting from the stern, it took longer to investigate the ship than they had at first thought. The vessel itself was less than half the size of any of the others they'd seen – Black Dog was obviously more interested in getting back out to sea quickly than in having a large ship, regardless of the fact that if he became becalmed then he would in effect really be all at sea – as, thankfully, it had no space for oarsmen. It smelt clean because there were no unclean bodies manacled below and it was light on the water. It was driven only by the wind so they hoped that the elements would be kind to them and keep them moving. Eventually the tour was almost over when, with some surprise, Bohai was reminded of Tiala by one of the women coming to find him; her head, as she looked down into the hold, was framed by the lightening of the sky behind her.

Bohai realised that unless they were very careful, the moving ship might be discovered, so after checking first to see if Tiala was well, he started giving instructions, first to Shen, 'Send a lookout aloft, Shen.

We cannot chance being seen. We may have to stop completely,' and then to all the others who ran to do his bidding.

The wind was favourable and it seemed foolish not to take advantage of it so he determined to continue on their course, giving orders that absolutely everyone needed to be vigilant. 'The first sign of anything unusual – and I mean anything – you have to let me know immediately. Do you understand?'

Everyone nodded or added their agreement to his command.

On the first day he sent two men down to the cabin to bring Tiala up on deck. 'The sea air and the light might do her some good,' he explained.

But he was shocked when he saw her. Gossamer-like to begin with she was now almost transparent.

"Never let your thoughts show; always keep the other person unaware of what you are thinking, whether it be joy or sadness, fear or triumph, sorrow or anger." Bohai remembered his teacher's warning almost in time.

'Come, Tiala, let the women make you comfortable over here.' He smiled at her and felt his heart almost break as he watched his sister bravely trying to return it. She started to speak but he knew the effect that effort would have on her.

'No, don't speak. Just relax and regain your strength. I will see if there is any medicine on board.

She merely looked up at him and surrendered herself to the ministrations of the women.

'Let her rest if you can; don't keep fussing around her. I shall be back soon.'

He walked off calling Shen over to him and instructing him to go and find some medicine, if they had any. While Shen went off to search, he went and found a quiet place to think.

Lost in his own little world and wondering what he should do next, it was some time before the noise penetrated his brain. Had they been discovered? If not, with all that noise going on they soon would be! Jumping up and running to the foredeck he looked around at the other men who were prancing about and pointing upwards. Superstitious at the best of times, some of the men were blanching with fear. It took him a few moments to gradually make out what they were pointing at.

There, sitting nonchalantly and quite easily along a faintly visible crossbeam were at least twenty extremely small people.

'Who are you and what are you doing here and how did you get here and...'

'Whoa! One question at a time please!' a tinkling voice broke through the general pandemonium. 'And in any case, His Majesty isn't used to being interrogated like this. In fact, he isn't used to being interrogated at all! If there is any to be done, well, it is he who always does it.'

'I beg your pardon. My name is Bohai and we, that is, these men and women and I, are seeking the treasure so that we can divest ourselves of some of the misery that clothes us.'

'Treasure you say?' Turning, he spoke to the man he'd addressed as "Your Majesty" and everyone waited until that man had nodded.

The little man stood to one side, bowed and then waited while the king arose.

'I am Ogwin, King of the Faerie and this is my wife, Queen Gisele and these,' he spread his arm from left to right, indicating those others that sat across the beam, 'are some of my subjects.'

'But – are you also dead?'

The king raised his eyebrows before he and the rest of his little band burst into tinkling peals of laughter. 'Dead? Gracious, no! We are the Faerie – we go where we please. There is nowhere barred to us, though this is one of our least favourite places to visit and we rarely take the trouble to do so; however, we have been drawn by unseen forces. But, getting back to you, I am intrigued; tell me about yourselves and this treasure. And who,' he waved an elegant hand in the direction of Tiala, 'is she?'

'She is our leader but she more than any of us has been cursed by the witch – doubly so. However, she has taxed herself selflessly and has in reality worn herself out on our behalf, and is now close to extinction. If she is not made well soon, we will no longer have her. We know, as we've seen it happen to several others of our people.' He was almost crying by now.

After looking intently at the young woman he realised that if they didn't do something very soon she would end up as one of the wraiths that float about scaring people in the night or, worse, be imprisoned inside one of the standing stones and spend eternity going round and round within it. 'Gisele,' he spoke to his wife. 'Go down and see what you can do for her.'

Queen Gisele danced lightly along the yardarm and almost skipped down the mast until she reached the deck. As she glided across the floor, men stepped back – some were very superstitious and believed that any contact with her might do them great harm.

'*Well, Queen Gisele, don't you have a "hello" for an old friend?*' Cabal peeked round one of the more opaque doors and, with tongue lolling out, smiled at her.

'Ogwin look, see who's here! *Perhaps you can tell me just what is happening?*' she added.

Cabal had remembered that the queen had the gift of mind speaking and so, while she ministered to Tiala, he got her up to speed with virtually all that he knew, Tiala adding a word here and there. Before long, however, she started to visibly strengthen and Gisele returned to her husband. The King, once apprised of all that had been going on in this awful place, became quite animated. 'Tell him where we have been,' he instructed his wife.

And so, as quickly as possible, she told him about Mab and me.

'Oh, the adventure begins! It's all coming together. And to think we will be able to do all this with Merlin again – what fun,' he chuckled. 'My dear it's been too long. I can't wait.' Turning, he instructed two of his guard to return for his army. 'We're going to need them. Bring the weapons – the secret ones,' he whispered to one of them, 'and meet us back in the Valley of the Shadow. Hurry men!

'Now,' he grinned as he joined his wife, Cabal and Tiala, 'what were you planning to do?'

'Come over here boy,' she yelled at me, as I, experiencing a mixture of emotions of fear, feeling sorry for myself and relief that I was still alive, lay slumped against the inside of the cave.

I knew from experience and to my painful cost that obedience was expected and had to be immediate.

'Now, I want to show you a map and I'll know if you lie to me. So, what do you make of this?'

She had removed the waistcoat from the Jackal and now laid it on the floor in front of me. I looked at a crudely drawn map that had been etched onto the inside of it and wondered just what I was supposed to say.

'Um, er isn't this where we are now?' I queried gingerly.

'Oh – give me strength; of course it's where we are now, you idiot! I don't want to know something I already know, I want to know what you know.'

Ever had that awful feeling of dizziness when you think your head is being squeezed in a vice – it's stuck fast and you can't do anything about it; there's no way of escape; there are no answers because there's been no real question? Or even if there had been a question you knew you had no idea what the answer was? Well, that's just how I felt then. I knew that I was for it! I knew that as soon as I said some inane thing she'd be all over me like a rash. If I made a run for it there was nowhere to go; even if there was, she'd throw some magic thing or other at me and turn me to stone or confuse my feet so that I went all wobbly and fell down. Oh well – here goes!

'Well,' and this was one of those very long drawn-out "wells" – more like a "wee-e-e-ll", 'the cross,' I explained as I pointed to the map and drew her eyes back to it and away from me, 'is just past Dragon's Reach, which is near enough the entrance to that tunnel over there which the river flows into. I mean,' panic was starting to grip my throat and almost stopped the words coming out, 'um, once you come up the river from those two statues you have to come through the tunnel and out here and we are surrounded by caves and there's nowhere else to go from here so the treasure must be hidden hereabouts, either in one of the caves or in the valley somewhere.'

Even to me I sounded like I was waffling. I waited, eyes almost closed, for the inevitable cuff round the ear but it didn't come and so, squeezing open one eye and peering cautiously round I was surprised to see the witch sitting chin in hands, elbows on knees and with her face screwed up in concentration. She sat for quite some time making rabbit shapes with her lower lip, with me trying hard not to breathe too loudly for fear of being noticed or clouted by her for interrupting, when suddenly she grinned – had she lost more teeth? – and, jumping up, ordered me to search the area and let her know how many caves, how many mounds of rocks (and there were quite a few of each) and other weird features there were. She was then going to do a systematic search of the area – well, she was at least going to get me to do a systematic search of the area, starting with the cave in which we had made our temporary home.

'*Home!*' I thought. '*Some home!*' A heavy curtain of despondency fell upon me just then as I thought of mum and dad and my brother, James; I suddenly missed them all very much and wondered if they were, even now, searching for me. Yes, they would be. Even though we had our ups and downs – and I did sulk a lot I have to admit – we really did all love each other. Yes, they would be searching for me! But, then again, Merlin always said that time stood still back in my real world when I was here in the past. Funny, that! I'd drifted off into some sort of reverie when Merlin first told me that, imagining everyone stopped in time – my dad, striding through our front door, suddenly stopping halfway and staying there with one leg sticking forward; my mum taking a batch of bread halfway out of the oven and getting stuck like that (would she end up with a bad back?) and birds flying in the sky or ponies jumping over the hedge (would they stay suspended in space or would they crash to the ground?). I must have been in that reverie once again and was now just about to suffer the consequences of it.

Clump! I got that thick ear! I knew it was going to come at some time or other; she never missed any opportunity to punish me. 'Get on with it boy, we haven't got for ever, you know!'

I rushed out, gulping down the uncontaminated air, and started yet another set of map making, wondering, like you do, whether that was what I'd be when I grew up – then I started worrying as to whether I might ever grow up or would actually leave this place alive. Shaking off the despondency that threatened to descend once again and grip me with its huge hands, I entered the cave next to ours and determined I would take my time. Can you imagine my surprise when, after my eyes adjusted to the darkness within it, I found myself face to face with the King and Queen of the Faerie?

Getting over the shock, and taking advantage of the short time I might have, I quickly told them what I was doing and we agreed that they would wait for me to come back there when it was safe. It would be a long wait but I would come back when the witch slept – and she would have to sleep at some time, wouldn't she?

It was well past nightfall before the ground started to vibrate as grating noises erupted from the witch's slack mouth and some far less pleasant sounds and odours started to erupt from elsewhere. I waited a further twenty minutes or so – which seemed like hours at the time – counting off sets of sixty seconds before venturing back out to the cave where the King and Queen waited for me. If Mab were to miss me, I'd just say I thought I had an idea where the treasure might be or I needed to spend a penny. They were sitting quite patiently either side of a very small green baize table playing whist with the smallest pack of playing cards I've seen in my life – even smaller than that small pack I'd once got out of a Christmas cracker. Another flitting remembrance almost knocked me off balance again as I thought of Christmas with my family. 'No,' I said to myself, shaking my head to clear it of the attacking homesickness as I walked over to the pair.

Collecting up their cards, King Ogwin somehow managed to fold them and the table into a packet the size of his palm and pop them into his pocket.

'How did you do that?' I enquired, without thinking how rude I sounded.

'Oh, it's one of my best tricks,' he winked at me and then changed the subject.

'Come now, get me up-to-date with all that's been happening.'

So I spent the next hour or so doing just that – well as much as the spell would allow me to do – the witch's spell was strong but the Faerie had ways of getting round it; only being interrupted by one of them if I found myself waffling because of the witch's binding or if I didn't explain myself too well or the truth had to be coaxed out of me by means of their magic. Thus it was that they, getting very excited, told me they could help and, blowing the whistle he always kept with him – that high pitched one that always knocks Cabal off his feet – summoned a small band of his subjects who'd been waiting high above the cliffs; after sliding down lianas and spiders' silken threads they stood and waited for his commands. It was almost morning before we all agreed on what should be done and watching them flit lightly up and away, I crawled back to the cave and lay down just outside it with my back against the wall, only to be roughly awakened at the most two minutes later by a grumpy woman yelling for me to go to her and a roaring Jackal screaming blue murder. I was dog-tired and, as I made a wide berth past the pirate, wondered how I'd get through the day.

'Shut him up!' she shouted. 'Stuff some rags in his mouth; no, wait,' she rummaged through her pockets, 'I'll spray him with this,' she grinned as she walked towards the man who was still hanging in the cave's entrance. Yes, you've guessed it – she didn't immediately throw her potion over him – that was too easy and not enough fun; she had to explain what she was going to do and what effect it would have on him when she did it.

This time, she told him that the powder would feel like a million red and poisonous ants crawling all over him, biting him to bits and making his skin feel like it was on fire and peeling off in thin and sticky strips. She watched him squirm and try to break free and was extremely amused at the look of both hate and fear in his eyes as he shouted his curses at her. 'But, of course,' she added, 'it won't really be happening, it's just how you will believe it is happening and, also, you will be struck dumb – well I don't want to hear you screaming – well I do really but I'm too busy to enjoy it – and you'll lose all sense of feeling in your body – well, what I mean is you won't be able to move but you will feel the pain – oh, and it is exquisite pain! It's going to be great fun watching you every time I pass by and see the agony in your eyes.'

The Jackal roared at her, threatening her with every bad thing he could think of until, suddenly, all went quiet. I watched as the powder, thrown high above him by the witch, sprinkled down over him and then all that could be seen was the horror in his eyes – the only part of his body that could actually move. He couldn't speak, cry, yell or even scratch – he just hung there in agony, just being able to watch us as we moved about.

I really felt sorry for him, even if he was a nasty piece of work; no-one deserves to be tormented like that. Then I, once again, got knocked flying by an impatient woman wanting the search to continue for the treasure.

Rubbing my ear I began to wonder if I was some sort of receptacle for abuse – always getting thumped on the back by my friends and then getting belted round the ear by my enemies! *'One day!'* I thought! I walked out of the cave and made my way, by a very circuitous route, over to the waterfall.

I made sure the witch was out of sight as I, remembering what Ogwin had told me, made my way round the rocks and disappeared through the fall of water where wet, but wide eyed, I discovered its secret. I stayed there for a very long time, ignoring her yells and threats as she called for me, and explored every inch of the large cave behind the falls knowing how safe I was – she wouldn't go anywhere near where she'd get wet – oh no, too much power would be lost for her to chance that! The waterfall caught the light which bounced back and forth over the walls, lighting up the cave's interior with its hidden cracks and crevices; I searched these as the treasure could be hidden anywhere. Then I found it hidden behind one of those boulders – a steep staircase cut into the rock that disappeared ever downward into darkness but to who knew where? Remembering what King Ogwin had explained to me I took that first careful step. The stairway, dark at first, gradually lightened as I came to a huge cavern lit by an eerie phosphorescent glow and there, right in the centre and raised on a dais and nestling on a deep crimson velvet cushion was the treasure.

I stood for ages just looking at it. It seemed so innocuous; however, Merlin had told me it could be used mightily for good or evil. Mab's yells were faint but persistent as I leaned my shoulder against the arched entrance to this secret place and it was very hard to block her out. I should have listened and obeyed straight away but you know what it's like! I'd done the same with my parents when I'd felt safe – and brave – only knowing that eventually I would have to pay the price for disobedience. Well, the price I was going to have to pay was just about to go up as I stood examining the spoon and blocking out the witch's yells.

Who would have imagined that this could be the treasure? Everyone here was searching for it, possibly thinking it was coin, gold or precious jewels hidden in many chests; but this spoon could hardly be called treasure. It was obviously made of silver, though the shine was more like satin than high gloss; it was roughly eighteen inches long and at the top of the handle sported the head of what looked like an identical replica of one of the bearded faces that appeared on the outside of Gundestrup. They must have been made at the same time and given the same magical properties; no wonder they were supposed to be powerful together.

The cavern, cool to begin with, became chillier and then extremely cold which, if you consider where we actually were, should have given me a clue that something was not quite right but I had been too busy studying the spoon to notice at first. It was when I found myself starting to shiver and my teeth began chattering that I thought I'd better go. I reached out towards the spoon thinking it best that I left this place before I froze to death when my hair, which had by now grown quite a lot since it had been shaved off, stood up straight while my eyes bulged out of their sockets and my mouth dropped open – not a pretty sight. There, between the spoon and me at least half a dozen apparitions rose up out of the stone floor and then stood between my prize and me. I didn't even consider how I was going to retrieve it now; all I could think about was escaping but, when I turned to leave, my reaction, now sluggish because I was so cold, was too slow. I think that even if I had been fast, I would still not have made my escape in time. At least another six of these beings rose up in the entrance to the cave.

Looking back, I believe that that witch didn't know where I was but she'd cast a spell and just sent it to follow me. The only other thing I could think of was that perhaps these were the guardians of the spoon. Well whatever it was, they had found me and now I was really stuck!

'What were they, granddad?' Ben asked before Jack could continue with the tale. 'Were they the Archers or the Swordsmen?'

'No,' Jack answered; 'they were even weirder and more scary than them. I'll try to describe them as best I can; they were quite unforgettable.'

They were skeletons, all of them were skeletons from the neck downwards at any rate but they had live heads, like you and me. All the heads were different – some were men and some were women but, as I said, you could only tell that by their heads because every body was just bones. It would have been quite comical if it hadn't been so serious as each of them had a different weapon in his – or her – hand and they were all starting to edge closer to me. I was spinning around like a top trying to keep an eye on the ones behind as well as the ones in front but every time I turned back they'd got so much closer it was scary. I knew they were moving quickly because of the clattering of their bones as they ran up behind me.

One of the women was really beautiful, except for the vicious look on her face that is: she had long, blue-black hair that was extremely shiny and she tossed it about as she got nearer; there was a man who looked just like a famous rock star I remembered and he held a club in his two hands like a guitar; some of the others looked famous but I was starting to sweat with fear by this time, even in that cold cavern.

I reckon they thought they'd have some fun with me before they laid into me and after being shoved about a bit by the ones behind me and then being pushed back again by the ones I'd fallen against I got so dizzy I wondered how I was going to escape. I hadn't taken any weapons with me when I'd entered behind that waterfall so after being pushed to the floor I looked around for something to defend myself with. The ground of the cave was strewn with rocks and so I quickly gathered up as many as I could and began to throw them with quite positive accuracy at as many of them as I could. One pebble shot into the mouth of a bald-headed man and I think all of us were mesmerised; we stood still and watched as the small rock dropped down his throat and then bounced backwards and forwards across and down his ribcage, just like a slot machine at the penny arcade, before dropping out through his pelvis and onto the floor. We all just stared at this weird phenomenon until it had run its course; then I felt their eyes turn once again toward me – they just laughed soundlessly as they rattled closer and then the mayhem began again. Without taking my eyes off my assailants, I crouched down and continued to feel around on the floor gathering more rocks and letting them fly almost as soon as I lifted them; then one that had a lot of dust on it flew into one of the women's eyes. She dropped her club and rubbed her eyes with bony fingers, contorting her features as she did so; without more ado I gathered up as much dust as I could and started throwing it everywhere. They really didn't like that at all and I was able to make my escape while they were trying to rub the dust from their faces. Remembering my quest just in time, I ducked between two of them, grabbed the spoon and fled back up the stairway, hiding it as the Faerie had instructed, then rushed out through the curtain of the waterfall and over to the far side of the valley before I made my way back to the witch.

FORTY-FIVE

It was dawn.

Again it came to mind – the dawn of what? There was no sun to herald her entrance, no lightening of the sky over the horizon, not even a blackbird to sing for joy at another day; no – it was as though darkness had swung its black cloak around itself and had hidden away in a corner somewhere, allowing the light to step forward and take a bow.

But Merlin made no fuss of it. He made sure all the sails were furled, the blades of the oars wrapped with rags and all loose material strapped down. He'd even had the wheel oiled, as well as every hinge on board ship. When he finally arrived in the valley, he wanted it to be on his terms and with complete surprise. He'd had virtually all day and all night to complete the plan he was now putting into action.

Patting the pockets of his voluminous robe to make sure he had stashed everything in its right place, he strode over to the grille situated in the middle of the deck. Peering down into the bowels of the ship and noticing that the awful smell, even after all that scrubbing and washing they given it, still remained, he spoke to the men and women at the oars. 'Now row as quietly as you can; follow the lead of the man in front of you; we can't beat the drum to keep you in time with one another or even speak above a whisper, so it's up to you. Once we have the treasure, we'll sail back to Raven's Harbour and you will all be set free.'

There was a mighty cheer at which Merlin held up his hand. Thanking them, he warned them that no sound should be made after they began their journey upriver beneath Dragon's Reach.

They murmured their consent and readied themselves for the off.

So it was that, as soon as it was light enough to see their way upriver and into the dark cavern from whence it emerged, Merlin softly gave the order to proceed, 'But slowly as we need to sound the depth. We don't want to run aground in these treacherous waters.' Tailor, with his sure knowledge of measurements, was seated on the plank beneath the figurehead where he would swing the lead.

Those on deck gazed upwards in awe as they sailed between those two gigantic statues, both of whom stared ahead with sightless eyes and grim mouths, swords held hard by their sides as they allowed the ship to pass.

They were soon swallowed up by the darkness of the cave as they made their way oh so slowly against the inky river's flow; men at the front of the ship held torches aloft for light, men at the sides held out long poles to feel when the cave narrowed and Tailor measured the depth of water below them. The serpents could be seen swimming alongside – in the darkness their usually flat, pale eyes shone red which, frightening as it made them look, helped a bit as the men could then tell that there must be water between the ship and the rock walls. The journey seemed to take a lifetime but it could only have been thirty minutes before light was seen at the end of the tunnel.

Torches were extinguished and the oarsmen were told to stop; the momentum would carry them a little way and they only then need row gently to stay in place.

Then they were edging into the light.

Many men were sent aloft to whisper down in relay fashion just what could be seen and where.

The first thing they saw was the Jackal, hung up on a hook and visible half in and half outside a cave. 'He might be dead,' was the message that reached Salazar, 'as he ain't moving! Looks like 'e been 'ung as a sheep!'

Mab emerged from the cave but unfortunately saw the ship – well its mast above the rocks – and ducked out of sight. You had to admit there was plenty wrong with that woman but there was definitely nothing wrong with her eyesight!

'Ah, that was a shame! I'd hoped to surprise her!' Merlin exclaimed softly when the news of their discovery reached him. 'Never mind, we will still overcome.'

He gave the order for the ship to sail on and anchor in mid-river. 'No need to be silent anymore,' he called out to all aboard, 'as she knows we're here.' He launched two rowing boats over the side, placing himself and Arthur in one along with six other men and Salazar and seven more men in the other, all made up from those who had guarded the cauldron; the fake version of which stayed on board ship.

As they made their way across to the shore, a short distance but awkward due to the fast-flowing river, Mab, who had snarled on first seeing the ship moving silently up-river, flew into a frenzy of equal amounts of rage and frantic activity.

I didn't know what had occurred at first until I managed to piece together the few disjointed words she was shrieking about the ship and the orders interspersed with those yells as she dragged me over to the Jackal.

'Get him down! Untie him! Oh, get out of the way, you dolt.' This said as she pushed me to the floor. Rummaging about in her pocket she found a small phial, uncorked the top of it and poured some foul-smelling liquid into the agonised man's slack mouth. His eyes rolled up into his head which flopped onto one shoulder as relief spread over his face – his torture ended; however, he was exhausted with the pain and upon being cut down fainted immediately away.

'Ooh – ridiculous man – and he's supposed to be a tough pirate! Help me get him upright,' she ordered me and between us we dragged the unconscious man to his feet and held him, as directed by Mab, face squashed against the cave's wall. 'Now,' she muttered as, to my disbelief, looking like he was being hugged, she pressed herself back into him until she was lost inside him. My eyes, like my mouth, were huge as I stared with disbelief at what was happening in front of me. Shaking my head to try and clear it I shut my mouth and rubbed my eyes, only to find that, on opening them again, everything was just as I'd seen it seconds before. There had been no fight this time, no pummelling inside his body – just a smooth transition from witch to pirate!

The witch, or should I say the pirate, threw back her, um his, head and laughed out loud. Then, recalling the urgency of the moment, she grabbed me by the collar and dragged me as far back inside the cave as we could possibly go, she telling me how clever she was to have kept the pirate while I, knowing that it was at my suggestion, was mentally kicking myself for doing so.

'Now I want you to tie me up and gag me.'

I goggled at that! What an opportunity! To get this horrible excuse of a woman, admittedly currently disguised as a man, captured; I could truss her up like the proverbial Christmas turkey ready for the oven – she'd be really stuffed then, wouldn't she?' I almost laughed as I thought that. But then my head rang as her currently large, masculine fist belted me round the ear.

'No, you won't be able to do any of what you're thinking,' she whispered hoarsely into my clanging ears. 'You are going to be bewitched again. You will do as you are told and then you will forget. You will only remember what I place into your mind.'

'*Oh, not again!*'

A quarter of an hour later, Merlin, Salazar and Arthur cautiously entered the cave. Holding their blazing torches aloft, it wasn't long before they found me, lying seemingly unconscious in the middle of the floor. I had managed to drag myself so far along to warn everyone of what had gone on but then, exhaustion had taken hold, my legs grew heavy as lead and I had collapsed and lapsed into the state in which they now discovered me. It took them minutes to bring me round and then ages to get any sense out of me.

Eventually Salazar realised that I had been placed under a spell, 'and until we can discover which one, we will have to be very careful indeed; we do not want to be fooled by the instigator of the spell and we certainly don't want any harm to come to the boy – any wrong move by us could send him mad,' he whispered to those closest to him. 'Be very, very careful and extremely vigilant.'

They all looked around to see what had happened to the witch or the Jackal.

I was still thanking Merlin and the others for saving me; at the same time trying to rub my pounding head when, suddenly, I remembered. 'Oh, there is a pirate here with me! He had his ship stolen by a witch and she left him here with me!'

Merlin and Salazar looked quickly at one another and then just as quickly away. No-one saw what passed between them.

We all made our way to the back of the cave where the Jackal lay squirming and almost choking on the gag that was in his mouth.

'And how long have you been here?' Merlin asked craftily.

'Oh, we've been here ages… ,' I was about to say but what actually came out was, 'We've only just landed. The Jackal and I were caught up by the witch and the dragon; she tied us up and left us here to die but I have only just managed to get out of my bonds; only I hit my head, I think, and then you came and, and, well, you know the rest.'

Arthur and a couple of the guards were untying the Jackal, who never took his eyes off Arthur. He didn't notice, well, none of us noticed, the hungry look in those eyes as he watched him. However, Arthur moved away from him and left the rest of the releasing to the others as he came over to me.

'It's great to see you again Percy,' he greeted me, giving me a rough bear hug. A huge improvement on the back slapping, eh? Perhaps they were accepting me now as more than just a boy! I grinned back at him. Looking back at that time, I realise now that I seemed perfectly normal to everyone; well, almost everyone as the Druids obviously knew something wasn't quite right. I was acting like I always did and talking the way I normally talked. The only wrong thing was that the witch had put a spell on me with regard to who she was, so even I thought of her as the Jackal.

Anyway, as soon as he was released and had given his thanks to his rescuers – and he was really over the top in his praise of them, Merlin eventually having to ask him to desist as he was becoming acutely embarrassed – we all made our way to the little boats in order to get back onto the galleon.

The Jackal never stopped talking. He told them about losing his ship to the witch; he asked if they might possibly help him recapture it; he wanted to know how they had managed to sail upriver, past those two giants – did he have a secret he could share about that for the future? He wanted to know why they wanted to go upriver anyway; was there anything he could help them with? The questions went on and on but Merlin, eventually holding up his hand to stem the flow, asked him to wait until they were on board and then he might be able to concentrate better. He noted the flash of anger in eyes that he thought he knew. Then, shrugging, he dismissed it as fancy – how could he have ever met this man before? He would originally have been about two hundred years older than himself!

The day wore on and everyone on board ate and rested until the time that Merlin said he would call them. They all congregated on the main deck, even the oarsmen, and for the next half hour or so Merlin set out what each had to do in order to achieve their goal.

'You all know your tasks,' he spoke to the gathered assembly. 'In about an hour, Salazar will take six of you to the waterfall. Behind it he will find the chandelier of crystals that has been pulled up to the roof of the cave in which it usually hangs and which has been tied securely to the ceiling. Ogwin has told us that on its release it will hang down just behind the curtain of falling water.

'We shall row over to that bluff of land over there,' he pointed to two or three guards and then motioned to the bank of the river where a sharp promontory jutted out. 'We will take up our positions and, when all is ready, do our part of the task.'

The Jackal, who had not been invited to this parley, had crept around and flattened himself to the side of the ship and was listening just out of sight, almost salivating as he listened to what was going on. He waited until all had been discussed and then made his way back to the small cabin in which he'd been installed. However, being the greedy type of person that the Jackal was, combined with the fact that he was also as nosy as the witch, he pushed open doors and peered under lids and generally poked into every corner on his way back. Imagine his shock and joy at discovering the cauldron.

'Oh, it's all coming together. What joy!' And with that he disappeared through the door of his cabin to make his plans.

The small boats were once again lowered and everyone went to his task with a will. Arthur and Merlin, with some of the men, set off in a third boat which, tied to the ship, merely waited on the river, although it rocked dangerously in that fast-flowing water.

One of the guards had originally been given the other task but it fell to me to perform it and before long, with me now up in the crow's nest, we were all in place.

Almost holding our collective breaths and hearing nothing except the torrent from the waterfall and the gurgling of the river, it was still a shock when we heard Merlin call out 'Now!'

Salazar had already released the crystals that initially swayed unseen and tinkled behind the waterfall and I, who'd had my hands clutched across my chest and hidden inside my jerkin, lifted my arms high and shone the two stars, which had initially adorned the foreheads of Castor and Pollux, straight at the waterfall.

As soon as the stars' lights hit the crystals, a blaze of amazing multi-coloured fire just like the aurora borealis filled the valley, shooting here, there and everywhere in a frenzied dance, almost blinding us – it had seemed so long since we had seen anything of such shining and stunning splendour; eventually and reluctantly it would seem, it settled and came together before the most beautiful rainbow arched over – one end starting from within the waterfall itself, while the other landed on the far side of the river close to the arched tunnel from which the ship had emerged.

Merlin, at the risk of falling into those serpent-infested waters, was standing with one foot on the edge of the boat and shielding his eyes while he searched. 'There, Arthur! Over there!'

And then we could all see it. Right at the edge of the water was a cave; a very small cave that would have been missed by anyone walking on the land, as it was obvious that it could only be seen and reached by anyone sailing into it from the river.

'Row, Arthur. Fast as you can,' he called excitedly as he untied the rope from the ship. 'Let's go and see if it's there!'

I held my breath and kept my arms aloft – easy at first but, boy, was I now getting a pain in my chest and weren't my arms getting heavy. Everyone watched as the guards rowed Arthur and Merlin in the small boat over to the cave. It disappeared inside. As we watched, steam or smoke started to waft out of its entrance, followed by low rumblings or growls. What on earth was happening? Had the dragon caught them? Had he eaten them? Again I held my breath as I waited and waited; it seemed as thought they would never come out again. Ten minutes, which seemed like hours passed and then they emerged, a grinning Arthur standing precariously in the rocking boat and holding one arm aloft, a silver spoon, as long as my forearm, gripped in his hand.

Everyone on board the ship started cheering, while the others were leaving their various places and heading back toward them; I lowered my arms and placed the two stars back inside my jerkin. Their sparkle went out! The rainbow and its beautiful colours evaporated! I noticed the Jackal watching everyone row back to the ship with a wry grin on his face; he must have felt my eyes staring at him as he twisted his head and then looked straight up at me!

I shivered. I didn't trust this man one bit.

Back on board, Merlin retrieved the spoon from Arthur and, smiling broadly – a very unusual thing for him, as you know – told everyone to ready themselves for the sail back.

'We now need to get back to the others and see what can be done about cancelling out the witch's spell.'

Now don't you sometimes feel that even thinking, let alone mentioning, something – or someone – bad, just conjures them up? Well, I do, and right then, all hell was about to be let loose – if you'll pardon the expression.

While we'd all been busy searching for the treasure and, of course, retrieving it from the cave, no-one, and I mean no-one, had given any thought to the Jackal. He, knowing what we were off to find, was making the most of every opportunity not only to steal the cauldron but also to somehow get the spoon as well. He'd dragged the cauldron to the stern, somehow – probably used magic – and had summoned the dragon.

We had just emerged from the tunnel and had turned the ship to sail on from the river and into the sea and then back to Raven's Harbour when it happened.

Although I didn't know it, I was still under the witch's spell and so it was that, when Merlin held the spoon and I was returning to him the two stars, I asked if I could hold it for a moment.

He should have said no! I know that now! He should have realised something wasn't quite right – there had been too many clues!

As he took hold of the two stars and I held the spoon in my hand it all went horribly wrong.

The Jackal swooped down, one leg curled round a rope and one hand holding onto it; he grabbed me and we swung back to the stern where we landed beside the cauldron. I tried so hard to throw the spoon to Merlin but even as I tried to toss it to him my hand just would not open, not until the Jackal wrenched it from my grip. I was yelling my head off as I called out to him to help me but everything was going much too fast.

As we dropped down beside the cauldron, which had been very well disguised and had also been tied into some sort of rope basket, the Jackal attached both of us to it and then, with the shortest burst of flapping wings I've ever heard, we were airborne. I don't know where the dragon had come from; I expect he had been lying atop the tunnel and was just waiting for us to emerge.

Away! We flew almost straight up, the galleon sitting very still on the sea and getting smaller by the second before it disappeared completely as we moved up and over the top of the cliff to our left and then past Castor and Pollux to our right – well out of reach of their slashing swords- and out over the open sea; and all this to the accompaniment of hysterical and maniacal laughter.

Then I froze as I recognised the witch's voice, 'OK Percy, this is as far as you go.'

She, still disguised as the Jackal, cut the rope and, with no land in sight anywhere, I fell and fell, screaming like a banshee I must admit, towards the sea and I knew not what end. Well I did really – knowing that if I landed inside the mouth of one of those creatures I would actually die a very painful and real death and have to stay here forever – but things were moving much too fast and I really did *not* want to think about that.

FORTY-SIX

Merlin stood very still watching us fly away. As soon as we were out of sight he moved – like lightning. He had known I was bewitched; I just wasn't my normal self; he'd tried to mind speak to me but there was a definite disconnection – he could only understand the odd word thought by me, so he'd taken as many precautions as he could to make sure I didn't give anything away – well, not unless he wanted me to, that is. That was really awful, if you think about it! Just try to put yourself in my position – my brain was being manipulated by two of the strongest mindbenders the world has known – only one of whom wished me well!

Shouting orders, the men at the oars started to drag them through the water; it was always hard work at first but as soon as the ship began to move the rowing got easier. The men Merlin had sent aloft doused their lanterns and scrambled down. The man at the wheel waited on Merlin's every word as, leaning over the prow, he yelled instructions as to direction until they came fully out onto the sea.

Passing between the two marble statues, he called up at them to find out if they knew what was happening.

'They flew off to our left; that is all I can tell you,' Castor called down. 'It might not mean anything but I believe they are heading for the Endless Hills.'

'I reckon the Jackal's been mesmerised by Mab and is going to take the cauldron and Percy to her and she's going to try and use the spoon and cauldron to take complete control over all the earth and all that is under it!' Salazar spoke into Merlin's mind.

'Well, she'll not accomplish that, will she?' Merlin responded. *'For a start she won't get the real cauldron and even if she did, she hasn't got the real spoon!'* A small twitch distorted the corner of his mouth but he managed to keep his mirth under control. He didn't want the rest of the men believing he'd gone mad with the disappointment.

'Let's get to Raven's Harbour,' he called out to everyone. 'When the witch finds she's been duped I reckon she'll make the Jackal go there and try and round up a mob to attack us, so let's get there first.'

'Castor! Pollux! Here are your stars.' The two marble men leaned down and held out their hands; once they'd retrieved them they placed them back on their foreheads, where again they glowed dully. 'I shall come back when we have defeated the witch and I promise I'll do all I can to set you free.'

The two giants nodded and as Merlin's ship sailed away – a stiff breeze moving them quickly over the waters – everyone on board watched as Castor and Pollux slipped back down below the sea, the waters churning around them as they disappeared.

Arthur stood leaning against the bulwark, watching until the water was once again calm before turning and following Merlin and Salazar to the prow. They all started at the CLANG CLANG when the wolf's eyes (that predator being the figurehead on this particular ship) opened.

'Well,' Merlin grinned. 'Seems we are now headed in the right direction. Full sail,' he shouted to the men and watched satisfactorily as they clambered up the ropes and along the yards to release the sheets. *'You'd think they'd been born to it,'* he thought, *'rather than only having been doing it for a few days!'* The breeze continued – to the relief of the oarsmen – and everyone on board, including those men, took turn and turn about to work or rest; they wanted to be ready for whatever they might have to face when they docked; and they all knew that something was definitely going to happen – you could just feel it.

FORTY-SEVEN

'Aarrghhhh.' Whoosh! Thump!

I almost crash-landed onto something that wasn't there. Well, at first I really thought that there was something there; that I'd landed on an awful being that was about to grind me to bits between rows of sharp and unmerciful teeth. Then, still seeing stars, I watched in absolute horror as a huge tongue wrapped itself around my head, curling itself over my cheek.

'Nooooo! Please God!' I called to Arthur's God, not knowing whether he would hear me or even whether he was real and at the same time trying to hope he had heard, was real and about to fight off the serpent. Well, I reckon my prayer was answered as a faint but real noise began to penetrate my terrified brain.

'*Stop it! Stop it Percy! GET A GRIP!*'

I opened one petrified eye, ready to shut it again if need be – I mean, who wants to see the object of their demise or actually witness an eye about to be plucked out of their head? Or worse, with that one opened eye, witness the rest of your dismembered body floating past it along the inside of that sea snake! Then both eyes shot open. The tongue did not belong to the monster from the deep and neither did the huge teeth!

'Cab!' I flung my arms around his neck and hugged him, almost sobbing with a mixture of sheer delight and huge relief. 'I thought you were a serpent!'

'*Oh, thanks! I really appreciate that!*'

I started laughing and then noticed that he and I were lying in mid-air about seven metres above the sea. I felt sick. Cabby, watching me and following my thought pattern quickly brought me up-to-date with my current home and with Tiala, recovering almost by the minute, and with some of the others adding bits and pieces, I soon knew pretty much what was happening. It was weird seeing the Faerie on board; they didn't tell me how they'd managed to get there from the cave, simply saying that it was one of their secrets and that only they could travel that way – they couldn't take passengers.

Then I, in my turn, was overjoyed and pleased to find that I was now free from the witch's spell; I wondered then whether because she thought I was now dead she had relaxed her enchantment over me. Well, whatever she had or had not done and after listening to their stories, once the Faerie had finished, I got them up to date with what had happened to me up to the point of being dropped from the air.

'Well, if the witch now has the spoon, I reckon she'll be trying to make some awful spells. They won't work, though, as we have the real cauldron,' Tiala spoke more strongly from her sick bed.

The Faerie, their laughter tinkling all around us, then explained that the witch not only didn't have the real cauldron but she also didn't have the real spoon. 'We arranged all of this with Percy when he excavated the cave behind the waterfall; Salazar was able to go and collect the real spoon while everyone else had their eyes on the one that we made-up to dupe the witch.'

'What witch?' more than one of the others chorused.

Ogwin went on to explain to Tiala's people that the witch they thought they'd left on earth had actually now made her presence known here – below it. 'The Jackal's body had been taken over by Mad Mab when they were hiding in the cave. We could see it was Mab and we believe Merlin and maybe Salazar could as well; she was extremely well hidden inside his body but not well enough to fool us.

'Anyway, the rainbow fell across the small cave and we were hiding with the false spoon almost at the right spot to go and hide it inside when the end of the rainbow fell there. We had merely to place it inside the cave and hide. What everyone else didn't know was that we had already found the real one inside the cave with the waterfall and the other end of the rainbow was inside the cave. Salazar merely walked over to the boulder upon which it landed, saw the cavity behind it and thus retrieved the real spoon where Percy had hidden it. So, all is well; Merlin has the real spoon and we have the real cauldron.'

'Perhaps we'd better see if we can get back to Merlin,' I suggested, relieved that it wasn't my fault any more. And so it was that as soon as daylight came King Ogwin sent half of his band on ahead with instructions of what they should prepare themselves to do once he arrived – but how they got off that ship in the middle of nowhere I am still puzzling about – while the rest of us headed back toward Raven's Harbour as we believed that that would be where Merlin would return.

Cabby took me round the ship and it was great fun hiding behind things that I couldn't see but still be well and truly hidden behind them. We and a few of the others played one or two games of hide-and-seek but I soon got fed up because Cabal always won – I just didn't have his sense of smell – but he could smell me a mile off. I remembered the time he first smelled the witch and had nearly passed out; his sense of smell was hundreds, if not thousands, of times stronger than mine.

We were just finishing a game and had come round opposite sides of the corner beside the main cabin when a sound penetrated our brains, and by "our" I mean mine, Cabby and Tiala's minds. She was resting amid a pile of cushions when Cabby and I rushed around the corner on either side of her – me trying to hide and Cabby pursuing.

'I know you're near. Answer me!'

Tiala opened her eyes at our sudden approach and looked from me to Cabby. Not knowing that I, too, had this special gift of the Old Way, she spoke only to the hound.

'What is that Cabby? Someone is trying to speak to us!'

'I don't know,' he replied. *'I've never heard that voice before. I don't think it's anyone on board as apart from Queen Gisele, and I know her voice, and us; oh, and Percy, of course...'*

Tiala looked quickly up at me before Cabal carried on.

'...there is no-one else.'

'Oh, I didn't know...'

'Sorry, Tiala, neither did I, about you, I mean. But let me put your minds at rest; the voice you just heard came from a pirate on the Raven's ship called Pick.'

'Hello Percy. So you did hear me?'

'Yes, we heard you. Why are you trying to contact us?'

'Where are you? You must be close now as I've been trying to call you for ages.'

'We passed the Swamplands yesterday and are heading for Raven's Harbour. Where are you?'

'Very near you, I should think, and we, too, are headed for the Harbour. Why are you going to Raven's Harbour? Have you seen the Jackal?'

It was at this point that I thought it best to say nothing more as I had no idea what the other ship and its crew were plotting. I turned to Tiala and Cabal with my fingers raised to my lips and, with more sign language, told them to close their minds to Pick's probing.

'I think the witch has captured the Jackal but I don't know where they are.'

Then their ship, or should I say two ships, came into view. I signalled to Bohai to come over to me and, with all my barriers in place, explained who they might be, suggesting that everything that wasn't invisible should be hidden; we mustn't at any cost be seen and must stay as still in the water as we could. He nodded and turned to give orders to the rest of the crew.

We conversed with Pick for a short while longer but it soon became evident that none of us wanted to give anything away and so with a cheery mental farewell from Pick we closed our minds off to him.

As Tiala was moved back into her cabin, Cabby and I ducked down behind the prow and watched as the two ships sailed on before us. We believed that their lookouts would be watching what was in front of them more than what was behind and we couldn't take the risk of them seeing the wake that would have shown very clearly behind our ship. Once they had passed us we set the sails again and, moving within their wake, followed them from a distance.

As evening drew near, we judged that the cloak and safety of night would bring the lights of the harbour into view. We needed to anchor as near to the quayside as possible so that we didn't have to row too far to reach the quayside but also far enough away so that no sharp eye would detect us or maybe an early fishing boat bump into us.

But we needn't have worried; nothing untoward happened as we finally crept into the harbour.

Pick kept trying to call out to us but we kept silent. We didn't want him to give us away, even though we knew he couldn't speak or write; but you never knew whether, by some fluke, he might give the game away or whether there might be someone else listening in. The witch, I knew, had the power to pick up the odd word or two and who knew where she was at the moment? No, we had to take care.

Slowly and silently we lowered the anchor whilst searching the quayside for signs of life. There were now three ships tied up alongside each other but, apart from two lookouts on each, there didn't seem to be anyone else around; even the lookouts were a waste of time – not one of them was awake even if he was sober.

Other ships were missing, someone had said as we rode at anchor, and so nothing would happen until they appeared. I wasn't sure what was meant and soon forgot it as sounds of shouting and laughter were heard from the square where it was noticed that the buds on the tree were just about to burst into flower. At that time I didn't know much about the Contest so couldn't understand the excitement that the tree evoked in almost everyone else.

Bohai and Shen lowered an almost invisible rowing boat down into the water and jumping inside whispered that they would see what was going on and then come back. Tiala, whose strength and solidity was much improved, thanks to Queen Gisele, leaned over the side of the ship and told them to take care and hurry back, watching until they covered themselves with an invisible blanket and disappeared from view.

King Ogwin and Queen Gisele had also joined them as they left, skipping nimbly down the side of the ship and, together with the rest of their subjects, landing lightly in the stern of the little boat.

'We're going to meet up with our army,' the Queen had whispered into Tiala's ears as she'd danced past her. 'We'll meet them at the Contest.'

And then, with muffled oars, the two men rowed slowly towards the jetty.

FORTY-EIGHT

Merlin's ship had sailed into Raven's Harbour earlier that afternoon. They'd charted their course into the quayside by the light of the three taverns and moored without being challenged by anyone; its original captain must still be drowning his sorrows for losing his ship! Having already been given their orders, everyone carried them out with a precision that any captain would have been proud of.

Once they'd disembarked, Merlin, Salazar and Arthur made their way directly inside the Blue Pelican with four of the guards; the rest of the guards and all of the former galley slaves skirted the area behind the inns and hugging the walls crept along their sides until some of its customers came out.

They didn't have to wait long. Two men stood ready either side of the door so as to move forward and grab anyone who came through it – most were drunk, so there was hardly a struggle – and then they ran him off to the water's edge and threw him in. There was more of a struggle in the water than out of it as the serpents, who very rarely had anything to eat from the harbour itself except the rubbish that was thrown into it, were in for a rare treat tonight and were jostling one another out of the way to catch the falling prey. The screams were awful but were swiftly cut off. As each inebriated patron emerged there were always two of Merlin's men ready to escort him to the harbour's edge. So it wasn't long before the Blue Pelican had a new owner, bartender, staff and clientele, the latter looking the worse for drink but not having touched a drop.

'We are not out to cause mayhem just for the fun of it, men, but to make the best of what we can in this awful place. Once we have achieved this, you will all be free to go; and if I were you I wouldn't touch the drink again – I should imagine it's being drunk that got you manacled to those oars in the first place, eh? And you have only to look at this inn's previous customers to see how weak they were because of it!'

There was a general nodding of heads and a few sighs but they were determined to stay out of trouble from now on.

A little later, Merlin and Salazar, standing outside the Blue Pelican, leaned nonchalantly against the wall and watched as more ships moved into the harbour and docked. Finally ducking back into the doorway of the inn they kept a wary eye on the men as they disembarked. The first off the gangplank of the biggest vessel was a large man with a huge hat sporting a foppish feather, all of which seemed to slip slightly sideways as he strode across the square and was continually and hastily being pulled back into place. Brosc and Wite and a funny little man whose eyes darted here and there as he seemed to search out minds accompanied him.

Merlin grabbed Salazar's wrist; nodding towards Pick, Salazar understood the warning and closed his mind to the man.

The Druids were still in their disguises, so Brosc and Wite stared straight through them without any sign of recognition as they headed towards the Minstrel closely followed by Nell's son, Shake Spear and Tailor from the second ship; Tailor looked over at Merlin, who could see him start to raise his hand to wave, but after a hasty warning sign he carried on towards the Minstrel along with the others, the raised hand pretending to straightening his hat. Just outside, the Raven stopped and, pointing to the two other inns, directed Brosc and Wite to the Nest to see what was going on there and Nell's son and Mongrel to the Blue Pelican. 'And get back here without delay! There's no time to be lost,' he shouted over his shoulder at them.

As Nell's son and Mongrel pushed through the doors, everyone stopped and stared at them. They would have felt very uncomfortable indeed if Merlin hadn't moved forward to greet them. Nell's son almost did a double take as he stared and then stared again.

'Merlin – it is you isn't it?' he croaked; and then, clearing his throat, repeated his name again, grinned and hugged the sorcerer. Still smiling and nodding over at Salazar and Arthur, he asked, 'How on earth… ?'

'Hush now,' Merlin quieted the man. 'We're not on earth, so things are very different down here. I'll explain later – there is too much to do right now. Salazar and Arthur will get you up to date with things while I get on. But, who's this?' he asked looking down at Mongrel.

Nell's son explained as Merlin stared, nodding as the tale progressed and then, cutting him short, told Honey that he'd sort everything out as soon as he could but that she would be her normal self by morning at the latest.

'I shall be back soon but right now, I'm going over to the Minstrel. Now, you stay here with the others. As soon as I can arrange things with Shake Spear and Tailor, I'll come back. Keep an eye out for trouble, Salazar, and call me if there is.'

Salazar nodded and watched his friend amble over to the other hostelry.

Merlin pushed the door open to find Shake Spear, as the Minstrel, being clapped on the back and being asked a million and one questions as to where he'd been and they'd missed his stories and who were his friends and would he like a drink. Merlin stood and watched this going on until the Raven, losing patience, asked if anyone had seen the Jackal.

It went deathly silent and one ugly looking customer – Black Dog – stared hard at him and said that no-one had and no-one wanted to and if the so-and-so should show his face round here he, personally, would wring his head off his neck, throw it in the harbour and then sail as far away as he could to throw the rest of him somewhere else. 'Then it'll take him forever to get himself back together again,' he bellowed.

Merlin recognised the man as one of the erstwhile captains that had lost out because the Jackal had not returned.

The Raven – not one to be put down, let alone by one as ugly as him – pushed his stubbly chin into the other man's face and, wig and hat only slightly askew – warned him to watch his tongue before it joined Pick's in the pickled aubergine jar.

Now you can just imagine how Pick's eyes lit up at this bit of welcome information. He knew the captain hadn't really tossed his tongue overboard because if he had it would have come back to him long before now but that he must have hidden it somewhere and up to that moment he hadn't known where – and sliced aubergines did look a little like tongues so he'd not even thought of looking in there, though he'd searched high and low everywhere else. He couldn't wait to get back to the ship. Then he noticed the captain staring at him. 'And don't you even think about it Pick or I might slice off a bit more of you and this time really chuck it over the side! No,' he grinned with sudden inspiration, 'I'd burn it and then you'll never get it back!'

Poor Pick felt crushed.

Turning back to the ugly man, the Raven continued his stand off. 'I think everyone should know that the Jackal has a trained dragon at his beck and call. He got carried off by this dragon and got past the guardians of the river. I imagine, even now, that he has got the treasure; so, if anyone knows where he is they should say. We need to band together as one, find him and fight now or he will take over everything and then we'll all suffer.'

The other man's face changed when he heard what the Raven had to say; he pulled his face away from the man and, standing up, roared with the rage that for weeks had been building up inside him and threatening to explode. 'Is he going to get away with everything?'

'Not if we forget our differences and work together.'

'We've never done that; it wouldn't work. You'd never take orders from me and I certainly won't take orders from you!'

'It's the only way!' the Raven's voice became more persuasive. 'If we don't, he'll win. And no-one has to take orders from anyone; we can discuss things and decide together.'

Black Dog's mouth dropped open at this. It was unheard of. No-one discussed anything down here – it was always serve or be served, steal or go hungry and fight, fight, fight – no grey areas! But, after considering it, even he could see the sense of it.

'Then let's sit down and talk,' Black Dog ushered the Raven over to a table near the fire, calling for the landlord to bring over some vittles, 'and some of that strong brew,' he yelled.

Merlin had made his way silently round the room until he stood immediately behind Shake Spear and Tailor. While the fracas between the captains had been in progress he'd whispered his instructions to the two men, who'd nodded almost imperceptibly now and then but, as directed, did not turn around. So it was that, almost without being noticed by anyone else, Merlin came in and went out, having achieved his aim.

I often wonder if he still does this today – in the 20th Century, I mean – but being caught up in the business of life we just don't see him. But *I* know he's there! Sometimes I've imagined that I may have heard him whisper something in my ear and have then shaken my head and smiled, thinking it all a figment of my imagination again, only to find that later on that day what I'd imagined I'd heard actually happens. Like the time I thought he'd told me to take the long trek home from school; I'd shrugged my shoulders and, being tired and my usual lazy self, started on my normal route only to find that the river had swollen, the bridge had been swept away and I couldn't get across. Well, as you can imagine I had to walk all the way back and then round the long way to get home. Halfway it started raining and I was cold, wet and starving hungry when I finally arrived home.

It wasn't until I was tucked up in bed that night that I thought I heard a faint tut-tutting echoing from a long way off and then I remembered thinking I had heard him speak to me earlier that day. I was a lot more conscious of being obedient to those "imaginings" after that.

Smiling and humming one of his tuneless tunes, Merlin walked back across the square to the Blue Pelican noticing, out of the corner of his eye, a shimmering, or an almost shifting of elements, some fifty yards or so offshore. Without letting anyone know that he was doing it, he tuned in to that movement until he was sure of what it was. And so, continuing to hum, he went back through the doors of the Blue Pelican.

FORTY-NINE

Mab was by now getting very irritated by the confining body of the Jackal and it was with a huge effort she stopped herself shrugging out of it. 'Not long now,' she told herself, 'and then I can dispose of him completely.' She chuckled and then, turning back to the dragon, ordered him to take her to Raven's Harbour. 'Put me down in the square,' she barked. 'I want to make a grand entrance.'

The dragon spoke back – well it was more a roar – and the witch was finding it increasingly intimidating when he did so as she had not been used to it before. 'I'd like to put you down completely. That would give you a grand exit, eh Mab!'

'Ahhh, not so loud. I can't stand it,' she yelled back at him, trying to ignore the threat. 'It's too much!'

'It would never do if I deafened you Mab! You would then not hear my threats; you would then not learn to fear me; you would then not tremble when you heard me approach!'

It did cross Mab's mind that there was just a tingle of apprehension dancing up and down her spine where he was concerned, but then, her pride getting the upper hand again she told herself that soon she wouldn't need him any more and would completely dispose of him this time without a second's hesitation. Well at best he'd be left here in the place of the dead where he was confined, as were all the dead, for all eternity and she would return to rule above the earth, would become supreme and would fear no-one; they would all fear her; at worst – well he'd probably just cease to exist – then again, which was the better option?

To be able to rule forever and to live forever all she needed to do was get rid of Arthur and me – her nemesis, she called me. She knew of necessity she had to get rid of Arthur and would do so as soon as the opportunity arose, but I was just a nuisance – and her times of daydreaming existed of thinking up pleasurable ways to dispose of me at her leisure.

Struggling to put all this out of her mind, as at the moment her rage threatened to unhinge her again, she took a deep breath, shrugged her shoulders merely reiterated, 'Just get me to Raven's Harbour, Hellion.'

FIFTY

Merlin left Salazar in charge of the Blue Pelican after telling him what he'd said to Shake Spear and Tailor. 'I'm going to visit the Nest now and see what is happening over there. Keep alert, my friend; you never know what might happen next in this place.

'Tiala and some of the others are nearby; they're a little way out in the harbour and their ship is invisible – well, almost invisible but I can see it. They need to be very careful as Mab might latch on to the fact that it's there; any untoward movement she'll not miss!'

'Can we get out to her?'

'No, Salazar – it's best we draw no attention to them. You never know what might happen if we give them away!'

Salazar stood in the doorway of the inn and watched Merlin make his way over to the Nest; his eyes scanned the horizon – well, what could be seen of it at night – and, like Merlin he, too, could just about make out the shimmering, or shifting, a little way out from the quayside. *'Take care, my friend,'* Salazar whispered.

'I will,' came the response.

'Are you there, Merlin?'

'Percy! Is that you?'

'Yes – and Cabal is with me! We're with Tiala!'

'Yes, I'm here, too,' Cabal replied.

'Ooh, who's that?' Pick tuned in.

'Shut down now!'

'Oh, don't do that! I haven't had a good conversation since the last time Percy spoke to me! Hello! Oh hello-o.'

But we all closed our minds to Pick; he kept on trying to break through and even though we could hear him promising not to give us away, I knew we would have to leave it up to Merlin to give the go ahead. But he did not.

So it was going to be much later that we would be able to catch up. It was very frustrating knowing that I was able to communicate with Merlin once again but could not because of Pick. Well, I knew that Merlin would eventually sort it all out so I just needed to be patient.

The man himself had by now reached the doorway of the Nest and pushing open the door recognised the scruffy manager of the bar – his hair had grown profusely since the last time he'd been in there and might now be large enough to house a whole family of eagles. The smell of smoke – more like old socks being roasted – hung in the air like a heavy curtain and gave way grudgingly as Merlin made his way up to the counter. Brosc and Wite were sitting at a table near the fire, talking to two skinny men who didn't appear to be too happy that they were being interrogated. A burly man – in fact Merlin recognised him as the man who had wanted to take Cabal off to the slaughterhouse – with a scar across his bare chest (a sabre cut, Merlin guessed) came thundering towards him obviously looking for trouble, (although it wouldn't have been a problem as Merlin was always able to deal with normal people – well, if one could call "dead" people "normal" and he had dealt with this one before) especially if they were off guard because of having either lost their temper anyway or because they had a permanent short fuse but he was saved this time by at least twenty manifestations. Everyone turned at once at the whooshing sound, that was soon followed by crunches and bumps when they appeared initially by falling from, well, nowhere really, down onto the top of the bar counter just to Merlin's right or in front of or behind it or on top of someone and, with arms flailing, all bounced a couple of times before landing in various heaps on the floor. Once they reached the ground they jumped up, some with hair alight or bodies steaming with black smoke, and, whilst patting out the flames, stared bug-eyed all around them.

'Where are we? How did we get here? Where's everybody gone?' and, 'Which idiot lit the fuse?' There were other questions and exclamations but soon, once they'd taken stock of their new surroundings, they all stood silent and in a state of shock – every face showing complete bewilderment.

Order was eventually restored when the burly man, turning away from Merlin, grabbed hold of two of the newcomers and, ordering the rest to follow, took them all out into a back room to the accompaniment of "don't usually get as many as that in one go" or "strange clothes" or "we'll get less booze now" and the like.

Brosc and Wite had jumped up all agog at the bizarre things that were happening before them. The two men who'd been sharing their table slunk off unobserved while they had the chance, relieved that they didn't have to answer any more of their questions.

As the scarred man ushered the new arrivals through into the other room, Merlin made his way over to his friends and sat down, waiting for them to return to their seats, which eventually they did.

They showed surprise as they turned to sit down at the fact that one strange man had taken the place of the other two men who weren't there anymore and, after the initial shock, looked around to see where they might have gone but neither exhibited any recognition of Merlin.

'I'm sorry, sir,' Brosc stammered, almost sitting down and then standing up again. 'We didn't know this was your table. Excuse us; we'll sit elsewhere.'

Merlin moved his hand directly over his face and the two men, once more goggled as they saw the face of Merlin appear and then disappear as he moved his hand back the other way.

After a shocked silence they both let out a sigh of relief at finding at least one of their original party but before they gave the game away Merlin held up his hand, palm facing them, commanding silence.

'Sit down men,' he ordered them. 'I am in disguise so you will have to pretend that it wasn't me when you leave this place. I've already spoken to Shake Spear and Tailor; Salazar is getting Nell's son up-to-date with the plan and now I shall inform you of the part you two have to play – but you mustn't give anything away to the Raven. Right?

They both nodded.

'OK, then. This is what you are to do.

FIFTY-ONE

'OK men. Quiet now! SHUT UP!' Shake Spear finally got their attention as he jumped up onto the bar inside the Minstrel. 'That's better.' Turning to introduce Ambrosius to the gathered assembly who, it must be admitted, didn't like having their drinking time interrupted, he started to let them know that the tree had now blossomed and that the morrow would bring the Contest. 'We have something more than just ships to fight for this time, men! We have the Treasure!'

There were gasps all round as tankards stopped halfway to lips and those walking about stopped dead, so to speak, in their tracks.

The Raven and Black Dog had almost come to blows several times as each one mocked the other's ideas on how to overcome the Jackal; they had been slumped for the last hour over several, now empty, jugs of beer, getting more and more despondent as each plan became more ridiculous than the one before. So it was that now, with hopeless expressions on both their faces, they looked up at this newcomer with the strangely piercing eyes. Black Dog could hardly lift his head, the depression hanging very heavily upon him, while the Raven was finding it increasingly difficult to focus.

Now having all their attention, Shake Spear went on to confide, conspiratorially, that they all had a good chance of not only getting at least one of the ships each but the Treasure as well – and Ambrosius was the man to show them how.

'Who's he? And how can someone who's only been here five minutes know about the Treasure or where it can be found? Seems funny to me!'

'Now, now, men,' Shake Spear spoke gently to Black Dog. 'Let's just listen to what he has to say eh? I mean, none of us has managed to find it so far, so let's see what he knows first.'

For half an hour it went really quiet in the Minstrel; men could be found huddled around hastily pushed together tables, occasionally nodding, occasionally asking questions, but all appearing to be in full agreement with what the strange man was saying. Even Black Dog's face showed a little animation and, could it be, hope?

Finally ending with, '…so I am now going to go to the other two inns to confuse them; you will then be sure to win tomorrow.'

''Ere – and just why are you doing this for us and not them and what's in it for you and 'ow do we know we can trust you anyway?' one brawny man shoved his toothy face into Merlin's, showering him with spittle.

'Now, now, Hyena, I know him and know you can certainly trust him. Would I lie to you? Besides, if you aim correctly enough tomorrow you'll drown everyone who tries to fight you!' Everyone laughed at Shake Spear's quip as he slung an arm around the man who grudgingly moved away from Merlin and then, before sitting down, started laughing like a drain himself, or should I say like the hyena he was obviously named after, and continued spraying spittle in every direction he faced.

'Sorry Minstrel,' he gasped between guffaws, 'but it's been so long since I had a ship, I thought there must be a catch.'

'*Oh man,*' Merlin thought, wiping the spit off his cheek with the back of his sleeve. '*If only you knew!*'

FIFTY-TWO

'We know the witch has been disguising herself as the Jackal and will most probably continue to do so at the Contest. What we need to do is make sure the other captains don't all gang up on her at once. But, from what Shake Spear has told me, it doesn't work like that. Apparently all the captains pick straws and decide where they want to make their stand and almost everyone wants to be in front of the Blue Pelican, and then the other inns so that they have something solid at their backs; when all the inns have been picked the other three captains have to choose a place for themselves and their men along the quayside. Then the Contest begins. It's awful as they use every imaginable weapon for hand to hand fighting – clubs, knives, swords, balls and chains – nothing that can be thrown as that would then leave them weaponless. Shake Spear said it's really weird as no-one down here has any blood – when people get their heads chopped off or a hand or something it doesn't bleed; the amputated part just drops to the ground. Now one of the things that the winner has to do is grab that part of the body and toss it into the sea before it has the chance to join back up again, so that his victim is disarmed! Disarmed!' Merlin's lips twitched at that! Disarmed?' He coughed trying to keep his wit in check. 'Now I don't know how he knows that, as he hasn't been down here long enough to have seen a Contest, but then again he seems to know a lot about the place; but apparently that's how it works! Hmm, I expect it's all part of his weird manifestation as the Minstrel! I wonder if there really was someone called Minstrel! Now that's a thought – surely Shake Spear hasn't been taken over by him, like the Jackal! No, I'd know if that had happened.'

'So, what happens after that?' Salazar asked, bringing him back to the point in question.

'The Year with the most men standing wins the Contest. They will then decide which six men from that year are to captain each vessel and then those six pick straws to choose the galleon they want until all six ships have been taken.'

By now Merlin had spoken to all the men in the Nest and the Minstrel. The burly man had got his newfound friends up to speed with what was about to happen and they were by now all fired up and sharpening their weapons in readiness for the fight.

'I think we should return to the Blue Pelican and get our own men ready.'

FIFTY-THREE

The trumpeting brought everyone bursting out of the inns and into the square, elbowing each other out of the way in order to get the best vantage point for the upcoming fight. But they'd got it wrong! It wasn't the signal to begin the Contest but the sound came from a more frightening source, so instead of standing their ground in readiness for the fight and putting on their best grimaces or practising their roars and yells, most of them lost face when they flattened themselves to the cobblestones in fear or elbowed everyone out of the way in order to get back inside the inns.

The dragon, tail swishing through the air, swept the ground angrily and dusted the sides of the inns with his wings before soaring high again. Many so-called brave men rushed back inside the nearest buildings or ducked behind any safe barricade; some were just rooted to the floor with fear – not a good idea as they were soon to find out; it took many a long time to recover from being batted around the square like skittles.

The witch, still clothed from head to toe in Jackal, shouted up at the dragon to cease before screeching up at him to set her down as near to the flowering tree as it could – a difficult task, as he was much bigger than the whole area.

'A magnificent entrance,' she called out to anyone near enough to hear; they were all near enough as she was still in screech mode. However, it was the Jackal they all heard and the Jackal they all saw who alighted from the wing of the fantastical beast. Black Dog, seeing his arch enemy – the thief of his ship, was striding out through the door of the Minstrel and it was all the Raven could do to pull him back.

'I'm going to sort that man out right now!' he muttered, struggling to free himself from the Raven's grip as he was pulled back into the inn. 'Let me go! It's been too long! He's for it and I mean right now!'

The Raven just about managed to drag him back inside and had to shout right into his ear that if he did so, all their plans would be brought to nought.

The extremely dark expression on Black Dog's face gradually eased as the sense of what the Raven was saying penetrated his overreacting and red-misted senses. Eventually flopping down into a chair, he let out a huge sigh and grudgingly thanked the man for cooling him down.

'We have to wait until we get the signal,' he told the still red-faced man. 'It will all work out – you'll see! Come, let's watch through the doorway.'

The two men leaned over the stable doorway to see what was going to happen next.

The Jackal was offloading something from the dragon's back and setting out various bits and pieces on one of the occasional stone slabs beside the tree. Two or three people who had taken refuge beneath those tables were creeping away to a hopefully more secure hidey-hole.

Once instructed, the dragon shook a wing and down its dull scales rolled a large pot that eventually came to rest just below one of the flowering branches.

'Blast – I can't see properly; the tree's now in the way!' Black Dog was starting to get agitated again.

'Well, let's go out and stand down the sideway,' the Raven suggested.

The two men and, well, nearly everyone else from the inn for that matter, followed them out and down the sideway, all trying to see what was happening over everyone else's shoulder.

Why they didn't rush the Jackal could only be attributed to Merlin's strict instructions and that the plan would go completely wrong and they'd not get the treasure if they did. So they waited – and watched.

By now the small stone table was loaded with bottles, phials, a huge book and a couple of scrolls, together with a large lamp, which was lit; beside it sat a huge pot and, underneath it, a pile of tinder with wood stacked nearby.

Mab, though looking engrossed in what she was doing, still kept a wary eye on all that was going on around her; she knew that the people here were desperate, mostly mad and had nothing – absolutely nothing – to lose and that a sudden rush might just be too much for even her to cope with. The dragon had moved off some way along the quayside; she could see his neck and head raised above the roofs of the sheds near the edge of the harbour but realised that she could now not count on him one hundred percent – he appeared to have a will of his own these days. Muttering under her breath at this turn of events she carried on observing everything around her. She had a quite powerful bowl of powder handy and all she had to do was hold it in her hand and say the spell whilst looking at her attacker. They would stop dead in their tracks, freeze, crack and then fall into a pile of splinters where they had once stood. Very effective but if there were too many it might prove difficult. However, her natural faith in her own ability took control and she carried on with what she was doing.

What she wanted to do was take control of all the ships. *'This is the Year of the Witch,'* she chuckled to herself, *'so none of you other Years will get a look in. In fact, you are never going to get a look in again! I'll see to that right now!'*

Screwing up her face with just a twinge of annoyance, she threw a blue-flamed ball up into the air; it went higher and higher as she chanted a spell until it burst into myriad of stars. Of course there were 'oohs' and 'ahhs' like there are at any fireworks display before, with a tinkling sound, golden coins dropped to the ground, bouncing and rolling until they stopped near the edge of the square.

Greed is a terrible thing! Four men, all of whom had been warned of what to expect, rushed out to pick up the gold. Big mistake! As soon as they had them in their hands they were enslaved. Some of the other men were shouting at them to leave well alone: "Don't touch!" "Come back!" But zombie-like they walked towards the witch who merely waited until they stood before her.

'Now,' she barked, 'pick up the tinder and light it; then, when it is well and truly alight, lay the wood on top of it. *Why didn't I think of this before? It would have saved so much hard work for me!'* She waited until the fire had died down to a red glow – I mean, she didn't want to melt her pot – before she got them to lift the cauldron onto its support. She waited until the metal became warm before returning to the table.

Turning over the pages of her huge book at the places she'd marked, Mab started measuring this and pouring in that until bubbling could be heard coming from within the cauldron's depths; coloured mists started to rise from within it and then it all started to get confusing.

The men didn't know what to do; they'd watched the Jackal alight from the dragon's back, not appearing to be the man they knew, and this uncertainty kept them glued to the spot. Not one of them wanted to be the first to chance his luck with him; they'd seen what he'd done to the men who'd chased after the gold – gold which was now shrivelled and crusty – like dried leaves. The men themselves were at that moment propped up against the tree as though asleep. So the rest just watched.

The mists rising from the pot began twisting into shapes, the shapes solidified – it soon became very clear that the Jackal was building his army. Rank upon rank rose out of the cauldron and began to fill the square; some of the onlookers recognised old foe: the Archers raised themselves high upon their hoofed feet as they landed before taking their places behind the Swordsmen. They didn't appear too frightening at the moment as they still had their weapons sheathed but those that had come across them before knew they need be very afraid; some crept away up the side streets – the fight for the ships seemed not worth the trouble any more. But, for the ones that remained, how on earth were they going to defeat this foe? And then, if that wasn't enough, the skeleton men and women began to appear, rising up and forming from the green smoke that now rose from within its depths; they clattered briefly as they landed in front of the other adversaries, taking their stand and keeping very, very still, their fleshy heads grinning back at the men from the Years who, with bulging eyes, were staring at them mesmerised.

FIFTY-FOUR

And then it began.

It had become apparent that the Jackal was determined to win again and must now be using darker forces than any that had been used before. Most of the captains were unsure of themselves but knew that the fight was worth the pain, so, egging each other on with yells, roars and beatings of chests and sword upon shield, they and their men took their places and readied themselves for this different type of Contest.

The Minstrel stood upon a dais that had been erected just outside his inn and raised a red silk scarf high above his head. As soon as everyone was in place, he blew a horn, dropped the scarf and the men, obedient at last to their lust for power, prestige and vengeance, rushed the Jackal with swords flashing, balls and chains swirling and all sorts of evil looking weapons spinning and crunching. The men, and some of the women, were yelling, roaring and screaming as they ran across the square towards their foe, urged on by those who were unable to fight as they called encouragement from around the square.

The Archers and the Swordsmen were very fast and adept at their craft – feinting here and leaping there; cutting and thrusting with their swords or aiming their arrows with cunning and an accuracy that would put Robin Hood to shame; the Swordsmen lopping off heads and arms as though they were made of straw – which body parts just bounced along the cobblestones, the heads like hard footballs and the hands still trying to grab onto something until their twitchings stopped.

The Contest was going very wrong for all the pirates and captains who thought they'd had a good chance to win this time round and the ground was soon littered with convulsing bodies; many of the sailors decided it was time to quit and could hear the Jackal roaring with laughter as they, using what little strength that remained, rushed out of the square leaving the Jackal's army almost intact. There were one or two Archers and Swordsmen who'd been wounded or killed but the majority of them had hardly been touched.

'So let me see what magic this cauldron can really achieve, now that I have the spoon!' Mab muttered. Turning to the book of spells she went directly to a page she'd marked.

'*I think it's time we acted, Prince!*'

'*I'm ready,*' he replied.

'Are you ready, Ogwin? You know what to do,' he turned to speak to the diminutive king who'd arrived around the same time as Mab. The tiny King nodded and led out his troops.

At first the witch was so caught up in preparing her elaborate concoction that she was completely unaware of the change in the atmosphere around her: she didn't hear the anxious scraping of the hooves from the Archers and Swordsmen as they looked around them or even hear the clattering of the bones from the skeleton men and women as even they became aware of something not quite right.

Merlin told me later that he was astonished and quite delighted at watching the Faerie at work. They fought like no-one or anything he'd ever seen before. They were so fast that you could hardly see them and really had to know they were there to appreciate that they actually were. He said he had to tune his mind in to fast forward so that he could see things happening at normal speed – well, normal speed for the Faerie, that is, as everyone else appeared to be moving in such extreme slow motion that they hardly seemed to be moving at all. They ran up the side of the legs of the goat-like men, pouring a concoction onto their hands which would have a peculiar effect on them: the Swordsmen's swords would rust and try as they might they would not be able to shoot their blades out of their hands again for a very long time; the Archers' bows would come out of their hands but the string would be rotted and fall away from the ends of the bows; also their arrows were becoming wedged inside their quivers as spiders, dropped inside them, weaved sticky webs that glued them together until they were stuck fast. And, so far as the skeleton men and women were concerned, they just blew Faerie dust into their eyes. Neither they nor the witch saw anything that was going on as it was all happening just too quickly for their eyes to capture and so it was, unfortunately for Mab, too late to do anything about it.

The now disabled Archers and Swordsmen took flight, disappearing up through the streets towards the Endless Hills as fast as their hooves would carry them, leaving the witch screaming dark threats after them if they didn't return – 'right now!' If she did throw some spell at them, we didn't know – their clopping soon faded until all that could be heard was the Jackal's deep, angry breath and the clattering of the skeletons.

Rushing up to the first skeleton, she grabbed her by the hair and screamed into her face – a face that was screwed up in agony by all the dust that she was trying, with bony fingers, to rub away; being jolted by the witch she lost her balance and plucked out one eye which her nail had dislodged from its socket. The witch watched slightly fascinated as it bounced across the square. Still not quite under control and showing her usual lack of compassion, she roared into the skeleton's ear, 'What's going on? What is causing all this confusion?'

The skeleton woman did not respond so the witch, exasperated, shoved her to the ground and grabbed the next one – a man. After going through another couple and still getting no joy – well she wouldn't, as they couldn't talk – Mab, never the gentlest of souls, started to chant a really nasty spell! In the back of her mind was the explanation that you have to have lungs to be able to talk, and they didn't have any so they weren't going to be able to let her know what had happened, but she was too far gone in her anger to listen to the back of her mind so she flung an enchantment at them and watched with a little sour satisfaction as they fell together into a huge pile of bones at the edge of the square, while their heads, in obedience to the spell thrown at them, bounced off into the harbour. She cocked her ear to listen for the splashes and then the inevitable rush in the water and wished the serpents well of their dinner, not noticing the mangy and skinny looking dog-like creatures that crawled upon their bellies towards the inviting stack of bones. Disappearing up alleyways there was soon no sign of the evening's cadaverous fighters. In fact the Jackal now stood alone against the people of the town.

Still not sure of what had caused the collapse of her army, the witch decided it was time to dispose of the confining body of the Jackal – this time for good. Murmuring a few chosen words, she, after the few moments of weird one-man fighting, shrugged out of his skin and tossed him into the pot.

'Now let's see what we can make of you,' she chuckled.

Engrossed in her wickedness, she didn't see, even if she saw them in the first place, the army of small people disappearing once again into the Blue Pelican. Merlin corrected the pace of his mind and vision and brought them back to everyone else's normal speed at just about the same time as the Faerie.

'Thank you, sire. I think the odds are now stacked more in my favour and I am very grateful. I would ask, though: could you make your way out to that ship and assist?' He pointed to our virtually imperceptible vessel. 'I need them to bring the ship into harbour; I want to transport the real cauldron well out of the witch's reach before she realises she has the wrong one.'

King Ogwin nodded to Merlin and in the twinkling of an eye he and his army of little men and women were gone.

Merlin walked out of the inn and stood leaning with his back to its wall. Still in his disguise he wondered if the witch would notice that it was him. She, he could see, now showed her true colours and Merlin stood amusedly watching her throw this and that on top of the Jackal. He, meanwhile, had regained much of his senses and, beginning to roar, climbed out of the pot and made a lunge at her. Well, Merlin had never seen the witch scared but for a brief few seconds fear contorted her face; however, luckily, she was holding a phial that contained the next ingredient that had been about to be poured on top of him. Overcoming that unusual feeling of panic, she pushed the whole contents of it into his face and watched with satisfaction as he dropped out of the pot and twitched violently before passing out.

Merlin started to give a slow handclap and waited for Mab to notice. It took some time as she was still congratulating herself on her defeat of the Jackal. Eventually becoming aware of the only noise in the square she screwed up her eyes to look around and find the source of it. Then she saw him! She knew who it was, even though he had tried to disguise himself. Quickly rushing in front of the cauldron to try and hide it from view and at the same time shoving the spoon down the front of her bodice, she curled her lip at him.

'So, now I know the cause of all this mayhem, Myrddin!'

'Mab, my dear,' Merlin cooed at her, knowing that this calm attitude usually caused her to lose her cool. 'I am the master of control; I think the perpetrator of chaos has to be someone else. But I must tell you that your army was not one of your more successful creations.' He waited to see how this might rile her; she was always ineffective when she lost her temper. Well, this time it only half worked; she lost her temper but not completely.

'Well, you are too late!' she screeched at him. 'You cannot win now! I have the cauldron!' At this, with a swirl of skirts she moved aside to reveal to the magician the truth of her statement, not bothering to notice the bedraggled and unsteady man who was crawling away from it. 'And not only that,' she whisked the spoon out of the front of her dress, 'I have the silver spoon!'

Merlin took a step forward but she pointed the spoon at him and commanded him to stand. He stopped.

'I don't think it wise for you to keep hold of that, Mab.'

'It has nothing to do with wisdom,' she retorted. 'It's all to do with power! Now that I have both artefacts I shall be all powerful.' She looked at him mockingly. 'Even more powerful than you, great and mighty Myrddin.' She bowed mockingly.

He took another step forward but she threw the spoon and herself into the cauldron and yelled for the dragon.

A flapping of wings, a snarling, an unbelievable roar and then Hellion was there, bending his huge head, grabbing the cauldron and its contents and they were gone, flapping out to sea in the gathering gloom; the last sight anyone had of the witch was a self-satisfied grin and a yell of. 'Just you wait and see what's going to happen to you all now!'

Looking across at where she'd once been, all that was left was a very unsteady Jackal trying hard to get to his feet and more than a handful of pirates, who were determined to wreak vengeance, closing in on him.

Ignoring all of this, Merlin returned to the Blue Pelican and called everyone over, explaining what was now going to happen. The oarsmen were told they were now free and should choose a leader as very soon he and his men would be leaving them; it was now time they began to look after themselves and get their own ship. 'Perhaps your leader could be called "the Albatross", he suggested. 'The Minstrel will commence the Contest proper in a short while now that the witch has gone and things should return a little to normal – *well, what appears to be normal in this awful place.* And don't go and get yourselves drunk again – always remember just how awful it was at those oars.'

Calling across to Shake Spear and whispering quickly to him, Merlin explained that he should get everyone that was left together and, now that the witch was gone, restart the Contest. 'Keep them all occupied, man; I have things to do and I don't want them watching. Join me as soon as you can.'

Shake Spear nodded and, clanging a gong, had all the participants lined up, once again, to start the Contest.

'You will fight for half an hour and then, when the trumpet sounds you will stop. A tally will be made of those that remain and where there are the least of a Year remaining, that Year will have to retire. Those that are left will fight for a further half hour and then another tally will be made. Finally, when there are only three Years left, you will have to nominate one contestant from each of those Years and they, as old or now new captains, will fight on in the square. They will fight until there is one winner. The winning captain will have the right to choose five previous captains or newly elected captains from his Year to take charge of the other five ships till the tree flowers again.

'Do you understand?' Shake Spear was nearly losing his voice as he tried to make sure it reached those at the back. They all nodded or called out that they did. 'Right, take your places and you can start when the trumpet sounds.'

So it was that, just as darkness was falling, which was just as well Shake Spear had thought – as if it was still daylight it would have been much too awful to watch, they took their places around the square, picked up their weapons, screwed their faces into what they hoped were some quite grotesquely fearful masks and, stamping their feet or beating their chests, worked themselves up into a fighting frenzy.

When Shake Spear left to rejoin us, he told us that there were just six contestants remaining – the Raven, Black Dog, the Unicorn, the Albatross, the Jackal and the Mule – two each from three Years. He told them to keep to the rules and stand by the judgment of the Year that wins. 'And I only just got away in time,' he added. 'I was just stepping down from my podium when I saw the real Minstrel walking back into his hostelry. He looked like he was out for trouble and he's a huge brute of a man. So I'm glad I saw him in time and got away.'

'Real Minstrel?' a few of us chorused.

'Yes. He and I had had a bit of a set-to when I first got here. Well, what I mean is not so much of a set-to but, well, I fell out of the sky on top of him and knocked him unconscious. He's been in the back shed for, well, for as long as I've been here and everyone said I had to take his place and pretend to be him or someone would come and take over the inn – it was the rules apparently – and then all hell would be let loose, and…'

'And now he's back?' Merlin interrupted.

'Um, yes! Must have come round. Still I don't want to go back there. I was getting a bit fed up with repeating my stories over and over again. And I'm sorry I didn't know I wasn't the Minstrel – must have happened when I hit my head on one of those low beams in the ceiling.'

He looked a bit sheepish but after Merlin flung an arm round him and told him it was now all right, he cheered up (and shut up, which was what Merlin had been hoping for).

Thinking back, Merlin was pleased that the Albatross was still in the Contest and hoped he would win, wondering if life would be better on the ships if he did – even in this awful, godforsaken place.

FIFTY-FIVE

The two Druids, along with those guards that had accompanied them, made their way down to the harbour. Ogwin had done well – the ship was moored and an excited dog and youth stood looking down at them.

I called out to Merlin before he was halfway across the square and watched as he raised his hand in greeting. Cabal rushed around in circles a couple of times before raising his front paws onto the side of the ship and watching the party approach.

Merlin called into my mind to try and be quiet; there were still people who could tune in whom he didn't want to know about our business.

'Oh come on,' that voice interrupted. 'I can keep a secret!'

We all locked our thought communications and waited until Merlin and the others had boarded the ship.

'Now, let's just talk normally so that he won't hear,' he said as we walked over to join Tiala and Bohai. Shen brought refreshments and over the next couple of hours everyone got everyone else up to date with what had been happening. After several hours Merlin set out the plan as to what was going to happen next and everyone was given their instructions.

'So the witch has the false cauldron but what she doesn't know is that she also has the false spoon!' He started chuckling as he recounted the way he'd swapped the real spoon for the imitation one while they were on the ship in the Valley of the Shadow and that he'd left it so that Mab would have no trouble in finding it. Then he looked over at my very pale face.

Turning even paler himself, if that were possible, he asked me what was wrong.

Beginning to shake, I stuttered out the explanation that I wished I didn't have to make and he began to fear that I would. 'I swapped the spoon too! So she now has the real one then?' I was hoping against hope that I had maybe got it wrong.

It all went very quiet and I just couldn't look into Merlin's face; though I could feel his eyes boring into my skull.

'Oh Merlin, I am so sorry; what can I do to make up for it?' Even I could just about hear myself speaking, my voice having almost deserted me.

He walked over to me and even now I can't believe how generous he was. 'Ah!' he exclaimed, looking not necessarily at me but, somehow, through me. Climbing back up from his deep reverie he brought his eyes once more back into focus and looked across at me with a little compassion. 'Now, now, young Percy, don't take on so. It's my fault entirely, as I should have told you what I had done. Maybe I would have done so if that pirate, Pick, hadn't kept picking up on our conversations. Hmm, he has the right name eh? And, young man, at least she doesn't have the cauldron.' He had flung an arm around my shoulders but now removed it and walked away deep in thought.

None of us interrupted him.

However, it wasn't long before things took yet another turn for the worse as someone else broke into his thoughts.

FIFTY-SIX

No-one saw what happened to the Jackal after he slunk away from the square while Mab was making her getaway. A few pirates had chased after him and one or two had had a pop at him but they soon returned – I mean, they didn't want to forfeit their place in the Contest. Unfortunately for the Contest, the Jackal was still the one to play unfairly and it would be another captain who would lose out once again. Creeping round the back of the Nest he waited until he found one of his men who, not wanting to be anything other than a sailor, was leaning up against the side of the building and watching the fight progress. Apart from not caring about being a captain he was, basically, not only lazy but a coward as well. So it was that he almost wet himself when a huge hand clapped itself upon his shoulder, nearly dislocating it.

'OK Piper, round up the men.'

'What? Captain!' he stuttered, getting himself back under control, 'they're nearly all fighting!'

The captain, still puffing and panting from his fight with half-a-dozen men who thought they could get the better of him, was regaining his strength and bad humour by the second; he dug his fingers quite cruelly into the poor man's shoulder muscles and, shoving his face close to the other's told him to stop wasting time and be quick about it or he'd be sorry.

With a helpful shove from his old captain, Piper moved away from his shadowy corner and sidled up to one after another of his shipmates; it wasn't long before they began, in dribs and drabs, to extricate themselves from the fight and make their way behind the Nest.

The Jackal, watching from what had originally been Piper's place of observation, soon had enough men to man the ship and pointing to the rear of the building it wasn't long before they were edging their way down to the quayside where they would soon sail off once again on a ship – he didn't care which one; just as long as they could get away. With luck he might be able to chase after that awful witch and take the treasure off her. Even so, he was determined to give her what was coming to her!

Two sets of eyes were watching these peculiar activities: one of them from the stable door of the Minstrel and the other through the window of the Blue Pelican. Both onlookers now made their way down to the harbour by different but almost parallel routes until they, almost bumping into each other behind a stack of barrels, found themselves almost beside the gangplank leading up to what was once the Raven's ship.

'Who are you?' one of them asked the other in a voice hardly above a whisper and worrying that he was discovered.

The other man – short, bald and swarthy – obviously a sailor – merely grinned and pointed into his mouth whilst shaking his head. The smaller man tried to speak to the other man using his mind but realised after only the first attempt that there was and would be absolutely no reaction; he just did not have this particular ability.

All this took place in a matter of seconds before, and without any warning, they were both lifted off their feet and hoisted aboard the ship. Again, before anyone could even draw breath, the sails were unfurled as silently as they could be and the ship crept out of the harbour.

Both men were shoved into a small cupboard on the main deck where they heard the bar drop across the doorway.

'Oh great,' Arthur moaned. 'Merlin is really going to be mad now! Why did I wait? I only wanted to watch the fight!'

The other man's eyes lit up and settling into the corner of the cupboard smiled and dropped into an almost trance-like state. Arthur tried talking to him and shaking him but got no response and so, settling down beside him, began to think of a way of escaping. *'But how – we are at sea? Even if we did get out, where on earth could we go?'*

He looked down again at the sailor slumped beside him but decided it best to rest while he could and try to think of what to do once they were let out. *'That is, if we ever are let out!'*

'Hello! Oh hello-o,' Pick reached out in his mind. *'You'd better speak to me now.'* He waited but there was no response. Trying again he added what he knew they would be powerless to ignore. *'I have one of your men with me! He said that Merlin would be mad when he found out!'*

He settled back in the cupboard and waited. He knew they would speak to him now. All they had to do was find out who was missing and then they would speak to him. He lay back, dreaming of how wonderful it would be to once again have someone to talk to. And – his eyes shot open – if he could only get to that aubergine jar; if he'd had a tongue he would be licking the saliva off his lips just thinking about getting it back.

'*OK Pick – what do you want?*'

'*Is that you, Merlin?*'

'*Yes, it is I. I take it you have Arthur with you?*'

'*I expect it is – if that is who is missing. He hasn't given me his name.*'

'*Describe him to me.*'

Pick stared at the other man through faraway eyes, exactly describing Arthur to Merlin. Salazar, Cabby, Tiala and I were listening in but had been warned by Merlin to make no comment and to definitely not open up our thought channels to Pick.

'*And where are you?*'

'*At sea.*'

'*At sea? Where? How?*'

'*We followed the Jackal and his men down to the quayside to see what they were up to. They'd crept away from the Contest, which is really not allowed, you know, so I went after him; that's where I bumped into your friend but we both got caught and taken aboard. I reckon they might just throw us overboard when we are well out to sea. I hope not 'cause it happened to me once before – when I lost my tongue – and it hurts like blazes when those serpents chew you to bits.*' He stopped for a little while, thinking, and then continued with, '*but I think it will have a worse effect on your young friend though, eh?*'

Merlin went quiet for a very considerable time. Pick had some idea of what might be going through his mind so he leaned his head back against the panelling and waited. He knew that this time they would come back and talk with him.

Merlin recounted to us verbally what had transpired. Tiala, who had been unable to hear every part of the discourse between the two, now raised a hand to her mouth and her eyes went wide with concern. The rest of us just stared at Merlin and waited for him to come up with a solution.

'Well, things are turning out quite badly at the moment. We have the witch to chase – we must get that spoon back – but, much worse than her having the spoon, we must save Arthur. If she finds out he's not under our protection any more, well who knows what will happen?'

He turned and looked at me. 'Percy, I want you and Cabal to come with me; as for the rest of you,' he looked round at the men he'd brought with him on this quest, 'I want you to take this ship and sail it back to the Valley of the Shadow: that, I believe is where we'll meet up with Mad Mab. But I must go ahead and rescue Arthur. Salazar here will let you know what you must do and he will speak to the Colossi; Nell's Son will navigate and I will meet you there.'

'But,' Tiala looked confused, 'how will you find Arthur?'

Suddenly he stopped his pacing. 'Well, I hope this will work! Having seen that awful Hellion, I believe it might! I'll call for the dragon' Merlin replied, looking down at her.

'Dragon?' more than one person echoed him.

'Moon Song,' he replied, his voice hardly above a whisper. 'We know that there are certain beings that can come and go as they please – like King Ogwin and his people,' he explained. 'I'll call for Moon Song and see if she, too, is able to come to this place. We will never catch up with the witch in these boats but with her help we might be able to reach Arthur before she does.'

And then he started that awful singing. I jumped when he began but this time I was able to put up the barriers to my thoughts before he was able to listen in to my derogatory judgment, even thought I wanted to laugh when I saw the surprised and shocked looks on Tiala and Bohai's faces – they, unlike the rest of us, had never experienced such an awful din before and it was some time before they could get their faces back under control. Nevertheless, he still turned a challenging eye toward me as he began to sing!

FIFTY–SEVEN

'But, granddad, how can Moon Song get to the place of the dead?' Daniel interrupted Jack's flow as, leaving off stroking Cabal, he pushed his hair back from his face and turned confused eyes towards his grandfather.

'Ah, well,' Jack looked thoughtful for a few moments. 'That's easy, but it turned out that it almost sent Merlin mad.'

'Mad!' both boys echoed the word and Cabal, who'd been nudging Daniel's elbow to remind him of what he'd been doing, also stopped and stared at the older man.

'Yes – mad, but are you going to let me continue?'

'Oh yes; sorry!'

'Ha! Pick!' the Jackal almost laughed, rather cruelly, as the two fugitives were brought before him. 'Lost your master, eh?'

Pick grinned rather sheepishly, nervously drawing unseen pictures on the floor with the toe of his boot, and hoped that the Jackal was not in one of his more callous moods. He needn't have worried; the Jackal was more than pleased with himself for securing one of the better ships and so, after staring at him for several moments, turned his eyes towards Arthur.

'I've seen you before,' he mused, stroking his chin. 'Where have I seen you before?'

As the question appeared more rhetorical than actual, Arthur held his tongue.

Shaking his head the Jackal decided that it wasn't important to know who he was; he was hardly more than a boy and yet there was something very familiar about him. Thinking out loud he continued as he waved a languid hand toward Pick, 'You I'll keep as you know this ship better than me or anyone else on board I reckon; the other one,' he pointed at Arthur and just as if he was deciding what pair of boots to wear today, uttered, 'hmm, I'll feed him to the fishes.'

Arthur blanched, knowing that he wouldn't stand a chance at escaping all the pirates on board this ship and also, now that they were at sea, there was nowhere he could run to. '*So this is it!*' he thought, eventually standing up as tall as he could and trying hard to show no fear.

However, he hadn't counted on Pick. He'd never met the man

before in his life, yet this little man seemed intent on keeping him alive.

Pick, grabbing Arthur's arm, turned and looked hard at the Jackal, shaking his head violently.

The Jackal looked quite amused for a second or two before asking Pick why on earth he should keep him. 'He'll only use up all the food; he's probably a spy for one of the other captains; maybe, he wants to captain this ship?'

After each point, Pick shook his head until in the end the Jackal agreed to keep him on board. 'But if I have one bit of trouble from him – over he goes!'

Pick grinned again and this time nodded.

'Now, get out of here. Redman!' he shouted, turning his face toward the door. Redman, who'd obviously been just outside, entered immediately. 'Take them out and find them something to do; Pick can show you where everything is on this ship. Perhaps the other one can go up into the crow's nest.'

Pick once again grabbed Arthur's arm and shook his head. Laughing at his antics, the Jackal, in a rare good frame of mind, agreed that the two could stay together.

'*And now I only need wait and hear from Merlin,*' Pick thought contentedly.

FIFTY-EIGHT

Then we saw her.

First the sky started to change colour – and that was a sight in itself; even though night was dark and day was light, there was never much colour in either – generally a uniform greyness cloaked everything. The sky during the day – that if there ever was a sky – was always just light: no sunrise, no sunset, no clouds, no constellations and definitely no colour.

But now the sky was, first, blue, then the blue was tinged with green, then yellow and orange until a veritable rainbow of colour lifted from the horizon and eventually shone above us.

Then she was there!

My heart caught in my throat as I saw her again – deep crimson but with such a wonderful metallic sheen that glistened and changed colour as she rippled and undulated; majestic, absolutely beautiful, powerful and so big. I had forgotten just how huge she was as she circled the ship, dwarfing it and us as she did so. She rose and swooped, joining in the song with Merlin until all that we could see was a wonderful waltz being danced to this marvellous melody of their duet. It was hard to think that Merlin, who everybody knew couldn't sing for toffee, made such a wonderful sound when joined by Moon Song.

The colours in the sky gradually softened as they merged into one and everyone watched in amazement as the dragon's circling slowed until she was finally able to settle onto the sea.

I looked on in horror thinking about the serpents and tried to call out to her in my mind that they were there and would harm her.

It was one of those "I'll remember this to the end of my days" moments when that beautiful creature turned one eye upon me and I knew; we couldn't mind speak, like I did with Cabal or Merlin and the others, but I knew what she was thinking. My fear left me and then I started laughing as I watched what was happening. It was almost like a starburst in the sea with Moon Song as the epicentre and every serpent in the area making a dash for it – if they didn't get away from this monster, it was they that would be dinner! I understood from Moon Song that there was absolutely no way they'd get even a mouthful of her beautiful body – anything that thought it could would break its teeth trying, as her body to them was like metal, yet I had experienced firsthand the silken softness of those glossy scales and trembled with excitement knowing that I was about to once again.

I was brought back to the present by a dig in the ribs from Merlin and was amazed to see that while I had been concentrating on Moon Song he and the others had cast aside their disguises and were, once again, their normal selves.

'Come along Percy; come along Cabal, we have work to do.' So, without more ado we were climbing over the bulwarks and, after drawing alongside, were sliding down Moon Song's neck. We were soon settled on her back between her wings and then we were airborne. I'm sorry, but I have to go over the top when I tell you about this because it is just so wonderful. Her scales, mostly red, glistened brilliantly and when stroking them it felt like silk; however, under all that you could sense her solid, muscular power as she flew and wow did she fly! We soared and dipped around the ship a few times, startling some and scaring many before, with Merlin whispering to her, we headed towards the Valley of the Shadow. Looking back we saw Nell's son at the wheel calling out his orders to the others; once the sails were unfurled the wind caught the sheets and the ship, finally, began its journey to meet up with us.

But we were now on Moon Song's back and were thus travelling faster than anything else in this underworld could possibly go. We would soon catch up with the Jackal, we hoped. It was imperative that we save Arthur first and then we had to get the spoon from the witch before she had a chance to use it. Still, she didn't have the cauldron so it wasn't quite as bleak as it looked.

Or was it?

FIFTY-NINE

It was well past the middle of the night when we'd first left the harbour and we sighted the ship just before morning the next day; it was in full sail and headed away from us as fast as it could travel – only a slight movement on the sea giving away the fact that it was there. Of course, the Jackal didn't stand a chance against the dragon but he had one great advantage – his ship was about to sail past the Wailing Rocks and as they couldn't make out anything at night they didn't wail and therefore couldn't warn the Colossi; well the ship sailed in, past where the Colossi usually guarded the entrance, up the channel and in through the tunnel in the rock towards the Valley of the Shadow.

Observing this, Merlin whispered to the dragon and she turned, flying low, north to the area where the Swamplands met the Red Hills; she settled down in a fairly dry clearing and we all alighted.

'Go gather some sticks, Percy. I'll find something to eat. And don't go into the Swamplands. Cabby, go with him in case he gets lost.'

Talk about stick your chest out and feel important one minute and then be brought back down to size the next! Still, I obeyed and Cabby and I strolled not too far from the dragon, whose glow lit up everything around, which didn't look very appealing as the Red Hills, to our south, still oozed thick red rivers. I shivered and tried not to look. We found some sticks but where they came from originally I have no idea; I had only seen one tree the whole time I'd been here and that was the one that budded in the square at Raven's Harbour; and again, where on earth (but then we weren't on earth, were we?) did they find the wood to build the ships?

Then it could be seen just exactly what the wood was, or was not! Dead serpents! Similar to naiad root I thought! As the naiad crawled up onto dry land and was unable to get back to water it shrivelled and died and looked very similar to the exposed roots of large trees – hence the name; now the same could be seen here, as some of the "logs" still had faces – and teeth. So that's how they got their fires and built their ships. Dawn was almost upon us and my eyes searched across the swamp – it was heaving with dead serpents – thousands of them – as far as the eye could see.

My mind was spinning when Cab and I returned.

The campfire was eventually lit and we all sat around it; I was mesmerised as I watched rows of teeth burning or cracking in the heat and wondered if I might catch sight of half-digested people. Trying not to think about it I concentrated on eating some cheese and bread while Cab gnawed on a bone.

'It's going to take the others at least all day today to get here,' he spoke quietly. I wondered why (with my barriers down) as there was no-one else around for miles to hear him except me and Cab.

'Concentrate, Percy!' he raised his voice slightly.

'Sorry!'

'They might get here too late to help us so we'll need to act as soon as it gets really light. If the Jackal has gone up the channel, he must know Mab is there and he has a double incentive: he wants the treasure and he wants to get back at her. He obviously doesn't know that he has a great bargaining tool with Arthur but he's a wily one and so I expect it won't take him long to find out just how much he's worth once the witch gets sight of him and he sees the look on her face.

'Obviously she's not going to give up her treasure but she'll be a little off guard and that might be all we'll need.' He looked across at the real cauldron and wondered if it had been wise to bring it along. If that mad woman managed to get hold of it – well, he didn't even want to think of what might happen, not only to Arthur but also to the whole of mankind. Looking across at me he told me that he'd wondered if I might even exist now or in the future – if I got killed by her now, well I would never get back to the future and then I wouldn't be sitting here with him now! He wondered whether I might not exist in the future at all or, after searching for me if I did exist, whether my parents would eventually give up and I'd be on that long list of people who'd disappeared and never been heard of again. He told me all this later, saying that the whole course of history might be changed should she gain the cauldron and, thus, ultimate power.

But, shaking his head to rid it of its negativity, he grinned and told himself that she only believed she was the most powerful of the two of them – he knew she only came second – at best!

'Get some sleep Percy – and you Cab – we need a few hours' rest before we set off once again,' he called the hound over to him.

'And you Merlin,' I urged him.

'No! I need no sleep! There are things I have to plan over the next few hours. And,' he raised his hand to stop my interruption, 'we may only have a few hours!'

Shivering at what might be the consequences if anything went wrong (and, oh, the amount of imaginings that reared their ugly heads in my mind) I accepted his declaration, giving up any attempt at persuasion and, shoving the edge of my cloak up under my head, closed my eyes, believing that sleep would evade me and I'd toss and turn for the few hours I had to rest. Ah, sweet youth! The next thing I knew was Merlin nudging me.

'Wake up Percy – now we fight!'

Rubbing my eyes to get rid of the remaining tendrils of sleep I tried to figure out where I was. It soon came crashing back into my memory and I wondered if Arthur was still all right.

'He is!' Merlin broke into my very unguarded thoughts. 'Keep your barriers up, Percy! You never know who might be listening in.'

'How do you know, then, that he's OK?' I asked out loud.

'I spoke with Pick, very briefly, just a few moments ago. They are still on board as the Jackal needs Pick's knowledge of the ship and Pick made it very clear to the Jackal that he needed Arthur. So everything is well for now. But it won't be when the witch sees him. So we have to move. Come along, get yourself ready – and you, too, Cab. I want to go at once.'

I don't know why, but I found myself looking at Merlin more intensely than I normally did; well, I mean, I always looked at him but it's like in a family when you are all seated round the dinner table – you eat, talk and look up but don't really take in the fact that they are there because you know that they are and they are just so familiar that you don't really look at them closely any more. Well, I mean, how many times do you look across at your mum or your brother and really look at every part of their face? You just don't! And being a child or young you are mostly caught up in your own problems, needs or wants and don't really care about anyone else. Oh the selfishness of youth!

But I did now as I looked across at Merlin. His face, normally pale, was almost transparent and his eyes were slightly red-rimmed. What had happened to him? Was he ill? Had he been crying? Did he know something that was very bad? Was Arthur really all right? Was *I* going to be all right? Did he know something bad was going to happen? Was it going to happen to me? Oh – we were not going to get back home, were we? Or perhaps it was just me that was not going to get home! I wasn't going to see my mum and dad anymore!

I'd let my barriers down again and, even though his eyes were very sad, they bored into mine as he told me to watch my thoughts.

'Everything is fine, I've worked out my plans and,' he slung an arm round my shoulder as he helped me up onto Moon Song's back, 'you will be told everything as and when you need to know. So,' trying to smile (it was very sad and lopsided) he climbed up after me and called Cabby up, 'let's go and flummox the witch.'

Pick had had a wonderful night. He had spent nearly an hour conversing with the strange man who had obviously been flying on the dragon that the captain had managed to evade as darkness fell. Oh what joy to be able to use the brain he'd been given; to be able to exercise that intelligence that no-one believed he had; they'd all considered him a moron because he had to act out his words in mime and, being short, with a comical looking face anyway, they'd all laughed at him. He'd put up with it because there wasn't anything else he could do about it. None of them were at all aware of how hurt and angry he felt inside or even, on a darker note, how he'd spent hours devising ways to get back at them. But he felt different after his conversation with Merlin and it was a very contented Pick that woke up early that morning; also he had some of his own plans to set in motion.

Arthur awoke about the same time and took mere seconds to remember where he was but, unlike Pick, almost allowed despair admittance. How on earth was he going to get away? And where on earth was this place? He looked over the sides of the ship and at the vaguely remembered valley; then over to the waterfall before it came flooding back to him. Then he saw the dragon! None of them had noticed it at first, which was very strange as it covered almost all the valley. It could, he supposed, have been mistaken for hills, as it was similar to the colour of chalk and as still as they would have been before a slight wisp of smoke from its nostrils concentrated everyone's stare to its head.

'So – I expect the witch is around,' Arthur thought. 'I hope she doesn't know I am. Why is she always trying to kill me?'

Pick, knowing Arthur had no skill at all at mind speaking and would not be able to answer him, was still able to pick up most of what the other man was thinking and decided, for some reason of his own no doubt, to keep him hidden, 'for his own good – or maybe mine!'

Beckoning Arthur to follow, he made his way down to the lower deck where food was being distributed. Arthur had forgotten how hungry he was and though he had no idea what it was he was eating, ate everything that was given to him, feeling better as he washed it down with some not very fresh water.

By the time they'd all been fed, the ship had nosed its way out of the tunnel where they now spied out the land; the Jackal decided that through sheer weight of numbers they would overcome the witch. At that time he had merely believed her to be someone who was clever at hypnotism or maybe drugged people so that they would do what she wanted or used some other piece of trickery; he believed that if they didn't look directly at her or were able to rush her, they would prevail. However, he was still very confused at some of the visions and dreams – and pain – he'd experienced ever since he'd escaped from her but he had no idea of just how wicked she was and the evil influences and spells she used to achieve her goals; if he'd had even an inkling of who and what she was, he might never have set out to take his revenge but would have shrugged his shoulders and put it all down to experience.

But, of course, that didn't happen! He'd already given his men their instructions and it was still just getting light as they lowered the small boats over the side of the ship. The four little boats bobbing on the fast flowing river each held ten men, the Jackal leading the way as they headed towards the cave where the witch had held him prisoner not too many days previously. He was standing with one foot raised onto the front edge of his vessel and directing the others with signals from his arms, all the while holding his short sword between his teeth in true pirate fashion.

Arthur, now that he knew it was definitely the witch they were after was more than pleased to be left on board with Pick and a skeleton crew to guard the ship, watched this exercise and was surprised at how silently and efficiently it was all carried out. The oars had been wrapped around with rags so that they made no sound in the water, no words were spoken and every move was conducted by hand signals.

The boats were moored quickly and silently and the pirates disembarked, creeping towards the entrance to the cave. Still taking their orders by the Jackal's hand signals, they separated into two serpentine lines and made their way to either side of the entrance where they stopped in amazement and watched what was currently happening in the centre of the cave.

Mab had a fire of logs blazing fiercely beneath the cauldron and was screeching spells one moment and then mumbling incantations the next as she hopped up and down, swirling around and cackling as she danced maniacally. She threw herbs, liquids, powders and who knew what into the cauldron as she continued to leap around it, screaming and prancing and laughing with, possibly, what sounded much like belching or worse! Bubbles and steam rose up from within the cauldron's depths; cracklings and miniature explosions that erupted from inside it could be heard bouncing off the walls of the cave and some of the pirates outside dropped to the ground as missiles appeared to shoot straight at them.

After a while the noises from both witch and cauldron eased and only the occasional plop or issue of steam could be heard from within it, while Mab, holding up a dilapidated scroll of parchment to the light, checked and double checked that she had done all that was necessary to carry out her plan.

The pirates, still watching from the safety of the clearing, saw the contented look that spread itself across the witch's face before she replaced the scroll into her cracked leather box and then, almost reverently, take out the spoon. Holding it aloft she turned it this way and that, allowing the different lights from within and without the cave to shine upon it and pick out the deeper glow that came from within. The cold silver began to take on an unusual warmth as she held it aloft and then, unable to contain herself any longer, she plunged it into the bubbling mixture.

The result was immediate and explosive: stars and swirls flashed out of the cauldron, multi-coloured missiles whizzed up and around the cave which was by now ablaze with light.

The pirates were finding it very difficult to stay where they were, their difficulty being that although the witch was scaring them to death – to coin a phrase! – they were equally as much afraid of the Jackal.

So they stayed put – bug-eyed – watching what might happen next!

All the coloured lights gradually coagulated before making their way onto the back wall of the cave, then hardening and giving off a soft glow as the witch moved over to it.

Having her back to the pirates, they, feeling less threatened, moved closer to see what would happen now.

Well, the witch stood in front of this new screen, raised her arms and chanted they knew not what but it made the hair rise on the backs of their necks – those that had hair, that is. They were used to wickedness and heartlessness in their lives but what they heard from this woman really made them afraid.

They waited. They watched.

First the outline of something started to appear; it was very indistinct at first but then at least one pirate nudged his neighbour with his elbow – it was their ship! The screen shimmered as they watched the picture get closer and then flow from the figurehead along the decks, finally stopping at two men who were watching something from the bow.

'Ah,' the woman breathed. 'Arthur!'

The picture moved on, showing the entrance to the river's tunnel, the cliffs, then back to the waterfall, along the length of the sleeping dragon until it eventually alighted on the backs of forty or so men who were staring into a cave.

The witch started laughing maniacally, slapping her thighs and almost falling over in her glee.

The pirates' eyes flickered between the screen and the witch before, almost simultaneously, they realised what was happening. Turning to run they were all caught in mid-stride as the mad woman turned, pointed the spoon at them and shouted a command. They stopped – one man was actually in the air in mid-run and stayed there – and she walked slowly over to them.

'So,' she grinned at the Jackal, 'we meet again.'

His eyes bore into hers with such hatred that if his feelings were power he would have been able to move and kill her on the spot – but they weren't and he couldn't so he glared.

'But I tell you what,' she wondered out loud after considering something that was nibbling away at her mind, 'I will set you free if you agree to do something for me. What do you say?'

She waited for a while and then, almost falling over with laughter at the thought of it, stated, 'Oh you can't say anything while you're like that, can you?' She cackled on for a while longer before, wiping away her tears, she added. 'And you can't even nod eh? OK, I'll just release your mouth!'

What could he do? He had to agree or they would be left like that for, well he had no idea how long! It could be forever or it could be when the spell wore off, however long that might be, if ever. No, the best thing would be to go along with this mad woman for however long it had to be and then to take his revenge on her.

'Good!' she exclaimed as she muttered something else, waved the spoon and they were all released, the one who'd been suspended in mid-air crashing to the floor and twisting his ankle.

'So now we'll all go back to your nice ship and see what we can do there,' she grinned.

Telling the Jackal to organise his men to carry the still rather hot cauldron on board the ship, she tucked the spoon into her leather box and followed them down to the boats.

'Now, Arthur, you are nearly mine!'

SIXTY-ONE

From a great height, Merlin and I watched the tiny ant-like creatures moving across the clearing toward what looked like little half walnut shell boats. As we circled and moved ever closer to the small band of men we were eventually able to make out the identity of one of them. From up in the sky we couldn't smell her but there was a distinctiveness about her that made her stand out from the rest – apart from the fact that she was the only one in skirts.

We couldn't hear her but it was obvious what she must be saying after she'd looked upwards and seen us; they all began to run, the men with the cauldron struggling to keep up as she screamed abuse at them but they eventually all made it safely into the little boats, Mab hugging close to herself and trying to hide what she believed to be Gundestrup.

We watched as she began to gesticulate and then, almost too late, we saw Hellion rise from his sleep. His huge, ugly head raised itself from his shoulders before almost like lightening, he stood on his short but sturdy legs, eventually running across the cliff top gaining speed all the time and was soon headed toward us, nostrils igniting as he worked himself up into a frenzy.

'Turn Moon Song,' I heard Merlin whisper the instruction into her ear. 'Run.'

I held on to Cabby's neck as we made a swift turn, swooping low and heading out over the cliffs toward the sea. Surprisingly Hellion did not follow but we made sure we were well out of reach before we turned and made our way back to our clearing above the Red Hills. It didn't take us long to reach it and all the while Merlin was laying out his plan, reaching out to Salazar with his part of it and finding out just where everybody else was at the same time. They were close but were they close enough to help? I could see by Merlin's face – unusual in that he never ever showed by any expression and rarely gave any hint of what was going on in his mind – that things were very serious indeed; perhaps he let down his guard when he was on his own. I personally liked to think that he trusted me enough to be himself in my company!

'Come Percy,' he helped me down from Moon Song's back (I didn't like to tell him that I would really have liked to have slid all the way down myself) and we walked over to rekindle the fire that still sparked a few embers.

We didn't actually need the fire for warmth but to boil some water for some tea (or what passed as tea anyway). It was never cold in this place, even on the sea; in fact it was always really much too warm. Then again, if we were in the Place of Shades (or hell if it was to have its proper name) well I had always heard that it was hot. Thinking of that I had to ask Merlin something that had been bothering me for quite some time.

'Merlin.'

'Yes, um what Percy,' he said, almost absentmindedly.

'If this is hell, well,' I then began to almost whisper, 'where's the…'

Still rummaging about in the pockets of his robe and only half listening to me, he tried to finish my sentence, 'Where's the what?'

'The, er, um, devil?' I finally found the courage to say it.

Merlin turned around and grinned at me. 'Oh, he's not here! He's up there!' He pointed upwards and carried on. 'He's busy up there trying to get everyone to end up down here! There are a few demons down here but they don't cause much trouble because they've done their job.'

'What do you mean "done their job"?'

'Well, they have to make sure that the people they've been assigned to don't follow the right path; they lead them up the wrong path and then they end up here. Once they've brought them here they don't have to do anything else. But the devil has taken most of his hoards "up there",' he pointed upwards again, 'to cause confusion and mayhem, work wickedness and make sure loads more of them end up here. Anyhow, don't you think it's bad enough with Mab down here?

'But forget about him, we have things to do,' he started bustling about again. 'Come, help me; we have to get this potion ready for the next meeting with that old witch.'

'What will the potion do?' I asked.

'Well, I'm hoping to have quite a few allies the next time we all meet up and if I get this right,' he screwed up his mouth as he struggled to free the cork from a very small bottle, 'she won't be able to see them coming. Now, no – don't ask any more questions – just help me. This,' he explained as he sorted out the ingredients, 'will make us invisible but it's a contrary potion – I only hope it works for as long as we need it; if it wears off too soon we could be in trouble.'

So we spent the next hour or so stirring, mixing, sprinkling and so on. Soon we were ready to wake the resting Moon Song and set off once again on our travels, but not before we had all drunk a small portion of the brew. I watched first Cabal become transparent before he disappeared, then it was my turn, then Moon Song and finally Merlin. Merlin had placed Cabby and I on Moon Song's back before he administered the potion; he then went to her head, whispered something in her ear, holding her close to himself as he did so and then things really did start to get weird! I could see the ground below me and it was some thirty feet away; I watched as Merlin seemed to climb an invisible staircase before nudging me and Cabal to move over so that he could sit beside us. Fortunately I was still holding on to Cabby's neck, otherwise I wouldn't have known he was there. Finally, Merlin also drank the potion and then we were all just not there, even though we were. Merlin spoke softly to Moon Song and we were airborne.

I had always loved the flight on the dragon's back and had cherished every journey I'd had with her but this one was scary. We climbed and swooped, sometimes so close to the sea that I could make out the serpents as they slithered about searching for food – which was always mainly people! I felt a bit sick.

'*Pull yourself together,*' Merlin broke into my panic. '*I'm here and so is Cabal and, even if you can't see her, so is Moon Song and she is as solid invisible as she is visible.*'

'Sorry!'

I felt a little better when Cabby's shaking made me aware that it wasn't just me. I hugged him closer and we gave each other comfort.

Before long the Valley of the Shadow came into sight and we became aware that things had moved on a bit since we were last there.

Hellion was once again snoozing as he lay along the cliff top.

All the little boats had been hauled up and some now dangled down the side of the ship and most of the pirates must have gone below decks. Of Mab, the Jackal, Pick or Arthur there was no sign.

We glided around for ages waiting to see what would happen next. Then we heard the witch's scream.

SIXTY-TWO

Salazar and Nell's son stood each side of the figurehead, straining their eyes as they approached the land. With as spectacular a performance as before the Colossi rose from the deep and prepared to make their assault on whoever it was that was trying to sail past.

Salazar called up to them that it was he and the men that would be helping Merlin defeat their foe.

The two giants had not been aware of the Jackal's ship passing them but eventually concluded that they must have arrived before dawn when the Wailing Rocks couldn't send out a warning.

'But they have not returned,' Pollux added. 'We know when something comes down the river and need no warning. Pass, friends, and good hunting.'

Nell's Son shouted his orders and the ship, looking tiny compared to the Colossi, edged cautiously between them and up the channel. After sounding the depths and measuring the sides of the cave they eventually saw light at the end of the tunnel; creeping even more slowly forward their virtually invisible ship poked its head out into the Valley of the Shadow, stopping about two ships' length from the Jackal's vessel from where they heard an unholy scream. Both Salazar and Nell's son looked at each other and mouthed "Mab".

And then they saw it: a very small boat, surrounded by serpents was being rowed toward them by one man they knew and another they didn't. 'Arthur,' they chorused again under their breath.

'Quick,' Nell's son called across to the men that were nearest. 'A rope – quick,' he added with more urgency.

They ran around, found the rope and watched as he and Salazar dangled it before the approaching boat.

Then everything seemed to happen at once!

Arthur and Pick, who had not been able to see the invisible ship, almost collided with it before seeing the disembodied faces of Salazar and Nell's son calling down to them to climb the rope.

The witch had run on deck to see the two fugitives rowing away from her.

Merlin, who'd been watching all this from above, gave Moon Song the order to dive and pick them up.

Well, it all went wrong! For everyone! Even the witch!

Mab shouted a spell just as the two men were about to catch the rope. She'd uttered something that would cocoon them so that she could draw them back to herself; and this, just as Moon Song was about to grab them in her mouth thus puncturing the cocoon. The hardened bubble burst causing a miniature tidal wave that rocked the invisible ship back into the cave and smashed the Jackal's ship against the rocks beneath the waterfall – it didn't sink but it got drenched – so you know what was going to happen to Mab! But she had seen the other ship – not too well, of course, but she knew it was there. The last we heard was Mab screaming at the Jackal to catch the fugitives.

Moon Song's mouth and nostrils were glued together with all the webbing from the cocoon which was quickly turning into a glutinous mess and Merlin realising that she would be in mortal danger unless she could be freed had no choice but to tell her to fly off and land somewhere so he could remove the suffocating material. By the time we landed once again, she was in real distress and night was coming on fast before the last of the smothering mess was removed. Merlin had had to reverse the spell and so, using some of the powder he kept in the folds of his robe, he brought us back to visibility. Now, however, she was completely exhausted. Merlin ordered me to try and get some rest while he ministered to Moon Song and so I leaned up against a fairly comfortable rock and managed to float off into a sort of dreamlike state – not really awake but not really asleep either. I had started by watching him as he cared for the dragon and was once again moved by the tenderness he showed her and the loving but painful look on his face as he did so. I gradually drifted away and, needless to say, dreamed of sorcerers, witches, dragons and the like, so it was with a trembling start that I awoke to Merlin's gentle shake which continued my violent shaking back and forth in the mouth of Hellion – in my nightmare.

'Come, come, Percy,' he called into my semi-consciousness. 'Wake up now; stop shouting.'

I realised that my dream, which was speeding away from my memory as dreams do on waking, was one of fear and horror. Of course Mab had been at the core of it but now, as I awoke, it disappeared.

Rubbing my eyes and scratching my lengthening stubble of hair – which was taking an exceptionally long time to grow in this awful place – I was soon all attentiveness.

'Moon Song will take at least this night to recover, Percy, so we will have to make our way back down into the Valley and see what is going on. I haven't been able to reach him but I sincerely hope that Salazar has been able to pit his wits against the witch; I really hope Arthur is now on board his ship.'

He looked slightly worried and unconvinced by his hopes but, turning his eyes on me, he rapidly removed all expression from his face, then smiled and said that we shouldn't worry – all would be well.

'Come – let's go down.'

I realised that Moon Song had not flown too far from the Valley. In fact we had settled just over the rim of the cliff and could see that we were directly opposite Hellion who was snorting out reddish puffs of smoke as he dozed on the opposite hilltop.

We looked down towards the river but could see no sign of life and then over to the cave that I had shared with Mab where there was just a hint of light, maybe from a small fire, that touched the edges of the entrance.

'She must have returned to the cave, Percy. We need to get down there without her knowing. Think you can manage it?'

I nodded – not too convincingly, but I nodded.

SIXTY-THREE

Nell's son called as many able-bodied men over to him as seemed strong enough to help. The wave had washed them back into the river's cave and had almost smashed them against its walls. The water, which had first risen and then dipped, finally levelled again but had wedged one side of the galleon under an outcrop of rock within the cave's entrance. The ship was dangerously askew and everything had rolled over to one side; more than one serpent was considering swimming between the cliff face and the ship to enable it to slide onto the decks but because they might get crushed between them had probably decided against trying.

Things looked grim and then even more so when Salazar was found slumped against the ship's wheel, a gash showing on his temple where he'd been knocked out by a falling rock. Tiala and Queen Gisele took charge, mopping his brow with cool water as they fought to bring him round, hoping that he didn't end up like Shake Spear had when they'd first arrived.

King Ogwin and some of his men ran up the ropes to see what could be done but finally admitted defeat as they slid back down, reporting their findings to Nell's son.

It was no good – the ship was stuck fast.

'Come on, let's try and see if we can wake up the Druid. He will know what to do. And for goodness' sake, shift that gear or we'll surely sink. And,' Nell's son yelled, 'get rid of those serpents!'

Tiala's men rushed at the few serpents who'd somehow managed to slither on board and with swords and brooms, bashed and slashed until they slid back over the side.

'Well at least no one will be able to get past us,' Nell's son mumbled as he looked back through the tunnel's entrance into the clearing.

'Yes, that's true!' Shake Spear agreed. 'But what about the dragon? She can fly above the cliffs and get away on that can't she?'

The witch, at the same time, had screamed blue murder at the fact she was about to become drenched by the waterfall; however, she'd been leaning over the bows when the wave struck and, fortunately for her, was therefore on that part of the ship that remained dry. Running at a speed I wouldn't have thought possible for such an unfit and overly large woman, she made it to the door leading to her cabin just in time and disappeared inside. Grinning as she slammed the door behind her she made sure she'd remained dry before yelling for the Jackal to join her.

'So, where is Arthur?' she purred.

'Arthur?'

Oh how she hated it when she was questioned. Didn't they understand that they should know immediately everything she spoke and jump to answer or obey? A frown not unlike the gathering of storm clouds gathered upon her forehead, compressing the ingrained dirt in the furrows of her brow and making her look more frightening than she actually was – no, she was scary – there was no doubt about that. Holding on to what little sanity she had left, she gritted her teeth (what was left of them) and through them hissed that it was the stranger with the dumb man.

'Oh him! Why yes, I'll send for him,' he breathed a sigh of relief as he remembered who he was.

Opening the door he called to Piper to bring the two fugitives to him and waited while his orders were carried out. The witch, meanwhile, was holding the silver spoon in one hand and slapping it into the palm of her other as she walked around the cauldron. Eventually slipping the spoon into a pocket of her dress her careless examination of the magical pot was suddenly arrested by something not quite right.

'Bring that lamp over here man,' she choked on her own voice, which was hardly above a whisper. 'Quickly!' she yelled as panic caused her voice to rise.

Unhooking the lamp from the panel above his head, the Jackal moved over to the witch and held it aloft. Its soft glow shone down, picking out the figurines and carvings on the outside of the cauldron.

'Lower,' she ordered the man, with a voice that once again seemed frightened to raise itself in case it damaged anything.

'No! No, no, no!' she cried as her finger traced the hardly visible line where the two sides of the cauldron had been welded together, the cry ending as a scream which bounced off the wall of the little cabin and rattled everything not only within it but on and out into the valley beyond.

Now you can say what you like about the witch – that she stank to high heaven (which was a position that she wasn't in at the moment or ever likely to attain, come to that); that her hair (mainly stuck to her head with grease but wiry and out of control at its frizzy ends) was definitely not becoming; that her skin, being sallow (where it could be seen) was engrained with filth and her teeth (those that remained) were loose, brownish-yellow and uneven – but you couldn't say there was anything wrong with her eyesight!

'It's a fake!'

'What do you mean, "It's a fake"?' the Jackal's gravelly voice finally broke into the witch's brain, obviously not realising the significance of the cauldron or the foolhardiness of his remark.

'What do you mean in asking me?' she screeched as she flew at him, talons extended. 'Don't you *dare* ask me to explain myself! Don't ask me what do I mean? I know a fake when I see one. But how? Who?' she muttered, turning back once more to examine the pot more carefully; and then she stood stock still in the middle of the room and the sound that came out of her mouth was a breath rather than a word.

'Myrddin!'

'Myrddin?'

She almost threw herself at the wolfish looking man but stopped just as she was about to pummel her fists into his head. Controlling herself – just – she turned and flopped down into the chair. She felt, rather than heard, the man start to talk and merely held up her hand to silence him. She could hardly speak herself as she tried to inflate lungs in a room that suddenly seemed devoid of air. Almost choking on the words she uttered, 'I have to think!'

Piper chose that moment to knock and enter with the information that the two men couldn't be found anywhere and that one of the small boats was missing.

Have you ever done that? I mean – walked into a room where people were arguing and then get dragged into the argument yourself and be forced to take sides? Then had both the quarrellers have a go at you because you wouldn't? Then they end up making you the object of their feud, eventually become friends themselves and walk off arm in arm and you end up the bad guy? Or, perhaps, you walk round a corner and literally bump into someone that you've been trying to avoid for weeks – even walking the really long way round every time in order to try and avoid them? Or, maybe, you get your mum to write a sick note to the school so as to avoid a situation? Well, I reckon Piper felt like that right then!

Poor man! Poor, poor man! What had he done to deserve it? He had merely been taking orders, carrying them out and returning with the information. Had he done anything deserving punishment? No! Had he been disloyal to his master? No! Had he whipped the men into a frenzy to mutiny in order to take over the ship so as to become captain himself? No! Did he do everything he was told? Yes! Without complaining? Always! Did he deserve to be thrown to the serpents? Never!

Splash!

'Now that was a bit extreme!' the Jackal complained to Mab as he followed her back down into the cabin. 'I needed that man!'

'Oh shut up! Shut up! I need to think!' She rubbed her face and eyes harshly, as if trying to rub away her problems, now extremely irritated that she had not only gained a fake cauldron but had also lost Arthur. *'Arthur -I almost had him in my grasp and with the cauldron and spoon could have disposed of him forever.* Anyway,' her hand brushed against the spoon in her pocket, making her feel a little better, as she turned to the captain, 'your man will come back sooner or later and perhaps he'll be a bit better at his job after the experience.'

'He was good at his job before!'

'SHUT UP!'

Just before darkness fell, the witch, along with the Jackal and most of his crew, got into the small boats once more and made their way back to the cave, Mab finally belting the captain round the head as she tuned into his thoughts of *why couldn't she have stayed there in the first place – all this dragging cauldrons back and forth; it's not even as if it was the real one...*

He had this vague but creeping suspicion that she could tune in to his thoughts and so, trying to mask them even from himself, he determined that now he knew that the spoon was the treasure he'd try to relieve her of it as soon as the opportunity arose and that as soon as that happened he'd make sure he disposed of her as well "one way or another".

SIXTY-FOUR

Pick and Arthur, hearts in their mouths, rowed for their lives after getting into the small boat they'd lowered on the far side of the ship while the captain was ashore. They, like everyone else, were unable to see Tiala's ship and so they'd headed for the waterfall; unfortunately the tide was on the turn so the river flowing back towards the sea was hindering the rowing. Arthur had remembered my recounting of the cave behind it and believed that they would be safe from the witch there. However, in the back of his mind he remembered the skeleton army so he told Pick to stop struggling and row with the river in the other direction, when they saw the rope and Salazar urging them to climb it.

One grin was all he was allowed and then all hell was let loose. Pick, too, had looked extremely pleased with himself but now, with their satisfied looks wiped from their faces, Arthur was too preoccupied with escaping to find out why. They rowed high on the wave back towards the waterfall and on through its churning waters until they entered the calmer waters on the other side. Securing the little boat, they climbed up the crumbling steps to the cave above.

Once again, Arthur marvelled at the speed with which his clothes dried. 'So now what do we do Pick?' he asked the funny little man.

Pick suggested, with many gesticulations, that as night was falling they should lie down and sleep.

'I don't know whether I will be able to,' he answered. 'And even if I can, I'm just so hungry I think I'd just keep waking up.'

Pick pulled some rather uninviting biscuits from his pocket but, well, beggars can't be choosers; the two men sat and nibbled at them, trying to make them last as long as possible, eventually feeling marginally better.

As nearly always happens with the young, sleep crept in on soft, velvety-slippered feet, wrapped them around like a blanket and rocked them gently down into the land of nod.

Mayhem! It was absolute mayhem!

We had disembarked from Moon Song, leaving her resting along the crest of the cliffs that overlooked the Valley of the Shadow. We noticed that Hellion was still sleeping opposite so Moon Song made certain she was silent; not even a puff of smoke stole from her nostrils.

Merlin had weaved some pretty powerful magic after we disembarked: one minute the cauldron was nestling on the ground, glowing dully in this weird place and the next it was gone. I stared and stared again, searching all around until Merlin, snorting down his nostrils, asked me if I still didn't know anything about him. 'Am I more powerful than you can remember Percy? I have sent it on ahead! It is not here!'

I still had a lot to learn from this amazing man but it was, as always, astonishing.

Merlin had reached out to the now conscious Salazar in a way that no-one else could tune into. Cabal drew close to me in a little distress as, he told me later, he could hear this high pitched whistling noise when Merlin and Salazar used that particular mode of communication: it screeched through his eardrums, almost sending his brain haywire.

Looking satisfied, we finally reached the valley floor and, keeping to the cliff edge, made our way toward the cave.

Merlin had, once again, used the potion that would make us invisible, however there wasn't enough left and, as we'd taken so little, cracks were beginning to appear – a sparkle of this or a wisp of that had started to flash here and there and Cabby was dropping some extremely vile, if silent, smells (not that the witch would know, smelling as badly as she did anyway), but I did keep kneeing him in the ribs every time he did it; well, I mean, some of the pirates might smell it, not to mention the fact that it was making me choke. Goodness knows what he'd been eating!

Merlin had his hand on my shoulder and I held onto Cab's scruff as we made our way towards the entrance to the cave; we stopped, finally, taking in what was happening within it.

Mab had somehow managed to line up all the pirates on opposite sides of the cauldron, well away from it and with their backs against the walls. She was standing behind it, almost facing us, with the Jackal at her side. Somewhere along the line the real Mongrel had been reinstated and stood beside his master.

A small fire had been lit beneath the huge silver pot. It had been its glow that had brought us here. We moved further into the cave so that Merlin could hear the enchantment that Mab was muttering and thus be able to countermand it. We were well hidden in the darkness and felt fairly secure in our invisibility. I was still holding on to Cabby's neck when I felt the hair all around my hand begin to raise.

As Merlin was still holding on to my shoulder I raised my hand and grabbed his to warn him of, well, I knew not what!

Then it happened!

Oh how I wish Merlin had been able to hear what that witch was mumbling before it all went wrong. But there's no use wishing for things with hindsight – it's always too late.

Crash! Crash! CRASH!

All eyes turned toward us – well, really, they all turned to what was happening behind us. We, too, turned around and horror of horrors, there he was filling the whole entrance to the cave – bulbous eyes staring at us not a million miles away; in fact his snout was almost touching us and then he opened his mouth and row upon row of sharp and jagged teeth greeted us in an evil grin. Then he spoke – well his voice hammered through our brains.

'You killed me Merlin!' He then turned his dead looking eyes upon me. 'He used you to do it! And now you will pay! Both of you.'

How could he see us? We were invisible I thought holding my hand up before me! But then I could see we were not! At the same time that we'd all turned to hear what was making that awful racket, Mab had thrown some sort of powder over us and now, there we were, our outline glowing with sparkling dust and visible to absolutely everyone – and oh so vulnerable.

The witch, cackling as though she would burst, finally got herself under control and was able to tell the dragon to speak more quietly. 'Yes,' she called up at him, 'but after me. First, I want that cauldron. So,' her tone changed from honeyed sweetness to one of complete evil as she minced over to Merlin, 'you'd better get it for me right now, or,' like lightning she grabbed me, holding me to her, and placing an extremely sharp dagger to my throat.

Merlin, showing no expression whatsoever, held up his hand and waited until there was complete silence; the pirates had at first been gobsmacked by the magical happenings but then – well they weren't such nice people were they? – they started whooping and hollering at the antics of Mab and Hellion.

'Burn him, monster.'

'Yeah, frazzle him up,' along with other less salubrious instructions.

'You win Mab,' Merlin croaked.

She looked smarmily pleased with herself as if to say that she knew she would all along, that she was wonderful and powerful and why on earth hadn't he given over his mantle to her long before this.

Of course, Merlin was able to gather most of her thoughts but gave no sign that he had. 'Come – I'll take you to it.'

Mab was then a little unsure believing there must be some sort of catch as she knew that if it was her she would definitely have something up her sleeve with which to fool him. However, she had all her pirates with her – and Hellion – and wasn't she as powerful as this sorcerer standing here, if not more so? – her confidence climbed back up again.

'Come Jackal, bring your men – we are going to gain complete power. Come along then!' she called again as they made no move to follow her orders.

'And what do we get out of it?' the Jackal, raising one eyebrow, asked.

'Joint power with me!' she lied. 'Everything your heart desires!'

'And the treasure?'

'Of course! I won't need it once this lot are dead, now will I?'

So he was won over and beckoned all his men to follow; Mab could almost read on his face the words that rushed through his brain at the thought of wielding power with that magical spoon.

And so it was, with me still in her iron grip, we waited until Hellion turned his head aside and then followed after Merlin, though I was a little confused as we moved toward the river and not to where Moon Song lay sleeping. Then again, the cauldron had disappeared from there and Moon Song was still weak. Scared as I was, I was still curious as to what the great man might now be up to.

Salazar waited as Merlin had instructed. The guards and most of the able-bodied men from Tiala's people stood beside him as they watched the little cavalcade move ever closer.

'Don't do anything until we get the signal.'

Bohai and Shen had worried about leaving Tiala on board the ship as it was still listing so much they thought it might sink if the tide rose higher. So they had carried her into the little boat in order to hide her in the cave behind the waterfall. She was so much stronger now and, with Honey assisting her, she stepped from the boat and the others watched as the two women made their way up the stairway in the rockface until they disappeared behind the falls. The men then rejoined the others at the far end of the river beside the tunnel's entrance.

They didn't have long to wait. It was still dark and dawn would not come for hours. However, it was just light enough to see across the Valley of the Shadow – perhaps that's why it had that name; it was full of shadows and shapes and moving things – and eyes. Were they really eyes or figments of the imagination? Perhaps they were merely some type of lamp to keep the place visible but shadowed.

I'd been so scared when Mab had first made me start searching the area; some shadows were just that – shadows but after one particularly bad experience when what I thought was a shadow had actually scuttled away when I approached, I kept alert. I mean, what if that "shadow" hadn't been able to get away from me and felt trapped? It might have attacked and swallowed me up and then I might have ended up a shadow in this awful place! Of course, I then got to thinking that that was what had happened here and these shadows were actually disembodied people – wraiths swallowed up in the darkness and ready to pounce – with eyes! Some of the men were trembling – it had to be fear, and fear seemed to be extremely catching here, as it was certainly not cold in that place – ever.

Shake Spear held the one and only spear in that place – he'd made it himself and was very proud of his achievement. He had seen how some of the smaller men were a little afraid and decided to encourage them but he could have been a little more diplomatic: 'Cowards die many times before their deaths; the valiant never taste of death but once.'

But it had the desired effect; they stiffened their backbones and resolved to make a good show of it. What had they to lose? They were dead anyway! However, they knew that Arthur was their only hope of reaching their families that were still alive back on earth to warn them about the witch.

Salazar had called some of the men over to him and using hand signals gave orders for Brosc and Shake Spear to go to his right, while Nell's son, Wite and Tailor took up their positions to his left. The others fanned out in rows behind them. Finally ready, they all watched and waited.

With Merlin leading the way, we all followed until we'd almost reached the river. Turning right we headed towards the waterfall where Mab decided that we'd gone far enough.

'Where are you taking me Merlin?' she yelled. 'I am not going into that water!'

'But Mab, that's where the cauldron is hidden!'

You could almost see what she was thinking as the thoughts raced across her face: the determination to get the cauldron; the fear of losing her power if she got wet; what might happen if she sent Merlin in to get it – would it empower him? Would he come back? Should she send the Jackal – might he keep the cauldron for himself? She might have to chance it.

It was hard to keep a straight face, but Merlin just about managed it.

Then the witch turned. 'Jackal! Go in and find the cauldron and bring it out.'

He hardly hesitated but called half of his men to go with him and told the rest to stay and guard us.

And so we waited again.

Then, as I said – mayhem.

It all seemed to happen at once – within half a minute, I reckon.

First we all spun round as a loud and clamorous army of solid, semi-solid and partly see-through men charged at us from behind; then the Jackal and some of his men rushed back down the rock stairway, struggling with what appeared to be another cauldron while at the same time two men erupted from the far side of the waterfall, dragging two women and a small boat with them; jumping into it they started to row with all their worth from one end of the river to the other to escape the Jackal and then, when they saw her, the witch. Fortunately the fast-flowing river was with them.

'Arthur,' she whispered under her breath. Swivelling round, she'd completely forgotten about me and I quickly ran across to where Merlin and Cabby were as they turned and waited for Salazar. The witch began calling for Hellion. While she waited for him she started chanting, causing many things to happen: as she aimed a curse towards Arthur's little boat we watched in horror as the river surged; she was obviously trying her hardest to smash it against the rocks. Without waiting to see the outcome of this assault she turned and cried some other incomprehensible chant until, flying towards us, we saw the Archers and the Swordsmen unleashing their weapons as they galloped down the cliff face. Unfortunately for the Jackal's men, this foe couldn't distinguish between any of us and so all ended up fair game to those peculiar creatures.

Salazar had been fighting hard with scimitar flashing through the air; his band of men had been caught up near the edge of the river in an extremely bloodthirsty battle with the rest of the Jackal's men. Shake Spear was doing his usual spear shaking and was making the most awful noise as he charged here and there, scaring off most of the Jackal's men and quite a few of ours as well. Then it got to the point where all the men had to take their stand against the witch's unnatural army.

The witch was screaming for the Jackal to leave the fight and hurry up with the cauldron and at the same time screeching above the noise for Hellion to come whilst watching Arthur and Pick row the two women downstream.

'Hurry, hurry, they're getting away.'

Merlin had taken himself off to a rock near the river and, facing it, was holding up both arms. He looked like a giant bat as he stood motionless atop the boulder and, as the river began to move a little faster, he started to, um, forgive me, sing!

Once more, with her strength returning, Moon Song's presence lit up the sky along with everything else. She soared and swooped, almost hypnotically holding the other dragon's dull, lifeless gaze with her bright and sharp eyes. The two dragon's made tracks in the sky as they soared around, neither wishing to be first to attack the other.

However, Mab had other ideas. Now in charge of the cauldron, she shouted at the dragon to stop horsing around and whistled for him to go to her where, with some difficulty, she, along with the Jackal and Mongrel hauled it onto his back with orders to take to the skies. She pointed down at the river and screaming and yelling wildly forced him to swoop as fast as he could and grab the little boat.

Arthur had seen what was about to happen and it was with superhuman effort that they just managed to enter the tunnel before they could be seized.

They could hear the witch almost crying with frustration at missing him and then attacking the dragon with words that I'm afraid are unprintable but it has to be said that if the dragon had not swerved just then he, she and everyone else on board would have crashed into the rocks and would have fallen into the river in bits where it is safe to assume that Mab would have been soaked at best, drowned at second best and eaten by serpents at worst. So, she was being a trifle unfair at her treatment of the dragon eh?

The inevitable smash hadn't been quite so inevitable as the witch had, out of the corner of her eye, seen Arthur, still intact, disappearing into the tunnel's entrance. Without wishing to stay around any longer she ordered Hellion to fly off over the cliff top towards the sea to lie in wait for Arthur when he eventually drifted out the other side of the tunnel.

As the witch disappeared, so did the Swordsmen and the Archers, swarming back up and over the cliff top. The Jackal's men looked confused and ran off towards the small boats, hoping to rejoin their ship and get away from the witch and the weird things that happened when she was around, all the while squabbling as to who should now captain the ship.

Shake Spear chased them for a while but stopped when shouts of his name eventually penetrated his brain.

Merlin and Salazar spoke for a few moments and then we were off again.

The river's ebb and flow and high waves had enabled the ship within the tunnel to dislodge. Salazar took the men back on board while Merlin, Cabby and I climbed once again onto Moon Song's back in readiness for our flight after Hellion, Mab, the Jackal and, of course, Gundestrup.

'So was that the real cauldron that Mab got?' I asked, thinking that somehow Merlin would cast a spell and return it to Moon Song's back.

Merlin said nothing but look grim.

So I kept silent as we flew on to catch up with Hellion and, hopefully, get to Arthur before she did.

SIXTY-FIVE

Pick and Arthur stopped rowing. Rubbing their sore hands together they leaned back and struggled to catch their breath; too tired even to call for help from their ship as they shot past it.

Tiala breathed a sigh of relief but still looked worried.

'You know she's going to fly to the other side of this river to get you when you come out!' Honey exclaimed. 'Do you think it would be better to go back?'

'No,' Arthur replied. 'The river is flowing too fast for that; we'd still end up coming out the other side and just be exhausted with trying to row against the tide. No, I shall just trust in Merlin and my God to save us.'

'Well, let's just hold our oars in the water to slow us down then, to give Merlin and your God time to catch up!'

Almost jumping out of their skin they stared, goggle-eyed and drop-jawed, at where that suggestion had come from, each one of their brains trying to compute the new voice that intruded.

'Sorry, I just had to try it out and see if it still worked.'

'Pick,' Arthur finally managed to find his own voice. 'How did you manage to speak?'

'Well I found the aubergine jar... ,' he started to say and then spent several minutes recounting what it contained, how he knew it was there and the fact that he was now all back together again. He told the story in such a way that, notwithstanding the fact that they'd only ever known him silent and having to mime his words, even in their dire situation he had them all laughing; laughter that would soon die on their lips as with just a faint outline of early morning they saw the ever-expanding entrance to the tunnel rushing toward them.

Pick tried, then, to call out to Merlin or me or anyone who might be listening but it eventually became all too obvious that, with the retrieval of his natural speech with his tongue, he'd lost his unnatural use of it with the mind.

'*Well, we will just have to put our confidence in those with whom Arthur puts his,*' he thought.

SIXTY-SIX

Morning was now rapidly approaching as we flew across the treeless rockface toward the sea, knowing in our spirits rather than by sight that Hellion was not too far distant. We saw him with a little difficulty; he was crouched on the cliff above the entrance to the tunnel, gripping the edge of it with his forepaws and, but for the odd wisp of smoke from those pug-like nostrils, appeared to blend in with the greyish white rocks. Mab and the Jackal, together with Mongrel, were on his back and tucked between his very still wings. All of them were staring down at the river as it flowed swiftly out of the entrance beneath them.

Merlin whispered quietly into Moon Song's ear and we flew silently in an arching direction towards the Red Hills where we, too, would blend in and, hopefully, not be seen.

We didn't have long to wait and needn't have worried about being discovered ourselves: the witch was fixated with the thought of her capture and disposal of Arthur. So when his boat suddenly shot swiftly out of the entrance to the tunnel, without hesitation Hellion swooped to pluck his prize from the river.

I felt rather than heard Merlin urge Moon Song into flight and with the added benefit of surprise we would hopefully get to Arthur before Mab. Swooping high above everything, we looked with horror as Hellion's jaws opened wider and wider.

In a split second Merlin spoke again to Moon Song and, raising her mouth to the skies, she let out the most blood curdling sound I've ever heard. I wished he'd let me know what to expect! My ears were ringing for a good few minutes afterwards as the clanging continued to bounce around in my head; Cabal was whimpering – it must have been much more painful for him with his sensitive hearing. However, I noticed that everything seemed to stand still for an age, as though we were watching a film and someone had paused it; all the time just Moon Song with us atop her were the only ones that actually could move. Then, again, as though they had pressed the "play" button, it all started moving again – this time crazily! Hellion swerved, preserving his tail by tucking it under his body, as Moon Song dived towards him. The witch was screaming blue murder and the Jackal had drawn his sword; Mongrel was just staring, drop-jawed.

I was watching this play being acted out in front of me when, out of the corner of one eye, I saw the Colossi rise from the deep. It all seemed chaotic, though a quick glimpse at Merlin showed me that he had it all in hand; or was that my imagination?

Back to our flight!

Hellion, ignoring Arthur and the small boat, flew back up the cliff face almost skimming it in the hope, probably, that Moon Song would dive right into it and crash; she was too good a navigator for that, and he hadn't counted on Merlin; I was watching him as he leaned against the dragon's neck, holding onto her with a grip of steel and whispering into her ear.

Moon Song shot out a jet of steam and flame that scorched the tip of the pale dragon's tail. Trumpeting into the air he shot upwards with absolutely no regard for his passengers while Mab, holding on for dear life, began screaming at him and pummelling his neck. He eventually evened out but not before the most precious part of his cargo so far as the witch was concerned slipped, rolled down his back and fell with an enormous splash into the water at the mouth of the cave where the river was assumed to be deepest, followed swiftly by Mongrel. The cauldron floated for a good minute before gradually sinking; Mongrel wasn't quite so fortunate – he sank like a stone (or had he been pulled under?). The witch, meanwhile, was digging her heels into Hellion whilst yelling into his ear to dive and retrieve her treasure. The Jackal, just about managing to hold on, breathed a sigh of relief as the dragon, completely ignoring Mab, righted himself.

However, Mab had by now lost it – completely! 'Get back to the valley,' she spluttered at him. 'We need that ship! You're going to have to drag the river for that cauldron,' she yelled over her shoulder at the Jackal.

The Jackal, on the other hand, had by now had enough of the mad woman. He'd gone along with her stupid schemes (and stupid they definitely were); *'I mean, just look at her!'* he thought. He sat back, nestling as safely as he possibly could in a fold of the dragon's back and, turning off his hearing, took time to have a good look at this weird excuse for a woman who'd made such a mess of his life lately. If he'd have known that the treasure was going to be this much trouble he'd have given up long before he started! And he determined to make sure she didn't take over his body again. *'I'll lay off the drink till I've disposed of her; it's when I'm drunk she takes liberties!'* He'd managed, over the years (but I expect this was while he was alive), to turn himself off so that he couldn't hear certain things and now that he was in this peculiar world he found that he was able to do it very successfully indeed. So, snuggling down for the duration of the short flight, he took a good look at her. Frizzy hair was tossed about wildly as she shouted and gesticulated at him; he almost laughed and wondered what she'd do if she found that he couldn't hear a word she was saying and that her lips (quite good lips really but spoiled by a perpetual grim and angry bitterness) looked ridiculous as they mouthed silent words at him; and, oh, those teeth! Very bad! What there were of them! Going back to the hair, though – close to her head it was greasy – plastered thickly to her scalp until it was able to escape – the wispy bits at the ends being frizzy and waving medusa-like as she moved. It looked as though she could have been pretty at one time or other as her features were fairly regular but marred by a permanent look of wickedness; however the overriding impression was of dirt – and, oh was there such a lot of it. There were rings of tidemarks around her neck where she sweated and the dirt had settled almost into black necklaces – row upon row of them. Now she was pointing at him, obviously shouting, and thick, dirt-encrusted talons tipped her filthy hands. Her dress was so dirty he had no idea what colour it could have been but it was old, torn and probably weighed three times what it should have. '*Yeuk!*'

He thought he'd better turn his hearing back on again as if his instinct hadn't deserted him completely it looked as though she might be about to either attack him or take over his body once more.

'…so come on – what do you think?'

'Um, you'll have to say it again. My ears have gone deaf with the er, um, wind rushing through them!' It sounded lame but it was the best he could think of at the time.

'Your men,' she yelled straight into his face, thinking he'd gone completely deaf. 'Will they stand by us?'

'Oh yes; they'll do everything I say,' he replied, choking on the fumes from her breath.

'Right, then. Let's go get them.'

The Jackal, with relief at the relatively fresh air, turned aside, peered ahead and continued making his plans as the dragon twisted and dived towards the clearing in the Valley of the Shadow, followed swiftly by Moon Song. If that cauldron was the treasure – well, he for one could live without it and it could stay where it had sunk. Right now he had decided he'd wait until they'd landed and had boarded his ship and then, well she would see, wouldn't she?

SIXTY-SEVEN

We flew after the other dragon, back over the cliff top until it dived and landed in the clearing. There wasn't enough room for us to land in the same place as Hellion had taken up most of the ground. So, circling high above, we watched as the Jackal and Mab slid down one of his front legs and made their way to the river where, shouting and whistling, they were eventually picked up by one of the small boats and taken back to the Jackal's ship, most probably to the disappointment of the new captain, where they disappeared below decks. Merlin, nodding with satisfaction, whispered into Moon Song's ear and we flew back to the river's estuary.

Landing on the spot that had so recently been vacated by Hellion that overlooked the sea, Merlin peered quickly around to find where Arthur had got to but they, their little boat and the Colossi were nowhere to be seen.

'We have to retrieve that cauldron before the witch comes back,' Merlin whispered. 'I'm going down to that outcrop of rocks beside the cave's entrance and you and Cabby must fly back with Moon Song to make sure I am warned should the witch and the other dragon head back. Do you understand?'

I nodded, as did Cabal.

Merlin walked around to Moon Song's head and spoke to her in a strange and new tongue that I had never heard before and did not understand but it was obvious to both Cab and me that there was a definite sorrow in both their demeanours.

Straightening up he came back to me, assisted me up onto Moon Song's back, Cabal jumping up nimbly beside me and, as I nestled between her wings, repeated all that I had to do before I returned to him.

Before long the dragon was lying full stretch along the hilltop on the other side of the river to where the Jackal's ship sat at anchor. Hellion, completely ignoring us – that is, if he knew we were there (but I reckon he did) – covered almost the whole of the valley floor, occasionally puffing out jets of smoke from his nostrils and mouth; his eyes were closed.

'*Do you think we might have to fight him?*' I asked Cabby.

'*Well, Percy, I hope you were really listening to Merlin and not pretending to! I know sometimes you go off into another world of your own but, hey, he did say just to watch and then warn him didn't he?'*

'Um, sorry!'

'Well, there's not much happening at the moment so let's take it in turns to be on guard. I'll go first.'

I settled down and closed my eyes to rest. I didn't realise just how tired I was; it had been a very long and stressful day and I almost had to tell myself to relax; my shoulders were hunched up almost to my ears and I had been breathing quite rapidly and quietly; I was in a bit of a state really.

'Percy – relax!'

'Sorry Cab.'

And then the next thing I knew Cabby was almost shouting into my brain.

'Quick Percy – he's gone!'

Who's gone?' I blithered, climbing up the spiral staircase of sleep – one of those awful awakenings when you are so tired you still think it's all part of your dream.

'Hellion! And the ship!'

Then I was wide awake! 'Where? How?'

'Look – he's there!' Cabby pointed with his nose, and I looked and could see the red smoke from the dragon's nostrils as it headed away from us – and toward Merlin.

In unison we both started calling out to Merlin in our minds. I soon gave up: it sounded wild and disjointed as we both cried out. But there was no answer. I held on to Cabby to quiet him and started calling him, getting quite panicky and very worried. Our calls echoed back to us. What had happened to him?

We awoke the dragon and she flew off immediately. It wasn't far but it seemed to take forever, worried as we were and Cabby almost weeping with, *'I only shut my eyes for a minute; well, I thought it was a minute and I tried so hard to make sure I opened them every few seconds or so! But I must have just been too tired to count the seconds!'*

In the end I had to give him a good shake and tell him to shut up. *'It was the place Cab!* I tried to assure him. *'I was in a dead sleep and I believe we've been enchanted by the witch or maybe someone even worse than her – if that's at all possible. We couldn't have done much about it if we'd tried!'*

And then we flew over the sea and could see why there had been no reply from Merlin. As soon as we had left him to carry out his instructions, Merlin had started his spell.

Arthur, as I have already said, was nowhere to be found and so Merlin believed that if he couldn't see him, neither could the witch. It was the best time now to sort out this matter, as he felt safe enough to do so. Then, whilst laying out all his paraphernalia on the flat rock in front of him, the ghostly ship sailed out of the cave.

'Salazar!' Merlin called as his Brother Druid leaned over the side of the ship. 'Sail on. Find Arthur and keep him safe.'

Salazar, recognising Merlin's voice, nodded and mind spoke his understanding before they sailed on past him and the rising Colossi and out onto the open sea. They couldn't be seen much anyway and so it was mere minutes before they couldn't be seen at all; except for the telltale wake that marked their progress.

The witch hadn't seen him! It was all I could do to make out he was there! He'd wrapped the cloak of invisibility around himself and Mab had flown straight over him and on out to sea.

Now that we could communicate, Merlin told Cab and I to stay with Moon Song; to scout around and keep him informed of all that was happening. We flew off, but not before noticing that Hellion was heading towards Dragon's Reach.

'Hmm, wonder what he's up to!'

Then Merlin was alone with his spell.

Arthur and Pick between them had been able to raise a short sail. The breeze, which was never much in this place anyway, apart from around the Unsettled Sea that is, was kind to them and it wasn't long before they were making good headway. They'd decided, long before the witch had started to chase them, that they needed to get back to Raven's Harbour; Pick had believed it one of the only places where Mab had been somewhat unsure of herself and not having any better ideas, that is what they set out to do, along with some enormous serpents that had chosen to escort them.

The wind slackened and finally dropped altogether. The small sail hung limply down the mast and the four occupants of the boat stared hopelessly at it.

'We'll have to row,' Pick stated as he looked around for the oars and, fitting them into the rowlocks, told the others to do the same.

'No, Tiala,' Arthur spoke softly. 'You couldn't possibly manage it! Pick and I will row and you and Honey can steer the rudder. Do you think you can manage that?'

Honey said that she'd take charge of that and suggested Tiala could be lookout.

Once everything had been agreed they set off, hoping that it wouldn't be too long before the wind picked up again.

'How weird!' Honey exclaimed, looking at the serpents rising up and sliding under the sea. The others looked to see what she was pointing at and, eyes bugging, exclaimed they'd never seen anything like it before; well, Pick had but only once before and that was years ago.

The sea, in the calm, was like glass; it was still and eerie in its stillness with no wave or even a ripple disturbing it; all that made any impression were those that moved within it or upon it: the serpents rose up and down, leaving holes in the sea where they'd moved; the boat left dents where the oars had come into contact with it and the wake left strands of water lying upon the sea like ribbons floating behind them, and all these marks remained, even after the instigators of them had moved on.

Then they saw them – footprints – lots of them – moving across the waters; they travelled as far as the eye could see, not toward Raven's Harbour but away from it.

'What should we do?' Honey exclaimed. 'Whose footprints are they? Are they friend or foe?'

'I think we should continue to Raven's Harbour,' Pick, looking a little concerned, interrupted. 'We know what's there! If we follow these footprints, well, we might end up anywhere!'

Tiala, who had been nodding or shaking her head as she sat in the back of the boat said, 'No, we have to follow the footprints – and quickly before they disappear!'

So, after looking at her for a few moments, they agreed and taking hold of the oars, followed the path trodden out for them. It soon became easier when an undersea current took hold of their little boat. Soon they didn't even have to try to row. But what had taken hold of them? And where was it taking them?

We were circling very high and it was getting quite cold, which is weird for the place we happened to be inhabiting at the moment, and with our bird's eye view could see quite a lot – that is, if it was big enough to be seen in the first place. We could see the Valley of the Shadow, which appeared at that time to be deserted with no people or ships – or dragon! Hellion, we could see, was miles away resting on top of his nest;

he must have known we were there but didn't acknowledge the fact.

We saw the waterfall and where its river ran along and disappeared through the cave's tunnel and then out the other side into the open sea and we knew Merlin was just beside its exit doing, well, we knew not what, but we thought he must still be there even though he couldn't be seen. Far out in the distance we could just pinpoint No Hope Island but we couldn't see any ships between it and us.

'Go lower, Moon Song,' I whispered in her ear. 'Let's see what's happening with Merlin.'

We circled until we could just make him out. He'd removed his cloak when he saw us approach and stood tall with arms outstretched and staff raised high in the air. His head, which had been held well back, now swung slowly forward as he looked down at the water just outside the entrance to the tunnel. We could just about hear him speaking but with words strange even to me. Then it happened!

Out of the still water it arose. First of all we saw a glistening that got brighter as it poked up out of the depths of the sea and, finally, disturbing the glass-like surface, eventually climbed into the air and floated across to the flat rock, landing gently just in front of the wizard. The cauldron had left a deep hole in the water from whence it had come and I could hardly take my eyes from it, noticing a very bemused-looking serpent sticking its head out of the deep hole that should really have been a flat sea surface.

I turned back to see what Merlin was now going to do and almost jumped out of my skin. He had climbed into the cauldron and it was floating up through the air towards us, finally landing between Moon Song's wings.

'Close your mouth Percy,' he said, only slightly sarcastically as he climbed out onto the dragon's back.

'How did you do that?' I was eventually able to ask.

'Not me; it was the cauldron! Just think how powerful it and anyone who gets it could become if they also had the spoon!'

And then we saw her ship nose very slowly out of the tunnel's entrance.

She looked up immediately and I ducked as she started screaming abuse as she tried, unsuccessfully I reckon because of her uncontrollable madness, to throw spells at us, although I blushed as I noticed Merlin's unbelieving look – did I still think she could get the better of him? Then their ship, which was struggling to move because of the glass-like sea, hit the hole that the cauldron had emerged from and everyone was thrown all over the place as, amazingly, it split in two and began to sink.

Merlin was chuckling as he urged Moon Song to fly off and find Arthur while looking over his shoulder at the chaos that was still in full force on the Jackal's ship. The last image he had was of Mab and the Jackal fighting each other as they climbed up the main mast which, as their half of the ship rolled onto its side, was lying horizontally and resting on the rocks at the base of the cliff; some of the other pirates were trying to run over the wickedly deceptive sea, which seemed solid but sucked them down into it without even a burp.

The waters looked really weird, as though it had turned to jelly – full of holes here and jagged edges there, serpents plopping up and down as if in glue and men and ship sinking but leaving impressions of their shapes where they had once been.

Forgetting what was behind us we strained our eyes forward and eventually saw the start of the wake of Arthur's boat and the footprints that led across the still waters, the wake separating from the footprints as each unexpectedly went in a different direction. Following the boat's wake, we hoped to be able to catch up with him before darkness fell once more and thus it was, with all eyes trained forward and totally oblivious to whatever else might be happening around us, we were taken completely unaware as another, larger beast, flew above us; before we could do anything we were falling and falling, wholly enveloped in a sticky web that cocooned us, disabling Moon Song's wings and almost suffocating us as we tried to claw our way out of it before hitting the water.

She was laughing – oh how she laughed, almost choking as she rocked to and fro on the dragon's back, pointing and spluttering spittle uncontrollably as they flew above and past us.

'Fall off!' was my subconscious thought as I continued to claw at the sticky webbing.

'Not so, Percy,' she hooted, and then, 'I can see the pathway,' she pointed at the wake in the stiff and unmoving waters that trailed off into the distance. 'You're dead this time Myrddin – you and your little helper! Ha! Ha ha ha! And so are your hopes – when I catch up with him – your future king! You must have thought I couldn't do it but you are wrong. And then I'll be back for that cauldron! I'd love to stay around to see what sort of a meal you are going to make for the little fishes,' she howled with laughter again, 'but I must get on – places to go! Things to do! Hah!' Her laughter gradually decreased in volume as they flew away but we weren't really taking that much notice of her; we were currently in a far more desperate state than to consider her future threats.

SIXTY-EIGHT

The lookout shouted down to the crew and, following his pointed finger, they all looked aft.

Salazar frowned – unusual in itself, as his countenance was almost always impassive. 'We can't do anything about the waters,' he spoke softly to Nell's son, 'as even if they were normal, they'd leave a sign that we had passed this way. However, I can weave a spell that will disguise them and us.' And this he did as he held up his arms and, with soundless words, began his spell weaving. Everything looked normal to them – they could still see each other and parts of the ship and the wake behind it but, obviously, the dragon and his passengers could not. It looked as though the spell was working!

'Get back to your oars men,' Nell's son called down to the six little boats that were pulling the larger ship along. He turned back to Salazar. 'Can you cause another spell to help us along? We're never going to catch up with Arthur at this rate and that witch is now in front of us.'

'That's going to take a lot of effort. Hold on, though; I think I know what might work. Keep the men rowing until I'm ready.'

And then the same current that had taken hold of Arthur and his little boat also took hold of them and their larger ship. The men who'd been trying to pull the ship along scrambled aboard as the smaller boats were hauled back up the ship's side; most of the crew rushing forward to see what was up ahead and wondering if they might be about to crash.

Salazar, looking larger than life, stood on the foredeck, arms raised and eyes closed. Nell's son and Shake Spear stood either side of him waiting on his command, occasionally holding up his drooping arms when they noticed the invisible battle he was involved in.

The Faerie, Brosc noticed, had returned and were sitting along the crossbeam looking serious; they were all armed to the teeth but he wondered how their tiny swords or other small weaponry would make any impression on the Jackal or any of his men. Then again, he had thought, they'd managed it before, so he left his wondering and returned his gaze to the glass like sea in front of them.

We were plummeting towards the sea and watched, well I did anyway, bug eyed as it rushed up to meet us. Well, I know we were rushing towards it, but it did seem to be the other way round. And also there were weird tracks in the water as the serpents rose up and down in an effort to be first at the feast. Then it happened! I had closed my eyes awaiting the inevitable splash into the sea and so, when it didn't come at the expected time, tentatively opened one eye and was amazed to find that we were still above it. Merlin had managed to somehow free Moon Song's legs and she was, at that moment, running along on top of the waters as he mouthed a silent enchantment and that, along with whatever powder it was he was throwing high into the air, appeared to be melting the web that had entangled us.

Then we were off and flying again; I couldn't help but laugh at the disappointed green faces that were staring up at us.

We flew higher and higher until all below us appeared like a picture that had been drawn and painted by a master mapmaker; I even expected to see names written beside places, or at least an arrow pointing north. Everything looked extremely small and Merlin, who'd gripped my shoulder and pursed his lips to keep me quiet, was surveying the scene intently. He didn't smile.

Heading toward us was almost a cavalcade of odd shapes and beings (well, we were really heading towards them but again it did seem the other way round).

First we saw the ghost ship – yes, we actually saw it! Whatever they had coated it with was wearing off in places and some of its sides and half of its prow were now visible; nearly all of the people on board were on deck and they, of course, could be clearly seen; about six or seven of them were leaning over the side and hauling in a small boat. Tiala, Honey and Pick, who were surrounded by half the crew, were now standing on deck and talking animatedly with Nell's son and Salazar. Pick was pointing over the port side and several men rushed across to peer into the distance.

We, too, looked and, because we were so high, were able to see that tiny speck – a speck that was pulling away from us.

'Moon Song, make haste!' Merlin whispered into her ear and even I could make out the urgency of that request.

I felt an unease in my stomach that was forcing me to start to ask the inevitable question but, once again, Merlin gripped my shoulder to keep me silent.

'She's got him; keep quiet! We mustn't let her get even an inkling that we are on her trail. She might try and kill him out of hand if she knows! If you have to speak to me, whisper; but don't mind speak as she might be able to tune in.'

I kept quiet and put up my barriers; I could feel instantly that Cabal had done the same, although he had already started and continued to shiver and shake.

Then we were on her tail. She didn't see us – not then anyway – as she was too intent on returning to the Valley of the Shadow. I tried to put out of my mind why she needed to go there and also what she intended to do to Arthur.

I had let my thoughts escape a little and once again felt the iron grip on my shoulder. Shaking myself and straightening my shoulders I swiftly shut them out.

We were still high above but gaining on her all the time when the Jackal turned around and saw us. We couldn't hear what he said but they were obviously going to try and shake us off or attempt to dispose of us once again. However, on this occasion she didn't have time to think of anything and so it was, that as we chased after her, we were able to see exactly what she had prepared.

In the centre of the Valley of the Shadow was a huge pile of wood and logs (I now knew what they were made of – dead serpents – as there just weren't any trees in this place- not any that I'd come across anyway – apart from the one that budded) – a bonfire ready to be lit.

'Yes, Percy, she intends to burn him on that!'

I went cold and replied that we must do something to save him.

Merlin turned and looked at me; his face was grim but he managed to raise one eyebrow at my ridiculous comment.

We swooped and dived, rose and fell as we chased the other dragon – he swerving at the last moment as he strove to get us to crash into the rock face or the valley floor, with Moon Song, almost like a pin to a magnet, staying right on his tail.

Mab, screaming and yelling at the top of her voice, eventually ordered Hellion to fly back over the cliffs to the sea.

We were still following as closely as we could and I can remember thinking that if our mission were not so serious I would have luxuriated in this flight with this most beautiful dragon.

I looked down and could see the ghost ship moored out at sea with Salazar and the others watching the two dragons as they swooped and dived above it. He once more held his arms aloft and I noticed that Shake Spear and Nell's son were each holding an arm – the fight going on in front of them must have been causing him an enormous effort of will to wrestle against.

The two dragons were beginning to tire and the witch must have been becoming aware of it. Merlin's face was like stone as he looked at her. The dragons were now flying at great speed toward one another and each time only just missed a head-on collision but it was enough to see what the witch had done to Arthur. He was trussed from shoulder to ankle with thick rope and with a huge stone attached to his feet. She hadn't gagged him – she obviously wanted to hear his screams as he suffered what she had in store for him.

As they shot past each other Mab called out to Merlin, 'You might still be alive Myrddin but I have your king! You can't save him now you know and if I can't burn him, I'll drown him. You can't stop that. You are too late!'

Merlin noticed that she had woven the spoon into the rope at Arthur's chest; obviously she had made a spell over it and it was now close to Arthur's heart. His mind was racing as to what enchantment she had used but he knew he'd never know what it was in time to save him.

Other measures had to be used – and fast! Sending a swift message to Salazar, he quickly spoke to Moon Song and we flew away in a wide arc over the sea, hearing, as we did, the echoing laughter from the most demented woman the world has ever known.

As we flew Merlin began chanting a spell. I could tell by his voice that we were in a desperate state but I sat back against Cabby and we kept as silent as the grave so as not to disturb him. Cabby even stopped shaking. I had my arm round his neck and laid my head against his. We began to disappear. We were becoming invisible once again.

SIXTY-NINE

We flew over the sea back toward the witch – and none too soon.

She'd pushed Arthur along Hellion's wing and was prodding him nearer and nearer to the edge. The dragon was flying straight toward the cliff face, with wings outstretched, just waiting for the order.

They had flown out to sea and were now heading back straight for the cliffs. I believe the witch's intention was to drop Arthur as they flew against the cliff face so that just as they shot over it he would be propelled forward and thus smash into the rocks, finally falling into the sea below: if the crash didn't kill him the waters or the serpents most definitely would.

They were almost there!

Merlin yelled!

Hellion, completely shocked, froze as his once supple body solidified and, as he had become on earth so now he became in this place; hitting the cliff at a rate of knots, his rocklike body shattered into a million pieces and everything seemed to stop as we watched them spiral down into the sea.

Arthur – sliding down the dragon's wing before the impact – was grasped by a huge hand and lifted to safety.

The witch, who'd been dislodged from what she had believed to be a place of safety just couldn't believe it as she and the Jackal were catapulted right over the sea in the direction of No Hope Island.

The Colossi had at the right moment risen from their watery depths and aided by the Faerie – once again in fast mode – and a host of spiders who'd spun their webs in moments between the giants – had effectively caught Mab and the pirate as they flew toward the cliff face and catapulted them into the air before batting them across the sea with the flat of Pollux's sword. Bat, crash -they were hit and flew high and long before disappearing completely. Castor, who in the meantime, had managed to grab Arthur was, even now, handing him over to the Faerie.

Moon Song flew in an arc over the heads of the Colossi and we watched as the last bits of Hellion sank below the sea. Gradually slowing down as she skimmed across the waters, Moon Song finally came to a halt close to the ghost ship and we clambered aboard.

'So, Arthur,' Merlin, who had joined the others on the ship, turned his satisfied gaze on the young man before him and, as he loosed him from his bonds, safely pocketed the spoon, asked, 'what say you, we now go home?'

Arthur, finally released and looking exhausted, rubbed his blistered hands and merely nodded.

'I have one more task to complete before we leave; Salazar, help me please.'

The two Druids walked aft and called up to the Colossi. The language Merlin used was obviously ancient; it evoked visions of a time long forgotten. I couldn't see them with my eyes but my imagination was conjuring pictures inside my head of a beautiful landscape with columns of white sculpted marble reaching up to the stars and what could only be described as human gods walking about dressed in shining material that floated elegantly as they moved. They looked contented; some were going off on adventures on ships the like I had never seen before; some were climbing into what I would now call space ships. It looked exciting – old but new at one and the same time. The picture faded as I was brought back to the present.

No-one on board could understand even a portion of what the Druids were saying but, still, it was exciting and continued to cause shivers to run up and down my spine; I could feel Cabal shaking beside me, so it wasn't just me that was experiencing it.

The Colossi leaned forward until their huge heads were level with that of Merlin. He had obviously somehow managed to get them to close their sightless eyes and then he placed his staff against their foreheads, one by one, continuing to speak those powerful words as he did so – wow, what on earth was going to happen now?

The two giants, standing straight again, began to glow silver-white; they raised their faces to the skies and held their arms aloft as they, too, joined in with Merlin's words. Then it all went quiet. Almost all of us were holding our breath as, frightened to blink in case we missed anything, we continued staring at the shining Colossi.

The sea became liquid again; the waters lapping softly against the side of the ship, causing it to rock gently and up and over the feet of the Colossi as one by one they lifted each foot from the rock to which it had been fastened for so long. They looked down at their own feet and then across at Merlin and smiled. Yes – they looked down – they had eyes.

How Merlin and Salazar achieved some of their magic is beyond me. They would never tell. 'Not until I can bring you into the mysteries,' he would say. I have asked him many times when that might happen but he has always just smiled and said that at the right time we would both know. Until that time his mysteries would remain just that!

The strange language passed again between the Druids and the Colossi for a few moments before it all went quiet and still.

Merlin spoke to Nell's son who, with a few shouted instructions, the ship was soon moving away from the giants. At a safe distance Merlin and Salazar raised their arms once more; Merlin turned his face to the horizon and shouted – those ancient, unknown words again raced across to the other side of the sea; this time it was deathly quiet and still for long moments; then there was an enormous rumble, a whooshing as of a great wind and finally we saw them – enormous footprints from an invisible force rushing toward us over the surface – this time disappearing almost as rapidly as they had been formed when the waters of the sea filled in the places where they had trod. I started to panic, thinking we were being attacked, but felt more than heard Merlin's acknowledgement of friend rather than foe.

The two mighty men of old – those two fantastic gods of mythology – were caught up by invisible hands and lifted into the night sky – shooting faster and higher than anything I've ever seen before, leaving a trail of a million bursting colours and flames swirling in their wake and thus it was that just as dusk had fallen – it was fireworks night! It was out of this world! We all watched dumbfounded until they were no more.

'What happened Merlin? Where have they gone? Who took them? What was all that about? Where did they get their eyes? Who were they?' The questions came thick and fast before Merlin, laughing, held up his hand for silence.

'Castor and Pollux had somehow fallen foul of Mad Mab. She had managed to trick them to come to this place and once she had them here had managed to secure them to the rocks beneath the sea; at the same time she blinded them. I have no idea why she wanted to do all this, except perhaps to try out some of her sorcery to see if it worked. Anyway, it turned against her, didn't it?'

'So where have they gone?'

'Castor was famed for training horses – he has used the horses of the sea, though they cannot be seen, to gallop across it, leaving the footprints – or should I say hoof prints – you have seen. Jupiter was riding the lead horse and you should have seen him Percy – like a warrior king of ancient times. But, sorry, you don't have that gift do you? Anyway,' he got back to the answer, 'you have just seen them riding across the sea to carry out my and Jupiter's will: he has carried them up to the heavens. Pollux was also famous in Greece but he was renowned for his skills in boxing – it was he with huge mighty muscles who batted the witch across the sea. But you will see them both again, Percy – nearly everyone on earth can see them on a clear night if they look. Though not you, Tiala, I am afraid to say.' He looked kindly at the young woman who smiled sadly back at him.

'I know,' she replied. 'But I am content if you promise to visit my people and warn them against the witch. Tell them to leave that place and find somewhere safe to live. You will do that for me, won't you?'

'I have made my promise and I will keep it. Arthur will accompany me. *You tell me that your people know of Arthur, even in China; that even there he is known of as a mighty warrior and champion of the poor.*' This last said so that Arthur was unaware of the prophecy: the time was not yet right for him to know.

'*Yes – many wise men have told us – that is why we sought him out.* Thank you Merlin and thank you also Arthur,' she said as she turned to him.

Arthur bowed.

We were alone for a brief few minutes so I asked Merlin again if he would tell me when I would see Castor and Pollux again.

'Ah yes,' he replied. 'You know your constellations, Percy?'

'You know I do!'

'Well, maybe you've heard of the Twins?'

'Yes – Gemini!'

'That's Castor and Pollux!'

I was dumbfounded.

'Merlin,' Arthur looked over at him. 'Why can't you do anything to bring Tiala and her people back to earth?'

'Arthur!' Merlin looked shocked. 'You can't mess with life and death! Even I can't do anything about that! Only God! And you should know that more than anyone here!'

He thought about it for a while and nodded. 'Yes, Merlin, you are right. Only God has the power over life and death and determines man's destination. How foolish of me; I should have known.'

'You have a good heart, Arthur. Your question was a kind one, not foolish!'

SEVENTY

The Colossi had gone! The Faerie, too, had disappeared and now that Mab was somewhere else Tiala and her people believed that the Valley of the Shadow could be a place where they need fear no evil – that they could make the best of it as their home.

They sailed their almost visible ship up the now unguarded river to make ready for their people to join them. The funny thing was that now that Mab wasn't throwing her weight around, Tiala and lots of the others had regained much of their physical form and were improving almost hourly. Or had Merlin managed this? Perhaps I would find out one day. As we waved goodbye I was sad to think that we would never see them again.

'Well, that's not true for all of us,' was Merlin wry response.

'Even so, I don't think I'd like to come back here!'

'You are free to make that choice, Percy! No-one else can make it for you!'

'What do you mean?'

'Look for the answer – keep searching until you find it!'

We had disembarked at dawn to allow Bohai and the men to prepare for their onward journey. Moon Song had flown up to the cliff top and was at the moment lying along its edge sleeping.

'Are we going to try and find that place in the Endless Hills so we can come out of that standing stone?' Brosc asked Merlin, starting Cabby off shivering again. I nudged him with my foot.

'No, Brosc, we are going home with Moon Song.'

I brightened and so did Cabal. 'How will she do that?'

'So you still think I'm going to let you into all my secrets?' he raised one eyebrow but his eyes were twinkling as he looked across at me.

'Come!' He made sure we were all there and then organised us safely on the dragon's back until he was satisfied that all was as it should be.

'Now, before we go home, I'd like to see what's happened to that witch. Honey said she still has a potion to enable her to return to the land of the living so she might have left already.'

And so we flew across the sea, eventually over No Hope Island where at least three of its previous residents couldn't stop chuckling at what they saw.

Mab, who'd obviously landed in the sea and had once again been completely drenched, was walking along the beach, dragging her feet and sodden clothes, with a bedraggled Jackal trailing along behind her.

'Don't keep following me – I don't need you!'

'Why not? You wanted me before.'

'Well I don't now, so go somewhere else!'

'There's nowhere else to go! Can't you use your magic?'

'What for? I don't expect it will work here!'

'No, I don't suppose it will. But there's still nowhere to go!'

'Don't be stupid. There must be! Find somewhere.'

'Oh, I can't be bothered!'

'Well, don't bother me!'

'There's a dragon flying up there.'

'Oh, happy for it! Clear off! I don't want you here.'

'I need you!'

'Well I need you like a hole in the head!'

'But there's nothing else to do!'

'Then what's the point?'

'Does there have to be one?'

'Oh I give up!'

'That's a first!'

'Shut up, shut up, shut up!'

And so it went on as we flew away.

We caught a few of the words being tossed backwards and forth between the duo until we were satisfied that the island did indeed have its grip on them – a double whammy for Mab, seeing as she'd also had, as she thought, all her power washed away.

I did wonder if she still had the magical formula to return or whether, being in that place, she might think using it a complete waste of time. We could only hope.

The smile on Merlin's face was a strange one as we circled the island once more (the witch didn't even look up!) and then we flew out over the open sea.

Throwing something into the air above us – was it dragon's droppings? – it wasn't long before a silvery mist began to float out of the dragon's nostrils – increasing rapidly, a haze of swirling, cool vapours soon enveloped us – we were all yawning in seconds and asleep within minutes. Except Merlin, that is.

And so we left Tiala and her people trying to make some sort of happiness in their eternity of hopelessness, and those mad captains running hither and thither across dangerous seas at the beck and call of those crazy clanging eyes of the figureheads.

SEVENTY-ONE

'Wake up Percy.'

I looked up into the beautiful, laughing face of someone I'd often wondered if I would ever see again.

'Rhianne!' I exclaimed.

Still chuckling she asked me if I'd been at the mead.

Recalling the last thing I could remember before waking up, I quickly looked around to see where I was and also who was there and was flabbergasted to find myself in Sir Ector's large hall where a fire blazed merrily in the hearth and the man himself was standing in front of it warming his backside, while I had been slumped in a large chair fast asleep.

Merlin was talking to him but as he looked over at me I heard him whisper into my mind to, *'Take care. Let me do all the talking.'*

We went on to have a merry evening with Sir Kay joining us and Merlin telling many of his stories (some a bit close to our recent home, I thought) accompanied by his harp.

I thoroughly enjoyed the food – nectar to what we'd been eating recently and had to laugh at Cabby who'd found the most enormous bone; he'd dragged it over to the hearth and was gnawing at it noisily. Again I was amazed that he didn't set himself ablaze – he couldn't have got nearer the fire if he'd tried!

It was good to be back. I spent a lot of that evening with Arthur and Rhianne and wondered if Arthur, too, had been warned not to speak about our recent adventure.

We met up with some of the men as they came to the caer on various errands but they, too, although friendly enough, didn't mention anything either. Mead and Hive (who almost smiled) had a joyous reunion with their sister and stayed on for a few days.

Merlin took me to one side some time later, when each one of us had recovered somewhat, and said that he would soon be off to China with Arthur and that I would also be going home. He said he'd made an enchantment so that most of the others, especially the ones without the gift, forgot their adventures, maybe believing them a dream.

I was disappointed at not being included in Merlin's forthcoming trip to the orient but, getting back to my imminent departure, felt a bit guilty when I thought of home; I always had such wonderful adventures back here in the Dark Ages that sometimes I wished I could stay there forever; then, again, I knew I would really miss my family. I knew they didn't miss me because Merlin had always told me that when I returned, no time will have elapsed, so I didn't worry too much about them. However, I was sorry to be going home as I'd only just met up with Rhianne again. It didn't seem fair.

'Don't worry Percy; you will come back again,' he said as we walked through the woods with Cabal at our heels. 'You'll see Arthur again before you go home; but maybe not me!'

'Why not you?'

'I'll tell you – possibly another time or maybe in a dream.'

I looked at him and he seemed not only extremely grim but also very sad. I put up my barriers as I considered what might be wrong but almost got a headache as I discounted one possible problem after another.

They were there for one more day and then both he and Arthur were gone.

I spent several days helping out around the Hall and enjoyed Rhianne's company.

But all too soon it was over. Arthur came back and recounted all that had happened in China, telling me that Tiala's family had packed up and set off for a distant place to live; that they'd thanked Merlin and him for all they'd done for them and spent a long time blessing Arthur for doing all that he had tried to do for Tiala and the rest of their family.

'I was really confused by it all!' he told me as we sat out in the late autumn sunshine. 'It's as though they knew me. But they couldn't have!'

I kept quiet – as instructed.

'But where's Merlin?'

'He's flown off with Moon Song. I don't know where but, and this is weird Percy, he was almost crying!'

I jumped at that. I would have asked more but could see that Arthur was as confused as I. Then I looked over at Cabal.

We had walked a good ten minutes into the woods before I spoke. 'OK Cab – tell me!'

Then he did. But I soon wished he hadn't.

'I spent some time alone with Merlin while we were in the Valley of the Shadow and he made me promise not to say anything until he'd gone.'

'Do you mean to say that he's gone? I mean really gone? Not going to come back again?'

'Well, I'm really not sure about that but while we were alone, at one point he almost went mad! I had to get him back together again. I think you saw him after he'd been weeping?'

I nodded, remembering how sad he looked when we were resting beside the Valley of the Shadow with Moon Song.

'Before we came to the Place of Shades we'd gone several times on flights with the dragon but, as you know, she was silent, apart from when she and Merlin sang together – well, more of a tune really – no words. Well, in that place, just like Hellion, she could speak!'

'No!'

'And what she said almost completely destroyed Merlin.'

'Well come on then,' I urged after he'd been quiet for such a long time. I really hated it when he did that; he knew it wound me up when I had to get him to carry on with a story.

'Do you remember Merlin telling us that Mab, a good few years ago, had Nimue as one of her apprentices.'

He was quiet again so I said, 'Yes, one of her apprentices. We know that. Then what?'

'She always wanted to know too much. We all thought, as no-one had seen her for so long, that she'd gone away to find another professional sorcerer to apprentice herself to. Merlin was sad because she was the only woman he ever really loved, you know.'

We were both quiet again as we thought about this.

'Go on Cab,' I urged, feeling a hollow, sickly feeling growing in my guts.

'She hadn't gone away! Mab used a potent, poisonous plant to try and kill her off, together with an ancient but banned spell; she knew she shouldn't use it as centuries ago it did such terrible things and caused such awful damage that all the sorcerers got together and made a solemn oath never to use it again – but Mab didn't care, she wanted to use it anyway just to see what effect it would have. You know what she's like! Merlin did say what it was but I can't remember. It nearly did kill her but she crawled away and, with the knowledge that she had gained whilst with the witch immersed herself into the standing stone that is Moon Song. She somehow knew that by doing this she *would live but also knew she might never be able to separate herself again from the dragon.'*

'No! So Moon Song is Nimue?' I cried.

'No, Percy, Nimue has been absorbed into Moon Song – she's the life force in the stone dragon and he is the body that enables her to live – they need each other. But the awful thing is she cannot escape – if she tries to extricate herself from Moon Song she will surely die and he will remain a stone circle. It has driven Merlin mad.'

'So where is he?'

'I don't know – he's flown off with her and has taken the cauldron with him. I believe he's going to try and do something to bring her back.'

Neither of us believed enough to think it would happen but kept these thoughts to ourselves.

Returning to the Hall I tried as hard as I could to join in the festivities. Well, Arthur and I had been found and returned to the bosom of the family – what could be better? However, even though I was trying to shut out the information that Cabby had imparted to me that afternoon, Rhianne knew something must be afoot – my mask of false jollity kept slipping, showing the sadness that lay beneath.

The room and the unasked questions were beginning to spin inside my brain and stifle me. I looked at all the faces – some smiling or laughing, some happily choosing from the wonderful table that was groaning with different types of food and drink, some just gazing around with satisfaction at the fact that all was once again well.

But it wasn't, was it?

Rhianne never got to ask me – well not then at any rate – what had caused my sadness. It was going to be many months – in fact a good year – before that would happen.

Pulling the stock from my neck – it was beginning to choke me – I left the room, thankfully without being followed as I just needed fresh air and to be alone, ran through the kitchens and out the door to the yard beyond.

Almost blindly reaching for the stable door I eventually pushed it to behind me, effectively drowning out the noises of the night, and leaned against it, the blood thumping through my temples as I thought about Merlin and the awful sadness that must even now be afflicting him.

Would he be able to release Nimue from her imprisonment within Moon Song; would Moon Song then be just a pile of broken-down ancient stones; would it all go very wrong and everything collapse altogether; would Merlin go mad; would I ever see him again? 'How rubbish is that?' I cried aloud.

These thoughts were crashing and spinning through my mind as I leaned against the inside of the stable door. I felt myself going. I didn't have the strength or the will to stop myself as I slid lower down until I was lying flat. My eyes, which I had been trying so hard to keep closed anyway were screwed tight. Then I heard them calling for me. I curled myself up into a ball. I didn't want to see anyone. I didn't want them to find me. Why wouldn't they leave me alone and go away?

'Wake up! Wake up!'

They were whispering my name now and gently shaking me.

'You're OK now! It's all over!'

I opened one eye tentatively and then the other widely because of the shock.

'How did you get here?' I croaked.

'We've been here all the time,' my mother smiled down at me. 'You've been very ill – measles,' she added as if to make it all clear. 'It affects some people quite badly,' she explained.

I realised that I'd been holding myself stiff and so, with an effort, tried to make myself relax. I almost cried. It had all been a dream.

My father lifted me by my shoulders and helped me take a drink of water. He felt my forehead and smiled with satisfaction at the fact that it burned no longer.

Both of them helped me out of bed and with weakened legs I flopped with relief into the chair while they stripped the bed of the old linen and replaced it with fresh, cool cotton sheets. After mopping my face and hands they asked me if I was strong enough to change and so left me to dress in clean pyjamas.

Still reeling from the fact that what had seemed so real had not really happened I changed and then sat weakly in the chair.

Dad popped his head round the door. 'Need a hand to get back into bed?' he asked, smiling.

I nodded.

As he lifted me up he said my illness must have made me lose weight; I was as light as a feather.

Then it happened!

Trying to keep my excitement to myself I asked if he'd close the curtains as the sun was hurting my eyes and I thought I might now be able to sleep for a while.

As he shut the door quietly behind him I waited until his footsteps had completely disappeared before I pulled my arm out from under the sheets. It had been stuffed down the side of the chair and now, holding up the dull silver spoon with the scowling face at the end of the handle, I smiled. No, it had not been a dream.

Jack and his two grandsons turned together and looked at the almost black spoon that hung from a hook on the side of the mantel; Jack smiled as the boys looked sideways at him – they never really knew whether those artefacts that littered his cottage really were from those days long ago or whether he just manufactured them to fit his stories.

Would he ever tell?

The following extract is from the next tale of Merlin –
Book 4 in the current series.

THE MASQUE OF ALL MYSTERIES
...A TALE OF MERLIN

The man stared ahead. He was covered from head to foot in glistening white silken robes and his face, the only part of his body that was visible, was inscrutable. Once in a while he would turn in his saddle and look over his shoulder, past the silk-draped curtains at the profile of the beautiful woman and his features would soften – but mainly he stared ahead. The horse he was riding, a glossy, black stallion, knew its master well and the two progressed almost as one in a graceful, smooth-flowing movement, not too fast even though an urgency could be felt by all in the little caravan as it swept through the desert. The small carriage was pulled by four equally stunning horses with a dozen men following on loping camels, each trailing a second beast loaded with bundles or crates. If anyone were to view the cavalcade from a distance they must think it a mirage or something from a fairy tale. Night was drawing in fast and it was with much tossing of manes and snorting from the horses – a good sign – and honking from the camels, that with enormous relief they spotted the oasis shimmering in the evening light. The man held up his hand and they all came to a halt and listened. There was no sign of life – no whinnying, braying or honking, no talking or whispering, no glow from cooking fires and no unusual smells wafting on the gentle, almost non-existent breeze; the man let out the breath he had been unconsciously holding in. He let it out slowly and then spoke in soft whispers to the woman in the coach.

Pulling back the silken screen she followed his pointing finger with her eyes and smiled. 'All is well. He will meet us there.'

The man nodded, accepting the woman's knowledge of the fact.

The stars looked enormous in the heavens above and they continued toward the oasis by their amazing light.

The man, recalling the enormity of their mission, looked grave and spoke so softly that only the woman heard. 'And then it must be buried deep – it must never be found again!'

'No – it must *never* be found again,' she responded solemnly.

www.jennyhall-talesofmerlin.co.uk